BLOOD
OF THE
STONE
PRINCE

by M. J. Neary

Chapter 1

The Purifying Properties of Pain

(Daniel Dufort)

Paris, late 15th century

I wrote my first polyphonic mass for choir and organ at age nine – alarmingly late for an alleged genius – or even a musically inclined idiot for that matter. I was standing on the Gallery of Kings, throwing empty wine bottles into the crowd, reveling in my immunity – and, let us be candid – impunity. Above my head the workers were doing repairs to the roof of the cathedral. The back and forth grind of the saw, the hammering of the sledge, the chiming of the shattering glass and the cursing below gave me an idea. I identified four distinct melodies racing, rivaling and taunting each other. Mother of God, Our Lady of Paris! Now I knew exactly what to do next. I would write my first full-length sacred composition.

I threw the last bottle off the gallery, hitting a cart with vegetables and soliciting a volley of curses. The poor farmer had no idea where the glass had come from. I was standing in a spot where nobody could see me from down below. And even if they did, there was not much they could have done.

Not that I was a malicious child. My talent and intellect, not to mention my physical beauty, had not corrupted my soul beyond repair. I still possessed enough humility and fear of God. (This is where you laugh. *Do* realize I am provoking you. Better get used to my sarcasm if you want us to be friends. And if you'd rather be enemies, well, that's fine by me. I know how to deal with enemies. I have already put a few of them in the ground. You can be next.) Like I said, I was not malicious. I was only trying to figure out the link between transgression and consequence.

Having spent my early years encased in stone, smothered in frankincense and drenched in holy water, I was not quite sure whether the societal laws applied to me. The circumstances around my existence, both privileged and precarious, obliged me to isolation. I could not test my strength by engaging in fist fights with other children. If given the opportunity, I could probably knock out a few teeth, break a few bones and gouge a few eyes. Instead, I was surrounded by adult men who had been instructed not to engage in conversation with me or even acknowledge my presence. However, I learned to read their lips and their thoughts. Let us just say, if the ordinary faithful knew what was going on inside the heads of some of the clergy members, they would not feel so guilty about their *own* sins. For instance, one of the tenors liked to look at drawings of naked maidens being tortured by demons. I have no idea where he procured those drawings. They were fairly well executed, too, with a great deal of skill and attention to detail, down to the expression of voluptuous agony on the maidens' faces. I have a strange feeling the artist was one of our own, residing in the cloister.

Well, the choirmaster confiscated the drawings, probably with the intention of keeping them to himself. This is just to give you an idea of what sorts of things excited those men. The conversations in the sacristy were not that different from those in the nearby military garrison. Fewer profanities, perhaps, but very similar topics.

Truthfully, Notre-Dame de Paris can crush anyone's spirit. Many of the canons found the experience of serving in the cathedral overwhelming. This type of assignment is not for everyone, certainly not for those who are too sensitive or too principled. The senior clergy will weed out the undesirables. Moreover, if the edifice itself does not like you, it will drain the life out of you; you will start having nose bleeds, headaches, chest pains and nightmares. I have seen too many men break down in the sacristy, turn blue in the face, gasp and faint. They would arrive at the precinct filled with euphoria, and a few months later they would leave looking haggard. Oddly enough, the cathedral appeared to like me, feeding me the life's energy it took from others. It definitely wanted to keep me. And I wanted to show that the amicability was mutual.

Over the course of the following week I wrote the first three movements: *Kyrie, Gloria* and *Credo*. I composed during the day and played late at night, after the main entrance was locked.

The organ was located on a high and narrow stone gallery above the western portal. In the early 1470s, it was not an impressive instrument by any means and it was not used much during services. Everyone agreed it was inadequate for a cathedral the size of Notre-Dame – it was an embarrassment, to be candid – but expanding it or installing a new one would be too costly and time-consuming, and the old bishop, Guillaume Chartier, simply did not care enough to release the funds. No, he was too busy locking horns with the king. Of course, he made sure that the roof did not collapse, but furnishing the cathedral with a decent instrument was not a priority.

Philippe Chauvel, the existing organist, a compliant, drowsy and unambitious man, seemed perfectly happy doing the bare minimum. He knew the pipes well and could make them sound decent. When I asked him for permission to use the organ, he merely shrugged and gave me the spare key to the lid. I could practice my pieces late at night without attracting anyone's attention.

One time I went a little wild and changed all the registers. The next morning it took Chauvel at least forty minutes to arrange them back to where they were before. In all honesty, I thought he would rip my head off. Any other musician in his place would. But Chauvel was no ordinary musician. He actually had a sense of humor. Imagine that? He made a joke that a demon had messed with the organ at night.

The first person to hear my compositions, however, was not Chauvel. It was my guardian, young Monseigneur Desmoulins. We did not have much time before the service, so I just played

Kyrie and the first half of *Gloria*. He did not say much, but that look of languid disgust on his face was sufficient.

"Do not let anyone hear this," he said. "People have been pilloried for less."

Before we get any further, allow me to make one thing clear: Monseigneur Desmoulins is not my birth father. We are some fifteen years apart, so from a purely physiological point, our blood kinship was possible, but not from the point of ecclesiastic etiquette. Parisian priests are the most cynical men in Christendom, and Desmoulins will be the first one to admit it. They make the most ludicrous and convoluted rules, only to break them later. Yet there is a certain amount of honor among those cassock-wearing thieves. There are still rules that even they will not violate. One of them proclaims: "Thou shalt not raise thine own bastard." That's right. Raising your own love child is nepotism, while raising someone else's is charity. Well, not exactly charity, more like a form of barter: you take my bastard off my hands, make it look like an act of selfless patronage, and I shall help you get that promotion or just pay you off for the trouble. There was an intricate underground system of bastard-swapping. My real father, as I would eventually learn, was far more influential and formidable than Monseigneur Desmoulins.

Alas, my master was not destined to shroud himself in bishop's robes. Paris has a long standing tradition of promoting intellectual mediocrity. Ambitious, forward-thinking men rarely make it to the level of archdeacon, and those who are truly brilliant do not make it to their thirtieth birthday. Their hearts shrivel up, and their brains explode. My master's tragic mistake was showcasing his erudition too soon. Mentally, he was already living in the sixteenth century. Potions, novelty gadgets and contraptions similar to that of Gutenberg excited him.

Most of the canons in the precinct only casually dabbled in physics and astronomy. My master, on the other hand, was a man of science first and foremost, begrudgingly married to the church. As most marriages of convenience, it ended in teeth grinding. He performed his priestly duties thoroughly yet without much enthusiasm, counting the minutes until he could seclude himself in his laboratory to dissect rats and play with explosives. He had been guilty of coming late to the morning mass after staying up all night melting glass. He had been spotted wearing secular clothes while harvesting sap from the trees. Still, his infractions were not egregious enough to merit harsh punishment. Chartier disciplined Desmoulins in his own passive way by refusing to fund his experiments or publish his scientific essays, saddling him instead with dull, uninspiring work that had absolutely nothing to do with science.

"That malicious old owl," my master would grouse of Chartier. "He wants me to listen to confessions and visit the sick, like I'm the last priest in this God-forsaken cathedral. He'll do anything to take me away from *real* work."

It would be worth mentioning that my master's original surname was either Von Müller or Van Der Molen. For simplicity's sake he changed it to Desmoulins, something an average French idiot could pronounce. His father was of German or Flemish extraction, and his mother, I think, was Venetian or Florentine. Ah, the curse of dual heritage! The German in him perpetually battled the Italian. His German side was methodical, analytical, austere and fatalistic, while his Italian side was theatrical, explosive and downright violent. I learned to stay out of his way, watching him from a distance and trying to mimic his mannerisms.

Desmoulins had three signature poses. One of them I called the Destitute Nobleman, for he was of aristocratic descent. It involved him sitting in his chair with his feet on the desk, arms dangling and head tossed back. The second pose was called the Inquisitor and involved him resting his elbows on the desk and propping his chin on his intertwined fingers. The third, most subtle, and yet the most poignant pose, I called the Alchemist. He would sit with one hand open, as if holding an invisible sphere. I tried practicing those poses, but they never looked or felt natural. We were made of different substances. He was made of ice, and I – of stone.

One thing I learned was that his statements did not always reflect his true feelings. For instance, he quoted Italian humanists right and left yet did not consider himself one of them. He claimed that one's lineage was inconsequential, yet repeatedly brought up his own aristocratic roots in conversation. He claimed that looks did not matter, yet was guilty of lingering in front of every reflective surface, including the cup of holy water. He complained about his physique. Indeed, being taller than most is a major inconvenience when your head towers above everyone else's, because it makes it that much harder to nap discreetly during evening prayers. And when your shoulders are so broad, people assume you are wearing armor under your cassock.

Would it not be grand if priests could wear ordinary clothes and carry weapons? Would it not be stupendous if they could marry – as often as they liked? In the same breath, he would assert that most women were stupid cows, a few of them were witches and sometimes he would point out a woman in the crowd and nudge me:

"What do you think, Monsieur Dufort? Does she look like a cow or a witch to you? I want your unbiased opinion."

I had no idea why he was asking me, of all people. Perhaps, he was probing to see if I would make a good Inquisitor someday.

"You know, there are ways to find out if a woman is a witch or not," he said to me once in that eerie, enigmatic voice that made the cartilage on my ears stiffen. "There are specific interrogation techniques. A few pokes with a heated needle in the right places, and you'll have your answer."

Desmoulins laughed, and I laughed with him, though I suspect I sounded like a bleating goat about to be slaughtered. My master was dreadful in his amusement. His hawkish Italian nose sharpened, the nostrils flared and his upper lip curled, revealing a row of dazzling teeth, while his dark hooded eyes exuded silent terror. I know those eyes had seen things that were a necessary part of his education and canonical duty, things that made his hands curl into fists, and the white of his knuckles peek through the golden pigment. We never discussed that aspect of his service at length. He threw random bits of his biography at me, when I expected them the least, in the form of grim jokes and eruptions of blood-chilling laughter.

I do not mean to brag, but I must be the calmest condemned girl in Christendom. When it is time for me to walk up to the gallows, I will handle it with the utmost composure. There will be no wiggling, shrieking or wondering what it feels like to have your windpipe crushed. And I owe this serenity to my illness. I rehearse my own death several times a day. With little warning my breathing interrupts, time itself pauses, and a perfect lull settles in. My free time is spent trying to connect the moving stars before my eyes, reassembling various images, trying to discern real events from dreams. I feel like I have been alive for a long time. And I have managed to keep my virginity until the age of sixteen! How many girls can brag of the same?

If someone ever decides to use the devil's invention called the printing press to immortalize my story, the title should be Nightmare on Rue des Bernardins. I picked that street because that was where I danced La Rotta for the public. And "nightmare" because these events would be frightening for a normal girl, which I am clearly not. A normal girl would not find herself in love with three men at the same time. At least three men, to be precise. Because there might be a fourth one on the horizon.

Good heavens, I hope that last potential affair does not transpire. Three men are more than enough for a girl who is running out of time. I have enough room in my heart, but not enough air in my lungs. Mother of God, our Lady of Paris! Wait, we are in Paris, aren't we? That is what Mathias tells me. He Blood of the Stone Prince 107 is the one who brought me here. Indeed, it is Paris, the city of Inquisition Fires. What year is it – 1476? No, not anymore. Which is a pity, because it was a good year. I learned this mind bending card trick called "Satan's Wheel." You can entertain yourself for hours, even if you do not have the deck with you. It involves manipulating numbers in your head. If you are sitting in a dungeon, awaiting execution, and there is nothing to do, try that game. It will calm your nerves. And when they come for you, at least you will face the executioner with a straight face. They ask you, "Are you prepared to meet God?" And you reply, "Take fifty-two weeks in a year and divide by thirteen lunar cycles and multiply by four seasons." The look of perplexity on their faces will leave you with that grim satisfaction that you will take with you to the gallows or the pyre.

His words regarding my early polyphonic compositions actually inspired me. Note, he did not say "ridiculed." The word he picked was "pilloried." It could only mean that my work was novel and significant, a challenge to the establishment. It has been almost a hundred years since the death of Guillaume de Machaut. France had not seen another prolific composer. So I continued polishing my composition and waited for my hour of glory.

And, sure enough, that hour arrived. When I was fourteen, Philippe Chauvel was found dead behind one of the pillars, his skull split. He must have slipped on a splatter of melted wax. My master broke the news to me in the same drowsy voice he used for delivering sermons. He then said that some people wanted to talk to me, since I was the last one to see Chauvel alive, and gestured for me to follow him. Those people turned out to be the new bishop and his first vicar.

By the way, did I tell you about the new bishop? Guillaume Chartier, the mean old owl, died and was replaced by Louis Beaumont, a much younger and even meaner owl. Unlike his predecessor, who did not concern himself with the day to day operations of his precinct and expended his last breath fighting the King of France, Beaumont made it his mission to, let us say, 'tighten a few loose bolts'. He wanted to make sure that every sou and every soul was accounted for. He needed to know the whereabouts of every deacon, every choirboy, what company they were keeping outside the service hours and what books they were reading. "Where is everyone?" was his signature phrase. Naturally, he was curious about the circumstances around Chauvel's death. It is not every day that one finds a corpse in the middle of the cathedral. Who needed rumors?

"Such a strange morning," Beaumont said, skipping the greetings. I noticed he was holding Chauvel's embroidered liturgical sash. "My young friend, I have a few questions for you. Exactly how much do you know –"

Suddenly dizzy, I leaned against one of the pillars. Vivid images of arrest, interrogation and execution passed before my eyes in a matter of seconds. Of course, they needed someone to blame for Chauvel's death. That was my punishment for writing that horrible polyphonic mass.

The bishop's fingers snapped right before my nose.

"Don't fall asleep, young man. I understand it's early in the morning, but we need your cooperation."

"I didn't do it!" I heard myself shout. "I swear to you on my eternal salvation. Chauvel was a friend. I could never harm him."

Beaumont's hooked finger lingered before my face, drawing circles.

"That's not the question I was about to ask you. What an ill-mannered child you are, interrupting your superiors. In my day impolite children were whipped. How times have changed. Getting back to my question: how much do you know about music theory?"

"Some."

That was a fair assessment of my knowledge.

"Did Chauvel give you private lessons?"

"He allowed me to sit in on a few rehearsals. I watched him practice. He showed me the notation and let me play with the registers. But I wouldn't call it formal lessons."

"All right, forget about Chauvel. He's dead. Let's talk about you. I understand you have been composing in secret."

"Composing is such a strong word, Your Excellency. I have been dabbling, yes."

"You are much too modest. I don't know who imbued you with such modesty. Clearly not Monseigneur Desmoulins. Play something for us."

I was not prepared to give recitals first thing in the morning, but it did not look like I had a choice.

"What would you like me to play?" I asked, flexing my hands. As if out of spite, they were cold and shaky. At least my voice sounded firm. "I know a few Vitry's hymns by heart."

"Why don't you play one of your original compositions?" Beaumont assumed a more leisurely attitude and interlaced his bejeweled fingers over his belly. "Surprise me."

I looked at my master imploringly, but he was sitting in his Inquisitor pose. I remembered his explicit instruction never to play my works in public.

"You heard the bishop," he said with a shrug. "Go on. Do as you're told."

Grateful for the chance to put some distance between myself and those men, I ran up to the gallery above the western portal. The organ greeted me with its multiple rows of teeth. I played *Sanctus*, my most convoluted and puzzling creation. His Excellency wanted something original? Splendid. I was eager to give him just that. The movement started off slowly and grimly, like a funeral procession, but then picked up speed and progressed to a gallop over the course of the next ninety seconds. Towards the end the pipes roared like wounded bulls.

Sanctus, Sanctus, Sanctus

Dominus Deus Sabaoth.

Pleni sunt caeli et terra gloria tua ...

After I finished playing *Sanctus*, I bent over the balustrade and looked down at the three men below.

"Would you like to hear more?"

"I think we've heard enough. Let's talk." Beaumont gestured for me to come down. A minute later I was standing before him once again.

"I've slept through many organ pieces, and this one definitely kept me awake. Show me your hands. Let me count the fingers. Are you sure there are only ten? There is no way you could have hit all those notes."

Then he took Chauvel's liturgical sash and threw it over my neck. "Well, that was easy. No need to rack our brains looking for a replacement. Congratulations to all of us. Notre-Dame has a new organist."

I had to find another pillar to lean against. This time I pressed my forehead into the stone. The bishop was not joking. He grabbed me by the shoulders and forced me to look him in the eye.

"Don't turn away now. There's no need to be shy. I don't believe I've seen you in daylight before." Beaumont glanced at his first vicar, who had not said a word up until then. "Does this child look like an ordinary human being to you? Why, he is a poorly sculpted angel! His hair is the color of Purgatory flame, and his shoulder blades stick out like malformed wings. I know:

he is an unfinished celestial being, expelled from Heaven at the last minute to live among mortals."

The bishop burst out laughing, amused by his own wit, and the first vicar joined him. There were only two of them laughing – my master remained silent – but they sounded like a mob. I realized their laughter was not malicious. It had a sinister, nervous quality. For Heaven's sake, only a few hours ago they had a corpse sprawled in the middle of the cathedral. Understandably, they were still recovering from the awkwardness of the situation.

"Remind me, child, what is your name?" the bishop asked once he managed to suppress the fit of laughter.

"Daniel … Daniel Dufort."

"Naturally! What a fitting surname. Dufort. Unbreakable. A fortress. Made of stone. From now on, we shall call you Stone Prince." He then turned to my master. "My dear Desmoulins, I cannot believe you've kept such a gem from us for all these years? We could've had him play for the papal ambassador. What other talents does your protégé possess that you aren't telling us about? Does he revive dead birds too?"

"I wouldn't know, Your Excellency." My master's shoulders rose and fell beneath the folds of the black cloth. "I have very little control over this child's activities. Obedience was never his chief virtue. At least he stopped throwing bottles into the crowd."

"Ah, a bit of juvenile mischief is allowed. You wouldn't believe the things I did when I was his age. I think the late Chauvel would be pleased to see this boy as his successor. What a relief!" Beaumont exhaled and fanned himself, the sleeves of his robe flopping like a pigeon's wings, his mood visibly improved. "I admit I worried we'd have to go for weeks without the organ accompaniment. I think that people would notice eventually. Well, we can return to work now. The delegation from Rouen is expected to arrive by noon. Stone Prince, you start tonight. I trust you to pick the pieces for the mass."

The bishop retreated to his palace, and my master to his cloister cell.

Left alone inside the empty cathedral, I dropped to my knees beside the pillar, in the very spot where my predecessor had died, and stood with my head hung for some time. The embroidered liturgical sash across my chest was choking me. I tried to pull it off, but it clung to my body. I struggled to process what had just transpired. At fourteen and a half, I was the youngest organist in the history of Notre-Dame. Traditionally the position had been occupied by older, mellower men, like Chauvel. The new bishop broke the custom. Maybe he got tired of being viewed as reactionary and decided to throw in a bit of novelty. Or maybe he was just anxious to put the issue to rest. Auditioning candidates could be time-consuming. All I knew was that in less than ten hours I would have to face the choir and the clergy for the evening mass. I could already see the antagonism in their eyes.

Make no mistake: I was accustomed to the stares and the whispers from those men, the same men who would not engage in a direct conversation with me. My main crime entailed being the protégé of Monseigneur Desmoulins, who was a little too Florentine, too sardonic and cryptic for their liking.

By the way, the comment about me looking like a sloppily made angel did not originate from the bishop. His Excellency was not imaginative enough to make that comparison. He merely repeated what was said by others. The comment came from Antoine Lasserre, one of the altar servers who had been a sculptor's apprentice; one of the few people who seemed benevolently disposed towards me. "Dufort, features like yours aren't found in nature, only in Gothic sculpture. I botched many angels in my workshop. You look like one of my unfinished commissions. It's as if one of my artistic blunders came back to haunt me!"

Clearly, it was not an insult but a rather accurate description of my physique. Indeed, I was abnormally tall, with prominent shoulder blades and hollow cheeks. As a layman, I was not required to cut my hair, so I wore it long down to my collarbones; I understand where Lasserre got his comparison. Coming from him, who had studied Gothic esthetics, those words were a jocose compliment. He knew how hard it was to make an angel.

It was also hard to *be* an angel, or even a decent human being.

At any rate, Lasserre had died of fever without completing a single commission, yet I remained grateful for that episodic friendship. The nickname 'Stone Prince' suited me well, reflecting certain physical advantages bestowed upon me. I was stronger than an average child my age, or even an adult. Although my musculature was not overly developed, the strength dwelt in my bones, smoldering, threatening to burst forth. Keeping it contained could be burdensome, even painful at times. Prayer and cold water did little to alleviate the symptoms. Still, I did not mind the throbbing tension in my limbs, my jaw and my spine. The only thing I minded was the circumstance under which I received my appointment.

Now the choir and the clergy had a *legitimate* reason to hate me. Of course, they would probably resent any man who would replace Chauvel, but I was not just a random outsider. I was Monseigneur Desmoulins' ward, which made everything worse. A horrifying thought occurred to me, one I could not chase away. What role did my master play in all of this? He did not look too shocked when he came to impart the news of the old organist's passing. He must have known about it before it happened.

I felt a light tap on my shoulder. It was a gesture of condolence rather than encouragement. When I turned around, there was nobody there. It was as if Chauvel's departing spirit brushed against me. I knew it was time for me to get up from my knees.

I ran through the Red Door into the cloister. My master was sitting in his Destitute Nobleman pose, twirling a pencil.

"Where are your manners, Monsieur Dufort?" he asked with more weariness than austerity. "Just because I saved you from the pyre years ago, it doesn't mean you can burst into my cell without permission. Even the bishop remarked on your rudeness, and he's a most unceremonious savage himself. There is a special place in Hell for children who don't knock."

He was right. I had completely forgotten the canon etiquette. I should have knocked and then waited for an explicit invitation. In my defense, I was not living in the cloister along with the clergy but in a tiny cell in the north tower.

"Maître," I started when I caught my breath, "how could you?"

"Oh, I didn't kill old Philippe, if that is what you are implying." He returned the pencil back into the skull that served as a holder for writing tools. "Chauvel's death was a pure accident, admittedly a very well-timed one."

"That's not what I meant. Do you hate me so?" I realized that last question was stupid. He hated everyone. I was no exception. "How could you put me in such a predicament?"

His index finger shot up towards the ceiling.

"Do you know how many beautiful, talented children with an actual musical education would love to find themselves in your ... predicament?"

"Of course, I know. But I did not ask for this honor."

"Well, sometimes we must accept things that we don't ask for. Did I ask to lose my mother when I was seventeen? Did I ask for my father to remarry only six weeks after her death? I sure as hell didn't ask for that baby brother. I rather liked being an only child. Unexpected competition was most unwelcome."

So he changed the subject, making himself the focal figure of the conversation. I was accustomed to that.

"I can imagine."

"No, you cannot imagine. You never had a real family. You don't know what it's like to be praised and doted on, only to have it all taken away."

"I'm afraid I don't. But I take your word for it."

"My mother was a scholarly woman," he continued, his indignation escalating, "who spoke six languages and played three musical instruments. Her successor was a vulgar wench around my age, who did a marvelous job playing stupid but in reality was quite cunning. She accused me of making lewd advances at her. Can you believe it? It's a miracle my father did not cut me off. Still, my relationship with him was never the same. I went from being his golden child to being a perpetual suspect, a predator who had to be kept away. Papa became cold and abrupt with me. He used to idolize me, and all that changed after he married that witch. She drained him of his last sou. Papa took her on extravagant trips. You know how it all ended?"

Of course, I knew how it all ended. I must have heard the story a hundred times. The Van der Molen couple died of smoke inhalation when a fire broke out at the inn where they were staying. The wailing infant was at home with a nurse. My master had to travel to the scene of the accident to recognize their bodies. But the most traumatic thing was not rummaging through the pile of charred bones. No. It was the realization that his carefree days as a student had come to an end. The wicked stepmother had depleted the family budget. The horrors! He would have to find a way to support himself. What could be more demeaning? He was a nobleman, not a tradesman. Indeed, it was the stuff of Greek tragedies to put Sophocles to shame. The gargoyles on the cathedral would weep. My master told this story every time with the same fervor. His anger had not waned over the years.

"I certainly did not ask to be burdened with the chore of raising you," he concluded. "It never was included in my plans."

"Then how did I end up here?"

I have always wanted to ask him that question, though I knew I could not expect an honest answer.

"You are too selfish and ungrateful to understand my motives," Desmoulins replied. "You relish your sense of victimhood too much. And I'm that tyrant who keeps you imprisoned. You always find something to complain about, be it loneliness, or the Greek alphabet, or a position you didn't ask for. If it is any consolation, the idea of appointing you the organist didn't come from me."

"Then where did it come from?"

"I cannot reveal his name at this time. It will suffice to say, that this man is of high rank."

"Our Lady of Paris," I mumbled, raising my eyes to the cobweb covered ceiling. "I have a father, who loves me."

Desmoulins hurried to drag me down from my clouds.

"Don't be ridiculous. Nobody loves you, least of all your father. Ask yourself: would he hand you over to someone like me? I assure you, there is no love in the equation, so get that idea out of your head. However, there is some minimal guilt and healthy vanity."

"Yet you will not reveal his name to me. Do you not trust me, Maître? Have I not proven my loyalty to you?"

Another stupid question on my part. My master picked up the empty ink bottle and squeezed it as if trying to crush it.

"You have an interesting definition of loyalty, Monsieur Dufort. For the past ten years you've done nothing but follow me around. I simply cannot get away from you. Wherever I go, I can feel your nagging presence and hear the shuffle of your boots behind my back."

"If I walk behind you, it is because you won't let me walk beside you in public."

"It's not just how you behave in public. You're always there, lurking in the shadows, spying on me. I wouldn't be surprised to learn that you've been reporting my activities to the bishop. God only knows what you've been telling him. Believe it or not, three days ago Beaumont summoned me into his study and questioned me for at least an hour. His Excellency wished to know what I have been doing in my spare time, namely what books I've been reading and what people I've been corresponding with. Apparently, he is under the impression that I practice black arts. Why do you think that is?"

"You tell me, Maître. Perhaps, it's because of how you quote Marsilio Ficino out of context. All your dinner conversations revolve around purifying metals. The walls in this cathedral are very thin. And if I follow you, it's to make sure that nobody else is following you. You get paid to protect me, while in reality I am the one protecting you."

I uttered those words in a surprisingly steady voice, because I knew them to be true. We both knew it. Desmoulins could not deny that the roles of protector and ward had been reversed. The empty ink bottle flew at me and by some miracle I caught and hurled it right back at him. The bottle shattered against the wall above my master's head.

"This isn't about me," he said, in a calmer tone. "I'm a lost soul, damned to hell. Everyone knows it. Today we are talking about you, Monsieur Dufort. Just because I am beyond salvation, it does not mean that you should continue being an omega Parisian. I have taught you many useless things over the years, from theology to architecture. You have to decide what you want to do with your life. It appears that the decision has already been made for you today. Take comfort in it. You do not want to teach at the University." Staring me down, he shook his head. "Surely, you don't want to take the vows."

"I don't know, *Maître*. You never asked."

"I don't need to ask." His dark liquid eyes flashed. "I'm telling you. You don't want my job. You will grind your teeth, pull your hair out and crack your knuckles. By age thirty, if you are lucky to last that long, you'll be toothless, bald and unable to hold a pencil because your joints will be shattered. Paris does not need another corrupt priest, or another alchemist. God be my witness, I've done enough damage to last us both throughout the end of the fifteenth century."

After leaving my master's cell, I spent the rest of the afternoon in the Gallery of Kings, fighting the urge to pick up another bottle and toss it into the crowd. I took a moment to grieve for my predecessor. Poor old Philippe! I was going to miss that man. What if I had some technical questions? To whom would I turn if I needed guidance on pitch adjustment? What if the old pipes refused to cooperate? Dabbling after nightfall is one thing, but playing for the people of Paris is different. Would they even notice the change?

At quarter past six, I went inside the cathedral. Chauvel kept his sheet music in the compartment underneath the bench. He usually planned his selection a week in advance. It had been less than twenty-four hours since his last performance.

Let the ogre hunt begin!

I tightened the neck strings of my cloak, adjusted the liturgical sash and immersed myself into my new occupation. The choir singers and the altar servers did not show much emotion on the first night I sat in Chauvel's place. I knew better than to take their lack of overt malice for acceptance. They were still in the state of shock. It was too early for me to rejoice or even exhale. It was only a matter of time before their puzzled ambivalence turned into full-blown hatred.

Things started getting interesting a week into my new job.

I overheard the clergy holding a prayer session in the sacristy right before the mass, asking the Blessed Virgin to protect them from the murderous devil's spawn in their midst. Once someone dumped a cup of holy water on me (supposedly by accident) to see if my skin would burn and blister; another time someone poked me with a processional crucifix. And the fact that my flesh did not sizzle perplexed them even more. They concluded that the demon had a protective shell around him that kept the holy artifacts from doing what they were supposed to do. Putting aside their ideological disagreements, they stood united in their antagonism towards me – from the altar boys to the senior deacons. For once, there were no quarrels in the sacristy.

Eventually I got used to the jabs and splashes and learned to enjoy my unique position of a privileged outcast. It was flattering and reaffirming. My detractors must have perceived me as quite a menace, since they felt the need to unite against me.

One Sunday Jean Ardon, one of the tenors, came by to see me after the mass.

"A word of advice, Dufort: tone down the volume when you play. You overpower the choir. The stain glass rattles."

"Non loqueris Gallico," I responded in Latin. I do not speak French.

Ardon gave me that one-sided smirk. "Very clever. It may not seem this way, but I'm actually trying to help you here. I'm one of the few people who harbor no malice towards you." He lowered his voice to a whisper, even though we were the only ones there. "You are probably oblivious to this, but people are talking."

I wondered who appointed Ardon the mouthpiece for the *people.*

"I understand you received no formal training," he continued, "and your compositions testify to that. One shouldn't judge you too harshly for breaking the rules you never learned in the first place. You pound the keys and the pedals at random without even trying to integrate into the service. Here's something you need to know about the essence of sacred music: the focus is on God, and not on the performer. You pour too much of your own juvenile melancholy into your music. It's distasteful and irreverent. You aren't some alley troubadour who bemoans his lonely heart."

The reprimands continued with impressive regularity. It was always the same combination of grievances. My rendition of the classics was too loud and aggressive, and my original melodies were too bizarre and convoluted. Apparently, my eyes were different shades of blue, and the right pupil was perpetually dilated – a sign of the Devil, no doubt. The veins on my hands also formed some enigmatic hieroglyph. My spine had too many vertebrae, my chest had too many ribs and my mouth had too many teeth. My hair was too long and red, my origin too obscure and my manner too brusque and disrespectful. One time I lost my temper and punched Ardon in the jaw, splitting his lip and loosening one of his molars. He ran to the bishop, screaming that he had been assaulted. Beaumont only chuckled.

"Ardon, you mean to tell me that you could not stand up to a fourteen-year old child?"

"Dufort is not a normal child!" shrieked the tenor. "His music is demonic. It poisons the minds of the faithful. Crime and suicide has been on the rise since he took over. Was it a coincidence? I think not. Everyone knows he caused Chauvel's death and usurped his place."

I laughed at Ardon's accusation, as it held no weight. He did not know it at the time, but I had an order of immunity issued by the cardinal himself granting me lifelong exemption from prosecution by the canon court. I do not know how to describe that peculiar document. It was not an indulgence per se. According to the stipulations, I could never be tried for sorcery or heresy as long as I remained in Paris. My master had a copy of that document. Do not ask me how he obtained it.

Ardon was given a piece of cloth drenched in holy water and sent home to mend his wounds as well as his pride. Two weeks passed before he resumed singing.

That incident took me to the next level of notoriety. The scandal actually worked in my favor. When the news of the demonic child prodigy who lashed out at the choir members spilled outside the cathedral into the neighboring precincts, people started coming just to hear me play.

Before long, new organ pipes arrived. Clearly, somebody had been listening and taking notes. The much-needed expansion work on the instrument commenced. Then people began requesting original compositions from me. At age sixteen I got my first commission. By eighteen I was drowning in them. Needless to say, funeral pieces came to me more naturally than wedding pieces. The people of Paris knew that my music was not light, cheerful or holy, and they kept coming for more. The surly, militant slant appealed to them.

The bishop profited from my sudden rise to fame. He kept most of the money and gave a small cut to my master, who in turn dutifully forfeited every sou to me.

"It's your money. You earned it. I'm sorry Beaumont is hoarding it. It's not fair to you."

In all honesty, those were probably the kindest words my master had said to me since my appointment. For the most part, his treatment of me was abysmal. I knew he was going through another internal crisis. He was still recovering from the blow of his thirtieth birthday. His scientific work was not progressing at the rapid pace he would have liked. He had been working on some optical contraption that consisted of a tube and a few pieces of glass that would allow one to examine the celestial bodies. Apparently, he did not have the proper tools, and his calculations were off. He believed that the key to his dilemma was found in the unpublished notes of Nicholas von Kues, a German astronomer who died back in 1464. The notes were either in Heidelberg or Padua, and Beaumont would not allow my master to go to either one of those universities. Night after night I heard Monseigneur Desmoulins growl in his cell. Since we shared a nervous system, all my emotions were closely linked to his, every fit of rage he experienced would thunder through me. I could not rejoice in my own success because he was feeling wretched. It was primarily his misery that nourished my music.

Shortly before my twentieth birthday, I discovered a new pleasure – making superficial incisions on my forearms and letting the rain water wash the blood off. It was in those moments that my muse lavished on me and I composed my finest works. The bleeding usually did not last long. The incisions would scab over. The cathedral never took more blood than it needed.

One time my master caught me in the act. I fully expected him to wring my neck or at least treat me to one of his condescending tirades. To my astonishment, he produced a weary, nostalgic smile and pulled up the sleeve of his cassock, revealing similar scars on his forearms.

"I did that when I was your age. It started after my father's death. It was such an odd, jumbled chapter in my life, written in gibberish. Now I'm thinking ... Maybe it was a mistake giving my baby brother to that childless couple. At the time it seemed like a wise decision."

I had never seen my master show such regret. He pushed back the hood, revealing grey hair on his temples.

"Do you miss that brat?" I asked. "Do you ever stay up at night wondering what became of him?"

"Hell, no! I do stay up at night, but not because of that. The Métiviers promised to pay for my studies. They sounded so eager, so sincere, and I was so naïve. I believed them. Of course, I did not see a single sou from them. They grabbed my brother and vanished, just like that." He snapped his fingers. "Had I done my due diligence, I could've negotiated a more advantageous deal. Of course, at the time I was so anxious to free myself of that wailing creature. I failed to see him for what he was: a valuable asset. A blond, blue-eyed child with all fingers and toes intact! I could've made a fortune on him. Then it hit me that I'd been duped. God, I was livid with myself. I deserved punishment for my stupidity. These scars serve as a reminder of my impulsive, erratic nature. Pain slows me down, but it doesn't stop me completely. I almost wrote an entire book on the purifying properties of pain. I'm capable of horrid things, Monsieur Dufort."

"So am I, Maître," I admitted, feeling a strange sense of solidarity with him. "Sometimes I fantasize about breaking your neck or smashing your skull."

"I admire your candor – and your self-restraint. No doubt, you've had more than one opportunity to act on your murderous impulses towards me. Indeed, you are made of stone."

"And what are you made of?"

"Hellfire and ice, dogmas and lies. After fifteen years in the Parisian ecclesiastic system, what can you expect? I realize I haven't been terribly kind to you, I don't know if I can change that. I've lost my capacity for kindness. It's a sad thing, isn't it?"

"Don't add another burden to your plate," I said, "not on my account. I'm used to being treated this way. I neither know nor expect anything different."

"How gracious of you! A tyrant like me doesn't deserve such a loyal, forgiving pet."

"I'm neither loyal nor forgiving. One day you'll find out. We deserve each other."

"We should try to become better friends, Dufort. Or at least give up the idea of killing each other. Now is not the time for bloodshed. The Church as we know it is cracking. Men like you and I are getting caught in the cracks. Who knows what will happen in the next twenty years. I have a feeling it won't be pretty. I'd like to think that we are on the same side."

Now, do not get excited. Monsieur Desmoulins and I never became friends. He continued treating me with his usual arrogance and condescension. It would take nothing short of an alchemic reaction to change the very substance of his character. I would be worried if he started showing collegiality and courtesy towards me. But we did talk more often. As it turned out, we agreed on many things. For instance, we both believed that the body and the intellect needed room to breathe. The severe restrictions on carnal pleasures and scientific pursuit stifled one's spirit. No, we did not think that all canons needed to immerse themselves in black arts and whoring. However, an occasional love affair does not do lasting harm to one's soul.

You must admit that even a one-sided infatuation stimulates one's creativity. I mean, look what Beatrice Portinari did for Dante Alighieri! My master believed that if he stumbled across the right woman, he would be able to finish that magnifying contraption for viewing the stars – even without help from Nicholas von Kues' notes. Alas, there were no women of

Beatrice's caliber in our immediate vicinity. One would need to travel to Florence or Bonn to find one of those. Remember what I told you earlier: there were only cows and witches in Paris.

It should not shock you to find out that my master and I had a similar taste in women, and that taste was, frankly, by no means exquisite or exclusive. I know that Desmoulins would never admit to it. He kept telling himself that when it came to the opposite sex, his standards were exceptional. In reality, he was too hungry to be picky, having reached his breaking point. Beneath that veneer of contempt, he was seething with desperation. It was the desperation of a man who had spent his prime fornication years repressing, sublimating, bartering with instincts, slashing his forearms, aspiring to God knows what. While waiting for his Florentine muse, he would gladly corner a compliant circus girl, as long as she was young and thin – Desmoulins was not an admirer of mature womanly forms. Of course, he thought it beneath him to pursue one, but if a street nymph brushed up against him in a dark alley, he would not cry "Be gone, Satan!" He would fully capitalize on the opportunity and get just as much enjoyment out of the encounter, minus the headache and the anguish of dealing with what he called a "scholarly woman".

At the last street festival on Rue des Bernardins we were ogling the same two girls as the rest of the red-blooded Parisian men – the two daughters of Mathias Eliade, a nomadic humanist and travel writer who had spent the last fifteen years roaming Europe and finally decided to settle in Paris of all places. Mathias had a handful of children, their ages ranging from ten to twenty. Some of them he had fathered to various women, and some he had adopted over the course of his travels. He filled their greasy heads with rather peculiar ideas about the equality of sexes and races as well as freedom of thought and love.

Of his own heritage Mathias spoke with that enigmatic once-upon-a-time aplomb. He cited Wallachia as his birth place, the land of blood-drinking princes, and claimed to be personally acquainted with Vlad the Impaler. He also spoke of the indigenous people of the land, who were descendants of Thracian warriors. "Can you name a famous Thracian?"

Mathias would then challenge his listeners. When met with a blank stare, he would proceed to tell the story of Spartacus, the avenger of the oppressed.

Having arrived at the festival after nightfall, my master and I caught the latest installment of that Bohemian mystery, that Transylvanian fantasy Mathias was trying to peddle to the people of Paris. His two daughters were on stage. The younger girl looked about twelve. Her most striking attribute was her white hair – not golden or even flaxen, but white as summer clouds, paired with equally colorless skin and garnet-red eyes. I have heard that in some places people with such complexion were regarded with suspicion. This particular child did not seem concerned for her life. Her costume consisted of an array of gauzy scarves wrapped around her tiny pert body. Her golden shoes with hard tips allowed her to walk and spin on her toes.

The older girl, about sixteen, looked like she was covered in a layer of grime. Later I learned it was her natural skin color. She was as swarthy as her sister was pallid. Her short brocade bodice barely covered her ribs. With every sway of her narrow hips, the ruffled skirt would slip lower. I found it odd that her abdomen was exposed, yet her hands and forearms were wrapped in colorful ribbons with coin bracelets slipped over them. I wondered if she had a secret like mine, if she also had a habit of cutting herself.

I would not mind running my hand over that strip of exposed skin between her bodice and her skirt; maybe even planting a kiss on her clavicle. I am sure other men in the audience had similar thoughts. Her pliancy was astounding. She could bend backwards with her arms intertwined above her head, as if she were made of reed instead of bone. At the same time, her fluid movements lacked energy. She moved like an autumn leaf kicked up by the wind, but I sensed she was not wild about being there.

My master and I were standing in the front row, dressed as Florentine noblemen – on occasion he allowed me to borrow his waistcoat. Strictly speaking, he was not supposed to keep secular clothing, just as he was not supposed to read certain books. But then, we were not supposed to be at the party either. This venue on Rue des Bernardins was considered exclusive, frequented by people who were too squeamish for the Feast of Fools. There was an admission cost, a surprisingly high one, which helped keep away university students and soldiers. The place was popular among officials, members of the academia, higher rank officers and even clergymen. The patrons from the last category took a few additional steps to conceal their identities and kept their faces disguised beneath masks and heavily plumed caps. Rest assured, Monseigneur Desmoulins was not the only one violating the vow of obedience. I recognized a few deacons from the St. Genevieve precinct, who did not bother to keep their voices down, because they were already drunk. The wine and the entertainment were supposed to be better quality.

Rue des Bernardins was also a great place to encounter all those forbidden, exotic women, the kind you would not normally see in daylight: English, Hibernian, Bohemian, Andalusian and Egyptian. Most of those women were transient performers looking for steady benefactors in the city. In addition to dancing, singing and juggling they possessed a few other skills that were better demonstrated behind closed doors. They were not common brothel whores. On occasion, they dispensed their caresses free of charge. They were capable of genuine attachment – sometimes to more than one man at a time. I imagined that my first time – if it was indeed in the cards for me – would be with one of such women. Even though I did not have much money, I wanted to believe that I was not entirely devoid of allure, and that my knowledge of Latin, ancient history, musical history, and Gothic architecture, as well as my original compositions counted for something. A marginally respectable woman would be more forgiving of my shady origin. She would not demand to know the names of my parents. Perhaps, she would welcome a lover who looked like a mangled angel. In return, I would dedicate one of my pieces to her. I would keep her warm and amused. I would do all the things I imagined my father doing to my mother. For some reason I always knew that I was not conceived in violence – in sin, yes, but a mutually gratifying sin. My natural parents may not have wanted me, but they had definitely wanted each other, however briefly. The image of them making love kept appearing to me in my dreams. I could not see their faces, just their limbs intertwined. I knew what to do – and what not to do. I would try my hardest to be tender, without unnecessary groveling, and leave a fond memory. If only I could get close enough to a woman. She would not regret it. Did I expect too much? I was about to find out. I was a few months away from my twentieth birthday. The party on Rue des Bernardins was a perfect place for such explorations.

We had a third man with us, an archer named Lucius. Not Lucien or Luc, but Lucius. That is right, like a Roman general. His surname had an odd spelling, either Castelmaure or Caestelmore. It meant something like "Moorish Castle" or "Castilian Lover." Lucius himself was not academically inclined enough to spell it consistently. He must have been handsome at some point, but now, at age twenty-three, his golden boy looks were beginning to fade due to various excesses. His bone structure was as close to that of a Greco-Roman god as it could get, but the tissue around it was already deteriorating. His musculature was beginning to soften, and his jowls to sag. His teeth and the whites of his eyes were turning the same dandelion yellow as his hair. The meat he ate was overcooked and too greasy, the wine he drank was poorly fermented, and the women he bedded were too filthy. I am afraid to imagine what his liver and kidneys looked like.

Lucius blamed his vice on his overall disenchantment with life, his enthusiasm for his profession having waned a long time ago. Yes, even hollow-headed soldiers suffer from vocational crises. He kept getting demoted and then restored, his rank fluctuating between lieutenant and captain. On several occasions he had voiced his desire to disappear, to run away from his military duties and the fastidious Parisian women, and start a new life somewhere as a tavern keeper or a brothel inspector. Monseigneur Desmoulins did not have a high opinion of Lucius, but he did tolerate his company. Can a priest and a soldier be friends? Yes, under certain circumstances. They both came from petty nobility, and that counted for something. They shared the same childhood grievances. The world does not know what to make of petty nobles. They are perpetually wedged between the high bourgeois and aristocracy, neither fish nor fowl, regarded with perplexity and contempt by both sides, awash in blue blood but not wealth, with very few prospects. It is such a tragedy when intelligent boys are forced into priesthood, and handsome boys are forced into military service. Brains and beauty were regularly destroyed by the Institution. If there was any justice in the world, men like them would be exempt from the drudgery.

So my master allowed Lucius to join us on occasion. Frankly, it did not hurt to have protection, especially at a place like Rue des Bernardins. The captain also gave us pro bono fencing lessons, even though the longbow was his forte. Lucius claimed that skill was on its way out, and the firearms would replace the bow and arrow the same way printed books were replacing hand-written ones. That realization exacerbated his sadness.

"You're as sick of your armor as I am of my cassock," I heard my master say to Lucius. "We deserve a chance to cast off our respective shackles for a night, don't we? Let us have ourselves a glorious time."

Alas, Desmoulins was not interested in having a glorious time that evening. He was determined to ruin the experience for everyone with his constant commentary on the girls' performance. He kept saying that their humor was lowbrow, their costumes too vulgar, and their choreography redundant. But then of course, he added, it was not high art by any means. And tambourine is really not a musical instrument. It should be used at executions along with the drums. All in all, the girls' contribution to secular theater was inconsequential.

When the musicians started playing *La Rotta*, an Italian piece written by a Hungarian composer, my master's breathing quickened, and a vindictive spark flashed in his eyes.

"I cannot take it," he moaned, tugging at the collar of his waistcoat. "This is utter blasphemy, an affront against Italian traditions. My Florentine ancestors are flipping in their graves. Look at their footwork! Those irreverent chits need to be corrected at once."

Monseigneur Desmoulins always has to be right. His dogmatic nature demanded it.

"Why don't you do the honors, *Maître*," I nudged him. "Alert them to their errors."

Not that my master needed any encouragement from me. He removed his plumed cap, shoved it into my hands and raked his fingers through his hair. I was shocked at how many grey hairs he had gained in the past few months.

Firenze, sono qui ... Florence, here I come!

He jumped up on stage, grabbed the older girl by the hair, wrapped it around his fist a few times, then pulled her head to his so that their cheeks were touching and whispered in her ear. His message to her must have been a matter of life and death. He was giving her some sort of ultimatum. I saw his fist contract and his jowls stiffen. He was waiting for an answer.

The music abated. The white-haired child let out a shriek and scurried offstage – leaving her older sister one on one with the belligerent stranger. The poor thing looked like a doe before a huntsman. When she finally nodded, my master released her hair and assumed his Alchemist pose with his hand outstretched and opened, except that this time he was not holding an imaginary sphere. No. He was holding his very own heart, offering it to the Wallachian girl, or to be exact, imposing it. "Take it already, god damn you!" he appeared to be saying. "Just take my bloody heart, or else ..."

The Eliade girl quickly recovered from the initial startle. This probably was not the first time that a spectator grabbed her on stage. She placed her small ribbon-bound hand in his, submitting to his invasive gallantry. Her father nodded for the musicians to resume playing. *La Rotta* picked up again, a little faster and louder than before. The adolescent white-haired imp, having regained her courage, reemerged from behind the curtain with a small drum and joined the recorder and the violin players.

A few steps from me, Lucius was sitting on the ground with his back against the stage, growling, complaining about the burning pain in his pelvis, saying he was in hell and wanted to die. I felt sorry for him, in all sincerity. He was missing a spectacular show, truly one of a kind.

Mother of God ... I had never seen my master dance before. That night I perceived a new side of him, a side that was both awe-inspiring and disturbing. He did not look in the least bit stiff or rusty. He knew exactly what he was doing, as if he rehearsed the steps every night. Every stomp of his foot was sharp and precise, every turn effortless. How quickly he responded to the call of his Florentine blood! Was there something in his drink? Perplexed, I stared into the bottom of my own empty cup. I believe we were poured from the same bottle.

The grimy girl followed his lead, having completely surrendered to her partner. He tossed, spun and draped her over his arm like a scarf.

When the music stopped, my master squeezed the girl's face between his gloved hands and hovered over her, his hawkish profile outlined against the glare from the fire. For a few seconds, an eerie lull enveloped the crowd. The spectators were wondering whether the Florentine nobleman was going to crush her jaw or kiss her. Perhaps, my master was not sure himself what he wanted to do. His breathing quickened. I saw his Adam's apple throbbing. As for the girl, she was not breathing at all.

Desmoulins ran his thumbs over her cheekbones and leaned in a little closer, angling his head, his mouth almost touching hers. Suddenly he released her and leaped off the stage, flying right over the captain's body.

"All right, time to go." He yanked his cap out of my hands and put it back over his disheveled hair. "I think we've had enough awkward shuffling for one night. I knew it was going to be dull here."

"Congratulations, Maître," I said as we were elbowing our ways towards the exit. "You have frightened that girl to death."

"Well, she should be frightened." He examined the palm of his hand, frowned squeamishly and wiped it against his cloak. "In fact, she should not be dancing at all."

"You're being needlessly harsh. Her footwork is not that abysmal."

"Footwork, my dearest Dufort, is the least of her problems.

That girl is unwell. Her fingers were hot and shaky."

"Perhaps, she was excited by your attention. I doubt that her other partners have your smooth moves."

"She kept wheezing throughout the dance. Something is wrong with her lungs. I think it's very poor taste on Mathias' part, displaying a sickly dancer. And that man calls himself a humanist! There's nothing humane about his behavior. I've seen traveling performers make sickly animals do tricks. There was that Moorish troupe from Spain. Their monkey looked emaciated, with bald patches. Eventually it snapped and bit the magician. A sad sight, indeed."

Yes, you heard me correctly. My master just compared a girl to a monkey, the very girl for whose sake he was willing to claw his heart out a few minutes ago. In his defense, he seemed genuinely concerned about her health. Perhaps, he did not consider her fully human – let us face it, a female of uncertain heritage who led an itinerant life did not stand on the same level as him – but he clearly considered her deserving of medical attention.

"Do you think she can be helped?"

"I'm afraid I don't have an easy answer for you. I don't know when the symptoms started. It's a treacherous disease. You can slow down the progression, but you cannot reverse it. I'll talk to her father about it next time I see him."

"Do you know Mathias well?"

"Well enough," he replied tersely and cryptically. "Our acquaintance dates back at least fifteen years. He ruffled a few feathers in the sixties, at the tail end of the plague outbreak."

"Would you consider him your friend?"

"That's what he wants to believe. Why else would he let us stand so close to the stage? Why would he serve us his best wine? He knew we were coming. That's why he put out his most delectable baits and played *La Rotta*. It was all a part of his plan."

Suddenly, I remembered that Lucius was not with us. We had left him on the pavement in front of the stage, twisting and groaning.

"Perhaps, we should go back and collect our friend," I

suggested coyly. "The poor devil was in agony the last time I saw him."

"He brought that agony upon himself. I told him to lay off the bottle. I'm sure he'll crawl back to the barracks eventually. He'll find his way."

"And what if he doesn't?"

"Don't worry. He's in good hands. The Eliade sisters will take good care of him. Let them scrub the vomit off his armor."

My master's flamboyant performance on Rue des Bernardins did not go unnoticed. Just a few days later the bishop pulled him aside after the mass. The cathedral was empty by then. The subject of the conversation was not grave enough to warrant seclusion. I was rearranging the music sheets on the gallery. They could not see me, but I could hear most of their exchange.

"How old are you, again?" Beaumont asked bluntly.

"Twenty … eight?"

"I don't have time for this, Desmoulins. According to my calculations, you're approaching thirty-five faster than the comet of 1465."

"*Mea culpa*, Your Excellency. I stopped acknowledging my birthdays years ago. I know, I don't look or act my age. What can I say in my defense? I have a young soul."

"I am relieved to hear that you still have a soul, that you haven't sold it to the devil. So you and I are roughly the same age. It would be safe to say, we have faced a similar amount of temptation. Maybe I am being a little presumptuous here. I can only guess as to what is happening inside your head and your heart."

"I don't recommend it, Your Excellency. Do not lose sleep on my account."

"But I have to, Desmoulins. I am still your superior. Despite being the same age as you, I am worlds ahead of you. I feel responsible for my men. It is my duty to look after your spiritual well-being. You know the penalty for breaking the vow of celibacy?"

Hah! I stifled a chuckle just in time. Even I knew what the penalty entailed: a scowl from one's superior, a penance and a fine. A good portion of the church's treasury was coming in via such fines. As for the woman involved, the punishment was a little harsher and usually entailed sorcery charges and death by hanging or burning. I am not entirely sure how the issue was handled in other cities. I only know how it was handled in Paris. The protocol was put into place not to discourage fornication altogether but to encourage basic discretion. So if a priest cared for his mistress even one bit, he would take at least some minimal precaution to keep their affair hidden.

"I haven't broken that particular vow," my master said.

Beaumont was always one step ahead.

"I did not ask you if you broke it. I only asked you if you remembered what the penalty was. I am merely testing your knowledge. Desmoulins, if you want to take my place someday, you'll need to modify your behavior at once. You'll need to give up certain eccentricities."

"What eccentricities, Your Excellency? I have so many."

"I'm talking about galloping through the square dressed in layman's clothes, quoting Italian humanists, toying with black arts and flirting with foreign women. It was brought to my attention that you were dancing with some mud-colored chit at the festival. What is she: a Moor, an Egyptian?"

"A Wallachian, I believe."

"Ah, related to the infamous Impaler. They are all blood-sucking baby eaters."

"We did not get as far as discussing her typical menu of choicest meats. I'm not even sure if she's Mathias Eliade's natural daughter. She could be one of the orphans he sacked."

"Regardless of her origin, she made quite an impression on you, I hear. Don't deny it. I know your weakness for those unusually colored females."

"I was merely teaching her the steps from *La Rotta*."

"But it didn't end with a dance lesson, did it? A few days later you were spotted in her company again, roaming the vicinity of Montfaucon."

"It's not what it looks like, Your Excellency. I do not know what your sleepless agents reported, but that girl is not long for this world. She's gravely ill. In all likelihood, Paris is the last major city she'll visit. Having traveled all over Christendom, she still had not seen the famous Montfaucon gibbet. We had to remedy that while there was still time."

"Oh, I see. So it was an act of charity?"

"Precisely. Christian compassion in its purest form. What other motive could I have possibly had? It was her dying wish to see the gibbet. I had to honor it."

The bishop rested his knotty hand on his heart and exhaled.

"That makes me feel so much better, Desmoulins. For a moment there I got worried. Next time take that little cousin of Dracul to the torture chamber right beneath the Palace of Justice. Show her what we do to those who do not obey the law. Let it be a message from our people to hers. Ensure that she has a comprehensive Parisian experience."

"What a brilliant idea, Your Excellency," my master said with a bow. "I'll consider it. Over the years you've given me plenty of invaluable counsel. You make me a better servant of God. Where would I be without your guidance?"

The bishop swatted away the flattery. Even he was not that dim. He knew when he was being mocked.

"Stop clowning around, Desmoulins. Don't tell me that serving God is your priority. Explosives and fornication – these are your two principal interests. And now you take our organist on your philandering expeditions. What are you teaching that boy? I've been far too tolerant of your antics, but even my patience has a limit."

My master bowed again, this time the gesture being deeper, slower and therefore all the more insulting.

"Forgive me, Your Excellency. I did not mean to sound irreverent. See, this is precisely why I need you. I'm still trying to break some bad habits. Your predecessor was so negligent. He allowed us to forget our place. We all got impudent."

"I'm glad you acknowledge that." Beaumont still sounded annoyed. "For one, stop implying that the Church needs to be reformed. There's absolutely nothing wrong with it. It's stronger, healthier and purer than ever – now that we've gotten rid of all the heretics. I hope I never have to regard you as one. I'd like to think that despite your many delusions and deviances, you are still a trustworthy member of our precinct."

"I'm trying, Your Excellency. And, while we are on the topic of ecclesiastic law, I hope you reconsider my request."

"Which request would that be? You present new demands every week."

"I was hoping to get your permission to carry weapons for personal safety. As you undoubtedly know, the streets are becoming increasingly unsafe. Last night I was attacked on my way back from a house visit."

"Tut-tut, my poor friend."

"You have no idea. I was called to perform the last rites on a dying man. It was already dark when I left him home. It happened not far from the Pont au Change. There were two of them, maybe three. The old man's family had given me a nice sum of money for the church, and the robbers took the whole purse. I tell you, some people will stop at nothing. They'll attack a man of the cloth. They have no fear of God." He opened the neck of his cassock and revealed a fresh cut right below the collarbone. "Fortunately, the stab was not deep."

The bishop did not look impressed or concerned. He tilted his head a little and squinted to examine the damage.

"Here is an idea. Don't stroll through the seedy quarters past midnight in pursuit of your brown-skinned harlots. Good day, Desmoulins."

I felt sorry for my master. After almost sixteen years of priesthood he still had not learned how to lie. I have no idea how much time he spent mapping that cat scratch across his chest. There were no other signs of assault. No bruises, no broken bones. Not to mention, the cassock itself was not damaged. The alleged attacker would have had to carefully undo the top buttons and the slide the blade across the victim's collarbone. The bishop was intelligent enough to spot a fabricated tale. Desmoulins must have realized his errors, because he looked like a heretic coming out of a torture chamber, his face red and his nostrils shivering.

"Are you sure that girl is ill?" I asked him as we were marching down Rue de Parvis.

"What makes you doubt?"

"You will not deny that some people will use a physical ailment or an injury to solicit pity. Some beggars attach morsels of rotting meat to their faces and necks to imitate festered sores. Is it so inconceivable that Mathias Eliade's daughter is feigning an illness to tug at your heartstrings?"

"I have no heart, Dufort," he reminded me hastily. "As I mentioned to His Excellency, I am motivated by pure Christian charity. You don't need a heart to be charitable. Besides, how can one feign a persistent fever?"

"She's a witch, after all."

Desmoulins slapped me on the back of my neck. "You find it amusing?"

"Hilarious! The whole thing, from start to finish, is turning into one gigantic farce. Jokes aside, there are herbs to keep one's body temperature elevated."

My master slowed down his pace and frowned.

"Well, if she is feigning, she's doing an excellent job."

"You could probably learn a thing or two from her, *Maître*," I murmured. "On the other hand, if you want to make your story more convincing, allow me to help you. Nobody will doubt the authenticity of your injuries."

Chapter 2

Because of People Like You ...

(Mathias Eliade)

What is my favorite thing about Paris? The people, undoubtedly. Their legendary hospitality. I could write ballads about it, seriously. Hear sarcasm in my voice? I love the fact that no matter who you are or where you come from, you can always count on being greeted with torches and pitchforks. You offer them free entertainment, free wine, free souvenirs from the countries you have visited, free puppet shows and even free kisses from your lovely daughters. And what do you get in return? Suspicious growls and accusatory stares. They think the songs you sing are demonic incantations, your puppets are possessed, the sweets you give out are poisoned, and your girls, your heavenly girls, are witches and whores.

Naturally, you are wondering why I would pick such an inhospitable place to settle. I am going to be forty-five this year. Do not think for a moment that I have grown weary of living the road. Never. I was born to lead a nomadic life. I feel most complacent when I hear the squeaking of the cartwheels. However, sometimes it is necessary to step beyond our complacency. I suppose, it is a challenge to take on a hostile fortress and turn it into your dwelling. You see, I'm not merely seeking a place under the sun. It is my wish to *become* the sun, to create an epicenter of enlightenment. I have so much to offer to this grim, backward city. With God's help, I, Mathias Eliade, former subject of the Kingdom of Wallachia, would transform Paris into an oasis of art, pleasure, compassion and social justice.

My two sons would inherit my empire.

I should mention that the boys were born just six months apart. Josef's mother was Hungarian, and Sebastien's – a Spaniard of Moorish extraction. Both women came from destitution and were all too eager to relinquish their children to me. I had invited the two women to join me in my travels, but they had both declined. My official wife, a Gascon, agreed to raise the boys as her own. Denise was a barren widow, so she lavished her pent-up maternal sentiment on my offspring, as I in turn lavished my gallantry upon her. I assure you, that woman was not exploited by any means. Her status was that of my consort, the revered matriarch. After ten years of being battered and belittled by her first husband for her inability to produce an heir, she certainly appreciated the freedom and adventure I had to offer. As time went on, we added more children to our family, those we came across en route.

How different can two brothers be? Since birth Josef had been prone to elopement. Sometimes he would disappear, and we would not see him for days. Then he would catch up with us on the road, ambushing us like a highwayman. Sebastien, on the other hand, the darker and the more disciplined of the two, was seriously contemplating a soldier's career. Jokes aside, I told him he would need to remove the hoop from his ear and give up the idea of injecting ink under his skin. I have seen men from my native Balkan region decorate their hands with permanent ornaments using a needle as a tool. Bosnians and Bulgars had adopted that fashion from their Turkish neighbors. I had seen some impressively elaborate designs, and I understood why Sebastien wanted to mark himself with one of those images. I was not sure if that fashion would be well received in France.

I come from a resilient, somewhat untamed Romanic tribe. My people have interesting neighbors, some more benevolent than others – Slavs, Huns, Helens, Ottomans, Bohemians and Saxons. I respectfully try to incorporate elements of their lore into my speech and clothing: belts, buckles, amulets, coins. All those artifacts came from my native soil before I headed westward. I had collected more trinkets while roaming Andalusia, Catalonia, Provence and Gascony. I have hundreds of tales to tell. If only the people of Paris would listen.

The first person we saw as we rode through the city's gate at daybreak was a lone soldier in an archer's uniform curled up on the steps of a tavern, weeping, shaking inside his armor. I could tell he had been quite handsome at some point, but now he looked like a pagan god stripped of his divinity and kicked off the Olympus. It was the saddest thing I had seen in a long time! It was even sadder than a beggar child with a missing leg. Of course, I had to stop and show some compassion.

"Pray, Monsieur, what makes you weep on this glorious morning?" I asked, placing my hand on his shoulder plate. "Tell me your sorrows."

"My horse died." He replied without as much as raising his head, but his voice communicated a strange familiarity, as if he had known me his whole life. "I don't know what happened to her. She was a healthy young mare in her prime, barely three years old. I was ready to go home, and when I returned to the stables, she was dead."

He succumbed to another volley of sobs, causing the breastplates to clatter. I gestured for my younger son to untie one of the Andalusian stallions we had brought with us with the intention to sell.

"Dry your tears, my friend," I said. "You are in luck, as I happen to have a perfect horse for you. This white prince of equestrians will serve you well. His name is Achilles."

The archer looked up and shook his head.

"I have no money. Beard of Muhammed! Take this fine creature away. Seeing him is torture."

"Consider it a gift, a token of amicability. We come to this city in peace. I think it was meant to happen, this encounters of ours."

"You are mocking me now." There was ineffable bitterness in his voice. "What for? I know I look pitiable, but I've done you no wrong. I don't even know your name."

"My name is Mathias Theodor Eliade, and I am not mocking you."

"Then I must be dreaming."

"Not dreaming. Listen to me. We are here to establish

horse trade. Even before entering the city I had resolved to give Achilles to an appreciative master, who would put him to work, and I cannot think of anyone more deserving than you. Having sold hundreds of horses, I've developed an eye for such things."

He looked at me with cautious hope. Those were not the eyes of a callous soldier. Those were the eyes of a boy who had aged before his time. "You truly think so?"

"Indeed. You and Achilles were made for each other. Why don't you try him out?"

"If I can get up ..."

Still a little unbalanced, the soldier struggled to his feet. A few seconds later he was in the saddle, galloping back and forth in front of the tavern, the wind tousling his greasy hair.

"You seem entirely in your element," I said to him when he dismounted. "Now, here is a gallant fellow who likes fast horses and beautiful women. Am I right?"

He was already out of breath. He had barely exerted himself, and he was already doubled over, panting, although with a grin on his face.

"I'm at a loss for words. How will I ever repay you?"

"You can help my younger boy Sebastien perfect his archery."

My words must have opened an old wound, because the captain let out another growl and squeezed his head.

"Don't bother with archery," he said after the spasm of pain passed. "In a few years it will become obsolete."

"I don't believe so."

"Well, I'm telling you so." He brushed back his oily yellow forelock. "With all due respect, you do not look like a military man to me. I'm well aware of the changes that are happening in warfare tactics. The infamous arquebus is replacing the bow and arrow. Archery is an elegant art. It requires finesse, discipline, precision. When you release that arrow, it's almost a religious ritual. You must find your inner Apollo. It elevates you, while shooting from firearms abases you."

His speech left me breathless. I must say, I had never heard a man speak with such passion of his bow and arrows. You would think it was an extension of his manhood.

"Firearms are great for shooting yourself in the foot," he resumed. "Last year my good friend crippled himself in that manner. He was cleaning his arquebus and accidentally fired into his ankle. Years of training and service – up the chimney. Why does your son want to learn archery, anyway?" I looked at Sebastien, giving him a chance to speak for himself.

"I'd like to pursue a military career."

The boy could really make a good impression when he put his mind to it. French was the language used within our clan in day-to-day interactions, so he spoke it without a trace of Spanish accent.

"How old are you?" the officer asked, assuming a more businesslike tone.

"Eighteen."

"I assume you have no prior training. It would be a rather late start. Fourteen is the typical age when boys are sent to the garrison."

Here I reentered the conversation and placed my hands on Sebastien's shoulders.

"Please, captain, do not let his age or lack of training discourage you. My son has cultivated many skills. He's already an excellent horseman. While we were in Granada, he took some fencing lessons. He understands marching commands in both French and Spanish." Then, seeing that the golden-haired captain was scrutinizing my son's complexion, I hurried to add, "Sebastien's late mother was a Spaniard. He spends a lot of time in the sun and tends to brown easily. Don't worry. There's no Moorish or Jewish blood in him. He's a faithful Christian. He can recite *Pater noster* for you to prove it. We have all the documents."

The captain looked perplexed by my last few sentences. Perhaps, he was still a little hung over from the previous night. "I am thinking what size uniform he needs. That's all. He is rather broad in the shoulders, and he's probably not done growing. I have a spare doublet somewhere. It's gotten a bit snug on me and doesn't close over the belly, but it should fit the boy, if it comes to that."

Words cannot describe the bliss on Sebastien's face. "Monsieur *le gendarme*! Does this mean ..."

Our new friend placed his large dirty hands over his armored chest. "I cannot promise anything, but I'm willing to mention you to my superiors. We always need good men."

"Are you sure you don't want to see his papers?" I intervened. "Like I said, his mother was a pure-blooded Spaniard, from a military family too. They are still in active service. Holy Brotherhood, you know? That new royal couple, Ferdinand and Isabella, they really like order."

Was I overwhelming him with too much detail? Did those words mean anything to him? Did he know the term for the peacekeeping force in Spain? The look of confusion and fatigue suggested otherwise.

"Personally, I don't give a damn if his mother is a Bedouin or an Egyptian," he said. "Lineage only becomes an issue when it's time for promotion. We aren't there yet." He looked straight at Sebastien. "I'll give you the directions to my garrison. Come by tomorrow morning and be prepared to demonstrate your skill in the saddle. Tell them Captain Lucius Castelmaure invited you."

His surname made me gasp. "Castelmaure! How do you spell it? Never mind. So you are a Gascon?"

"So they say. My father was born outside Auch. He came to Paris seeking glory. I'm a first generation Parisian – with Gascon roots."

"What a coincidence! My wife is Gascon, from Lupiac. We are practically neighbors! Not often do you see such fair-haired people from that part of the country."

"Well, it's from the English side, going back to King Edward I." Lucius winced, like a schoolboy preparing to receive a whack on the knuckles from the headmaster. "At least I think that's what the English king was called."

I patted him on the shoulder to reassure him I was not going to judge him or his knowledge of history. The province of Gascony was a beast of its own, having changed hands a few times between England and France. The past of my own country was even more convoluted. "I knew you were an extraordinary person, Captain," I said, "with an open and welcoming heart. Your father knew what it was like to be a stranger in Paris. It is because of people like you that people like me want to come to this city."

Two days later Sebastien donned his new commander's spare doublet and commenced training, having passed the preliminary testing. The recruiting committee was outrageously impressed and agreed that he was a natural. One of the officers even joked that from now on they would only recruit from Spain. And three weeks later, twenty horses rode through the city gate. My partners in Catalonia had received my message and driven an entire herd into Paris. Each horse already had a new owner waiting for it. Lucius was enjoying Achilles immensely and put in a good word for me to his fellow officers.

His comrades paid me well in advance, which enabled me to buy a two-story house on Rue de Mouton. The building itself was in a decrepit state. The interior walls were fragile, which I actually liked, as I was going to tear them down anyway to form one enormous room for hosting festivities and performances with musicians, poets and acrobats. There would be no tables, only rugs. We would sit on the floor and eat with our hands. Utensils take too long to clean. We would sleep on the same rugs with sacks under our heads. It worked with my philosophy. A house without walls. A country without borders. Other people would see our way of life, fall in love with it and eventually adopt it. That was my ultimate goal. And those who would find our ways odd would not dare to speak against us if we had the right allies.

Befriending Captain Castlemaure was our first fundamental success. We had the military on our side. But there was more ground to conquer. I was going to need my girls to help me accomplish the rest of my diplomatic goals.

Elinor, my snow-haired imp, was making quite a splash. As soon as we arrived, she captured the heart of a certain lecturer of English extraction, a Chaucer expert, who was teaching drama and dialectics at the College of Lisieux. Being of revolutionary mindset, he insisted on being addressed by his nickname,

Blackfeather, outside college walls.

He confided in me that his dream was to establish a permanent theater that would produce tasteful, thought-provoking secular plays, because that was where his passion lay and not those cryptic morality productions that followed a strict formula in terms of content and presentation. He found religious drama as a genre rather stifling, and he did not like being stifled. He wanted more freedom. A man after my own heart! I knew he and I would get along.

His chief grievance was that the city never gave him enough of a budget for sets and costumes, and as result, his productions came out looking lame and farcical. People were already confused and did not know when to laugh. Parisians, he concluded, have an odd sense of humor, making it hard for an author from the English tradition to connect with them. Plus, there was that instinctive residual animosity left over from the Hundred Years' War.

"They are beating me down constantly," he lamented to me once. "I'm good enough to organize street festivals, but not to teach higher level courses. I get a small segment on Chaucer, that's all. They will not stage my plays in any respectable venue. What can I say? Parisians simply do not like foreigners."

A part of me was itching to tell Blackfeather that having an English great-grandmother did not make him a foreigner, but another part, the diplomatic one, did not want to look like I was downplaying his plight. Clearly, he felt ostracized due to his origin. To contest that would make me look dismissive and unsympathetic, and I wanted to remain on good terms with him. After all, the man had access to that diabolic device called the printing press and expressed interest in printing my travel memoirs.

For the record, I really was acquainted with Vlad the Impaler. This is not one of my tall tales. I was his stable master during his second reign which lasted from 1456 until 1462. That was where I learned to appreciate horses, to breed and train them. I left Vlad during the conflict with the Transylvanian Saxons. He really did carry men, women and children from a Saxon village into Wallachia only to have them impaled. I wanted no part in that, so I split from my master, taking along a handful of his best horses. I am sure he bemoaned the loss of his stellar equestrians. Do I have stories to tell! I just was not sure if the dainty academician had the stomach for them.

The important part was that Blackfeather was already making grandiose plans involving Elinor. He was already writing dramatic works, crafting his leading female characters with her in mind. He said in England they only used male actors for female roles, which he found disquieting.

On the other hand, my older girl, Agniese was worrying me. Ever since we left Lourdes, she had not been herself. She must have contracted some disease while we were crossing the Pyrenees. She spent much of her time in the back of the van, sleeping on a pile of costumes. I could not tempt her to lift her head and look at the magnificent scenery. I touched her forehead, and her skin felt a little warm. During her performance she would run out of breath quickly, take frequent breaks and drink from the flask attached to her belt. She was becoming unpresentable – and therefore unmarketable.

One night I overheard her talking to Elinor about their future. Even though they were not related by blood to me or to each other, they shared a sisterly bond that was stronger than that between my two boys. To confuse you further, Agniese, despite her dusky skin and raven hair, was French, at least on her mother's side, as far as I knew.

It was Elinor who came from a Moorish tribe. Her natural parents were at a loss. They did not know what to make of their white-haired child with garnet eyes and pink skin that burned in the sun so easily. I jumped at the chance to take her into my family. I knew I would find good use for her. The girls did not know much about their heritage, so I allowed them to believe whatever they wanted; it was better that way.

They were tenderly attached to each other, my two adopted daughters. Ever since Agniese had started showing symptoms of a malady that seemed awfully like the infamous "white plague," Elinor had been sleeping next to her.

"When I die," I heard Agniese say, "I want you to continue dancing *La Rotta*. Promise me, you will remember everything I taught you. All the songs, all the dances, all the card tricks. As long as you remember those things, I shall live in you."

Her words disheartened me, to say the least. She truly believed she was dying and seemed at peace with it. I did not detect any desire to fight. She spent most of her time combing and braiding Elinor's hair and humming old Spanish ballads.

Agniese, no! Not now, my mud-colored lamb. I have grand plans for you, for you are an exquisite, mystical beauty, the kind that appeals to men of refined taste, men of knowledge and power who do not crave buxom tavern belles. We will find you a lover who will treat you like the divinity that you are and give our family the much-needed patronage. In this time of uncertainty, you cannot have enough friends in high places. Your little sister understands that. She is getting cozy with that scrawny academician fellow. I am already building a stage for his next play. Now we need to get the church on our side. You have already made quite an impression. Do not stop now!

A few days after the festivities at Rue des Bernardins my wife dressed Agniese in a dress made of green brocade with long sleeves ending in flared cuffs, a low cut bodice, and a full skirt with very minimal under-petticoats, which allowed the outline of her long legs to show through when she moved. Denise arranged the girl's wild hair in the most flattering fashion, braiding it at the crown only, leaving the tresses to flow freely. Then we took her to the early mass and put her as close to the altar as possible in hopes that she would catch the eye of some senior clergy member. The foolish girl coughed, wheezed, shivered and nodded off throughout the service. And to whom did she end up speaking after the service? The nineteen-year old organist, naturally.

He took her up to the gallery above the western portal. Seeing them standing very closely, their heads almost touching, I could not ignore the esthetic poignancy, the contrast between them: bronze and charcoal next to marble and fire. Through the recessional chant of the choir, I could hear Monsieur Dufort utter the word "immunity," placing a great deal of emphasis on it. Perhaps, he was referring to some privilege he enjoyed under the auspice of the bishop. I picked up the triumphant and vengeful notes in his voice. *Immunity!*

Dear girl, I do not deny that this youth is a musical genius and does exude a certain Gothic allure, but he cannot repeal execution orders. I do not know how to put it politely. His possessions consist of a half-melted candle and a music theory textbook. The bishop hoards his commission money. I have a more suitable match in mind for you: Monseigneur Desmoulins.

Now, do not start protesting; let me finish. I would never subject you to an unpleasant experience. Believe me, my girl, he will devour you tenderly. I have known that man for many years and am familiar with his taste in women. He is not keen on those who are grounded or respectable. A frail sorceress is more to his liking. Tomorrow we shall go to mass again and bring one of our famous Andalusian paintings as a gift. Do not reject his advances. Let him do what he wishes and try to enjoy his ministrations. Yes, he is in his mid-thirties, but very well preserved for his age. He still has his teeth and his hair, which is far more than most men can say for themselves. He goes hunting and takes fencing lessons. If you touch his shoulder, you will notice how solid his muscles are. If he wraps his arms around you, I do not think you will be disgusted. Imagine his long fingers running through your hair. He will lay you down and croon Italian lullabies. He will ask for your consent before he tries anything too bold. I would never, ever give you to a man that I believed to be licentious and greedy and crude.

And when he is done with you, he will send you off with charming souvenirs, the kind you could not expect from a secular lover. Monseigneur Desmoulins had been very generous with his first mistress. He had continued giving her money even after they had stopped sharing pillows. And they had parted under the most hideous of circumstances. Do not ask me how I know this. I just do.

Oh, did I mention? Men of God take exceptional care of their love children. Being fathered by a priest is a tremendous advantage, especially for a boy. There is a secret section at the cloister attached to Notre-Dame where high-born bastards are being kept. They all receive a stellar education. Some rather formidable figures have come out of that place: physicians, prosecutors, artists. I believe your copper-haired composer is one of the alumni. Ask him next time you see him. However, do not lead him on needlessly. Save your energy for Monseigneur Desmoulins, and you will not be sorry.

I know I sound like such a hypocrite sometimes. Here I am, preaching free love in one sentence and then instructing you whom to bed in another. I know you have plenty of affection for all the men of Paris. Your body is a bottomless vessel of pleasure. All I am asking is that you let our friend Desmoulins drink the first sip. Priests assign a great deal of significance to a woman's virginity. The very thought of initiating a girl into womanhood drives them wild. They are willing to pay a handsome price for the privilege. Afterwards you can squander yourself. You can have your haunted organist. You can even have that archer fellow with an unspellable surname, who trains your brother. I know you like him too, though he does not look too fresh. I am begging you about one thing. If you find yourself alone with Captain Castelmaure and notice any sores or rashes on any part of his body, please feel free to stop him. There is no need to go any further out of mere pity and a sense of obligation. You do not know where that man has been. Making love to a soldier is like bathing in a public bath at the end of the day. Seriously, there are polite ways to decline a man's advances even after the clothes are off. Tell him you have a headache or that you are feeling suddenly nauseous. Agniese, do you hear me?

Here my dusky angel stirred, lifted her disheveled head and glanced at me over her shoulder. "I do not think it is such a good idea to give Monseigneur Desmoulins one of your paintings."

Thank the gods! She could still talk.

"Why not?" I asked. "Don't you think he appreciates art?"

"Precisely. He's an astute man, who can spot a fake. He'll realize the painting was not done in Granada. He'll know it came from your attic workshop. The paint is still wet and soft."

"I assure you, my lamb, he will not mind if the gift comes from your hands. I saw how he looked at you that night on Rue des Bernardins. Have pity on the poor man. He is positively smitten by you."

"Papa, there's a tournament tonight," Sebastien told me one Saturday when he came home from the training. "May I go?"

"What sort of tournament?"

"*Les gladiateurs urbains.*" His carbuncle eyes flashed. "A clash of urban gladiators. It's taking place on Rue Grenier-sur-l'Eau, across from the Port-au-Foin. Scholars versus beggars. Rowdy boys from the College of Lisieux will fight those from the slum in a curated brawl. May I go, please? Oh, Papa, I've been so good all week. Haven't I earned a bit of fun?"

When Sebastien mentioned gladiators, my ears perked up. He knew my obsession with Spartacus.

"I don't know about it," I replied with affected austerity. "You've just started training with the archers. Do you think your new commander would approve?"

"Why, Papa, he presides over the event! There's nothing unlawful about it. Nobody is cajoling those men to fight. They do it of their own free will. It's only a game with titles and prizes. Nobody has gotten killed so far. And it's taking place in a part of the city where they won't disturb anyone. Please, Papa?"

I was so moved that my eighteen-year-old was still asking my permission. It would never occur to his brother to ask me anything. Josef came and went as he pleased, and when he deigned to have dinner with us, he always sat in a corner with his back turned to his family, pulling apart a pork shank and licking his fingers. Sebastien would still lean on my shoulder and kiss his stepmother on both cheeks before leaving for the day. For a future lieutenant, he was unusually affectionate. And there was nothing false about his tokens. He did not do it to soften us. It must have been that warm Spanish blood. He was perfectly sincere. But to be fair, both my boys were.

"So, on whose side are you fighting?" I asked him, throwing my arm around his neck. "Beggars or scholars?"

"Oh, I'm going as a spectator. I'll be standing right next to my commander. If things get out of hand, at least I'll be there to help him."

"You're so dutiful. I'm sure he appreciates your loyalty."

"You're welcome to come with me, Papa," he said. "It will be merrier that way."

To be honest, I was a little tired, and the prospect of watching an orchestrated street brawl did not excite me, but I did not want to disappoint Sebastien. It meant the world to me that he wanted to include me in all his youthful adventures.

"All right," I said, ruffling his dark curls. "We cannot stay too long. I have carpenters coming tomorrow to build the stage on the second floor."

"So we're going to have our own home theater, just like those noble Italian families?"

"Where have you been, my boy? We've been talking about it since we arrived in Paris. There will be hanging lanterns, curtains, a holding place for costumes and props, benches for the audience."

Speaking of the curtains, Denise was busy sewing square pieces of fabric together to make them look like a motley chess board. She was a virtuoso with a needle. Every piece of clothing we wore had been crafted by her hands. I urged her to start taking clients. She could make good money sewing for the wives and daughters of officials. Experienced seamstresses were always in demand. Some of her designs were truly fanciful, with Basque and Spanish elements. I only worried about Denise's temper being a little wild and snippy for the pampered Parisian damsels, who were hard to please and prone to swoons. Her gaze was sharper than the needle, and her tongue was faster than the scissors. She had already shot a few venomous comments. Denise did not like how much time I was spending with some officer's widow, even though I assured her that she was free to explore the pool of potential paramours. Still, according to her, I had an unfair advantage. She maintained that a man over forty has more intimate prospects than a woman the same age. I kept reminding her she was not a typical forty-three-year old woman. Having never been through childbirth, she was still taut and pert in all those places men like to touch. With her girlish figure, she could easily get herself a younger lover. I would only cheer her on. It would do her good. It would smooth out the wrinkles forming around those gorgeous mahogany eyes. It killed me to see her wilt away, sinking deeper into jealousy and bitterness that had not afflicted her before.

Before leaving for the night, I blew her a kiss across the gutted room. She responded with a long, intent "I-am-on-to-you" stare.

"Where's Agniese?" Sebastien asked casually on his way out. He may have as well asked where his hat was. "I haven't seen her all day. Is she hiding in the corner somewhere? She's been sleeping an awful lot."

"Your sister is on a rendezvous with our priest friend," I replied, mimicking his flippant tone. "He promised to take her on a tour of dungeons."

"Ah!" Sebastien grabbed a wrinkled apple out of the basket and took a bite. "So she must be having a marvelous time wrapped in the sleeves of his cassock."

"I highly doubt that they are still fully clothed. I say, his cassock and her dress are on the floor in a pile. What do you expect? The man is famished. It's been ages since his last affair."

We put on our night cloaks and mounted the horses. We were still getting used to the smell of the city. No, we were not in the Pyrenees any longer. The air did not get any fresher as we approached Rue Grenier-sur-l'Eau. A few times we had to pull out our sacks with dried lavender and hold them to our noses. We smelled the crowd before we saw it. The beggars were clustering quietly alongside the wharf. I counted about twenty filthy heads wrapped in rags. They were better behaved than their opposing party from the University. The scholars, their faces painted in mud and soot, jumped and made savage grimaces as if to mimic their opponents.

The master of ceremonies was a short, blond, round-faced youth dressed in oversized chainmail. Standing on a makeshift podium made of old vegetable crates, flanked by two burning torches, he was holding a horn that also doubled as a staff. There was something tyrannical and comical in his figure. One by one, the contestants from both sides approached him for inspection. He made sure that they did not have any hidden weapons – the combat was to be strictly unarmed. The participants could only use their limbs, heads and teeth.

Lucius, atop his horse, was positioned in the shadow, his hand on the hilt of his sword. He had a few younger archers with him, poised to intervene. I assumed that Sebastien would join his comrades, but instead he chose to stay by my side.

"The fight will last ten minutes," he explained to me in a secretive whisper. "The ringmaster has a sand timer around his neck. The goal is to put as many opponents on their backs as possible. The winning party gets a barrel of wine."

"These men are willing to risk their necks for a chance to get drunk?"

Never mind. That was a pointless question.

The first blow of the horn signaled the commencement of the battle. The beggars and the scholars rolled into one mass that looked like a disturbed anthill from a distance. To my surprise, there was very little grunting or shouting.

Sebastien was bouncing on his toes, his fists clenched and his eyes exuding childish bliss. Which side was he rooting for?

As for myself, I struggled to stay awake. Having witnessed real hostilities between the Wallachian soldiers and the Transylvanian Saxons, I found the urban gladiator tournament boring. I did not know how to communicate it to Sebastien that if he was going to become a professional soldier, eventually he would have to experience real warfare. Truthfully, I was more interested in learning how Agniese fared on her rendezvous with Desmoulins.

The second blow of the horn broke my reverie.

"Who won?" I asked Sebastien in a sleepy voice.

"Papa, you weren't paying attention!"

"I was, too! But it's hard to tell them apart in the dark. So, who won?"

"It was a tie. Six men down on each side. Which means, they have to patch up their wounded and come back in two hours to finish the tournament."

"I'm not staying here for another two hours. I'm anxious to talk to your sister."

To our surprise, when we came home around midnight, Agniese was still not back. Little Elinor was fast asleep on a rug, wrapped in the embroidered scarf she had received as a gift from her playwright admirer. Denise was still awake, sewing the curtain for the home theater. I noticed she had made some progress in the past few hours. There was not much left of the candle, but Denise did not need light. Her fingers were moving with the same tireless vigor. Every time she stuck the needle into the fabric, a soldier dropped dead somewhere.

"Back so soon?" she asked with a noticeable hint of displeasure. "Sebastien didn't stay with his new friends at the garrison? It's unbecoming for a young man of eighteen to spend his nights at home. You do not want your son to become a laughing stock, do you?"

Your son ... Ooh ... That was serious. I had not heard her use those words in a long time. She was sewing her venom into the motley muslin, stitch by stitch. Having decided not to press her any further, I stretched out on the mattress next to Sebastien. Within minutes my boy was asleep, which was more than I could say for myself. I kept thinking about my little girl in the arms of Desmoulins. I hoped, I prayed she was enjoying herself.

Agniese came back in the early hours of the morning, disheveled and limping, with a strange mad fire in her reddened eyes. It was Lucius who brought her on his new horse. I had to chuckle at the irony of the situation: she left with one man and came with another.

"What did you do, silly girl?" I asked her when she plopped down on the rug next to her sleeping sister. "I told you not to fight him. It's useless to fight a man like Desmoulins."

"You're asking me what I did, Papa?" Rocking back and forth, she began rubbing her ankle. "I did everything you told me. I pretended to be interested in his ideas and his work."

"Good. That's all good. And then?"

"And then, I couldn't pretend anymore." She looked down and stuttered with embarrassment. "I became genuinely interested. I wanted to know more."

"That's even better! I told you, Desmoulins is a fascinating man."

"That he is. I kept asking him questions, and then he ... he showed me a few things, things I wasn't prepared to see. Now he probably thinks I'm some skittish chit."

"Surely, Desmoulins doesn't think that. But why are you

limping? What happened to your foot?"

"I don't want to talk about it."

"That's all right. You don't have to."

I gave her some of that herbal brew Denise had prepared for her the night before. Her terror was a good sign. If she still could get frightened, it meant she was not quite ready to die. Her sickness had not progressed that far. While she was drinking, I examined her foot discreetly. It did not look bruised or swollen. I had no idea what she was complaining about.

"This much I will tell you, Papa," she whispered after emptying the cup with the brew. "Monseigneur Desmoulins is *not* a man of God."

Chapter 3

A Perfect Name for a Heretic

(Monseigneur Desmoulins)

If I ever decide to leave the church and start a new life far away from this bleak city, I shall change my name to Nicholas. There are two great men by the same name who influenced me greatly. One of them is Nicholas Flamel, the legendary scribe and alchemist, whose empty house I pass several times a week. The other one is Nicholas von Kues, a German astronomer whom I had met briefly before his death. I am not fond of my real name. It is dull and weak, and you will never hear it for the reasons I just mentioned. I think I shall revert to the original Germanic version of my surname. Nicholas Van Der Molen. A perfect name for a heretic, wouldn't you agree? You may have heard this already: I am going to hell. I made my peace with it. I know I will be in good company. Do you hear how calm my voice is? No anxiety. However, there are some things I cannot speak of without my hands curling into fists.

You know what makes me sick? Pierre de Laval is only a few years older than me, yet he is already the Archbishop of Reims. I understand, not everyone can be archbishop, live in a palace and have regular audiences with the King of France. Someone must do the mundane work. Someone must hear confessions, deliver and dispense the body of Christ, burn heretics and hang witches.

"I don't know how you do it," Laval said to me once. "I have so much appreciation for your work. It's people like you who preserve the glory of the Church."

Pierre de Laval and I met back in 1460. His boarding school came to Paris to visit the College of Lisieux and attend a few lectures. Being the two most intelligent boys in the whole group, we quickly singled each other out and bonded as scholars over the early writings of Nicholas Flamel. The disparity in our social ranks did not seem to matter. Laval's family was far, far more prominent than mine. For Heaven's sake, his older sister Jeanne was married to King Rene of Anjou. My father was just an untitled Flemish nobleman.

Before parting ways, Pierre de Laval and I made a pact – and I do not take pacts lightheartedly – that if one of us moved up in life, he would help the other rise. It was rather clear which one of us would ascend to power first. By age twenty-one Laval had been appointed abbot of Saint-Aubin in Angers. He and his older brother, count de Gavre, attended the Estates General held in Tours in 1467, rubbing elbows with royalty. What was I doing at the time? Don't ask. I cringe when I look back at my early dabbling in medicine and theology.

Laval remembered our pact. Shortly before the legislative assembly, he paid me a surprise visit. One morning I received a message that the Abbot of Saint-Aubin was waiting for me on the Pont Saint-Michel, which was an odd place for a meeting. But sure enough, Laval was standing on the corner of the bridge, tapping the pavement with the tip of his boot. When our eyes met, he ran toward me, nearly tripping over his robe.

"*Mon Dieu*, Desmoulins! Look at you. You're wearing a cassock. So it's done?"

"For better or worse," I concluded with a shrug. Truth be told, I was still getting used to wearing a black sack with sleeves. "What brings you here?"

"A dire emergency. I need your help."

"To write a speech?"

"No, it's a matter of life and death. I don't know where to begin, but there's a child in grave danger, a four and a half year old boy, who desperately needs a home."

I could feel my right eyebrow arch. Since when did Pierre de Laval, brother-in-law to the King of Anjou, worry about orphans?

"There are thousands of children in France who need homes," I said. "What makes this particular child so special?" Then it dawned on me. "Oh ... Oh! Never mind." My friend was chewing on his lower lip, his fingers interlocked, waiting for me to assemble the pieces of the puzzle. "It all happened so quickly." The sleeves of his robe rolled back as he threw his arms up. "My head is still spinning. The boy's mother died, and now this poor creature ..."

"Laval," I said sternly, "we've talked about it on many occasions. You were the one who always lectured me on taking precaution."

He launched forward with the ferocity and desperation of a cornered schoolboy.

"Don't give me that look, Desmoulins. I don't need your judgment. I've already torn three layers of skin off my back for that. I was bewitched!"

My opinion of him suddenly plummeted. Bewitched! A strong statement coming from a weak man. *Bewitched.* Truly, Laval, was that the best you could manage in self-defense? Knowing his low threshold for pain, I surmised that his mortification of the flesh involved whacking himself over the shoulder with a switch a few times. That was supposed to atone for his stupidity and recklessness?

"How did the mother die?" I asked him in the methodical voice of a procurator.

"Most unnaturally, by her own hand. The villagers found her with her wrists cut. The child was crouching in the corner. The bane of unwed motherhood must have gotten too much to bear. I'm still in shock, Desmoulins."

He leaned in, and for a moment I feared he was about to fall into my arms and weep, so I stepped back.

"Collect yourself, Laval. There are people around. I must say, you picked an interesting place for this conversation."

"I don't understand," he continued mumbling, staring into the pavement. "I had done everything to ensure her comfort. I'd rented a lovely cottage outside Angers and even procured a fake death certificate for a fictitious husband. Elisabeth could have easily passed herself for a young widow. The villagers didn't need to know the truth. She could've gotten married. I wouldn't have minded. How could she do this to me? After all the kindness I'd shown her. You realize I haven't slept in three months?"

"And you think everyone else is getting ten hours of sleep each night?"

Laval raised his eyes at me and slapped himself on the forehead.

"I'm such a callous idiot. Here I am wailing about my own pain. I'm so sorry about your parents. You must be ... Ah!" He locked me in his embrace. This time I did not have a chance to recoil. "How are you holding up, my poor friend?"

I politely brushed off his condolences.

"I never cared much for my stepmother. And my father pretty much stopped existing for me after he married that avaricious harpy. One could say I've been an orphan since my mother's death. Right now I don't feel an acute sense of loss, only the comfort of closure."

"Thank God for that." Laval made the sign of the cross. "And your little brother?"

"That whimpering bundle? He's in good hands. I think I made the right choice. An older childless couple. They promised to pay for my textbooks, but I'm not too optimistic. I've yet to see a single sou from them." I shrugged, having made peace with the thought of having been duped by the Métiviers. "That's what you should do for your son. Find an adoptive family that's discreet and not too prominent."

"You don't think I've tried that route? It's not that simple. Right now he is in a very posh orphanage, which is more like a miniature boarding school for children ... in a similar predicament."

I knew the institution to which Laval was referring. It was an idyllic rural estate on the outskirts of Orleans – a paradise for high-born bastards. A jovial middle-aged couple was running the enterprise. They had a cook, a laundress and a grammar teacher on staff. As you can imagine, the place was not cheap. Only the wealthiest could afford to send their unwanted male offspring there.

"Your son should feel right at home among his own kind," I said, "playing all day with the children of Cardinal de Bourbon. I wouldn't have minded spending my own childhood there."

"I told you, it's not that simple. Daniel doesn't get on very well with the others."

"Is he violent?"

"Not outwardly. I've never seen him lash out at anyone. He mostly sits in a corner, bangs his head against the wall and hums something. I think he's composing music!"

"And his compositions aren't well received?"

"Strange, sinister things started happening shortly after his arrival." Laval's lofty brow clouded as he narrated the story. "The other boys started falling ill. Some of them died within a very short span of time. It was some sort of mysterious disease. Understandably, the boys' fathers were upset. They demanded answers. The owners of the school were terrified. Now they are accusing my son of sorcery. They claim he cast a spell on the other children to get rid of the competition, like a cuckoo hatchling that kills its nest mates. Can you believe it? I'm worried about them burning Daniel on a pyre. When people are frightened to such an extent, they are capable of anything."

"It's an awfully sad story, Laval," I said, "but what do you want me to do about this?"

"The right thing, naturally." He placed his hands on my shoulders. "I know I can count on you to follow through."

"The right thing ... And what would that be?"

"You will raise my son."

Just like that! I was fairly certain that I heard him correctly. "You ... you want me to come forth and claim him as my own?"

"Of course not. You'll make it look like an act of charitable patronage. We'll come up with a plausible story. Those things are done all the time. Surely, you've been serving the church long enough to know that."

"Yes, I'm still learning. I catch bits and pieces of sacristy gossip. I just didn't think I'd find myself entangled in such an alliance so early on. Why did you approach me of all people? I don't even like children. Did you miss that part where I disposed of my little brother?"

"But Daniel is no ordinary child. He is *my* child, a Laval through and through. Above all, he's a musical genius, the next Guillaume de Machaut."

"Then maybe you should let your *own* family raise your genius."

"My family doesn't know about him."

"For the love of Christ, don't tell me he's the first bastard in the Laval dynasty." For a second I thought my friend was going to recoil, but instead he moved his hands from my shoulders to my throat.

"You picked a bad time to flaunt your moral superiority, Desmoulins. Forgive me for not being as holy as you. We're running out of time. My son is in danger of being burned. The world turned its back on that poor innocent."

"Correction, Laval." I finally brought myself to remove his hands. "You were the one who turned your back on him. His birth is on your conscience."

"And his death will be on yours! His ashes will settle on your skin. His cries will echo in your ears every night. Have you no pity? Do you not see the tragic irony of my position? There are many things I can do except recognize my own child." Now that his hands were free, he could use them to enhance his narrative with some choreography, like drawing circles in the air. "I have my family's reputation to consider. I'm not some provincial choir boy, I'm going to be a cardinal someday! I cannot disappoint the people who have already done so much to advance my career."

"Sure, present it like an act of altruism. I love how you put a heroic spin on your every blunder. Did you learn this in dialectics class?"

"Easy for you to judge me, Desmoulins! You're a penniless orphan. You'll never amount to much. You think your intellect alone is enough to propel you? It won't. Your languages and formulas are worthless. Just because you got your dual doctorate in medicine and canon law, you aren't unassailable."

"Triple doctorate, actually," I corrected him. "Don't forget liberal arts. I took it up just for fun, so I can ridicule pretentious dramatists. It's amazing how much useless knowledge you can rake up if you don't let the lower half of your body run ahead of the upper half."

"Keep saying that, Desmoulins. You'll be counting your doctorates on the way to your execution. Your erudition will land you on a pyre. It will be your turn to burn. And it will be my turn to point my finger at you. Ha!"

Laval's chest-beating and arm-flailing was getting tiresome. I had never seen that man so fired up. His wild mimicry was attracting unnecessary attention from the passers-by.

"Fine," I heard myself say. I really did not want to quarrel with him. "I'll take your bastard. Send him to me. Just do it after Easter. The next few weeks are going to be insanely busy. The bishop is running me ragged."

This time Laval did not throw himself on my neck. He simply crossed his arms and smirked complacently, his agitation instantly cooled.

"Grand. I'm glad we achieved an understanding. You won't regret this arrangement, Desmoulins, I promise you. Tell me what you want. Anything at all. I'll see that you get it."

Now it was my turn to dictate the terms. "For starters, I'd like some books. There's nothing good to read."

"In all of Paris? I find it hard to believe."

"Maybe I'm not looking in the right places. The cathedral library is surprisingly meager. It's the same old: Aristotle, Thomas Aquinas. Things I've read a long time ago."

He squinted with a conspiratorial air. "Well, what kind of books would you like?"

"Laval, you know all too well what kind of book I like. You and I have very similar interests. There are some … esoteric titles. I don't have to spell them out."

"Oh …"

"Yes, those titles. Every abbey library has a secret room where ordinary brothers are not allowed. Can something be arranged?"

"I think it can. Transporting those items can be perilous and costly, but I cannot have Desmoulins get bored for lack of good literature."

"Intellectual boredom can push a man to horrible deeds."

Completely reconciled, we embraced. I felt him slip a bag of coins into my sleeve. It felt pleasantly heavy. I knew this gift was not intended to belittle me. It came from Laval's frazzled but deeply loyal heart.

"Promise me, my dear friend," he whispered before we parted ways, "that if you ever find yourself bewitched, you'll tell me. Come to me. I don't want you to go through this torment alone."

I was not as ignorant of matters of the flesh as Laval surmised. Despite our friendship, I kept some things from him, because otherwise he would start smothering me in sympathy and calling me a brave, strong boy. At some point I had enjoyed the company of a certain lady friend, whose name, just like my own, I shall not reveal. I would not go as far as saying that she was my intellectual equal, but she, beyond doubt, was a few steps above most females. We had engaged in a few stimulating debates. Through the veil of girlish coyness, I perceived a bold, stubborn streak. She took genuine interest in physics, mathematics and astronomy. I had even allowed her to read some of my books – the more accessible ones.

Her Latin was very basic. Still, it was stronger than that of some of my fellow students at the University. The family she came from was quite removed from all things scientific. They neither encouraged nor threatened her when it came to scholarly pursuits. Her father was dead, and her mother was too sickly and apathetic. In that sense, my lady friend possessed enviable freedom. There was nobody to push her into marriage. Having no dowry except for her glistening dark eyes, a fatalistic sense of humor and a talent for adding a row of numbers in her head, she did not make an attractive bride. When I started coming by their house, nobody asked me about my intentions. Marriage was not one of them. I taught her a few things from the realm of Greek philosophy. She taught me a few things too, like self-restraint. We learned to give each other wicked pleasure without consequences. We spent countless evenings exchanging bold caresses and irreverent jokes. No topic, no experiment was off limits. While my fellow students from the

University were seeking relief in brothels and taverns, I was getting the same favors, only more skillfully executed, free of charge, from a clean, disease-free girl, who had no other lovers. She and I made plans to open a laboratory and create a device with a magnifying glass clear and powerful enough to see the celestial bodies up close. I could have spent another twenty years like that, beneath the orange trees of the long neglected orchard, with a stack of books, a bottle of excellent burgundy and my mistress.

Alas, someone up above decided I had been spoiled long enough. My life had been so alarmingly, so criminally pleasant. I found myself fatherless and penniless overnight. Suddenly, the idea of joining the Church did not seem so absurd. As most boys, I had imagined myself in that role. I had delivered improvised sermons to wooden soldiers and dispensed pieces of maize cake in lieu of communion. I had even burned a few soldiers for heresy. What child had not? In my adolescence I had wondered what benefits the Church could offer me. It had always been a possibility. After losing both parents, I revisited the idea with a renewed earnestness. I had taken enough courses on theology and canon law, I could take the vow tomorrow and free myself of headaches once and for all – I would never have to worry about making a living or deciding what to wear. My sensual escapades were not public knowledge. My University peers, whose company I scorned, were familiar with my arrogant, sardonic side. If I were to appear on the street shrouded in black cloth, it would not come as a massive shock to them.

Above all, it would silence my Italian and my Flemish relatives, who kept inquiring about my career and my marital prospects, yet were not in a hurry to provide any monetary support. "What a brilliant, gifted boy!" they would gasp. "What will he do for a living? Handsome too. Look at him. Long legs, regular facial features. A little austere. If only he'd smile more. But that scowl becomes him. Too bad he's so poor. What sensible woman will have him for a husband?" For once, they would leave me alone and let me focus on the things that interested me. All the gossip and tongue-clicking would stop.

Yes, I lacked humility, patience and a few other qualities

that it would be generally useful for a priest to have, but so did most young men entering the Church. Besides, I looked good in black. It matched my inner disposition. Nobody would expect me to smile now. I would have a perfect justification for my unfriendliness.

When I told my lady friend about my decision, she did not take the news well, much to my surprise. I had expected some initial bewilderment, but I was not prepared for that torrent of tears and reproaches. I gave her some time to grow accustomed to the new way of things. I tried explaining to her that it was not the end of us. Serving as a canon would give me access to the knowledge I needed to advance my scientific work. We could continue seeing each other, perhaps not as frequently as we did before, but that would only make our meetings sweeter.

Still, she could not reconcile with the idea of being a priest's mistress. No, we were to part for good, as much as it ravaged her. With trembling hands, she returned all the books I had lent to her, including those I told her she could keep. I wanted her to continue working on her Latin grammar. No, she insisted on returning them. Clearly, I loved those books more than her. I had made my choice, and she would not stand in my way. Nor would she tolerate her demeaning position. She had waited for me long enough. You see, she wanted respectability. And she started looking for it in very peculiar places – like other men's beds.

After our separation, she came totally unhinged. Every night she would stroll through Rue de Parvis with a new soldier, each one drunker and lewder than his predecessor.

Understandably, I was irked. I thought she and I had an understanding. To the best of my knowledge, the expectation on both sides was that there were no expectations. Free love without complications. Carnal joys without consequences. A bright future without obligations. Right?

Wrong. As it turned out, she and I had been playing the same game by different rules. A lifelong erotic friendship was not enough for her. All that time she had been dreaming of becoming Madame Van der Molen. She had envisioned us repairing the old house, pruning the overgrown trees in the garden, replacing the old furniture and building a cradle for our future offspring. *Mon Dieu!* Had I known about those fantasies, I would have broken off with her a long time ago.

Truth be told, I never wanted a family. The thought of a whining brat, soaked in snot and milk, made me shudder. The incident with my stepmother left me traumatized for life. For the last time: *I did not violate her.* Well, not quite. She was asking for it. That first Christmas after my mother's death I did not want to come home, knowing there was another woman there already. I tried to study, and she kept coming up, sneaking up behind me, leaning on my shoulder, touching my hair. "Let me see, let me see …" It was hellishly aggravating.

One day I snapped and pinned her against the desk, the very same desk on which I was writing my dissertation on Aristotle's usage of comedy. I did what I had to do. I gave her what she wanted, though maybe not exactly in the way she wanted. Otherwise, the bitch never would have left me alone. Eight and a half months later she gave birth to a yellow-haired, blue-eyed, button-nosed twerp. He could not have been mine. There was not a drop of Italian blood in him. I was not even sure it was my father's child. God knows how many other men she had dallied with. Mind you, it all happened while I was still with my first lady friend. She never found out. There was no need for her to know. What I did that Christmas break had nothing to do with her. It was an act of retaliation against my father who had replaced his first wife with a low-class harlot. I am only sharing this with you to show you how I felt about the prospect of having a family.

Someday I would meet a woman who would love me for my intellect, who would put up with my arrogance and occasional explosions of temper, who would assist me with experiments and not demand unreasonable sacrifices from me. I believed such a woman existed.

Nicholas Flamel, my idol, had a wife who assisted him with alchemy experiments and helped him decode *The Book of Abramelin* and replicate its recipe for the Philosopher's Stone. There was no reason to think I would not get lucky like Flamel.

Forgive me my lyrical digression. Back to business.

I had a new role to assume, that of a guardian to Laval's bastard. In preparation for his arrival, I tied up my cloister cell and put away some of the glass tubes. I was actually looking forward to meeting that child who had been accused of murdering seven or eight of his fellow students by means of sorcery.

When I pulled the sack off his head, I understood why Pierre Laval wanted to keep him as far away from himself as possible. The child was a caricature of his father, and a most unflattering one, almost incriminating.

The resemblance was undeniable: same glossy, copper-hued hair, same eyes the color of cracked ice, same harsh lines of the jaw and brow. There were no identifiable flaws in the child's visage, yet the overall impression was strangely disturbing and off-putting. The same traits that made Pierre de Laval so regal and magnetic made his son appear malicious and revolting. It was as if he embodied his father's hidden vice. I had no idea what the boy's mother looked like, but I began wondering if Laval was right in saying she was a witch.

Later I realized that Daniel Dufort represented much more than one man's violation of his vows. He symbolized everything that was wrong with our church as an institution. The collective grotesquerie of Catholicism was staring me in the face.

My theories were confirmed when in lieu of a greeting, he blurted out a random stanza from Virgil's *Aeneid*.

Musa, mihi causas memora, quo numine laeso,
quidve dolens, regina deum tot volvere casus
insignem pietate virum, tot adire labors
impulerit. Tantaene animis caelestibus irae?

The flat tone in which he recited those words suggested that he did not know their meaning.

O Muse! the causes and the crimes relate;
What goddess was provok'd, and whence her hate;
For what offense the Queen of Heav'n began
To persecute so brave, so just a man?

Perhaps, he was merely repeating what he had heard from

his previous caregivers. According to Laval, the boy's mother was a learned woman, who loved reading the poets of ancient Rome in the original. Or, perhaps, someone had instructed him to memorize those lines to impress me. And impressed I was. Not bad at all for four and a half. Even if he did not know the meaning of every word, the fact that he had memorized them in order implied that dark forces were aiding him. He could probably recite them backwards. Another mark of the Devil, no less.

"Just don't recite Latin verses before strangers," I said to him sternly. "We don't want anyone to get the wrong idea. People have been pilloried for less."

That last phrase became one I would use frequently. It was my duty to warn him about the fantastic dimness of the men in the precinct. My statement was broad and a little inaccurate. Technically speaking, you did not get pilloried for sorcery and cooperating with the Devil. You got burned at once. And Daniel could not be tried under the canon law. The order of immunity protected him. But he did not need to know those details. I wanted him to get in the habit of filtering his words and actions.

He touched his forehead, moving a strand of copper hair, and I noticed a huge gash above his left eyebrow. The pupil remained dilated. He must have put up a fight on his way to Paris. Apparently, those entrusted with transporting him to the capital did not care that he arrived intact.

Suddenly, blood gushed out of his nostrils, like water out of a gargoyle's mouth, soaking his clothes and pooling on the floor. I found myself disquieted. What if he died right there in my cell? What would I tell his father? Pierre Laval would blame it on me.

Fortunately, the bleeding stopped as suddenly as it started. Over the course of the ordeal, the creature did not make a single noise. I wiped his face with my handkerchief and helped him remove his stained vest.

"Now listen to me. I don't want you to have any illusions about this city. The only things that happen in Paris are student riots and plague outbreaks."

Daniel's father kept his side of the bargain, at least in the beginning. Mysterious parcels started arriving, anonymous gifts, delivered straight to the step of my cloister cell. They were mostly books, rare books that you would not find in most church libraries; books that could lead one to the gallows or the pyre. The canon law is like a dark, convoluted maze full of dead ends and surprising escape routes. I learned to navigate that maze. My cell and the possessions inside were inviolable and not subject to inspection. The bishop himself could not enter my personal sacred space. Outside the cell the book became perilous and incriminating.

One time Laval sent me a charming eleven-year-old Flemish girl with sand-colored ringlets and sapphire eyes. I received a note instructing me to go to the second story of a tavern on Rue de Saint-Jacques to receive my surprise. The girl was waiting for me there with a plate of freshly picked strawberries. She tore off her white cap and began some sort of harvest dance. The performance started in the middle of the room and ended in my lap. She smelled like milk and wild flowers. The poor creature looked a little nervous. Or maybe she pretended to be nervous to create an illusion of chastity. Either way, I had no desire to unlace her bodice. In her faltering descant she asked me what I craved, so I told her about the nagging cramp in my right shoulder. Indeed, I had spent a lot of time writing, and my entire right arm was feeling a little stiff. My request must have struck her as odd. Nevertheless, she dutifully kneaded the sore spot with her tiny hands. I have to say, for a Flemish girl, she was rather weak. Her tentative pinches got boring very soon. I gave her a few coins and told her to come back in a few years, if she was still in business. She slipped off my knee and ran off spryly, before I changed my mind. It must have been the easiest money she had ever made.

At any rate, I thanked my friend for the unique token and politely asked him not to send me anyone under the age of fifteen. Oh, and no blondes, for the love of God. They reminded me of my stepmother. To be blunt, I was a little offended that Laval would send me a gift of such kind without inquiring first about my tastes. He assumed that because he, the Abbot of

Saint-Aubin, was wild about fair-haired women, the rest of us were too.

In addition to the condemned books and the Flemish maiden I also received two Italian riding suits of superb quality, tailored to fit me perfectly, with gloves, belts, boots and plumed hats. The fabric on those suits was so fine and soft, they were practically unnoticeable under the cassock. I could easily walk around the city, wearing two layers of clothes. I saw undeniable poignancy in the duplicity of my situation. Everyone thought I was visiting the sick – and, for your comfort, I did some of that too, just not fourteen hours at a time – but then I would leave the city and go hunting.

I had a tiny lodge in the woods, old but surprisingly sturdy, the only piece of property left from my father. There I kept my longbow, a supply of arrows and a few knives for cleaning game. The walls were decorated with the heads of the animals I had killed. It would make a nice love nest, it really would. Cozy with a touch of macabre, with all those dead deer and boars staring from every angle. The only problem was that I had nobody to bring there. I apologize in advance for another lyrical digression. I had not given up on the idea of finding a replacement for my first lady friend. In fact, I was very much open to that possibility.

In reality, finding a new paramour proved to be more difficult than I had originally thought. Paris was not exactly swarming with erudite maidens who took interest in astronomy. Talk about a shocking discovery! I had underestimated the repellent powers of my cassock. Sometimes I forgot I was a priest. In my mind I was still an unattached college student. Apparently, that was not how women perceived me. When passing me on the street, they would bow their heads and avert their eyes. How would I even go about approaching one of them? "How do you do, mademoiselle? Come by my cell sometime. We'll read *De arithmetricis complementis* and quench our lust afterwards." Clearly, I had not thought through the details.

One time I overhead Chartier, the old bishop talk to his first vicar in the sacristy. They were making a schedule of services for the upcoming Easter season and wanted to solidify the rotation of canons.

"Put that handsome Italian where everyone can see him," the bishop said. "Give him as much pulpit time as you can, especially on the nights when you expect an affluent crowd."

"I don't think Desmoulins likes giving sermons," his vicar replied. "His public speaking skills are solid, but you can tell he doesn't enjoy it."

"Enjoy? He's not here to enjoy. He's here to serve a purpose. Desmoulins possesses that perfect combination of morose and sultry that women find so intriguing. A touch of mysticism, a touch of inner turmoil to kindle fantasies in their bovine minds. There's nothing like a tormented young priest to convince the wives of officials to loosen up their purse strings. We need money like never before. This is not the time to be proud. When his hairline starts receding, then we can stuff him in the confessional booth, but while he's young and good-looking, we should capitalize on it."

Grand! So I was the tasty Italian bait for the cows of Paris. Was that what my life had become?

After nearly vomiting into the cup of holy water, I retreated into my cloister cell, my thoughts turning to my long lost lady friend. Was she even alive? How many lovers was she bedding? Or had she given up on men altogether? I recalled our last encounter, of the horrific deed she had done and my part in covering it up. She could not stay in Paris after that rancid incident, so I gave her money for the road. If captured and convicted, she would be imprisoned for a long time, and I simply could not let that happen. So I helped her flee. I owed her that much. I could not deny my part in her downfall. She had become that sad, vile being mainly because of me. In my juvenile hubris I had assumed that I could expect the same level of interest and devotion from other women. I had viewed my affair with her as my first step into manhood. By my mid-twenties I realized how mistaken I had been. There never would be another woman of her caliber who would lavish her favors on someone like me so fervently.

1473 started off terribly with some turnover in the precinct. Guillaume Chartier died after having held the bishop's seat for twenty-five years. I had never thought I would actually miss him. While he was alive, I prayed for God to take him. *Mea culpa*! Little did I know what this succession would mean for me personally.

Enter Louis de Beaumont, a rabid reactionary. He was around my age, mid to late twenties, and full of energy, most of which he was going to spend on reversing whatever progress had been made. He refused to fund any scientific endeavor and instead got chummier with the Inquisition. France was already a few decades behind Germany, and a good century behind Italy. The new bishop was determined to keep us stuck in the fifteenth century. His first initiative was a massive purging spree, and I was his first target. We had loathed each other since day one.

"Desmoulins," he said, "I give you twenty-four hours to remove your love child out of the cloister."

"Your Excellency, you know that Daniel Dufort is my ward."

"All the same. If he's not a member of the clergy, he does not belong in the cloister. Put him up in the vacant cell in the north tower."

"He'll freeze to death. Have you ever been there? In the winter months you won't even find rats or pigeons there."

"Discomfort will strengthen his character. There are thousands of people in Paris who sleep under the stars every night. You don't want to coddle the boy. Allow me to remind you: this is a cathedral, not a boarding house. I don't care whose child he is. I want him out of the cloister."

"What trouble does he cause? He stays behind closed doors most of the day, studying Latin. Your predecessor did not object."

"Well, my predecessor is dead. I inherited this precinct in a very sad condition. There's a lot of damage to be fixed."

I shook my head. "Unbelievable."

"What part do you find hard to believe?"

"That you would take out your personal antipathy towards me on a poor orphan."

"That child is not an orphan," Beaumont said, unblinking. "He is someone's bastard. And he's not poor. His natural father has money. You don't expect me to believe that you took patronage over that boy out of pure compassion, do you? You wouldn't feed a stray dog, let alone shelter some random foundling. Someone is paying you to keep him, and I have a pretty good idea who that man is. I know you a little too well, Desmoulins."

"How do you know me? We just met."

"Let's say, I've heard enough about you from trustworthy sources. You'd never shoulder such an inconvenience unless there was some substantial benefit for you."

"Fine," I said, a little stunned by my own boldness, "if I am such a lost soul, go ahead and excommunicate me."

"Then I would have to excommunicate a good three quarters of the precinct and find replacements. No, Desmoulins, I am determined to reform you and remind you of your duties. You'll find me to be reasonably merciful. Now move that boy out of the cloister."

"If anything happens to that child, or he falls ill and dies, it will be your fault."

"No, it will be the will of God."

Daniel, who had overheard the conversation, was already dragging his mattress and his books down the hallway of the cloister. The prospect of relocating into the tower actually excited him. It gave him easier access to the Gallery of Kings from which he could throw bottles into the crowd in the middle of the night, urged by his invisible friends, the same ones who told him to compose music. I knew about these friends, because he drew them for me. It was a group of fanciful monsters assembled out of various animal parts.

"Where are you in this picture?" I asked. He pointed to what looked like a wolf with antlers of a deer and the wings of an eagle. "Very imaginative. Is this how you perceive yourself?"

"It's what the mirror tells me."

"Where's that magical mirror? Can you show it to me? I'd like to look in it as well."

He tapped his forehead. "It's in here. I close my eyes, and this mirror appears, and it shows me things, like the way I really am."

"And where am I in this picture?"

"You're not in it."

"Why not?"

"You're not my friend. You're my master."

It made perfect sense. Fair enough.

"Show this to the bishop," I said. "Maybe he'll have a heart attack and die."

"Not any time soon," he replied. I could tell it saddened him to disappoint me. "Louis de Beaumont will be here for a while."

"Your friends told you this?"

"Uh-huh ..."

"Did they say how long?"

He picked up a pencil and wrote down the number 1492 in the corner of the drawing. "You and I won't be here by then. We'll be long gone."

Now I was genuinely intrigued, for that number had appeared in my head as well. Some significant event was tied to that year. "What will happen in 1492? Will it be the end of the world? Tell me."

He only shook his head with a cryptic smile. So I was right about the approaching Armageddon. There were still a few astronomy projects I needed to complete. I had also taken on a few translation jobs. With time running out, I had to pick up the pace.

That child definitely possessed a vile streak. I say "vile streak" because the rest of him was generally benevolent; astoundingly so, in light of my unkind treatment of him. I had never caught him torturing animals. On the contrary, he doted on God's creatures. I made sure not to dissect rats in front of him. One time he brought in a one-eyed cat from the street. Another time he brought in a sparrow with a broken wing. The cat ended up eating the bird. Imagine the boy's surprise when he found a pile of bloodied feathers and a severed beak. If anything, it was a lesson in social hierarchy.

"It's never a good idea to lock two wounded, hungry beings together," I told him. "Just as it's not a good idea for me to be in the same room with the bishop. Poor Louis de Beaumont wouldn't stand a chance."

As I had feared, the boy fell ill within the first week of staying in his new lodging in the north tower. Having spent one night running up and down the gallery in the rain, he fell asleep in the draft and woke up with a fever. His cough echoed through the tower. I had to spend three sleepless nights sitting next to him, pouring warm chamomile brew down his throat and making sure he did not suffocate. If he died, I would be next. His father would find me, and then I would never get to complete my optical contraption.

Thankfully, the boy recovered and resumed drawing monsters, studying Latin and composing demonic tunes. I noticed the first grey hairs on my temples. At first I thought it was chalk dust or ashes from the furnace, but the grey streaks would not come out when I tried to rinse them off in front of the water basin.

I hoped Pierre de Laval appreciated the inconveniences I was enduring for the sake of his son. His gifts were getting scarcer, cheaper and less thoughtful. Worst of all, they were getting repetitive. For my thirtieth birthday he sent me a copy of the same book he had sent me a few months earlier for Christmas: *The Divine Comedy*. What could be more mundane? I knew the piece by heart, in both Italian and French. It happened the same year his son was appointed the organist. He could have done something to recognize my contribution to the boy's success. He sent us two identical statues of Mary – one for Daniel and one for me. And the clothes he was sending me were not in the latest fashion. One of the hunting doublets was also the wrong size: too loose in the waist. Did he assume I had gained weight? Was it expected that a man unburdened by marital obligations should turn into a pot-bellied boar after the age of thirty? My only explanation for Laval's sloppiness was that he had gotten "bewitched" a few more times and flooded the kingdom with more illegitimate red-haired offspring.

Still, I wanted to give him the benefit of the doubt. He could not have just forgotten about me and our pact. Perhaps he was preparing something truly exceptional, truly unique, for my thirty-fifth birthday; something that would make my head spin.

My long-awaited birthday gift came not from the bishop but from the Devil himself.

One afternoon, on my way through the University district – I gave occasional astronomy lectures at my alma mater – I ran into an old student of mine nicknamed Blackfeather. Or rather, he ran into me. His stringy flaxen hair was sticking out from beneath his cap. He looked like he was about to inform me about the second coming of Christ.

"There are wild festivities on Rue des Bernardins tonight," he imparted between gulps of air. "You absolutely must come. I want to show you something – or rather someone. Maître, I think I've found my new muse. It's serious between us."

I did not like the sound of it, for I had heard those proclamations before. Blackfeather had a tradition of putting his muses into the ground. By age twenty-five, he had already buried two official wives, both young girls, barely out of adolescence. Blackfeather surely liked his bedmates slender and playful. He found their curiosity and spontaneity charming. Not that I ever condemned his tastes, for they were not that far removed from mine. There were also several nymphs in between. They kept dying of natural but nevertheless mysterious causes, ranging from fevers to pregnancy complications. My personal theory is that they all died of starvation. Whatever money he made from teaching and his occasional commissions he spent on books. He did not need to eat. He could run for days on literary inspiration alone.

Alas, his female companions had more grounded physical needs. They needed to eat at least three times a week, as most of them were still growing. A few wilted cabbage leaves with a side serving of sonnets did not count as a meal. Blackfeather erroneously assumed that just because he was not hungry, his girls were not either. Either they were too shy to vocalize their needs, or he was too oblivious to their pleas.

"That someone … How old is she?" I asked, heavy-hearted.

Blackfeather wrought his hands. "She's just a child with snow-white hair and garnet eyes, but I've already written a few dozen sonnets in her honor. You can tear me into pieces later. I just wanted you to take a look at her and give me your opinion."

"My esthetic opinion?"

"No, medical. I need you to tell me if she is ready for ... you know?" He made a few discreet but characteristic movements with his boyish pelvis. "I could devour her any second, that nymph is so delectable. I just don't know ... Maybe I should wait?"

"How old did you say she was?"

"Thirteen?" he ventured, pulling his head into his shoulders. "You're going to kill me, aren't you?"

"Relax. I'm not going to kill you. I don't have any tools on me. See?" I held out my empty hands. "When is she turning thirteen? If it's in three years, then yes, I'd say we have a problem."

"In a few months. Maybe?"

"So, she's twelve."

"Technically speaking, if you insist ... Yes."

"Then she's ready. I don't see a reason to agonize. I don't know how enjoyable the experience will be for either one of you, but I don't see any medical catastrophes. You poetic types always create problems where there are none."

"It's just that I am still reeling from my last experience. Liénarde was fourteen, and you know how that ended. She suffered terribly. There was so much blood."

"A woman can die in childbirth at any age." I was starting to grow impatient. "If you don't want such risks in your life, don't get involved with women at all. Become a priest instead. Now, if you don't mind, I have a lecture in ten minutes."

I was ready to brush past him, but Blackfeather blocked my path again. It was amazing how such a skinny man could occupy so much space.

"So you'll marry us? I want you to be the one to perform the ceremony."

"I performed the two previous ones, didn't I?"

"And you'll come to the soiree on Rue des Bernardins?"

"I shall – barring the Armageddon or rainy weather."

"Just wear something more festive. More ... worldly, perhaps? No disrespect."

"Understood. There's nothing like the sight of a cassock to kill the mood."

Once again, I made a step towards the lecture hall, but the Englishman had more news to share.

"One last thing, before I forget."

"What is it?"

"I have some important and exciting news to share. The rector at the College of Lisieux is expanding the faculty. He invited a new astronomy lecturer from Amiens."

"Did he?"

"Yes! You'll meet him very soon. He's coming with his wife in a few weeks. What's his name? Ah ... Adrian Satigny! I thought you'd want to know. He does work similar to yours. Apparently, he's a little farther along in the process. He'll demonstrate his latest developments. Perhaps, you two can collaborate?"

It distressed me how poorly my former student knew me. "Collaborate" was not in my vocabulary. This enamored English clown was flailing his arms, kicking up a storm of enthusiasm, while my own heart sank deeper into melancholy.

"That's ... marvelous," I managed. "Though I don't think he needs my help. That Satigny fellow, if he is as advanced as you describe him, will probably want to take full credit for his achievements. Surely, he won't want to share his glory with others. I know I wouldn't."

"Oh, Satigny isn't greedy or egotistical like that. He believes in imparting his knowledge freely, for the benefit of humanity."

It amazed me how Blackfeather always rushed to the defense of utter strangers.

"What do you know about his beliefs?" I said. "You've never met the man."

"But the rector has, and I trust his judgment of character. I feel like I know Satigny already. I'm looking forward to his arrival. We'll become good friends, no doubt. I hear his wife assists him with research. They say she's a real scholarly woman. Quite a beauty, too! Not extraordinarily young, but very well preserved, with a girlish figure, a smooth, dignified face and dark eyes. God hasn't given them children, but that's such a trifle in the grand scheme of things. There are so many couples procreating. How many couples can say they are making scientific discoveries?" The Englishman raised his eyes to the overcast sky. "Can you imagine what it's like, a marriage of two intellects? How much closer to heaven on earth can you get?"

"Not much closer," I muttered.

I must have looked rather glum in that moment, because Blackfeather's beatific grin turned into a scowl of concern.

"Is something wrong, *Maître*?"

"Yes. I'm going to be late for the lecture."

Still mystified by the cause of my melancholy, the Englishman nevertheless stepped aside, letting me through. Honestly, I had no desire to speak before a group of young scholars that day. My lecture was even less inspiring than my sermons. At the same time, I realized I needed to keep their attention and their interest, especially in light of a potential rival.

I asked Dufort to join me. I gave him one of my Florentine doublets. It occurred to me that he and I had a similar body composition. We were both mostly bones. I liked to think that mine were a little better assembled than his, as my ribs were spaced out more evenly. Not that any woman was going to run her fingers over them any time soon. But then, what did I know? Maybe, I would get lucky that night. Maybe both of us would. Dufort deserved a bit of enjoyment. I did not say "happiness" because it is such a frightening, obliging word that I feared it would hinder his creativity. His work was fueled by hunger and frustration. If, God forbid, he found some semblance of harmony, his compositions would devolve into sweet, shallow, forgettable anthems, the kind that Philippe Chauvel must have written in his youth.

No, I needed to keep Dufort comfortably miserable. Just one sip of warm spiced wine for the Stone Prince! By age twenty I was already done with carnal love. He had not even started, at least not to my knowledge. I wanted him to try it once, preferably not with a prostitute, and then decide for himself if it was worth the trouble.

I had to admit, he looked good in that doublet. I toyed with the idea of letting him keep it. After all, it had been given to me by his father.

We all had a bit too much to drink that night. Being in the company of Lucius Castelmaure did not exactly help. The captain procured a large bottle of some sweet, sticky substance. When I drink alone, I remain myself, more or less. But when I drink in public, I turn into someone altogether different. In the privacy of my cell I know that the wine is of good quality, the kind that my Florentine ancestors would approve of. God knows what Mathias Eliade was serving his guests. Lucius was used to gulping poorly fermented substance, but clearly, I was not. The first few mouthfuls went to my head. I forgot what year it was and the name of the king. Apparently, I got up on stage and danced *La Rotta* with one of the Eliade girls. No doubt, Dufort has already described the incident to you in copious detail.

Now, do not judge me too harshly. Whenever I hear *La Rotta*, I turn into that spoiled, arrogant adolescent my Florentine mother had left behind. That night I was not in control of myself, ruled by my Italian blood, bad habits cultivated in the first seventeen years of my life and the repressed urges. The tune pushed the bubbling lava to the surface. The skinny bronzed arms of the dancing girl wrapped around my neck. My belated gift to myself for my thirty-fifth birthday that had passed unmarked. One thing I remember is that I had enough willpower to leave the soiree before things got out of hand. Walking down Rue des Bernardins, I could feel the gaze of Mathias Eliade burning holes in the back of my doublet. If someone told me it was a bizarre dream triggered by the spice in the wine, I would gladly accept that explanation.

A few days later Mathias brought his family to mass.

He was standing on Rue de Parvis, his hands on the shoulders of his eldest daughter. I finally saw Agniese Eliade in daylight. Avian features drowning in olive pigment. Yes, her eyes indeed were green. Not like emeralds, but a swampy, murky green, suggesting an equally murky soul behind them. Greasy raven ringlets draping over her frail shoulders, earlobes pink and slightly distended from her oversized earrings. All that drenched in rosemary and mint oil to cover the smell of progressing lung disease and overall confusion. In other words, she was perfect! It was as if Lucifer himself had read my juvenile fantasies and incarnated them. The thought made me wince. I was already in my mid-thirties, and my tastes had not changed in twenty years. Frail, bird-like brunettes had always been my weakness. In some ways she reminded me of my first lady friend.

"It's been a long time," Mathias said with that false please-do-not-kick-me humility. "Fifteen years, if I am not mistaken."

"Who is counting? Nothing significant has happened in Paris. It's practically the same city you left so abruptly. We're happy to see you again, Monsieur Eliade."

"We brought a present for you." Mathias cleared his throat and rubbed the girl's shoulders with his blackened fingers. "A little souvenir from Andalusia. Agniese, do the honors and present the gift to Monseigneur Desmoulins."

I noticed the girl holding what looked like a painting draped in a piece of cloth. She stepped forward and gave it to me. I could smell the fresh, cheap paint.

"It was done by a famous artist, whose name escapes me," Mathias continued. "I'm sure it will come back to me. A few of his landscapes decorate the halls of Ferdinand and Isabella."

"A masterpiece like this belongs in the cathedral's library." I took the canvas from the girl's hands, noticing that they were covered with long gloves almost up to the elbows. "It's only for the eyes of the select. I don't want unappreciative outsiders to ogle this gem."

I do not know if Mathias picked up the sarcasm in my voice. Being a perceptive, intelligent man, he probably surmised that I had already condemned the painting without even looking at it.

"My daughter has a request," he said, rubbing his fingers together as if conjuring a spell. "I must warn you: it is of a most unusual nature."

It sounded promising. Whatever request this enchanting brunette had for me, I was prepared to fulfill it.

"Speak, my child," I said, looking the girl in the eye. I tried to make my voice sound tender, but instead it came off sounding sinister. "What do you desire?"

"I'm speaking on her behalf," Mathias intervened. "Agniese

is a little timid with strangers. She's entirely uninhibited when it comes to dancing and doing tricks in public, but when you address her in broad daylight, she gets a little tongue-tied. She would like to see the Gibbet of Montfaucon. She's looking for a burial place for herself – a little prematurely, in my opinion. She's been talking of nothing else. Do you think this can be arranged?"

"I see no reason why it cannot. I was going to spend the rest of the day working on a Greek translation, but taking some respite won't hurt. Meet me at the corner of Pont au Change in thirty minutes."

"Excellent." Mathias rubbed his fingers again. "A horse will be waiting there for you. I only had one available. I hope it doesn't present an inconvenience. You don't mind sharing a saddle with my daughter, do you?"

Did I mind? Hmm … It had been a while since I had ridden with a woman. This one was slender enough to fit in front of me.

I went into the cloister to change, carrying the fake Andalusian masterpiece under my arm. Needless to say, I had no intention of hanging that monstrosity in the cathedral library. It was something for me and Dufort to laugh about. And yes, I found the whole situation darkly comical.

I was not going to tell my ward about my upcoming rendezvous with Eliade's daughter. There was no need to tantalize the poor devil. I suspected he was quite taken by the greasy-haired enchantress and would absolutely adore the chance to take her to Montfaucon himself. After all, his tastes were formed under my pernicious influence. If the girl indeed was mortally ill, and he was infatuated with her, that would make her death all the more traumatic for him. I was callous and accustomed to handling loss, but the Stone Prince was still a naïve, susceptible boy. The only thing in him that was not made of stone was his heart. I do not believe he would go as far as throwing himself off the roof for love – he was too pious and God-fearing to take his own life – but he would resume slashing his forearms. I could easily picture him coming to the service with dried blood stains on his sleeves. On the other hand, think of all the funeral music he would write! Before letting him get any closer to the Wallachian dancer, I needed to gather a few facts about her. If Dufort was to experience his first major heartbreak, I would rather have it happen under my supervision.

Once in my cell, I put on my riding suit and pulled the cassock over it. I also grabbed a small bottle of burgundy, just in case Agniese got thirsty on the way. I wanted to celebrate her arrival in Paris and officially welcome her to the city of Inquisition Fires.

My eyes fell on the crucifix above my desk. Christ was looking at me indifferently, without any condemnation.

Walking down the cloister hallway, I encountered a young deacon who was running messages for Beaumont's and his first vicar.

"His Excellency would like to speak with you in his quarters," the youngster said. "Stop by an hour before the evening mass. I was just coming to tell you that."

"I'm afraid it's not possible on such a short notice. I've made other plans."

"But His Excellency made it very clear ..."

"There's a fatally ill child who needs me." I did not feel guilty saying these words to the vicar, as there was a hefty dose of truth in them. "Surely, old Louis will understand."

As soon as I crossed the bridge and got off the Île de la Cité, I stepped into one of the narrow alleys, quickly pulled the cassock off and rolled it up into a bundle. By the time Mathias and his daughter saw me again, I looked like a typical petty nobleman. The horse they brought was a chestnut stallion with a mane a few shades lighter. When I took the reins, the beast snorted through its nostrils.

The girl was the first one to climb into the saddle, swiftly and methodically. Her skirts rustled by my ear. I joined her a second later.

"I cannot thank you enough, Monseigneur," Mathias said with a bow and a grin. The black stubble on his chin made his teeth look whiter. "God sees what you are doing to indulge my precious Agniese."

"We'll be back by nightfall," I promised.

"Take your time." His fangs flashed again. "You can even bring her back in the morning."

As much as I appreciated Eliade's leniency, I had no intention of tempting fate. It was bad enough I was going to miss the evening mass. I could not afford to miss the one the next morning. The young rat-faced deacon would notice my absence and report it to the first vicar, who in turn would go straight to the bishop. I would have to fabricate another sob story involving a dying child or a blind old man. My immediate task was getting out of the city without being recognized. I lifted the hood of my riding cloak to hide my face and spurred the horse.

Eliade's daughter was sitting in front of me, the back of her head resting on my shoulder. She was definitely running a fever. I could feel the heat radiating from her neck. Listening to her noisy, shallow breathing, I tried to think of tactful ways to ask her how long ago the symptoms had surfaced and what kind of remedies, if any, she had been taking. At the same time, I did not want to break the amorous ambience with medical jargon. The girl did not seem to mind our physical proximity. She emitted a low droning sound, no louder than a bee's buzzing. It was some Spanish ballad. The tiny pendants on her bracelets jingled with every step the horse took.

The destination landmark was located on a small hill outside the city walls. The construction had been in existence for over two hundred years. It was a full service butcher shop with a platform for carrying out executions, be it by hanging, beheading or quartering. The structure had three sides and forty-five distinct compartments in which criminals could be both hanged and hung on display following execution elsewhere. The bodies were later dumped into the massive tomb through the terrace grates. The edifice was highly functional and served multiple purposes. My German side was impressed.

"Thank you, child, for giving me a reason to come here again," I said when the horse stopped. "I had forgotten how enchanting this place is."

The girl instantly revived. With a melodic giggle, she

jumped out of the saddle and ran up to the platform, her ruffled skirts billowing, her raven locks blowing in the wind and her countless trinkets chiming. Unfortunately, there were no corpses on display at the time, so she had to be satisfied with the sight of bare hooks and chains.

Oddly enough, in all that time, she had not said a word to me directly or even looked me in the eye. Not that it bothered me. Just watching her climb the gibbet gave me great pleasure. She stood in one of the windows, raised her hands above her head and started swaying her hips, repeating the dance she performed that night on Rue des Bernardins.

I heard myself humming an Italian love song, to the accompaniment of the rusty chains. In case you did not know, I have a decent singing voice – one thing I inherited from my Italian grandfather. He had a potent, liquid baritone that drove women wild, and he used that tool often. I wondered if Eliade's daughter would appreciate it.

She spent the next hour dancing and playing on the terrace, while I sat on a rock and watched her. We still had an unopened bottle of wine.

When the sky started to darken, I stood up from my rocky throne and stretched my hands towards her.

"Come down, mademoiselle. It's time to go."

Agniese shook her head with the obstinacy of a four-year-old. She was enjoying herself too much in the company of the dead. I had to repeat my request. "Come down at once. We need to get back before they close the city gate. I promised your father I would bring you home by nightfall. Otherwise he'll never let you come here again."

"Catch me, father!"

It was her first time addressing me directly. The last word jarred me for some reason. Did the mad creature expect me to climb the gibbet and chase after her? A second later I realized that was not what she meant. She flailed her arms as if they were wings and leaped off the platform straight into my embrace. I caught her just in time. Entangled in the folds of my cloak, we nearly tumbled to the ground. Miraculously, I kept my balance. The small wine bottle was still in my pocket. For a few seconds we stood face to face, panting.

"You don't have the key to the crypt, do you?" she asked.

"I'm not an executioner, mademoiselle. I don't have a key to every door in Paris. Next time, perhaps."

"Good. I want to see what my future resting place looks like on the inside."

"I can describe it for you. It's just a pile of bones at various stages of decomposition. Nothing complicated."

I took her hands, and she pulled them away. The gloves came off, revealing an expanse of purple knotted scars that covered her palms and wrists. The nails on several fingers were disfigured or missing altogether. Leaning on my superficial medical training, I determined that those scars resulted from a severe burn.

"You're about to ask me a question, aren't you?" she said with a squint. "Go ahead."

"You don't have to answer it." I gave her back the gloves, still getting over the shock of the discovery. "It's none of my business."

"Perhaps. But you'll make it your business. It's what you do, isn't it? Well, if you insist on knowing, I had a spat with the Inquisition."

For the first time, I got angry with her. She must have sensed it, because she lowered her eyes, shivered all over and recoiled.

"You want people to believe you, don't you?" I said. "Believe me, I like macabre jokes. It's one of my many guilty pleasures. And perhaps, your Inquisition story entertains your father's guests."

"I don't really show my hands to anyone. You weren't supposed to see them either. There's a reason why I keep them covered."

"Yet you have a tall tale prepared. I assure you, when one has a spat with the Inquisition, one does not live to brag about it. An insider, who is familiar with the interrogation process, will know at once that you are fibbing, my girl."

She looked up at me again. "And you are one of the insiders?"

"I'd been present at interrogations, yes. They'd invited me mainly for my medical expertise. It was on me to keep checking the accused and tell the torturer when it was time to stop or apply a lighter technique. Crushing all the bones at once is … counterproductive. But my contributions do not end there. You know the unguent they put on the backs of scourging victims to close the wounds after the punishment is over? Well, I improved the consistency of the substance."

"The truth is I don't know how it happened. I must've been very young. Mathias says I was this way when they took me in. Denise jokes that it's a blessing that my palms are disfigured. Otherwise I'd spend all my time reading the lines. The map of my future was completely effaced by the fire."

So she referred to her adoptive parents by their given names. The whole situation was becoming increasingly intriguing. Agniese's scorched hands and the swampy eyes filled with riddles hinted that there was something peculiar going on inside the Eliade family.

The hue of the sky was deepening. It was time for a drink. I pulled out the wine bottle, uncorked it and pressed it to her lips. She gulped obediently, eyes half-closed, her slender throat vibrating. With my free hand I patted her on the head. She did not recoil. On the contrary, she pressed closer to me and slipped her fried fingers under the collar of my doublet, moaning between the gulps. In all fairness, the wine was excellent. I had been saving it for an extraordinary occasion such as this one.

"I have an idea," I blurted out. "Let's run away. Someplace warm."

Mon Dieu! That came out sounding terrible. *Someplace warm*. I knew I was damned to hell, but I was not sure this girl deserved the same fate.

"I'm tired of running," she said, wiping the drop of wine off her chin. "I came to Paris to die, as you know. But I am grateful to you for showing me the Gibbet of Monfaucon. It's where I'd like to be buried."

"Dear child, this place is for traitors and criminals."

"In that case I should commit a crime, so I have the honor of being buried there. Unless, Monseigneur, you can pull some strings and make special arrangements. It is my dying wish."

"And I shall honor it. But it will cost you."

"Name your price. Another dance?"

"I have something else in mind. A kiss, perhaps."

"That's easy enough." She pressed her lips against my knuckles. "There. Your hands are like ice, father."

"But my chest is on fire. That hollow space where normal people have a heart is a raging inferno. It's the strangest feeling. Any theories?"

"It will pass," she said sympathetically and rubbed my knuckles one more time. "It's just a whim of an aging heretic."

"No, my child." I cupped her wine-stained chin. "When I cosigned twelve executions in one day, that was a whim of an aging heretic. This is just a harmless game. Would it kill you to play along?"

Ah, who was I deceiving? It was not a game any longer, and I was not the only one making the rules.

Having made sure that her future resting place was everything she had envisioned, Agniese calmed down a bit. At last, she had a burial plan that satisfied her. She had my word. There was nothing else for her to do except recline against the trunk with costumes, hum her Spanish ballads and wait for her lungs to abdicate. Still, I was not convinced that her condition was hopeless. I wanted to believe that her disease could be reversed or at least halted.

Talking to Mathias Eliade was futile. I would need to converse with Agniese directly. No intermediaries. The extent of her attachment to her adoptive parents was yet to be determined. While referring to them, she never said "my family" or "my people." It was always "Mathias and Denise." I did not sense any fervent filial loyalty, which means that prying her away from them would not prove too difficult. It would be like cracking an oyster shell that was already half-open. If I could win her trust by further indulging her macabre curiosity, perhaps she would allow me to treat her illness. I had a few concoctions that I wanted her to try. The ingredients were said to reduce internal inflammation and deepen the breathing. Some physicians promoted another, more radical method that involved piercing the lung and collapsing it to give it rest, but I was not confident in my medical skill to subject Agniese to such an experiment.

After hearing about my part in the Inquisition trials, she wanted to know more. So I decided that instead of merely describing the process, I should show her the actual tools and even let her touch them.

For our second rendezvous I took Agniese into the dungeon beneath the Palace of Justice. The idea came from Louis de Beaumont, who half-jokingly chastised me for cavorting with a dark-skinned woman.

This time we needed to be extremely cautious, since we were navigating a densely populated area where my face was well known. We had to wait until the building was vacated for the night before entering through one of the many side doors. It gladdened me that Agniese was not wearing gloves. She allowed me to hold her scorched claw as we walked through the hall of the dark court-house. We cut across the main chamber where the trials took place and where I had spent so many late nights in the early days of my career. I paused and held up the lantern to show the girl the intricate *fleur-de-lis* design along the ceiling. As I led her through the maze of corridors, I felt her withered fingers wrap tighter around mine.

"Are you sure we're alone?" she asked me in a whisper. "I hear voices."

"Those are the spirits of the condemned." I wanted this excursion into the netherworld to be every bit as thrilling as the last one. "Their cries live in the stone of the walls. Only the chosen can hear it."

She let out a squeal of delight and jumped. Her long braid with golden strings and beads woven in whipped me across the face. That sting was more invigorating than a kiss.

We wound up on the doorstep of a circular chamber without windows. The shape of the chamber without corners was to conjure the image of a hell circle. The furnace after having blazed all day had already cooled for the night. The iron grating over the opening of the oven was shut, giving it the resemblance of the mouth of a sleeping guard dog. Saws, hammers and pincers of various sizes were laid out on a piece of cloth on the floor. The official torturer, with his penchant for neatness, liked to wipe the blood and soot off his arsenal at the end of the day.

Overwhelmed by the assortment of devices, Agniese released my hand and fluttered into the chamber. Once again her skirt inflated, and I caught a glimpse of her ankles and calves. The vaulted ceiling distorted her hoarse laughter. After spinning a few times around her axis in the middle of the chamber, she paused in front of me, reeling and panting.

"You know how these things work?"

"Why, I practically invented half of them." I tried to sound casual, not boastful. "Well, to be more accurate, I improved them. Many of the early designs were crude and destructive. They did too much irreparable damage too soon. The point of enhanced interrogation is not to kill the accused on the spot but rather to extract a confession. If you make the tools look intimidating enough, you won't even need to use them. It makes the torturer's job easier, and the judges appreciate not having to wait. It may not seem this way, but I am a very compassionate man. It pains me to see people suffer needlessly, regardless of how heinous their crimes are. I'd rather see them walk up the gallows with all their limbs intact."

Again, I tried not to make myself the center of the conversation. I was not sure if my words made any impression on Agniese. She resumed making circles around the chamber, patting the instruments with her withered hand, every tap bringing them to life, making them sing in their metallic voices. I have to say, the equipment was very basic. Some of the more intricate tools were not there. The torturer did not like to clutter his work space with things he did not use on a regular basis. The classics included the rack, the thumbscrew and the chair for the water torture.

She plopped on the leather mattress in the middle of the room. "It's so soft," she said, pounding it with her fist. "Softer than anything I've ever slept on. It's a little slippery and sticky."

"Yes, the underlings try to keep it clean, but, as you can imagine, it's a little hard, given the amount of work. Make yourself comfortable."

She sprawled on the mattress, her hair and the fabric of her dress slathered over the sticky leather. The strings of her bodice were starting to come undone. "What happens now?"

I hung the lantern on the wall, sat down next to her and placed my hand on her calf. "Do you really want to know?"

"Everything."

"Are you sure?"

"Yes."

"All right, then. Where should we start?"

The first thing I did was close a leather strap around her waist. She giggled when the cold buckle touched her belly. For a few moments I sat there, allowing her to get used to the sensation. Then I lifted her hands above her head, bound them with a shackle attached to a chain coming out of the wall. Agniese tolerated my manipulations, though her breathing quickened. A few times she lifted her head to see what I was doing.

"Remember what you told me the other day at the Montfaucon Gibbet," she said suddenly with just a hint of tremor in her voice.

"I told you many things."

"This is only a game, right?"

"Of course. Not too tight?"

"No. I can still breathe."

Once she was securely attached to the mattress, I smoothed the folds of her skirt beneath the straps. There was an eerie sense of familiarity and recollection about that act. I had stroked those thighs before – in another life.

I became an eighteen-year-old student again, hovering over the lean body of a young girl who was sprawled before me with her head thrown back. The memory triggered a physical response, but thankfully, the folds of my cloak concealed the evidence of my arousal. The wavering shadows on the ceiling and the creaking of the metal ring in the wall enhanced the ambiance.

What happened next? I remember uttering some absurd, laughable things. I told Agniese I was completely taken by her. I did not use the word "bewitched" – that was from Pierre de

Laval's vocabulary. My hands slipped up and down her legs and her torso. Between my insistent strokes and compliments, I revisited the topic of elopement. I bade her to run away with me to a place where we would not be bothered. I do not think we ever reached an agreement. Her answers were evasive and vague. I am sure she was playing with me as I was playing with her.

In the meantime, I needed to proceed with the demonstration. I slipped her foot between two blocks of wood. Her toes curled.

"What was that?"

"Oh, just a device to improve the circulation in your lower extremities. It's called the Spanish boot. I guess your acquaintances of the Inquisition did not introduce you to it?"

She started fidgeting in her straps. "My arms feel numb."

"Good. It's a vital part of the experience. Patience. You want to know how these things operate, don't you?"

"It's all right. I got the idea. You can untie me now."

"In a minute. I don't want you to miss out." I cleared my throat and hovered over her, my hand still on her hip. "Do you confess?"

"To what?"

Our lips were almost touching. If I leaned in one inch farther, I do not think she would recoil. Not that she had much wiggle room. "Do you confess that this is the most magnificent interrogation chamber in Christendom?"

She shook her head waywardly. "I deny."

"All right then. You leave me no choice. Should I proceed?"

I turned the handle of the screw-jack half a degree at most. The boot contracted, barely touching the skin. A second later I heard a blood-curdling scream. A sound more piercing and horrifying could not have erupted from a single person's chest. I swear I heard several voices. I looked up at Agniese's face. It was not the same girl who skipped into the chamber with me ten minutes ago. It was someone else, someone from my distant past, or rather, several individuals, their features blended into one mask of terror and agony.

Opening the buckles on the straps proved harder than closing them. The fact that Agniese was writhing and kicking did not help. I tried to talk her down, using the calmest voice, but she continued shrieking.

Once I finally succeeded at freeing her, she bolted past me like a cat that was let out of a bag, scurrying on all four of her own limbs out of the chamber. To make matters worse, she bumped the lantern on her way out, leaving me without a source of light. Grand! I really should have kept her tied up until she calmed down a bit. The prospect of having to look for her in the dark halls did not appeal to me. What would the prosecutor think if he found a feral adolescent with scorched hands in the morning? The girl would have a hellish time explaining how she found her way there. What if she told everyone that I dragged her into the chamber by force and tortured her? I could already picture the quizzical stares, the raised eyebrows and the lopsided smirks. *Tut-tut, Desmoulins.*

Finally, I found her crouching under the table in the trial room, rocking back and forth and shivering, clutching her ankle. By then my eyes were adjusted to the dark and I could see that there was no bodily damage done.

"See? Not a scratch, not a bruise. I'd never harm you. I promised Mathias I'd bring you back intact. Whatever you felt there, it wasn't pain, at least not yours."

"Don't touch me."

"I'm not touching you." I held my hands up. "See?"

I could not tell if she was laughing or crying. The tip of her nose would not stop twitching, giving her the resemblance of a frightened mouse. For a second I thought that she was playing a trick on me and that frantic fit of hers was staged. Did I not invite her to play along? Perhaps, she got immersed in her role even deeper than I did into mine.

"You are not a man of God," she declared.

"Finally." I let out a sigh of exasperation. "It took a long time for you to figure it out. I've been trying to tell you that since the very beginning. Someone thought I looked good in black. That's a great reason to become a priest! Come on. I'll take you home."

I pulled her out by the arm a little rougher than I would have liked, threw her over my shoulder and carried her outside.

Thankfully, she did not protest. Once the initial wave of terror had subsided, she was probably feeling a fair amount of embarrassment. "It wasn't real," I said, putting her down. "It didn't happen to you. You must've smelled someone else's blood. Sometimes our imagination deceives us. Let's forget about what happened tonight. I have other ideas for games."

As soon as she felt the pavement beneath her feet, she wiggled out of my arms and resumed her flight. She ran rather swiftly, which gave me further reassurance that her foot had not been damaged. I decided not to chase after her. It would only fuel her anxiety.

Turning the corner, she nearly collided with an armored horseman. He jerked in his saddle and pulled the reins.

"Horns and thunder," he growled in a sleepy voice and raised the visor on his helmet. It was Lucius, in flesh and metal.

"Monseigneur? Oh ... *Bonsoir.*"

"*Bonsoir,* Captain."

"Lieutenant, to be precise," he corrected me with a sigh.

"Have you been demoted again?"

"Alas. I fear this time I won't be restored. I've committed too many infractions. One more misstep and I'll be court-martialed."

"Rest assured, I'll continue calling you Captain. If it's any consolation, I'm in the same predicament. Just waiting for someone to pronounce me a heretic any day now."

"You missed one hell of a spectacle," he said. "Urban gladiators. Scholars versus beggars. It was a royal melee, surprisingly quiet but brutal."

"I'll take your word for it."

He was not even looking at the shivering chit clinging to the neck of his horse. Words rolled off his tongue like beads of sweat off his forehead. "You should come next time, Monseigneur. There will be a vis-à-vis tournament on Rue St. Denis between a librarian and a scribe."

"I'll think about it. You look tired, Captain."

"I really am. What time is it? You know, I was on my way home from the tournament, and then I heard cries."

"Cries of ecstasy," I assured him, gesturing at Agniese.

"I was showing this lovely mademoiselle some of the finer interrogation artifacts."

"Ah! Did you show her the new and improved model of the rack?"

"Among other contraptions. She squealed at the sight of such fine craftsmanship. But, I think we've had enough excitement for one night. Why don't you take mademoiselle home?"

Lucius helped Agniese climb into the saddle behind him. While putting her foot in the stirrup she winced with pain.

I felt perfectly at ease sending the girl home with the officer. She would get to Rue du Mouton unviolated. Lucius Castelmaure was as good as a eunuch. Over the past week the itch and the burning had gotten worse, compounded by night sweats and swollen lumps in his neck and groin. He cried to me in the confessional almost every day about his worsening condition. Carnal delights were very far from his mind. It was agonizing enough for him to empty his bladder. Do not think for a moment I gloated. I had no reason to wish him ill. That man had given me countless fencing lessons.

"I think you should consult a physician." Those were my parting words to him. "You look abysmal."

"Don't listen to him, Lucius," Agniese said, wrapping her arms around his waist. "You look magnificent, like a prince. He's a cruel, vicious, deviant man."

She wiped her nose against his doublet. I could not suppress a chuckle. *I* was deviant? She was the one who wanted to climb the gibbet and test out every piece of equipment beneath the Palace of Justice, and *I* was the deviant one? The same thing kept happening to me. A woman provoked me, I gave her what she wanted, and then I was branded a monster. All I did was pamper Agniese's morbid fancy, and now she was hiding behind the armored back of a drunk, who could not consummate with her even if he tried. Had she met him a few months earlier, it might have been a different story. Oddly enough, even if Lucius had not fallen ill, I still would not have felt too threatened. Even when he was in his best health, I could compete with him. Not every girl dreams of a knight in shining armor. Some girls secretly pine for an inquisitor in black. It was possible that Agniese was one of those girls. She simply was not ready to admit it to herself yet. Or maybe I was the one not ready to admit that she was just another primitive wench. Did I expect too much of her, comparing her to Beatrice Portinari and Pernelle Flamel? Did I allow myself to get distracted by her accent and the trinkets around her neck? Beneath that veneer of pseudo-Bohemian mysticism she was just as dull and inadequate as the rest of them.

I could easily imagine the conversation she was having with Lucius to the clopping of hooves:

"How do you like your new horse, Captain?"

"It's the best horse I've had. A horse like that deserves a better master."

"And your fellow officers, are they pleased with their horses too?"

"Exceptionally so! Tell your father to bring more."

"He will in a few months. And my brother, does he show any promise?"

"Sebastien is making excellent progress. He's a fast learner."

"You honestly think he'll make a fine solder someday? Just like you?"

"Oh, he'll be better than me. That boy has a glorious career ahead of him. I'm past my prime. My days in the service are coming to an end."

"Don't speak ill of yourself, Captain. Just because a coin lost some of its shine, its value doesn't decrease. It's what Papa says."

When I returned to my cell that night, I found the crucifix on the floor, face down. The nail holding it to the wall must have loosened. I do not think I need to comment on the symbolic poignancy of that. I picked up the crucifix, blew off the dust and just put it on the desk. Perhaps Christ got tired of it hanging in the same spot. He craved a change. And what did I crave?

Leaning over the cup with holy water, peering into the glistening surface, I scratched the word *damnum* into my chest with the nail. Latin for "damage." Such a short but loaded term that had so many interpretations. A point of no return, when a game gets out of control, when a disease can no longer be reversed, when the key to the prison cell is lost, and the Feast of Fools turns into a massacre. I looked for traces of my former fury against destiny, against the mediocrity surrounding me, but found only fatigue and disgust. I saw the red scratches appear on my chest but felt no pain. To be precise, the pain did not give me the same satisfaction. In the past I could count on some temporary relief. Not anymore. Seventeen years ago I had torched my own pyre. I had walked away from a learned woman. And now I was lusting after a dusky twig in ruffles. Well done, Desmoulins! So much for your triple doctorate.

A few drops of blood fell into the holy water.

With all those amorous distractions, I had completely neglected my research. I had to resume constructing that infamous optical device. My newest colleague named Satigny was due to arrive shortly, and I needed to have something formidable to show to him. It was crucial that I meet him in full armor, so he would not get too comfortable on my turf.

I'm sure you know this by now: Agniese had another brother named Josef, born to some Hungarian or Bohemian woman. He found the experience of living in a city oppressive. His vagrant soul longed for the open roads of northern Spain.

"I hate Paris," he lamented to me once after the service. He was the only Eliade who came to mass on a regular basis. "I'm sick of it already. I'm sick of that house that looks like a barrack, of the parties Papa throws, of the people he tries to befriend. Last night he made me put on a puppet show for the children. Would you believe it? We were invited to some official's banquet – not as guests but as entertainers. I had three squeaking girls hanging on me all night. And then they asked me to teach them a Hungarian dance."

I heard him out with a great deal of sympathy as I knew a thing or two about feeling stifled and embarrassed. I could tell he was hungry for a task, one that would give him a sense of purpose without hindering his freedom.

"How would you like to run an errand for me?" I asked him. "It concerns a matter of great importance. Believe me I wouldn't insult you with some trivial request. You'll be paid well for your time."

The corner of his stiff mouth curled. "I'm listening."

"I hear you like to travel and you have a talent for finding what's hidden."

"I have many talents, Monseigneur. There are some I don't care to cultivate."

"There's a Benedictine abbey outside Amiens. I just learned that their library contains a manuscript I have been trying to find for a long time. It is instrumental to my research. I don't suppose you've heard of Nicholas von Kues? He was a German scholar. At any rate, I will give you a letter of request. When you reach the monastery, ask to speak to the librarian. Give him this letter, and he will give you the manuscript. Your job is to deliver it into my hands. Don't worry, there's nothing heretical or incriminating in it. You won't be endangering your life by carrying it. Make sure you protect it from the elements. No wind, and no rain should touch it. Can I count on you to perform that task?"

Josef shrugged his shoulders. "When do you need me to leave?"

"Immediately – if possible. Would it be a problem?"

"I don't see a problem. I'll need money for the road, though."

"Of course."

I went back into my cell and came back with the letter and a bag of coins. He put the letter into his breast pocket and counted the money in front of me. "Well, this is more than I'm accustomed to holding in my hand," he said, tossing the coins up and savoring the jingling sound. "At this rate I'll never have to beg Papa again. He'll be the one begging me."

"This is only half," I replied. "I'll give you the rest when you come back. If you perform the task to my satisfaction, I'll send you on more trips."

For some reason I trusted Josef. He did not seem like he was interested in making quick money and running off. Like Mathias, he was looking to make lasting alliances, only apart from his family. The idea of helping him achieve that independence appealed to me.

However, after a week of his absence I started questioning my decision. According to my calculations, it would take three days at most to reach Amiens by horse. The entire trip back and forth should have taken no more than six days. Was he not anxious to get the rest of the money? There was no reason for him to take longer, unless he got lost or detained. By the end of the tenth day I began contemplating asking the bishop for permission to go to Amiens myself. I knew that Beaumont would not honor my request without asking a million questions regarding the purpose of my journey. I was not looking forward to that conversation.

Finally, after two weeks, Josef rode up to the cloister entrance, moaning about being fatigued, even though his relaxed appearance testified to the contrary. He did not look like he had spent all that time in the saddle.

"Here's your manuscript," he said with a yawn and handed me over a velvet bag covering the flat wooden box. "The librarian at the abbey was a rather obstinate owl. I showed him the letter, but he refused to believe it was genuine. Those damned Benedictines! That is why it took me so long. I'll just take the money and go home."

Before paying him the rest, I pulled off the bag and opened the box to examine the content.

"What   is   this?"
"The papers you'd asked for."

"Not quite. These are his religious works."

"So? Aren't you a man of God?"

"I think you know the answer to that. These papers are of no interest to me. I know perfectly well how von Kues felt about Jews and Muslims sharing Heaven with Christians. His metaphysical speculations are of no value to my research. I needed his notes containing sketches and mathematical equations."

Josef's gloved hands curled into fists.

"I told you I'm deadly tired," he growled through his teeth. "And even if I wasn't, I still wouldn't be able to keep up this conversation. Look, I'm just a messenger who can barely read. If you have a grievance, take it up with the librarian. I wasn't told to inspect the manuscript. Feel free to delegate your next task to someone more scholarly. I'm done running errands for the clergy. I still expect to be paid for my troubles."

I threw the sack of coins at him. "Just go."

Josef spurred his horse. Before leaving, he glanced one last time over his shoulder. "You know, it's people like you who make Paris such a bleak place."

I did not waste another minute being angry at the Wallachian hothead. I had a bigger riddle to solve. What happened to the document I was seeking? I knew the librarian at the abbey in Amiens. He was not the most jovial man – not that his position required that – but he was reliable. He knew what material I was requesting. If von Kues' calculations were not inside the box I was holding or at the library, then where could they be?

My misfortunes were only beginning. I had more vexatious discoveries in store. That night Dufort appeared at the door of my cell, covered in blood and grime, wearing some bizarre round metal plate around his neck.

"Do not be alarmed, *Maître*," he said, collapsing into the chair across from me. "Not a drop of this blood is mine. You are looking at the champion of Urban Gladiators. I won the battle of precincts. Notre-Dame against St. Genevieve. I took down their choirmaster, and I have the medal to prove it."

He held up the gaudy trinket so I could have a better look. The head side of the medal depicted a lion with its mouth wide open, and the tail side depicted a semblance of a Gothic rosette similar to those in cathedral windows.

"Brilliant! Of all the filthy pastimes Paris had to offer, you had to take up Urban Gladiators."

"I didn't even know such a thing existed. *He* sought me out. He approached me after the morning mass and personally invited me to the tournament. He said he had a perfect opponent for me from St. Genevieve's."

"Slow down. Who is *he*?"

"The organizer, some fellow by the name Johannes Métivier."

I felt a pinch between my ribs, followed by a wave of shallow nausea. "What did you say his name was?"

"Johannes Métivier," he repeated, unperturbed. "That's how he introduced himself. He looked about sixteen or seventeen.

Short, blond, a little pudgy. I could easily break him in half, yet he looked at me without fear. In fact, I detected some mockery and provocation in his eyes. He carried himself like he had an army of allies behind his back."

The queasiness intensified. Was Dufort saying this to aggravate me? No, playing mental tricks was not like him – that was something I would do. The name he uttered was that of my younger brother. The physical description and the supposed age also matched. I had not seen that twerp in over fifteen years, pretty much since I had dumped him into the eager arms of the elderly Métivier couple, but what Dufort described to me sounded about right. Blond hair, round face. God, that was the last thing I needed!

"He resembled a piglet with his snub nose and rosy cheeks," Dufort resumed. "Oh, and he asked me to say hello to you on his behalf. He promised to stop by the cathedral and visit you. Apparently, he had some personal issues to discuss. He would not disclose any details, but his tone was foreboding. Is he one of your astronomy students?"

I spent a few more seconds scrutinizing Dufort's mien. No, he was not feigning ignorance. The name of Johannes Métivier really meant nothing to him. He did not make the connection to my half-brother's adoptive family. The idea of my estranged relative roaming the streets of Paris was too disturbing. And I thought I had tucked that loose end of my past for good.

"Eliade's oldest daughter has not responded to my last letter," I said, changing the subject abruptly. "Do you know what happens to women who do not respond to my letters?"

"They get more letters."

"And then what happens? Do you remember what happened to Heloise de Cressay?"

"One never forgets the smell of burned flesh."

So he remembered! The burning of Madame de Cressay was one of the first executions I took him to see. We had a spectacular view of La Place de Grève. The sight proved to be too much for Dufort. At some point he closed his eyes. Still, he could not get away from the smell and the sound. I wanted it be an educational experience that engaged all senses. See, this is what happens to women who dismiss my advice. I had warned Heloise on several occasions. I had told her to leave the city. But had she ever listened? No. She thought I was pursuing some licentious goal. Female delusion knows no boundaries.

"Why is it that every witch in Paris thinks I'm in love with her?" I asked out loud.

"I'm at a loss, master."

Dufort hated being at a loss and admitting to it as much as I enjoyed prodding him. Even though he was in no danger of facing the Inquisition, I wanted him to stay alert and be able to answer potentially incriminating questions.

"I remember how uneasy you were watching Heloise de Cressay's execution," I said. "Of course, you were younger then. We wouldn't want the same fate to befall Mathias Eliade's eldest daughter, now would we?"

Dufort stopped playing with the medal. A crease appeared between his copper eyebrows. "Is she in danger?"

"Not yet. But you know how things are in this city. We are all one step away from the gallows, one accusation away from the pyre. I won't go into details now. I need to see her. It's extremely important. The fates of several individuals are at stake. The swarthy runt has been avoiding me. Since she will not talk to me, maybe she'll talk to you?"

"Eliade's daughter doesn't strike me as someone who responds well to threats."

"I'm not asking you to threaten her, Dufort. There are more direct and effective ways of getting your message across."

Direct. That word disquieted him. The wrinkle between his eyebrows deepened.

"Oh, *Maître*, I hope you're not suggesting that I apply force."

"Not at all. The only thing I'm urging you to apply is your masculine charm. And yes, you have enough of that."

"Enough to frighten the hell out of a statue! What am I going to say to her? *Bonjour, ma belle! I write demonic music for a living, the kind that makes people go mad and slit their own throats. And for fun, I draw monsters and break other people's bones.* That will win her over!"

He resumed toying with his medal.

"Granted, your charm is not of pedestrian kind, but Eliade's daughter is not your typical Parisian nitwit. She's a worldly, Bohemian nitwit. Some women like that gaunt, angular, tortured look. Agniese could be one of them. You won't know until you test your seduction skills on her."

"You mean to tell me that you are done with her already?"

"Done with her? I haven't even started! Yes, she's been evasive, to my great annoyance, but we'll take care of that. Rest assured, the girl is mine. And what's mine is yours." I straightened out in my chair. "Tomorrow night there's going to be a major soiree at Eliade's house. Blackfeather is putting on his play. They are expecting a sizeable crowd. You'll go there and try to become friends with her. You'll soften her up with some small talk about demonology. Then, as soon as she drops her defenses, you grab her by her greasy roots and bring her here. And if you snatch a few favors from her on your way, I promise I won't get angry. You're old enough. We can share toys. And that's just what she is – a toy. A pretty little trinket from a foreign land, with beads and ribbons. Let's face it. She's not long for this world. We may as well use her for our entertainment while she's still breathing."

You should have seen that look on Dufort's blood-stained face! Oh, maybe I shouldn't have. Yes, I should have! Hell, yes! I just could not resist. I needed to utter something truly horrific and watch his reaction.

"Sometimes," he managed after a few gulps of air, "I don't know whether you're joking or being serious."

"Sometimes I don't know myself. However, I did resolve that no woman would ever come between us, my son ... my beautiful, loyal, talented son."

God have mercy on me! I was overstepping every boundary that existed between me and Dufort. The burning need to challenge, taunt and provoke him was too overwhelming. It had been an exhausting month, filled with disenchantment. I must say, he handled my onslaught with remarkable composure.

"Now, Maître, try to get some sleep."

"Sleep? You think it's as easy as closing your eyes? It must be for you. After all, you're sinless. That is about to change.

Go after the Eliade girl. Be yourself. Who knows? Perhaps, she'll love you for your soul. And, if that doesn't work, I have something that might help. Women like shiny things."

I pulled out a plumed helmet from under my desk and handed it over to Dufort. Judging from his suspicious glare, the prop looked familiar to him.

"Where did this come from?"

"From the blond, hollow head of Lucius Castelmaure."

"Mon Dieu ... Is he dead?"

"Don't worry. The head is still attached to the shoulders – more or less. He forgot his helmet last time he came to confession. He took it off and started pulling his hair and bemoaning his condition. Halfway through his confession he jumped up and ran off, before I even had a chance to absolve his sins. He never came back for the helmet. I assume he has no use for it anymore. I thought it would look good on you."

"You cannot be serious. It's blasphemy to wear another man's helmet. Imagine if someone wore your cassock or your cross in jest?"

"Ah, but that's what makes the act all the more delectable. Don't tell me you've never dreamed about mocking Lucius. That golden boy deserves a lesson in humility. Pretend to be him for one night. See how far it will take you. And if you succeed at winning Agniese's good graces ... there will be a reward waiting for you."

Dufort blanched beneath the layer of blood and grime.

"What kind of reward, *Maître?*"

"I'll introduce you to your real father. You'll finally meet the man who abandoned you."

Stop, stop, Desmoulins! Nobody is to blame for your disappointments, least of all Dufort. He does not deserve such cruelty. Don't test his loyalty. He is like a dog that growls at its master but would never lash out and bite. Still, you never know. Or maybe it's your secret wish, to die by his hand?

My body was shaking with low, hoarse laughter. I needed to wait for the fit to pass. It is not a good idea to pick up sharp objects while your hands are still trembling. After Dufort left, I performed my nightly ritual and traced the letters on my chest with a knife. The cuts were scarring over nicely. *Damnum*. My tombstone inscription. The letters were the same size and spaced out evenly. It was the only endeavor in my life I had any control over. After rubbing some melted wax into the fresh cuts, I closed the cassock with a sense of satisfaction.

Suddenly, I heard a scratching sound outside the cell. It did not sound like a mouse.

The creature standing before me was a pudgy child in chainmail. Unruly flaxen curls. Round pink cheeks speckled with pimples.

"Bonsoir, brother. We meet at last. Your pet demon let me through the gate. May I come in? See, I'm trying to be observant of your rules."

So it was true. Dufort had not been playing games with me. Johannes Métivier was very much alive and in Paris. The little twig on my family tree that I had broken off and buried was peeking through the ground.

It all came back to me, that stuffy summer night, the last time I saw my brother, the thoughts that were passing through my head. After burying what was left of my father and his wife, I spent an hour sitting in front of his cradle, watching him squirm and listening to his wails. He sounded hungry, frightened and indignant. I could have sat there for a few more hours. I could have allowed him to die of starvation. There would have been no consequences for me. At the time those thoughts did not strike me as horrifying. I was not assessing them from the point of view of morality, only practicality. Yet it was not in my heart to let that creature die, just as it was not in my heart to love him. He needed to go. And there he was, more than a decade and a half later, standing a few paces away from me, separated by the threshold of my cell.

I gestured for him to come in, mainly because I did not want anyone to overhear our conversation. Somehow I sensed that simply telling him to get out would not work.

"What do you want?"

"I need you to intercede on my behalf once again. I will be direct. My adoptive parents are both dead. Some sort of fever. It did not take much. They were old and feeble. That puts me in a predicament. I need a new family. Do you think anyone would want to adopt a compulsive fornicator?"

His voice was low and devoid of any anger, and his tone businesslike. His gaze glided from one object onto another.

"Where are you staying now?" I asked him.

"Oh, here and there. I don't have a permanent home yet. But I've met some nice people through some of my ... activities. Some of them are students at the University. One of them is a soldier. He gave me a key to his lodging. He uses that place for bringing random women, though he hasn't been feeling well, so the place remains unused. It's not very clean. I do hope to find another family. This is where you step in, dear brother. But I want a better experience this time, so you'll have to try harder."

"What didn't you like about the Métiviers?"

"Oh, they were fine people, just not exactly my dream parents. I would have preferred a younger, wealthier couple, with more ... what's that word I'm looking for? Prospects. The Métiviers had nothing to offer except for blind, unconditional love. All they wanted was a pretty baby to squeeze and pamper. And look at me now, brother! That worked out well, didn't it?"

"Believe me, a day doesn't go by that I don't chastise myself for my mistake. What makes you so sure I won't repeat it? I don't have the best judgment. I trusted the wrong people. I chose the wrong profession. I fell in love with the wrong woman. You really shouldn't come to me for guidance."

"I don't buy this self-deprecating bosh. You'll do right by me this time. You won't get rid of me so easily –"

No! He was about to call me by my name and thus take our familiarity to a new level.

"You can pick your own adoptive family," I said to him. "I'll be sure to write a letter of recommendation. Does that sound fair?"

He shook his round blond head. "Fair? Hell, no! Nothing is fair about this situation. You grew up surrounded by books, paintings, Italian music, science. What did I have? Food. Sweet, greasy food. Buttered rolls with honey." He lifted the chainmail and pinched the cushion of soft lard around his waist. "They kept filling my stomach, but it didn't occur to them that I had a brain too. They never asked me if I wanted to be a physician or an attorney. Look at you! You're a man of the cloth. You can have any woman you want, including Queen Isabella. A little intimidation is all it takes. All you have to do is wave a crucifix in front of her nose, and she'll be on her back, ready to indulge your every whim."

"You've got it all wrong. There's more to sexual conquest than raw intimidation. There's much to be said for diplomacy and self-restraint." I could not believe what I was saying after the dungeon episode with the Eliade girl. Were those words really coming out of my mouth? "Otherwise, it's abduction – not seduction. And if you are paying for her favors, it's a purchase."

"And you're telling me all of this *now*?"

"Monsieur Métivier, you are still very young. Your finest conquests are in the future. Whatever bad habits you may have picked up can still be reversed. After a few weeks of starvation, your fat cushion will melt. You'll look as pitiable as any Parisian urchin. Please, go home now – wherever that is."

"Is that all you have to say to me? I came all the way from across the bridge to see you at this hour, and you kick me out? I know damn well you have wine in your cabinet, good Italian wine. You didn't think of offering me a sip. You replaced me with that … Dufort creature. It sickens me how you dote on that freak."

"Daniel is not a freak," I corrected coolly. "He's an eclectic idol."

"I've met many unsavory characters in my first few weeks in Paris, but I've never met anyone who enjoyed thrashing others as much as he does."

All right, now the chubby brat was attacking my protégé. If I had any sympathy for Johannes Métivier in the beginning of our conversation, it had all dissipated.

"He brings money into the precinct," I said. "The cathedral has made a fortune on his commissions. Thanks to him, we can repair the roof. And if he derives his inspiration from street brawls, so be it. If this is what nourishes his creativity, neither I nor the bishop will move a finger to stop him. Dufort is someone who isn't afraid to break a few rules – or bones, if necessary. At any rate, I am not sure what compelled you to seek me out. What exactly are you hoping to get from me at this point? Don't bother to answer. I'll see what I can do for you. I'll give you money for food. I'll help you find work. Now, get out."

When I told you my soul was as black as coal, you did not believe me, did you? You thought it was just self-deprecation or some internal ecclesiastic humor, didn't you? Well, now you know I was telling you the truth. I gave you an accurate description of my spiritual state.

Yes, in my next life, I want to be called Nicholas.

Chapter 4

Nightmare on Rue des Bernardins

(Agniese Eliade)

I do not mean to brag, but I must be the calmest condemned girl in Christendom. When it is time for me to walk up to the gallows, I will handle it with the utmost composure. There will be no wiggling, shrieking or wondering what it feels like to have your windpipe crushed. And I owe this serenity to my illness. I rehearse my own death several times a day. With little warning my breathing interrupts, time itself pauses, and a perfect lull settles in. My free time is spent trying to connect the moving stars before my eyes, reassembling various images, trying to discern real events from dreams. I feel like I have been alive for a long time. And I have managed to keep my virginity until the age of sixteen! How many girls can brag of the same?

If someone ever decides to use the devil's invention called the printing press to immortalize my story, the title should be *Nightmare on Rue des Bernardins*. I picked that street because that was where I danced *La Rotta* for the public. And "nightmare" because these events would be frightening for a normal girl, which I am clearly not. A normal girl would not find herself in love with three men at the same time. At least three men, to be precise. Because there might be a fourth one on the horizon.

Good heavens, I hope that last potential affair does not transpire. Three men are more than enough for a girl who is running out of time. I have enough room in my heart, but not enough air in my lungs. Mother of God, our Lady of Paris! Wait, we are in Paris, aren't we? That is what Mathias tells me. He is the one who brought me here. Indeed, it is Paris, the city of Inquisition Fires. What year is it – 1476? No, not anymore. Which is a pity, because it was a good year. I learned this mind-bending card trick called "Satan's Wheel." You can entertain yourself for hours, even if you do not have the deck with you. It involves manipulating numbers in your head. If you are sitting in a dungeon, awaiting execution, and there is nothing to do, try that game. It will calm your nerves. And when they come for you, at least you will face the executioner with a straight face. They ask you, "Are you prepared to meet God?" And you reply, "Take fifty-two weeks in a year and divide by thirteen lunar cycles and multiply by four seasons." The look of perplexity on their faces will leave you with that grim satisfaction that you will take with you to the gallows or the pyre.

Ah, who cares what year is it? It's the year I'm going to die. I know where I'm going to be buried. And I'm taking a few others with me. Who wants to join me in the tomb? Time will tell. And there is not much of it left. I am running out of air. Vertigo sets in, lifting me above the rooftops and the steeples. There is the dirty little hovel on the edge of Pont Saint-Michel and the broken cart that had been sitting there since January. There is the main library of the University district and the pillars of the Palace of Justice. I see some commotion in Place de Grève, the butchery of Paris. Another execution. Someone is getting hanged or pilloried. Another judicial misunderstanding. My memories muddle, like bones in the Montfaucon tomb.

The three extraordinary men, three beasts, each hideous and exquisite in his own way who filled the last few months of my life with terror and passion blend into one. Please, forgive me if my narrative makes no sense, if I describe the events out of order. Let me draw one last deep breath. By the way, feel free to embellish my story. You can change the names if you want to. Make it as bawdy and raunchy as you see fit. There's a collection of stories set in Florence during the plague. What was the author's name? Boccaccio, I believe. He really has a talent for compiling wit and practical jokes, high morality and erotic escapades. I do not claim my story comes anywhere close to that of Boccaccio, but you can turn it into anything you wish.

Where was I? Oh, yes. Act two, scene four: I am sitting on some officer's lap, who wants to pull out and show me his sword.

"Come on, touch it," he urges me. "You'll never see such a fine artifact anywhere else. It's the sharpest, sturdiest weapon in France."

Thankfully, the sword remains in its sheath. The officer, whose name is Lucius Maximus Octavius, or something equally ridiculous, buries his nose in my hair and salivates all over my bodice until we both fall asleep. I condone the smell of sweat and cheap alcohol, because the man is so puzzlingly handsome. Indecently handsome, I would say. You can look at his face and find new things to admire about it. Just his eyebrows alone are worthy of a poem, the color of white gold, perfectly arched and a perfect distance from each other. I doze off running my finger over those eyebrows. He grunts complacently. Sticky fog envelopes us like a curtain after a show.

Then I wake up in some freezing basement, chained to a bench, with a man in a black cloak standing over me.

"Give me your answer," he says. "Have you decided?"

"Yes," I hear myself say. "I mean, no. Yes, I have decided. But the answer is still no. I will not go with you to Catalonia."

I can tell that my answer drives a dagger through his heart. The lantern on the wall casts a glare on his gaunt face, making his features look predatory. His coarse black hair with a few streaks of grey resembles a wolf's fur.

"What am I doing wrong? You have no idea what you are declining. We could have a divine time together."

"Not in Catalonia." I hold my ground. "Why? Because I have already been to Catalonia. It was not my favorite place on earth. The people are crude, and not in a charming way. I cannot stand the sound of their dialect. It is neither French nor Spanish."

"Then let us to go Florence, the land of my maternal ancestors."

"I have an even better idea, Monseigneur. Some say the world is round, and there is another continent. We could run away there. But what if it is populated with people who are more savage than Parisians?"

Finally, we agree on England. It is a fair compromise. In his excitement he nearly crushes my ankle with the Spanish boot. Later he apologizes profusely and assures me the damage is not severe. Somehow I do not believe him, because it hurts like hell. That smell of candle wax and frankincense will follow me into the afterlife.

I close my eyes, and when I open them, I am standing on the Gallery of Kings next to this creature which looks like an angel that had a massive falling out with God.

"Allow me to apologize on my master's behalf," he says, his hair streaming like licks of flame in the wind. "I don't know what came over him. Or rather, I do know exactly what it was. We all had a bit too much to drink. But you have nothing to fear from him. He is like a hawk who likes to hover but he almost never swoops down. Still, I would like an opportunity to make amends on his behalf. I'd like to dedicate my next musical piece to you. How would you like to be immortalized?"

Of course, I say yes, even though the word "immortality" makes me a little nervous. I know he will keep his promise. It is not some hollow compliment of a court troubadour. Angels do not lie. Ordinary men do sometimes. But this one is no ordinary human being. He has a hymn vibrating in his every knuckle. His skeleton is a library of ecclesiastic music yet to be written.

The fact that all three men are divine does not make it easier for me. I wish I could take their virtues and fuse them together to form one perfect creature. But it does not work like this, so I must divide my affection among the three. Is this what Mathias had in mind when he told me to mingle and make friends with all the alpha-Parisians?

Sometimes I envy my little sister Elinor, who does not face the same dilemmas. She only has one admirer, a scrawny drama lecturer from the College of Lisieux. His street name is Blackfeather, and he's known for putting his wives in the ground due to neglect and malnourishment. I hope that Elinor is luckier than her predecessors. She is small and does not require a lot of food. She can live on compliments and innovative drama. I have seen some of Blackfeather's plays, and let me tell you, the man has talent; too much talent, perhaps. What he does *not* have is an appreciative audience.

Parisians are obtuse and inattentive. Any playwright who has tried staging a performance in Paris will tell you the same. Metaphors fly past their ears. You have to wrap them in strips of bacon and dip them in cream sauce to make them palatable. Blackfeather gets nervous every time someone mentions food. I told him not to take my advice so literally. Sometimes the 'bacon' is something as simple as a comely female performer with a naked belly. The first time I brought it up, he nearly fainted. The concept of throwing bits of sensuality into his shows was so novel. Apparently, in England, where his great-grandmother came from, they do not use female performers at all. Listen to this: they use boys whose voices have not matured yet to play the parts of maidens. And then what happens to those boys? They take their maiden personas offstage and fall prey to deviant men. France has enough perversions already.

"Blackfeather," I said to him once, "let me help you. I don't know how much time I have, and maybe that will be my last good deed. It kills me to see your work trampled every time. You need more skin. My naked belly and Elinor's are at your disposal. You have two skilled dancers to draw the crowd. In the name of Jupiter, use us!"

The Englishman was overwhelmed. His brittle blond hair sprung up. He kissed my hands through the gloves – he never found out what they looked like under the fabric.

"Agniese," he said, "if only you weren't dying, I swear I'd marry you."

"Why don't you marry Elinor instead? She's already twelve. In a year or two she will be quite ready for consummation. In the meantime, you can enjoy an idyllic engagement. She can be your muse, the diamond of your productions."

"A diamond," he whispered, his pale boyish face lighting up. "That's what I shall call my next play. *La guerre des bijoux*. The War of Jewels. It's brilliant. Elinor can be the diamond. You can be the emerald. There's a Spanish girl I know who can be the ruby, and another English girl who can be the sapphire. You think four girls will be enough? You can dress up in colors that correspond to your jewel. Your mother is an expert seamstress, isn't she? And the costumes will grow more revealing as the plot advances. With each scene there will be less fabric and more skin."

"That's the spirit! Now we are talking."

"We can stage the show at your father's hall and invite only the most discerning spectators. And if the show is a success, we shall take it to larger venues. Before long, we shall be performing for the King of France!"

The Englishman squeezed my face and planted a chaste kiss on my crown. Elinor got more intense, more intimate caresses later that night. "Nothing rough, nothing deep," she assured me afterwards, as I was wondering about the possibility of my little sister losing her virginity before me.

The script for *La guerre des bijoux* was ready within two days. Blackfeather could be very prolific when he felt inspired. The stage and the costumes were ready within the same week. The other two girls brought in by the author: Inez from Spain and Maude from England became frequent overnight guests at our house on Rue de Mouton. They seemed grateful for the food offered by Denise but not keen on talking about their lives, which led me to believe they had nothing to brag about. Perhaps, they were in between benefactors and looking to Blackfeather as their *souteneur* – God forgive me for saying this. After all, as a college lecturer, he was surrounded by young men, some from rather wealthy families, who would not be averse to taking steady mistresses. It was hard to guess what was happening inside the heads of Inez and Maude without knowing what they were doing during the day.

One time I ran into them on Rue de Parvis. Both were wearing scarlet bodices and massive earrings. To be fair, their attire was not that different from mine. They pretended not to recognize me, and I did not press them to exchange greetings. How did they come to know Blackfeather? The Englishman claimed he saw no difference between a tavern wench and a queen. To him all women were nymphs and goddesses. I had every reason to believe he was being sincere, and he was not just fibbing to entice desperate girls to be in his smutty shows. Of course, why would he not idealize women? He had never provided for any of them, including his lawful wives. All his muses had died before they had a chance to grow old and fat. In that regard he was lucky, having kept his illusions into his mid-twenties. I liked that rapturous, excitable part of him. To have buried so many women and children while still retaining those boyish antics was truly impressive.

Between us, the script for *La guerre des bijoux* made no sense. There were very few lines. If I understood it correctly, four jewels were competing with each other, and the rivalry involved seductive hip-swaying and slow removal of garments, with a little bit of singing. My lovely Elinor was the swiftest and most agile dancer of the four. She got rid of her clothes in no time. I knew many men in the audience would be disappointed to find out that she was already spoken for.

Before the opening performance I had purposely spent the afternoon on the mattress in the corner to make sure I had enough strength. Alas, bed rest no longer gave me the feeling of invigoration. Still, I donned the green dress tailored by Denise. The skirt was loose in the waist, so I had to pin it to keep it from slipping off.

After an hour of rocking my hips, swaying my hair and singing in Catalan to the accompaniment of mirthful howls, I was ready to stick my foot into the Spanish boot again. Blackfeather, to his credit, had kept his promise. The hall was filled with students from the University. I did not see any of my three prospective lovers in the crowd, which was probably for the best, as my performance that night was mediocre at best. Nevertheless, I got my share of applause. Thankfully, nobody approached me when I got off the stage. I threw a ragged shawl over my costume and slipped outside.

The smell of midnight Paris immediately made me want to go back inside. I remembered it was July, and it had not rained in a week. The collective legacy of every horse, stray dog or beggar that had passed through Rue du Mouton was very noticeable, and I did not even have a sack of lavender on hand.

For some reason I remembered that time in Andalusia when we ran into a band of African travelers, either Egyptians or Moors. They were sitting around a campfire, passing around a smoldering pipe filled with herbs and inhaling the smoke. I wanted to take a puff of that pungent ambrosia. My inflamed lungs craved it.

Suddenly, I forgot the heat and the stench. The sordidness of the night dissipated. I saw *him*. Or rather, I saw his helmet. The tiny dent on the side and the tattered plumage testified to the courage of the man wearing it. There he was, my golden archer, fairer than sunrise. My Olympian. My Lucius.

"Captain Castelmaure! You came."

I leaped across the puddle of horse piss straight into his arms. He lifted me off the pavement and clasped me to his breast. I noticed that this time he was not wearing his chainmail or armor, only a doublet over a wrinkled but clean shirt. I had often wondered what he looked and felt like beneath all that metal. Now I welcomed the opportunity to touch the man beneath the armor. With one arm thrown around his neck, I ran my free hand over his torso. His physique was different from what I had imagined. I had expected more muscle, but it was mostly bone, or rather, hot stone.

He had a broad chest, with large, palpable ribs encasing a set of powerful lungs. Feeling the rhythmical thuds of his heart through the linen excited me. I noticed that his hands were dry and warm. Moreover, instead of the usual smell of cheap wine and sweat, I picked up a faint scent of incense. Could it be that Lucius had gone to mass instead of the tavern that evening? By God, he was sober!

"Oh, Captain," I said, "I'm so glad to see you. Not a single familiar face in the crowd. You came at the right time. You didn't see me embarrass myself on stage."

Without saying a word, he clasped me tighter and started carrying me down a dark alley, his gait firm and determined. His visor was down, so I could only guess the expression on his face.

"Captain," I stuttered, "where are you taking me? Mathias … he'll wonder. It's opening night. I really should go back. The guests are waiting. Please, put me down."

To my surprise, he complied and put me down gingerly,

holding me by the sides to prevent me from tipping over. Alas, I rejoiced too soon. A second later I found myself pressed against the wall of the building. The metal helmet clanged against the brick. This time I feared that the sword would come out of its sheath. I could feel the hot throbbing pressure against my stomach. His swift fingers found the strings that held my skirt up. Usually, Captain was not good with hooks, pins and laces. Perhaps, he was accustomed to women undressing for him. This time he was doing the tedious work himself. Amazing how one night without alcohol transforms a soldier! Or maybe it was an entirely different person altogether. Not that it mattered to me at that point. I had a very strong premonition that Lucius – or the man wearing his helmet – was going to free me from my virginity and also from the agony of having to choose my first lover. With his visor down, he could not even kiss me. The mystery and the anonymity fueled my excitement. I felt my knees unlocking and my thighs parting. This man, whoever he was, suddenly made my life so much easier. I did not fight him. Trapped between the brick wall and the hot heaving chest of my midnight companion, I surrendered. More so, I made his life easier by holding onto his shoulders. I knew there was going to be pain, so I bit into the collar of his doublet, determined to pass this trial with dignity.

Through the veil of jagged breathing I heard the stomping of boots. The large warm hands of my would-be lover shuddered and suddenly released me. Knocked out of my reverie, I opened my eyes and beheld the face of Lucius, the real Lucius, glistening with sweat and crimson with rage. I had never seen him in such a state before.

Horns and thunder!

Before the infuriated captain could utter those words, my anonymous companion was thrown to the ground, with six soldiers surrounding him, kicking him from every angle. Still leaning against the wall, I did not intervene, at least not immediately. In the meantime, every second was accounted for, with so many men jumping on the same victim at once. Lucius was not taking part in the battery himself. He was standing in front of me, scrutinizing my face. Finally, he reached out and touched my neck. As usual, his hand was cold and moist. Now that was the Lucius I recognized.

"Captain, tell them to stop," I said, my tone more imperative than pleading.

"You want them to stop, do you?" A spark of malice flashed in his blue eyes, something I had never seen before. "You're defending this animal?"

"It's your men who are acting like animals. It's really sickening, this … this display of valiance. Six against one? Put an end to it at once."

"So I should have let him molest you then?"

"Did I call for help? Did you hear me screaming? Do you have nothing better to do at this hour than ambush couples?"

"Mademoiselle Eliade, what is it I'm hearing? Have you taken a lover?"

"And what if I have?"

"When were you planning on telling me that?"

"I don't know, Captain. You haven't stopped by in a week. A girl cannot wait indefinitely, especially one who's short on time. Then this decisive stranger turned up. How could I refuse?"

Lucius leaned forward, probably with the intention of pressing me against the wall and forcing me to watch the battery, but I was swifter than him. I slipped under his arm and ran towards the scene of the melee, probably risking having my jaw shattered by someone's elbow. The men were too engrossed in their task to notice me. Nevertheless, I darted right through the ring of muscle and chainmail, throwing myself on the body of the trampled man.

"Stop it at once!"

They obeyed. By God, they froze, heaving and growling. Yes, they took an order from a sixteen-year-old chit! I am sure Lucius was not thrilled about it. For a split second I sequestered command of his unit, but that second sufficed to salvage the man on the ground.

"Step aside!" Lucius barked, reclaiming control. "Let's see who this bold prankster is. Mademoiselle Eliade, why don't you do the honors? Show us his face."

At first I tried to lift the visor, but the hinges got bent during the battery. I had no choice but to remove the entire helmet. If only I knew how it was done. Having Lucius and his seven henchmen watch my every move did not add confidence. At last, after fidgeting with the side buckles, I was able to detach the leather strap that went under the chin and pull the iron contraption off the man's head, exposing the gaunt face framed by copper hair strands.

Lucius blanched and backed away from his victim.

"*Sang Dieu* … Is this a joke? Dufort!"

Indeed, it was the nineteen-year-old organist. I had only seen him up close once before, right after a morning service, and his striking appearance had left an impression on me. It was hard to forget that titanic statue, those enormous sinewy hands, hollow cheeks, flaming hair paired with shockingly light grey-blue eyes, one of which had a perpetually dilated pupil. I remembered that hoarse monotone voice – hoarse from inhaling incense all day and monotone from limited association with other human beings. Equally memorable was that air of detachment and superiority from knowing that most rules of the Parisian society did not apply to him. What he endeavored tonight was a manifestation of that belief.

The helmet had saved his nose and jaw from being fractured, though there was a gash along his hairline. I knew it would have been a good idea to examine his ribs just to make sure that chipped bones were not puncturing the lungs. Still, I was even more concerned about his left hand. It looked like someone had stepped and bounced on it, leaving the fingers purpled and curled up.

"Well, Captain, I hope you are satisfied," I said to Lucius. "You have successfully debilitated one of the best musicians in France. The bishop will thank you for it. I'm glad you've put your military training to good use."

One of the soldiers slipped me a half-empty wineglass. God only knows where it came from, but the timing was perfect. I pried Dufort's jaws open and poured a few drops between his teeth. He started coughing and choking immediately, but at least he was breathing. I helped him sit up, his back against an empty wooden crate.

"May Neptune spear me," Lucius muttered. "I don't understand. I thought Dufort was unbreakable. Isn't he supposed to be made of stone?"

"He *was* unbreakable," I explained somberly, "until he put on your helmet. In that moment he forfeited his powers. He became you, if only for a short stretch of time. It was enough to weaken him, to make him assailable. I don't know if he'll ever revert to his old self."

I could tell that my words had a terrifying effect on the men, even though it was not my intention to frighten them. There was mystical truth in what I said. See, this is why I had always been wary of masks and costumes. For that reason I was against Elinor acting. She was so young, and her spirit was still in flux. She should have just continued dancing and doing tricks. By having her act in his farces, Blackfeather was tainting her. I learned that wisdom from my adoptive mother. Denise believed in keeping personal property to the bare minimum and never swapping it with others. She discouraged me and Elinor from wearing each other's skirts and jewelry. Looking back at my last rendezvous with Desmoulins, I probably should not have tried on the Spanish boot in the dungeon. The sufferings of others have been permanently etched into my muscle and tendons. When people's powers and memories become entangled, it leads to chaos.

"All right, who put you up to this?" Lucius asked, bending over the battered man.

"Nobody." Dufort wiggled the fingers of his unharmed hand. "It was my idea, a belated Feast of Fools prank, if you will. It almost worked. Captain Castelmaure arrived just in time."

"Do you not know it's blasphemy to wear a soldier's helmet?"

"I know," the organist replied, his air flippant and languid. "That's what makes it so enjoyable. Blasphemy is so delicious."

"I could have you pilloried for this. You'll see how delicious that feels."

"By all means, Captain. It would only boost my popularity. I'm already swimming in commissions. The bishop is thrilled. He's raking in the money. Haven't you heard? I'm the new alpha Parisian. If you send me to the wheel, my loyal patrons will bring me a barrel of burgundy. And you, Captain, will look vindictive and petty, especially when your superior finds out about your negligence. What kind of officer loses articles of his uniform? You won't be doing yourself any favors by drawing attention to this. I just thought I should warn you."

Dufort's tirade took my breath away. I could tell that he did not get many opportunities to humiliate a fellow human being, let alone someone of Captain Castelmaure's caliber, so he relished every second of it. He also must have been in a great deal of pain, and spouting insults acted as soothing balm. Blood was dripping out of his mouth, which made me conclude that he did suffer from internal injuries.

Despite having been knocked down, Dufort acted as if he had actually won the fight. He looked more triumphant than defeated. Lucius must have agreed with the warning hurled at him, because he dropped the idea of sending the offender to the pillory.

"I cannot believe this," he muttered. "After everything I've done for you? I gave you free fencing lessons. For years I was your only friend. And how do you repay me? By stealing my helmet and groping my woman!"

Gulp. So I was Captain Castelmaure's woman? The declaration was a little startling. Not that I protested. Not in the least. What sixteen-year-old girl would decline a handsome officer, even if he smelled a little rancid? Not that I expected him to smell of frankincense and candle wax like Desmoulins and Dufort did. Those two never broke a sweat or got their hands dirty. They could sit for hours in the bathhouse on Rue de la Savaterie, after the custom of ancient Roman senators, chewing on mint and thyme. Lucius risked his life every day, and for that alone he deserved respect. He had no time to pick out the strings of beef trapped between his teeth. In light of his heroism, things like foul breath and rampant promiscuity seemed like such minor offenses.

True, my lungs were abdicating, but my other body parts were still alive and responsive, very much so. The trouble was that he kept stalling. The last time we were alone, he did not go farther than nuzzling and drooling. He had yet to kiss me on the lips. Something was holding him back, and it clearly was not a sense of chivalry. Perhaps, he did not know what to make of me. I was versed enough to know where I stood in regards to a man from a poor but noble family. I was not respectable enough to be seen with him in daylight. At the same time, he did not see me as another disposable wench. He could not discard me after one night, since Mathias was selling horses to his fellow officers. So he kept me on hand, marking me with his scent, priming me with his saliva and sweat. I do not think he was that ceremonious with his other concubines. It appeared that I occupied my own unique place in his lap and in his heart. At least, that was what I wanted to believe.

Of course, Dufort had to open his mouth and shatter my girlish delusion. "Now, Captain, you are being a little unfair. All women in Paris are already yours. At least they have been until recently. It was your immense success with the fair sex that has led to your downfall. I hope you can perform on your wedding day."

Now it was my turn to ask Lucius a few questions.

"Is it true, Captain? Are you to be married?"

"And what if I am?" he replied with a defiant shrug, ignoring Dufort's stab against his masculine powers. "What's the matter with that? You give yourself to strangers in a dark alley, and I give myself in marriage."

"Nothing is the matter. I'm thrilled for you. Is she rich? I hope so."

"She's rich enough."

"When is this supposed to happen?"

"As soon as my current wife expires."

"Your current wife …"

"Yes. I need to become widowed first." Lucius was playing with the buttons on his doublet. "This is how it works in a proper Christian society where marriage is sacred. I expect to gain my freedom within the next few months. The current Madame Castelmaure is not in good health. She lives in Gonesse, and I haven't touched her in years."

"Do you have any children?"

"Yes, two girls. Marie is three years old, and Amelie is four months."

"How is it possible? You just said you haven't touched your wife in *years*. Your youngest is four month old."

"Nine months after conception plus four equals thirteen. That was how long ago I bedded my wife last, making it just over a year ago."

"Are you absolutely sure the infant is yours?"

"Positive. I mean, I've never seen her in person, but I'm told she has my nose, the Castelmaure nose. At any rate, Amelie's birth put a deep dent in her mother. The poor thing started wheezing and spitting up blood. I suspect it's the same disease you have. White plague, they call it. Again, I haven't seen her. There is no need for me to aggravate her with my presence. But I hear she looks ghastly. The house lackey is detailed in his letters. She wasn't exactly a picture of health when I married her, but now she's a walking skeleton with bulging eyes. Who wants to look at that?"

Lucius cringed at the memory of his dying wife and gave his top button one more twist, severing it from the fabric.

"What does your fiancée think of all of this? I assume she's privy."

"Oh, she and I have an understanding. We've known each other since birth. It's practical to keep the fortune in the family."

The story was getting absurdly good.

"You two are related by blood?"

"Not closely. Our fathers were second cousins. Her father helped mine get established when we came to Paris, so there's a bit of debt to repay on my side of the family. Besides, the young lady is not entirely sane. She's fond of me in her own peculiar way, but not always predictable in her expressions. Some of the things she does are a little ... unnatural. An outsider might be taken aback. Luckily, I'm tolerant of her antics, as she is of mine. For her, the alternative to marrying me would be confinement. There are certain convents that take disturbed women." Lucius stammered and shook his head, suddenly hit by the realization of having shared too much. "I'm not sure why I'm telling you this."

"I'm not sure either, Captain. My guess is that you're desperate for an audience. This is what I gathered: you are marrying your insane cousin, so your daughters from the first marriage do not starve? Did I understand you correctly? Is this how it's done in your circles?"

"Yes, this is how it's done!" he exclaimed defensively. "People with surnames, titles, reputations and fortunes to protect do those odd things the likes of you cannot comprehend."

"If your daughters ever need a meal," I said, "bring them here. Mathias and Denise will feed them."

"Horns and thunder! You must be daft to think I'd let my daughters come here and mingle with the Bohemian riffraff."

"You have no qualms about coming here yourself," I reminded him. "You don't disdain our company. Or, if you do, you surely hide it well."

"Our men go many places where they wouldn't bring their women. You truly believe that I'd let my girls sit on the floor, eat with their hands and listen to your father's tall tales about Vlad the Impaler? You think I'd let them flash their naked bellies in front of the clergy?"

I did not take offense to his words. He was not accustomed to being made to look like a fool. He only started attacking my origin out of desperation. Dufort, on the other hand, looked indignant.

"Hey, Captain!" he cried out, craning his neck. "Show some respect for the hostess. I won't have you insult her family. The Eliades are no worse than the Castelmaures."

"Like you should talk about respect! A minute ago you were about to molest her, and now rush to defend her honor. That's rich, Dufort."

"I still have one good hand, Captain, and it's itching to loosen your jaw. You're just bitter, that's all. I may be half the human, half the Parisian you are, but I'm twice the man. Be thankful that your cousin-fiancée is, as you put it, unnatural. If she possessed natural womanly appetites, you wouldn't be able to satisfy them, not in your present condition."

God knows, Dufort was in no shape to fight, even though he was trying to get back up on his feet. The men accompanying Lucius assumed more militant positions, preparing for another grapple.

"There will be no more bloodshed." I nearly had to throw my arms around the organist's neck to restrain him. "Tonight belongs to Blackfeather and Elinor. I won't let a theatrical celebration turn into a massacre. Stop it. I am addressing every single one of you. That includes you, Dufort. Stop provoking the captain. He had no idea it was your head inside that helmet. You did a splendid job fooling everyone."

Lucius was no longer listening. He let out a string of curses and walked away, leaving his dented helmet on the ground. His men followed after him. I remained sitting on the pavement, propping up the battered organist, whose bravado was fading away as quickly as blood was leaving his body. I knew my green costume was soaked. The skirt could be salvaged, but the bodice would probably have to be thrown away.

This was probably one of the most bizarre nights in Paris. In some fifteen minutes I had nearly lost my virginity to a perceived stranger, witnessed a brawl and learned a few curious facts from the private life of Lucius Castelmaure. Now I had to figure out what to do about Dufort. He was in a sad condition. It made sense to carry him to our house for the night. I would need my brothers' help. I would need to concoct a plausible story about the origin of Dufort's injuries. On one hand, I trusted their sense of humor. If they learned about his prank with the helmet, they would probably laugh. But I did not want to take any chances, especially since Sebastien was under Captain Castelmaure's command. It would be safer to say that Dufort was assaulted by beggars while defending a little orphan girl. I'm not a convincing storyteller, am I?

"I'm afraid you overestimate Parisians and their loyalty," I said when we were alone. "If you do find yourself at odds with the law and tied to the wheel, do not expect anyone to come to your aid."

"I know that," he whispered and blinked slowly. "There won't be a barrel of burgundy awaiting me at the pillory. I only said it to annoy Lucius. Any time someone mentions wine, his eyes blaze up. If he goes through with his threats and personally introduces me to the torturer, I won't expect any sympathy. All the better! Afterwards I will go back to my cell and write my finest piece. I'll call it *Blood of the Stone Prince*. And I'll dedicate it to you."

He was one of those men who derived pleasure from suffering. Pain made him brazen. Pain made him prolific. It also made him alluring in a way that the yellow-haired soldier could not be. Dufort looked beautiful with blood on his face.

Next came the awkward part, the one I dreaded. It was time to examine the damage inflicted by the soldiers. I picked up his injured hand, flipped it with the palm facing up and tried to straighten out the spasmodically curled up fingers.

Instead of wincing, he smiled, blood caking in the corner of his mouth. I never considered myself a healer by vocation. Denise was the medicine woman in the family, and she never bothered to share her knowledge with me. Still, I knew that prayers and medicine were futile in Dufort's case. Only through black sorcery could the broken bones be reassembled. I pulled one of the scarves off my belt and started bandaging his wrist only because it seemed like a tactful thing to do under the circumstances. It was like wishing a speedy recovery to a person whose illness is known to be terminal.

"I'm sorry about your costume," he said.

"Don't worry. It's just a piece of fabric. Denise will make another one."

"You're very forgiving."

"No, I'm not. What makes you think that? As a matter of fact, I'm prone to brooding and holding grudges. I can put on curses and give an evil eye. But you haven't done anything wrong." The bandaging job looked ludicrous. I unwrapped the scarf and started over again. "I have no idea what I'm doing. In case you haven't noticed, I'm not a medicine woman."

"Keep doing what you're doing. I could sit like this for eternity. I'll have some explaining to do in the morning. Not looking forward to that. My master ..."

"You think he'll kill you?"

"No, that's not what I was about to say. He really wants to see you."

Ah, so that was the reason for Dufort's visit! Now the truth was emerging. I did not think he would come to the play of his own accord. And the idea to wear the captain's helmet did not originate from him.

"That wretched, vile man," I said. "What does he want from me?"

"Your safety and your well-being above all things. He's very concerned about you, though he won't tell me why. It sounds serious, a matter of life and death."

I covered his mouth with my hand. "No, don't venture there. There are no matters of life for me, only matters of death. I've already discussed that with your master. He knows where I want to be buried."

"And how long do you suppose I shall last after you are gone?" he asked after I uncovered his mouth.

"Daniel," I addressed him by his given name for the first time, "you've lived without me for twenty years. You can live just as long after my death. You've only seen me once before."

"That's not true. I've seen you twice. The first time was on Rue des Bernardins when you danced *La Rotta* with my master. The second time was after the service. So tonight is the third time. As you can see, I had three opportunities to fall in love with you."

I let his hand drop into my lap. "Mother of God …"

"You feel nothing for me."

"No, I'd be lying if I said that. I'd also be lying if I said you were the only one. There are two others, and I don't need to utter their names. Do understand it was never my intention to fall in love with three men who are so closely linked. It poses certain complications. My heart is not divided. It expanded three times its size. I am three times the woman I was before I came to Paris. As you can see, it is not my whim but fate. Somebody up above wills it. I don't know how long it is going to last, but we must try to enjoy it, all of us. We form a tight love quadrangle, don't we?"

"We surely do," he confirmed, melancholic resignation veiling his features, deepening every hollow and highlighting every angle.

I was very pleased with my speech. I did not believe half of what I was saying, but, damn, it sounded good! Any time you bring up fate, it instantly justifies everything.

"But the other two are not here this very moment," I added, "so why worry about them?"

"Indeed, why worry?" he echoed, leaning in and tilting his face.

I had a suspicion that he was going to attempt to kiss me, so I blotted the blood off of his chin with the hem of my skirt. I had already decided I would let him. After the interrupted copulation in the alley, it would be endearing to revert to a more chaste form of courtship. I just did not want a trail of red prints all over my cheeks and neck.

Just as we were about to sear the beginning of our affair, we heard slow, intent applause above our heads. I turned around and saw a blond youth around my age, with a round malicious face.

"Well done, Dufort," he said. "Very convincing. You know, for a reclusive freak, you're rather smooth. My brother will be thrilled to hear about your conquest. But he won't be so happy to see your mangled hand. How do you intend on playing the morning mass?"

"I still have one good hand," the organist replied. "Trust me. The people won't notice the difference. Besides, it might heal by tomorrow."

"You expect your bones to grow back together in ten hours? Here's to hope!" He came closer to us. I have seen that hovering posture before. For such a small person, he had a heavy gait and a threatening presence. "What about the upcoming tournament? I had a delegation from Reims coming to fight you. I had my money on you. If you let me down … You'll curse the day you were born."

"I curse it anyway. But I won't let you down, Métivier."

"Very well, then. Come with me."

It was a little shocking how eagerly Dufort slipped out of my embrace and followed the order. Wavering and wincing, he struggled to his feet. It was comical to watch the lanky red-haired giant stand up and obediently follow the pot-bellied blond dwarf. In that moment Métivier looked like a demonic puppeteer.

After the night of the performance my condition took a rapid turn for the worse. Yes, apparently, there was still room for deterioration. The symptoms intensified: the fog in the head, the pain in the chest, the cold sweats and the weakness. Add sensitivity to light to the list. The tiny window above my mattress had to be shuttered. It seemed like every day a new symptom would surface. Who knew that a human body could ache, sweat, shiver and burn all at once? I spent the next three days curled up under a pile of disarrayed blankets. Shifting position no longer brought me relief. I tried sleeping propped up on a sack filled with fabric scraps left over from Denise's sewing, but that did not make my breathing any easier. I started wondering if that episode in the alley was my last excursion outside. Would I ever again set my foot on the filthy Parisian pavement?

Little Elinor sat dutifully by my side, braiding my hair and kneading my shoulders. I loathed keeping her tied up. A dazzling girl of twelve, whose dance had aroused so many men in the audience with one sway of her adolescent hips, had better things to do than tend to her ailing big sister. She should have been with her playwright suitor, learning new amorous tricks and rehearsing for the next production. Elinor felt guilty for basking in her success, and I felt guilty for souring her joy.

I had no heart to tell her that her constant presence was not making me feel better. It was rather annoying, actually, the constant touching of her tiny hands, the chirpy voice singing ditties in my ear. And for God's sake, how many braids could she weave on my head? I realize she was frightened and puzzled, seeing me in that state, and did not know how to hide it. After my death she would be left without an ally. How reliable was Blackfeather? He seemed generous with lush, breathy compliments but not too hasty with nuptials. He used her tender age to justify his delay, but was it only an excuse? I had heard of girls younger than her walking to the altar.

Elinor had been getting her monthly bleedings for close to a year now and appeared primed for carnal knowledge. As far as I knew, Blackfeather had not crossed a certain line in his affections. I imagine Elinor would have told me otherwise.

Artistic men are flighty. I knew that better than anyone. I could only pray that the skinny Englishman was different, that he would not glaze her with flattery, squeeze her for inspiration and then replace her with another muse. You are probably wondering why I am so preoccupied with my sister's chastity after my recent escapades. My illness afforded me the luxury of taking multiple lovers and not giving a damn about my reputation or my long-term future. God willing, Elinor had a long life ahead of her. Nobody said she would spend the rest of it with the Eliades. In fact, I wanted her to split from them. Do not ask me why I wanted it. I just had some inkling that she would not be happy with them after my death. I could see her becoming a burden to them if she failed to secure an advantageous alliance. After all, that is what Mathias had been grooming her for. Feel free to call me an ingrate.

Denise kept placing the jar with her herbal brew next to my bed, insisting that I drink it, but at some point I could not force that substance down my throat. The very smell of it nauseated me. Denise kept making it darker and stronger, insisting that the brew was halting my disease, claiming that without it I would have died a long time ago, but somehow I did not believe her. I had a feeling she exaggerated the depth of her knowledge of herbs. One time, while she was not looking, I poured the content of the jar down the floor crack. It suddenly dawned on me that if I did not pull myself from under the covers right there and then, I would never come out of that room. I could not continue being selfish, bemoaning my symptoms, like I was the only patient in Paris. There were other people who were suffering, including all three of my lovers. Did Captain Castelmaure regain his manly potency? How was Dufort's hand healing? Then there was Desmoulins, a particularly hard case. Yes, I did worry about him too, for his illness was not physical but spiritual. The darkness in his soul could not be diffused with herbal concoctions and compresses. I needed to see them one last time.

One morning, as soon as Denise stepped out to visit one of her customers and take her measurements, I crawled from under the blankets, forced myself to eat half of a wheaten cake with a few slices of apple, drank a pitcher of tepid water and put on my dancing shoes – for my regular street shoes could not be found.

"Where are you going?" Elinor asked me, lifting her disheveled white-haired head from the pillow.

"To look up some friends," I replied.

"When will you be back?"

"It depends on how quickly I find them. If Denise starts questioning you, tell her that I left before you awoke. Go back to sleep."

"I may do just that." She stretched and collapsed back onto the mattress, her hands above her head in dulcet abdication. "I won't get much sleep tonight. Blackfeather wants me to spend the night at his lodging. I've already agreed."

"Is this what you truly want?"

"Yes. I like him. And I like what he's done with me so far. I want the rest. Besides, he promised to print Papa's memoirs."

I fought the temptation to sit down next to that girl, look her in the eye and tell her that Papa's so-called memoirs were mostly tall tales. Those bits about Vlad the Impaler and the Moors? Nine out of ten things never happened. But how could I rob Elinor of her last childhood illusion? For God's sake, the poor imp was about to lose her virginity. Too many revelations at once would prove overwhelming.

"That Englishman is a tasty catch," I said out loud. "Just don't be shy about making your desires known. If you get hungry in the middle of the night, tell him."

Elinor did not see me blow a kiss in her direction. She was asleep again, dreaming of her leggy playwright. I grabbed my shawl off the hook and slipped outside.

After three days of imprisonment, the stench of Rue du Mouton seemed heavenly. Every breath I drew reminded me that I was still alive. As I passed by the alley where I had almost bid adieu to my maidenhood, I paused to survey the stains on the wooden boxes. *Blood of the Stone Prince* ...

My first destination was Île de la Cité. I realized that by seeking out Dufort, I ran the risk of encountering his master, and I wanted to postpone that encounter, if possible. Morning mass had ended about half an hour ago. The cathedral was empty except for a few altar servers giggling on the gallery. Nothing is more aggravating to your ears than the laughter of adolescent boys with their cracking voices. I imagined those boys falling off the gallery and breaking their necks. I knew if I asked them where the organist was, they would start whistling and howling, and the sound would become unbearable. So I went to look for Dufort myself. He was not in the music loft or in the north tower.

Finally, I spotted a demure-looking young deacon. He seemed like someone who would not make any bird noises or snide remarks.

"I'm looking for Daniel Dufort," I said.

His sallow face widened in a grin. "Why, isn't he in demand!"

"What do you mean?"

"You must be the third or fourth woman who came looking for him this morning. Two of them dropped off a barrel of burgundy."

My blood ran cold. "Did he get pilloried?"

"Pilloried? Who would dare to pillory the most coveted composer in Paris? The wine was a gratuity gift for a commission. We'll be drinking it tonight with dinner. He could not possibly drink it all himself."

"I wanted to make sure he was all right, that's all. Where is he now?"

"Oh, he left right after the service with another group of women."

"Those women, are they ... of the street?"

"Heavens, no! They are fine, honorable young ladies from good families, polite and well-dressed. I believe they were going to a banquet. At any rate, it pains me to interrupt you, but I must return to my duties. I'm not good with names, but when Dufort returns from his rendezvous with the procurator's niece, I'll be sure to tell him that an Egyptian circus girl came looking for him. I hope he'll know who you are."

"I'm not Egyptian!" Of all the things I could say to that arrogant beanstalk in black, I chose to justify my heritage. "The people you call Egyptians are not from Egypt."

"It doesn't matter to me where they are from. They are not real people with feelings and rights like the rest of us. Even if Dufort throws you against the wall, it won't make him less of a man – or you more of a woman. Good day, mademoiselle."

I was walking down Rue de Parvis, overcome by that delicious feeling of impending doom. Something dreadful was going to happen. So I was not too shocked when a cold hand fell on my shoulder. Over the past few months I had grown accustomed to being grabbed and jostled. What surprised me was that the one standing behind me was not a man but a woman with violet eyes and thin light-brown hair mercilessly braided. I guessed her age to be early twenties. She looked like she was rehearsing for a life as a nun, so plain was her attire and so stern her expression.

"My name is Aurore St. Laurent," she plunged into the introduction. "I am Captain Castelmaure's cousin. And you must be the Transylvanian hussy."

Stupendous! We just went from an Egyptian circus girl to Transylvanian hussy. The compliments kept coming.

"Is that … is that what Lucius called me?"

"No, that's what I call you after having seen you with my own eyes. I like to call things by their proper names. Not bad. A little uncouth, but definitely an improvement on my cousin's usual fare. You should have seen the last three. *Mon Dieu!*"

Aurore stepped back and surveyed me. Her bloodless lips curled. Oddly, she did not look like a jealous woman evaluating her rival. She looked more like a man evaluating his latest pick.

"You are not exactly as Lucius described you," I said, still reeling from her bluntness which I found oddly engaging. "The words he used …"

"Here's something you need to know about my cousin. He is not good with words. He can follow simple commands, but don't believe his descriptions. At any rate, I'm not here to scratch your pretty eyes out. I'd have to blind half of the women in Paris."

"You don't love Lucius at all?"

"Surely, I do – as a relative, as a black sheep of our rather disjointed family. If he never gets his flaccid, infested rod, I won't be disappointed. I'm twice the man he'll ever be, and Lucius knows it. My fencing technique is better than his. I don't have much use for men in general. This is why I am breaking the engagement and joining a convent. Believe it or not, becoming a nun had been my plan all along, until my darling Maman, may the devil take her soul, started swaying me towards the hearth. Honestly, I can't wait for that clucking hen to die." She looked away and cracked her jaw. "Once you reach the age of twenty, having a living mother becomes a real nuisance."

"But … Lucius said he was *saving* you from the veil. He made it sound …"

Aurore smiled without showing her teeth and nodded, her nostrils flaring. "I have no doubt how he made it sound: a dashing officer rescuing his eccentric cousin from a spinster's fate. In reality, I was the one saving *him* from the gutter. That golden boy is in serious debt. Not to worry, he'll get a portion of what would've been my dowry. He counted on that money. The rest will go to Chelles Abbey. My friend Diane and I made a pact to become nuns. We'll be sharing a cloister cell."

"Does Lucius know about your change of plans?"

"Not yet. That's the problem. He's nowhere to be found. I have a bit of sad news for him – not related to our engagement – and no way of delivering it to him. It would be a nice gesture for him to show up at the funeral."

"Is it Madame Castelmaure?" I asked. "Has she finally died?"

"No, it's his younger daughter, Amelie."

"Mother of God … How did she die?"

"Most peacefully, in her cradle. She just went to sleep and never woke up. Her older sister found her and, apparently, played with her corpse for an hour – before the mother opened her eyes. It's awful all around."

One had to admire how calmly and flippantly she spoke about death. I would love a girl like her by my bedside for comfort.

"Don't you think it a little cruel to break the engagement now?" I asked. "Can Lucius handle two blows at once?"

She shook her braided head. "There will never be a good time. Perhaps, you can find a way to soften the blow? You seem like the mystical, sensitive type. I know you'll find the right words - if you see him, that is. I don't expect you to hound him down. But if he turns up at your father's house, please give him the message. Will you do that for me, little hussy? I doubt his family will postpone the funeral on his account. It would be nice of him to come and pay last respects to his daughter."

"I'll see what I can do."

What else could I tell her? After being called an Egyptian circus girl and a Transylvanian hussy over the span of fifteen minutes, I felt strangely honored to be given such a task.

Before leaving, Aurore squeezed my arm above the elbow. "And listen. If you ever get tired of being groped by the clergy, come and visit us at Chelles. You'll receive a most cordial welcome." Her fingers slipped up and down my arm a few times, stirring an unsettling shiver. Her violet eyes lingered on my face and neck. "Extraordinary girls go there from all over the country and never look back."

Even though Aurore had graciously excused me from the chore of finding Lucius and delivering the news of his daughter's death to him, I simply could not wash my hands and step back. Clearly, she thought I had influence over him, which was flattering in itself. Otherwise she would not have sought me out. It would also give me an opportunity to make amends. Since the night of Blackfeather's play Lucius had not stopped by our house. Believe it or not, we still had his helmet. He never reclaimed it. Perhaps, he thought it tainted? I had no idea how much it would cost to get a new one. I imagine, for a man like Lucius, replacing a helmet was a greater ordeal than replacing a mistress.

I wondered if Sebastien knew anything about his commander's whereabouts, but my brother was not expected home before dusk. I did not want to waste any time. Then I remembered the pudgy blond youngster who came on the night of the performance. Blackfeather told me that he was Desmoulins' estranged half-brother who suddenly resurfaced after fifteen some years and became the ringleader behind *Les gladiateurs urbains*. Now he was working as a library clerk at the College of Lisieux. His job involved cataloguing and organizing the books. I knew that he and Lucius were friends, sharing lodging.

Walking through the University district even in broad daylight posed certain problems. The moment I set my foot on St. Genevieve's Hill, I was greeted with a surfeit of whistling and tongue-clicking. If you are an unescorted female between the ages of twelve and forty, good luck proving to those satyrs that you are not there to peddle your body. I should have brought one of my brothers with me, or disguised myself as an old beggar woman, or attached a few morsels of rotting meat to my limbs to imitate sores.

To be fair, I did look like a cheap street harlot. The realization struck me a little too late. I had left the house that morning wearing a Spanish shawl with tassels and sequins. I moved it from my shoulders onto my head to cover my face from both sides. It did not help. The red lace was attracting too much attention. The sleeves on my chemise were too short and too transparent, and my skirt had too many ruffles. At least I had left my bracelets at home. Thank God for that. The chiming of the trinkets would have them would draw in packs. In my defense, when I got dressed that morning, nobody told me I was going into the very heart of the University district. Otherwise I would have put on Mathias' long cloak. My trek through the narrow streets in the vicinity of the College of Lisieux was nothing short of an obstacle course. On every corner I encountered another 'yellow beak', as first year students were called. They pulled off their caps before me and doubled over in mock bows. I would sound incredibly stupid if I tried to rebuff their solicitations, given my apparel, so I just let their howls glaze over me.

"I'm looking for Johannes Métivier," I said to one of them.

The scholar's plump, brazen mouth curved. I was prepared for him to say something to the effect of Métivier being one lucky bastard, but, to my surprise, he said nothing. He only pointed to the massive four-story tower with narrow windows.

"Am I allowed to go in there?" I asked.

"Hell, no. But that's where your fellow is. You'll have to wait for him to come out, which may not be until dusk."

I did not cherish the prospect of spending another few hours in the Mecca of wanton Parisian manhood.

"I'm afraid I don't have time," I said brusquely. "I need to see him at once."

"What can be so important?"

"The gladiators," I fibbed in an ominous whisper. "It's about the upcoming tournament. One of the contestants is gravely wounded and sent me to deliver the message."

It worked. It wiped the flippant grin off the scholar's face. The gladiators were sacred. "You stay right here. I'll go fetch him."

Two minutes later he came back with Johannes Métivier. Instead of his usual half-dismantled chainmail the boy was wearing an austere tunic, his blond curls flattened beneath the cap. Seeing the sixteen-year-old dressed in all black for the first time, I suddenly noted the resemblance between him and his older brother.

The resemblance was not physical. Desmoulins was tall, dark and angular, with a hawkish nose, whereas Métivier was short, round, ruddy and snub-nosed. Still, both had that air of superiority shrouding them. The two brothers were shaped differently but of the same substance.

"It's not about the tournament, is it?" he said when we were alone.

"No," I replied unapologetically. "I need to see Lucius. You've been lodging with him, haven't you?"

The scholar adjusted the belt over his tunic. "My dear brother wouldn't help me find suitable quarters. He wants me to make my own money. So he helped me get this job. Can you believe it? The man has never worked a day in his life. He's always tapped into the church's treasury to fund his demonic experiments."

As much as I sympathized with the scholar, I had to interrupt him. "I'm sorry about your plight, Johannes. We can talk for hours about your brother's unspeakable cruelty, but right now I must find the captain. It's rather urgent."

I was prepared to be met with a cryptic sneer and a string

of questions regarding my business with Lucius. To my amazement, Métivier only tapped his chin before blurting out the directions.

"There is a row of homes at the end of Pont Saint-Michel. Don't curl your lip when you see the place. The people living there are mostly butchers and boatmen. They have better manners than the ones you've met on the University grounds. Find the filthiest, most decrepit building on the block. Go up to the second floor, then down the corridor, take a left, then another left, then take a right, and you'll find a room with one small window overlooking the river."

"The filthiest house at the end of Pont Saint-Michel," I echoed. "Easy enough."

"Good luck. I am not sure if you'll find Lucius there. I myself haven't seen him in days. Last I heard he was having friction with his superiors. He could be at the garrison. Oh, and tell him the landlady wants her rent. The old hag threatened to throw out his things and change the lock if he doesn't pay up."

"Thank you, Johannes," I said, fighting the urge to reach out and pinch that pimply soft cheek. "Why cannot everyone be so blunt and agreeable?"

"It's my father's Flemish efficiency."

The scholar shrugged and ran back into the tower.

On my way out of the University district, I saw a handful of guards marching by. The scene struck me as somewhat unusual – guards in broad daylight. What sort of crime could have brought them here? They looked determined to make an arrest. Obeying their commander's abrupt commands, they entered one of the lecture halls with the stealth and swiftness of water running down the drain. A few seconds later I heard muffled cries and the sound of toppling furniture.

Wrapped within my shawl – and with a false sense of security – I proceeded towards the bridge.

Captain Castelmaure, whatever your superiors say, whatever they do to you, I want you know that in my eyes, you are the most valiant soldier in Paris. Moreover, I cannot think of a worthier contender to claim my maidenhood.

On the way to Pont Saint-Michel I rehearsed my speech

for Lucius. I wanted to keep it brief and sincere. Of course, I wondered if it would sound convincing coming from a love-struck Wallachian chit so far removed from the military world. As an officer and a nobleman, how much value did he place on my adoration?

The directions given to me by Johannes Métivier were very clear. It did not take me long to find the ugliest, filthiest looking building on the corner of the bridge. The front door was unlocked, suggesting there were very few valuable items inside that could tempt a looter. *Go to the second floor. Take a left, then another left, then a right …*

There was no bed in the room, just a massive trunk covered with a blanket. Lucius was lying on his back, his head turned towards me, eyes closed, one hand and one leg dangling off the edge. Judging from his ashen pallor, I concluded that the news of his daughter's death had already reached him. A part of me was relieved that I had been spared the unpleasant task of devastating him. Now it was my privilege to comfort him.

Even at that stage of devastation, he looked princely – his flawless Olympian features stiffened by grief. There was no room for me on the trunk, so I sat on the floor and took the captain's hand. It was moist and flaccid. Here came the hard part. I had so many things to say, all the words of praise I had prepared on my way to his lodging, and they all seemed lame and stupid now.

"Is there anything I can do for you?" I mumbled. "Talk to me, Lucius. I could shine your spurs or dust your riding boots. Water your horse, perhaps?"

He did not as much as stir, so I shut my mouth. Sometimes it is the best thing to do. Wise, delicious silence. For a few minutes I simply sat on the floor, my head leaning against the edge of the trunk, kneading the captain's cold fingers. There was no sound except for the faint wheezing coming from my chest and the drip-drop of water. That vicious landlady! She had the cheek to threaten Lucius with eviction when she had not even bothered to fix the cracks.

I lifted my eyes upward. The ceiling looked surprisingly sturdy and clean, with a fresh layer of plaster; the walls also did not have any visible cracks. Where was that steady splattering sound coming from?

I stood up to survey the room and gasped, seeing a pool of blood forming behind the trunk. The blood was coming out of a stab wound in Captain Castelmaure's back. So that was the cause of his listlessness and pallor. How deep was the wound? How long had he been lying there? Did anyone know of his condition? Or was he hiding from the world like a shot-down beast? I had an inkling that wound had not been sustained in the line of duty but that he must have gotten stabbed during one of those gladiator tournaments. Suddenly the prospect of court martial seemed real and daunting. What would he say to his superiors if they asked him how he got the wound?

I was afraid to move him as much as I was afraid to release him. All I knew was that one of the men I loved was bleeding right in front of me. So I stood over him, cradling his blond head. Suddenly, I heard a grim, sardonic voice behind my back.

"Is this the lair where you bring your prey, Captain? My brother described this place in great detail. I didn't believe such a filthy place could exist. Now I see it with my own eyes."

Glancing over my shoulder, I locked eyes with Monseigneur Desmoulins standing in the doorway. He seemed to have grown even leaner and greyer since our last encounter.

"You again," he said, stepping over the threshold, his movements slow and liquid. "As if it was not bad enough that you've saturated my nightmares. Now I must see you in daylight. You're like a demon that replicates itself, present in several places at once."

"I can say the same about you, Monseigneur."

"You really should not be here. Your presence is not doing the captain any good. Your mousy voice is nothing but an irritant. You are nothing to him."

"I love him."

"You and three thousand other women in Paris. You don't see them forming a queue to pay their last respects, do you? That is because they have enough courtesy to stay away. You know, death is a very delicate and private event. It is impolite to gawk and intrude."

"And what are you doing here?"

"Performing my duty." He placed his leather bag on the windowsill and pulled out a prayer book and a flask with holy water. "Death is my profession. But you … it's never enough for you, is it? I've taken you to the Gibbet of Montfaucon. I've shown you the interrogation chamber. You've touched the hooks and the chains, and you still haven't learned respect for death."

"Why do you speak of death?"

"You see our friend's condition. You see the puddle of blood on the floor."

"But you'll make him better, won't you?" I loathed the treacherous tremor in my voice. "Isn't this what you are here for, to mend his wound? What about your medical training?"

"It's true," he said with a nod. "I'm a man of many skills, and medicine is just one of them. But today I'm here to give the captain his last rites. Dull as it sounds, I'm actually about to do a priest's job. Imagine that."

"How did this happen? You must know."

"My informed guess is that it's the idiotic gladiator game. God knows, I warned him. But, look at the bright side. At least, he'll die with his title intact – captain, or lieutenant, or whatever it is. His superiors won't lay their draconian paws on him now. You cannot court-martial a dead man. And you too, mademoiselle, can let go of his head, pretty and hollow as it is. Let go and make it easier for everyone."

I do not know why I complied with Monseigneur's demands. Releasing the captain's head and watching it tilt backwards was nothing short of devastating. My gaze shifted back to the man in black.

"How can you mock a dying soldier?"

"I'm not the one making a scene." Desmoulins rolled up the sleeves of his cassock. "Everything was perfectly dignified until you showed up and started wailing and salivating. I have good news for you. With Captain Castelmaure out of commission, there has been some shuffling in the company. I heard your brother Sebastien got promoted. Well timed and well deserved. Wipe your tears, child. Go home and celebrate. There's nothing else for you to do here, except … kiss the captain."

The room was so tiny that it only took me a few steps to cross it. I stood in front of Desmoulins, my fists pushing against the tabletop. "What did you say?"

"You heard me. Kiss the captain. His last earthly sensation will be that of your tongue between his lips. What more can a dying man wish for? You wanted to make yourself useful, didn't you? Kiss him and leave, so I can get to work."

He was flipping through his prayer book, shifting pieces of paper that served as bookmarks.

"What's this?" I asked, lifting the flask. "Tears of the pope?"

"You're still here, child." He raised his large dark-grey eyes at me. "You're looking at me in that peculiar way. Well, if you won't kiss your captain, perhaps you'll kiss me instead? That's right. You've never been kissed by a *real* man. We should fix that."

The prayer book went flying over his shoulder. The flask slipped out of my hand. Desmoulins grabbed me by the sides, seated me on the edge of the cleared table and set off to finish what he had started in the dungeon beneath the palace, reverting to the role of the lovesick inquisitor. The pressure of his mouth was as fervent and steadfast as the grip of his hands, punishing and mentoring. With that kiss he narrated the story of his past. I saw images of a spoiled Flemish-Italian youth kissing another dark-haired girl, taking off her clothes, doing wicked things to her beneath the blossoming orange trees. I could not see the girl's face, but I could see her back arching, very much like mine was. Once again, my body welcomed the assault, just like it did in the dark alley. Being forced into a place with very little wiggle room felt strangely liberating.

When I opened my eyes, the room was filled with archers. Desmoulins was whispering to them with a look of sad disgust on his face, pointing his finger at me, shaking his head, and they were nodding sympathetically. I overheard a few flattering words like "deranged" and "unhinged". He snapped his fingers, and they dragged me away.

I woke up in a private room above one of the cleaner taverns in the vicinity of the Pont Saint-Michel. Whoever left me there was kind enough to cover me with a blanket that was not stained with bodily fluids or crawling with insects. How long had I been asleep? I glanced out the window overlooking the Seine. The color of the sky suggested it was early evening. A part of me wanted to go crawl back under the blanket for the rest of the night. I could not remember the last time I had a whole mattress, let alone a room to myself. I always had Elinor's restless feet kicking me, her greedy little hands yanking the covers.

Then it occurred to me that I had no way to pay for those lush accommodations, having left home without a single crown. With luck, I would be able to slip out unnoticed. Mathias had done that on occasion. His trick was telling the innkeeper he was going out for some fresh air and leaving behind some useless article of clothing like a vest or a scarf as a form of proof that he would come back. In the end, that article of clothing would end up serving in lieu of payment for the food and lodging. He spoke of those episodes from his youth without pride and stressed that the trick was only to be used in extreme cases. Given that I had been dragged into the tavern after watching one of my lovers bleed to death and being kissed into oblivion by another one, I thought my case was extreme enough.

Leaning onto the railing and simulating fatigue, I went downstairs. The dining hall was filled with the smell of roasting pork and teeming with merchants and shopkeepers. Suppressing a thief's grimace, my stomach churning from what I was about to do, I hung my whorish Andalusian shawl on the hook. "I'll return at once," I muttered to the portly woman behind the wine stand. "Just a gulp of air."

"No need to pull tricks on me, sweetheart," she replied. "The room is paid for. The good officers took care of it."

I pretended not to hear her words and walked out of the tavern, leaving the shawl hanging. I really had no more use for that gaudy rag. It was made of the same fabric as a bullfighter's cloak and drew the same response.

I did not make it far from the inn. A hoarse exclamation reached my ears. "Beard of Mohammed! What do I see? My dark Bohemian angel."

Those were Lucius Castelmaure's words on another man's

lips. That man who materialized before me was Daniel Dufort. He simply slipped out from between two buildings and blocked my path. The scarf I had used to bandage his hand was still in place, tattered and stained. I noticed nefarious red marks on his neck that looked an awful lot like love bites. I wondered if they came from one woman or from several.

"I have not forgotten my promise to you, mademoiselle," he continued. "I've started writing that piece *Blood of the Stone Prince*. It's progressing nicely. Since my left hand is still in pieces, I have been spending most of my time composing. During the mass I've been playing with one hand. The people of Paris haven't noticed the difference."

"So I worried for nothing."

"You worried about me? That's so damn sweet! No need to worry your greasy little head, *ma petite*. Dufort is fine, just fine."

He was referring to himself in the third person!

"You're not fine," I said. "I fear that in addition to your hand, your head may have suffered. You're not acting like yourself. Someone else has moved into your body and taken hold."

"No, it's still me, *ma belle*. Strange things have been happening," he imparted in an enigmatic whisper, leaning closer to me. "What you said about fates and powers getting entangled? It's true. That night Lucius took something from me, but he also left a few things behind – like his vocabulary and his taste in wine." He held up a bottle of cheap spirits. "See? This is the very substance that corroded his liver."

"Lucius is dead," I blurted out.

Dufort let out a nervous growl. "Don't tell me: his mannish fiancée ripped his head off." The tentative grin vanished from his face. "You're joking, right?"

"Alas, I'm not. He was stabbed in a brawl. That's my guess. A nice, deep puncture wound just below the neck. I saw it myself. "

"Oh …" He stepped back and lowered his eyes, but only for a second. "In that case, we should light a candle for him."

"Damn well, we should. His soul needs prayer."

Dufort rubbed his forehead. "Which reminds me: I need to get back for the evening mass. If I don't show up at all, the choir boys will gossip. Let's go."

He placed his good hand on my waist and we headed over the bridge towards Notre-Dame. We walked in silence. Dufort looked subdued, his breathing labored and spasmodic. A few times he slowed his pace and shook his head. I confess it was a little puzzling to see him so distraught by the news. Perhaps, I had underestimated his friendship with Lucius. The two men had so little in common apart from their lust for the same woman. And yet, so many things were coming to me as revelations. For instance, I had not known about the captain's convoluted family life.

"I never got a chance to apologize for ridiculing him that night," he said when we were inside the cathedral.

"Now, there were plenty of insults on both sides."

"But I started it."

"Do you remember that for certain? Who threw the first punch? It was dark, and everyone was a little drunk."

"I don't regret donning his helmet – that part was amusing – but I shouldn't have mocked him. I've never mocked anyone before. Would you believe it? But it gave me such pleasure. Insults taste like honeyed wine. I can see how one can become fond of it. I understand why Lucius was tempted to pillory me."

"His men gave you a sound thrashing. The score is even. That should alleviate your guilt. You paid for your insolence with your blood."

My words seemed to provide little comfort for Dufort. He continued brooding and gnawing himself internally. It did not help that the candle refused to stay lit. The flame kept going out. Was it some sort of omen? It took us three attempts to ignite the wick.

"Guess who is in Paris," Dufort said suddenly, changing the subject. "Anselm Viteri."

"Is that name supposed to tell me something?"

"If it doesn't, consider yourself fortunate. He's one of the most brutal inquisitors, originally from the Basque country. His surname means 'wolf'. How very fitting! The Wolf of the Inquisition! I do not know what brought him here. Perhaps, he thought that old Louis de Beaumont needed a hand. Listen to this. Viteri is the one who issued my execution warrant fifteen years ago. I never told you the story, did I?"

I do not believe he did. Dufort and I never had a lengthy discussion about his past – or mine. All I knew was that he had some special order of protection straight from the Vatican exempting him from prosecution in a canon court. I had a feeling his story would be good.

"Tell me."

We stood in the shadow of a pillar. Dufort kept his eye on the front entrance as people were starting to trickle in. I could tell he needed to tell the story before mass. His head would explode otherwise.

"It's almost droll." He lifted his bandaged hand to his mouth and laughed. "When I was four years old, I was accused of killing seven other children. It happened shortly after my mother had slashed her wrists. A fever ripped through the boarding school where I was staying. My main crime was surviving the outbreak. It led to me being marked as a sorcerer. Anselm Viteri – who was just an insignificant young deacon at the time – was pushing to have me burned. He took an active interest in the case and led the miniature crusade against me. I wonder why. His bastard must have been among the dead children. I see no other explanation."

The flippant tone in which he related that grisly tale made me smile. Because he spent so little time conversing with other people, he did not know what kind of responses to expect from them. He took my smile as a sign of encouragement.

"At any rate, I learned a new word: *grotesque*," he added boastfully. "That is what Anselm Viteri called me at the dinner table."

"What were you having for dinner?"

"I don't remember. I had no appetite. It's hard to swallow a morsel with Viteri sitting across from you and staring you down. I wasn't looking at the plate. It could have contained hearts of unbaptized infants for all I know. At any rate, it's a new word, stems from Italian '*grotto*'. Apparently, they found some ancient artifacts in a cave outside Rome. It means something like hidden treasure, an oddity discovered by accident. Well, Viteri says that my whole persona is grotesque. I don't know what to make of his statement."

I also loved learning new words and using them later to perplex my brothers and make them feel inferior.

"It sounds like a compliment," I said to Dufort. "A treasure from a cave …"

He shook his head, anxiety flooding his eyes. "What if Viteri is right? What if I am a monster without realizing it? Everyone I befriend ends up dying. It must be some sort of curse my mother put on me before she slit her wrists.

"It started with the children at the boarding school. I played with some of them. I was the tallest, and they loved to hang on me. I felt like a giant tree. My red hair fascinated them, so they yanked at it mercilessly, and I let them. To me the warmth of human hands was a novel sensation. My mother seldom touched me, unless she was swatting at me while telling me how I ruined her life. So I didn't mind being jostled by my schoolmates. I rather enjoyed it. I let them ride on my back and bury me in the sand up to my neck. They all died when the fever struck, the ones to which I was the closest.

"Then Philippe Chauvel, the previous organist split his skull, followed by Antoine Lasserre, the sculpture apprentice. Now Lucius. We just had our last fencing lesson a week ago. There won't be another one, ever. Is that string of deaths a mere coincidence or a sign of something greater?"

"I don't know about your other dead friends, but Lucius got stabbed in a trivial brawl. The only mystical force involved in his death was his own stupidity. Don't flatter yourself by taking credit for the deed. Besides, Desmoulins is still alive, isn't he?"

"But he's not my friend. He's my master. It's not the same. I hate that man. I'd put my hands in the fire for him, but I hate him nonetheless. Does this make any sense? He saved me from the pyre. Now I wonder if it was such a good idea after all. Maybe he should have allowed the Inquisition to follow through with the burning. Viteri must have an instinct for such things. That's why he's so good at his job of spotting demons."

I did not doubt Dufort's sincerity for an instant. He was not saying those things to gain pity. He believed every word he was saying, at least in that moment. The cuffs of his shirt came undone, and I caught a glimpse of his scarred wrists and forearms. I had not seen those thin pink indents on his skin before. It was dark when I was bandaging him after the run-in with the archers, and I was not paying attention to what I was doing. There was a pattern to the incisions. They ran perfectly parallel and evenly spaced, like the lines on music sheets. He must have inflicted them slowly and methodically. I wondered who had introduced him to the ritual of self-mutilation. Or did he discover the gruesome art on his own?

I put my hands on his shoulders and shook him.

"Stop it! You spend too much time talking to statues and ghosts. Now listen to a living human being – if I can call myself that. You had nothing to do with those deaths. You are not cursed, and you have no power to curse others. As much as you'd like to believe that you possess those demonic abilities, you do not. Do you hear me, Daniel?"

Once again, I called him by his given name. I did not know if he captured my words or how he interpreted them. He tilted his head and leaned in, just like he did in the alley. I had exactly two seconds to slow him down.

"Not now," I said, slipping my gloved hand between his mouth and mine. "I'm still recovering from your master's kiss."

Dufort's eyes widened. "Did he hurt you?" he asked, his voice muffled by my fingers. "Look, if he did anything to you ..."

"Calm down. Your master did not hurt me. He tried to ... comfort me in his own way. He saw how distraught I was at the sight of Lucius in a puddle of blood. We were both caught off guard. When two people are frazzled, sometimes they do odd things, like kiss." Should I have told him the truth? "You and I should wait until tomorrow." Before pulling my hand away, I stroked his lips and his chin. I was not ready to take off my gloves and let him see my hands. That revelation was going to take place in a very near future. "If we kiss now, it won't come out right. We must abstain, if only out of respect for Lucius. Today is a somber day. Let us hope that tomorrow will be brighter."

"Perhaps it's for the best," he agreed with a sigh, as his hollow cheeks suddenly reddened. "Because I just spent the whole evening kissing some random wenches whose names I do not know. Upon my life, I have no idea how it started. I was walking past a tavern, and these girls came out of nowhere and just flung themselves on my neck, as if I had saved the kingdom from an English invasion. It did not occur to me to resist. Now with Lucius gone, someone needs to take his place. I must say, it's a very time-consuming occupation, being the golden boy. Maybe it's Lucius sending me a sign that he is not angry with me and that he wishes me well."

"Forget about the tavern wenches," I said, smoothing the collar of his doublet. "They don't count. Tell me about your rendezvous with the procurator's niece. Now *that* I'm dying to hear about."

Dufort looked genuinely surprised. "I wouldn't be caught dead with that prude. What made you think something outlandish?"

"Don't play innocent now, Dufort. That sallow-faced deacon told me all about your recent amorous adventures. You know? The barrel of burgundy, the herds of high-born women whisking you away every morning."

"Are you talking about Benedict Lomont? Oh, he's such a prankster. You cannot believe everything that comes out of his mouth. Rest assured that whatever he said to you was in good humor."

"Including that part where he called me an Egyptian circus girl?"

"Really, is that what he called you?" I saw the awkward lopsided smile return to Dufort's face. "That brazen bastard. So, what are you, anyway? I don't believe you ever told me."

"I don't know. That's the problem." Now it was my turn to wring my hands. "I tell the world I'm Wallachian, just to keep it simple, even though nine out of ten Parisians have no idea where the deuce Wallachia is. What if I am of some heathen descent? Mathias maintains my mother was French, though he won't go further than that. He's not above telling a charitable lie. What if my mother was a prostitute and my father a Moor or, even worse, a Saracen? Would you still ..."

"Yes, I'd still dedicate my music to you," he vowed fervently. "I hope it's true, and your father was some brown-skinned rake.

That would make us perfect for each other. Suppose the worst we believe about ourselves is true. A monster boy and a heathen girl can do incredible things. Think of all the damage we can cause. Oh, I've waited for this."

"So you've never been with a woman before?"

"No," he responded with a sort of cheerful hopelessness, as if he had been expecting that question.

"I find it hard to believe, in light of all your accolades."

He let out a terse laugh that sounded like a gasp from being punched in the chest. "You think women give a damn about accolades? It's apparent that you don't have female friends."

"That's true. I do not."

"If you think my commissions boost my popularity with the opposite sex, think again. Even if I am a genius, as some of my followers maintain, it means next to nothing. I write a polyphonic mass, and nobody cares. I maim another musician from St. Genevieve's on a whim, and suddenly I'm coveted. *Behold the beastly fellow who breaks limbs!* This is what Parisian beauties find impressive. You know, you were the first woman to approach me after a mass, in the five years that I've been playing here. That tells me something. The rest of them are deaf and blind. My master is right about one thing. Most of them are cows, and every cow needs a bull. No judgment, only observation. I have no right to begrudge women their tastes. If I'm not what most of them desire ..."

He tried so hard to glaze over his bitterness with a sort of philosophical resignation, but I could tell he was vexed to his core. I had seen that bitterness before on Blackfeather's face when he complained about most women not recognizing his dramatic talent. One time the Englishman wrote a string of sonnets for a maiden, on her request, no less, and she never even bothered to read them. Dufort was in the same predicament. Being an ecclesiastic musician and composer did not boost his amorous prospects. I knew it was time for me to step in before he plunged deeper into his melancholy.

"I knew it wasn't Lucius inside that helmet. I had a feeling it was you. That was the reason why I didn't fight." Then I heard myself utter the words I nearly uttered over the cooling body of

Lucius. *"I cannot think of a more worthy contender to claim my maidenhood."*

What can be more gratifying for a girl than the sight of a man in turmoil? If you drop a declaration like that in the same unflinching tone you would use while giving a testimony in court, it is like telling a condemned person the execution had been cancelled. No coy sighs or sheepish giggles, only the determination of a woman who has chosen her lover and was merely informing him of her decision. Try that next time then watch the man's reaction! The look of bliss mixed with panic on Dufort's face made up for all of my past tribulations.

The cathedral was filling up. I heard rustles and voices coming from the sacristy.

"Don't go," he said, stroking my hair with his intact hand and glancing nervously at the entrance. "I want us to continue this conversation. Please stay for the service. I'll show you my cell in the north tower, and I'll honor your wish to abstain. We'll just talk. There are many things I wish to say to you."

"There are many things I wish to say to you as well, but I must go home." Gently, I pushed away his hand, but not before rubbing my cheek against it. "My sister is leaving with Blackfeather tonight. I hope to catch her before he whisks her away. I'd like to give her my final words of encouragement. Let me do my last sisterly duty. Then I can think of my own pleasure. After today, there will be no more soldiers for me, or wenches for you. I'm all yours, Daniel."

In that moment I believed my own words. There really was no other man except for the organist with his jarring pale eyes. I was pleased with my choice.

"I'm afraid to blink or move," he confessed. "A big part of me still thinks it's a dream or a joke."

"It's neither, as you will soon find out. But, there's something I need to show you." I exhaled and put my hands in front of him. "Do the honors and remove my gloves. This time tomorrow these hands will be sliding up and down your bare back; I want you to see what they look like first. Go on, Daniel."

Except for a faint twitch of the eyebrows, his expression did not change much after the gloves came off. "I suspected something like that," he admitted. "You can tell me about it when you're ready."

"It's a part of the mystery, just like my origin. And what if the burns were on my face?"

"Then you would be wearing a mask instead of gloves."

Before heading back to Rue du Mouton, I stood at the edge of the bridge and stared into the dark water. There really was no desperate need for me to go home that evening. In all likelihood, I was not going to catch Elinor. She must have already left with her Englishman. Nor did I believe it was necessary to observe a period of mourning for Lucius. I just wanted to make Dufort wait one more night. It was my gift to him – that of anticipation. I wanted him to spend one more night tossing on his mattress, pondering all the delicious liberties I was going to allow him.

As I was passing by the tavern Les trois grâces where I had slept for a few hours, I saw my red shawl lying on the pavement. Someone must have taken it off the hook and discarded it. As gawdy as it looked, it was a gift from Mathias. Feeling a subtle pinch of guilt, I bent down to pick it up. A cold man's hand intercepted my wrist.

"There you are." I heard the foreboding baritone of Monseigneur Desmoulins. "I've been waiting for you for the past few hours. I had to miss the evening mass. The bishop will give me hell for it."

"What else do you need from me?" I asked wearily. "It was a long and puzzling day and I'd like to go home."

"There is nobody waiting for you there; at least nobody who wishes you well." He threw his cloak over me and pulled me into the drafty gap between two buildings. "Listen to me. I don't advise you going back to Rue du Mouton. Your family has been arrested."

"Elinor ..." I whispered, overcome by vertigo.

Honestly, she was the only Eliade whose well-being concerned me.

"Your sister is safe," Desmoulins reassured me, albeit reluctantly, for it pleased him to see me in the throes of anxiety. "She's with her English lover. She owes her salvation to her adolescent whorishness. However, your parents and both brothers have been taken into custody. You would be with them right now, beneath the Palace of Justice."

I leaned against the wall, hoping my knees would not buckle. I would hate to slip to the ground in front of that man of all people. "Mother of God ... What did Mathias do this time?"

"You tell me." Desmoulins spread his black sleeves. "You know him better than I. From what you are insinuating, this wouldn't be his first tiff with the authorities."

"It wouldn't be," I echoed. "As much as it pains me to agree, it sounds like Mathias."

Indeed, it was entirely in his character. That was why we could never settle in one place. It always played out by the same scenario. Mathias quickly charmed everyone around him and became the crowd's favorite. But those golden days never lasted long. His new friends would quickly turn against him. The gold in his hands inevitably turned to rust. Before we knew it, we were on the road again. We were cursed, condemned to truancy. I truly thought Paris would be my last city. I even picked my burial site.

"Life is full of surprises, pretty child." Desmoulins proceeded to swaddle me in his cloak, as if he was afraid that I might break free and run away. "It simply isn't safe for you to stay here."

"If you ask me to flee to Catalonia with you one more time, I shall ..."

He inclined his ear, as if preparing to hear a confession. "You shall do what?"

My shoulders rose and fell. I really did not have a convincing threat ready. A few times I opened my mouth only to discover that I was completely lost for words. "I shall ..."

He repeated his question. "What shall you do – scream? Go ahead. Scream away. The guards will scoop you up and put you with the rest of your family. Believe it or not, I was not going to propose fleeing to Catalonia. There's not enough time for that. We'll be lucky if we manage to sneak out of the city. How about we go on a boat ride instead?"

A boat ride down the Seine after nightfall was one thing I had
not done since arriving in Paris. I could not think of a more
compelling companion than the dour, silver-haired heretic.
He had already shown me a few interesting places in the city.
What did he have in store this time? Once again, I found my
limbs bound by his gaze. I knew I was supposed to feel like a
queen, enthroned at the stern of the boat, protected from the
night's chill. While wrapping me in his cloak Desmoulins had
remembered to pull out my hair so it would not tangle around
my neck. At the mooring he had picked me up in his arms and
lowered me into the boat, lest I should inadvertently get my
clothes wet. His every gesture towards me was laced with a
mixture of cruelty and gallantry, sadness and mockery. His kiss
– the first adult kiss I had received from a man – had the power
to exalt and demean. He was capable of doing horrible things,
yet I sensed those things were necessary to the fulfilment of
some greater plan. And yes, that plan involved bloodshed. I
knew there would be more corpses. Poor Lucius was only the
first casualty. Fate was only cracking its knuckles, flexing its
long fingers, warming up for what was promising to become a
royal massacre. Desmoulins did not want to see me amongst the
victims. He seemed determined to do whatever it took to keep
me alive. I had value to him, if only as his plaything. You know
how learned men love their toys and contraptions. In his eyes
I was that rare alchemy gadget, that vessel for mixing potions.
I had as much power over him as he did over me. I agreed to
follow him, did I not?

Of course, that was my understanding of his motives. I
could have been entirely wrong. It flattered me to think that I,
whose honorary place was between that of a prostitute and a
show monkey, made such an impression on this austere man,
an aristocrat and a scholar with a triple doctorate, that he would
endanger his reputation and his very soul to skip the evening
mass just to protect me.

Yet something was missing, some vital component to
complete the ambiance.

"Aren't you going to sing for me?" I asked him, breaking the
silence. "How about one of your Venetian boat songs? Why are

you so somber on this beautiful night?"

"You're asking too much, pretty child. I cannot row and sing at the same time."

"Let me help you row. Look at you, Monseigneur. You're out of breath. It must be hard to acknowledge you are no longer twenty ... or thirty."

"I don't trust you with an oar," he said. "It probably weighs more than you do. Under less pressing circumstances, I would let you splash around, but we cannot lose any more time."

Truly, it was painful to watch him row against the wind. I could tell he was not accustomed to such intense physical exertions. Casual fencing lessons with Captain Castelmaure could not have prepared him for such a feat. The tension in his jaw and the perspiration along his hairline betrayed his exhaustion. I probably did not make matters any better when I let out a lament.

"Poor Lucius ..."

Do not ask me why I did it, what possessed me to say that name. I would not blame Desmoulins if he hit me over the head with an oar.

His response was surprisingly calm. "For the love of God, let the man rest in peace. Don't disturb his spirit with your wailing."

"You could have saved him, and you chose not to," I continued. "You let him bleed to death. You are vindictive and cruel."

"Is that so? Next time I stumble across a man with a knife wound in his neck, I will let you perform a miracle."

"How could you let this happen?" I asked, remembering that he had some additional explaining to do. "Forget about Lucius. I'm talking about my family now. I thought you were supposed to protect us."

"That was your father's assumption. I do not know where he got the idea that I can save anyone from the gibbet or the stake." He stopped rowing and we just rocked on the water for a few minutes. "Not all cassocks are created equal. My influence is limited – as is my physical endurance."

"Don't you have a part in the Inquisition?"

"It's very peripheral. I told you this already. A few times I got invited to the interrogation chamber for my medical expertise. I've never sat amongst the judges, nor have I embellished my powers. Your father's confidence in my patronage came from his lack of insight into the ecclesiastic system. At any rate, without knowing what crime he is accused of, I cannot say anything about his chances of being acquitted. I shall do what I can, though I suspect it will not be much. My immediate goal was to get you out of the city, so excuse my silence."

He resumed rowing. I closed my eyes and leaned back, listening to the rhythmical splashing of the oars and my companion's labored breathing, wondering how long it would be before his heart gave out. It would grieve me, losing two lovers in one day. Desmoulins was putting himself through hell for me. Assuming his rescue plan panned out, I could only imagine what he would expect in return. I knew what I would have to say to him, *"I cannot think of a worthier contender to claim my maidenhood."*

When a man imposes his love on you, however dark, heavy and scary it may be, you must accept it, even if you cannot reciprocate in full measure. Refusing it will not make it go away. That love will only grow darker, heavier and scarier, spilling over and smothering others. So much for my plans to give my virginity to the tormented organist.

Knowing Desmoulins and his possessive nature, I surmised he would not be satisfied being my first man. No, he would want to be my *only* man until the end of my days. Since I did not have much time left, the chances of him growing bored with me and releasing me were rather slim. That predatory man would maul me even on my deathbed. I would draw my last breath underneath him. I could not forget that I was dealing with a spoiled, uncompromising, Italian brat in the body of a thirty-five-year old. From what I understood, he was far from omnivorous and had gone through long periods of starvation, but when he sniffed out something that was to his liking, he would sink his fangs into it. I just happened to be his latest prey. He would never agree to share me with his own protégé.

Poor Daniel, my grotesque angel! Gro-tesque … That was

the word he used, wasn't it? And I was beginning to feel earnest attraction to him. Come to think of it, I liked him even better than Lucius. It was a very close competition, but the organist's unearthly exterior, superhuman strength and inexhaustible talent placed him above the officer. I had looked forward to spending a night in his cell in the north tower. Now my beloved Daniel would never know the feeling of my scorched hands on his shoulder blades.

Perhaps, it was for the better. He would find himself a deserving girl, one who did not come from a family of criminals, whose lungs were not crumpling and whose fingers did not look like fried sausages. Although, he said he wanted an Egyptian sorceress. Maybe he was just being charitable. Bah, what a shame … I could not bring myself to get angry at fate. I was so tired, even though I was not the one rowing. The black cloak felt so snug, and the rocking of the boat so soothing that I dozed off.

I could not tell you how much time we spent on the water. I awoke when the bow of the boat jabbed into a sandy bank.

"Don't get too comfortable," Desmoulins said. "The journey isn't over."

Having moored the boat to the protruding root of a tree, he yanked me up to my feet and dragged me into the woods. Accustomed to broad, open roads, I had no sense of direction walking through the corridor of prickly shrubs. A few times my hair got caught on the dry branches, and I covered my eyes with my free hand to make sure I would not get blinded. Desmoulins seemed to know those paths well. He walked fast – without any consideration for me – his hand firmly on my wrist. That iron grip was oddly comforting. I felt as safe as a half-smothered rat in a badger's mouth.

Finally, he slowed down his pace and announced, "We're here."

Still panting from the run, I opened my eyes. We were standing in front of a low wooden lodge. Desmoulins unlocked the massive oaken door, and before stepping inside, he lifted me up in his arms. "Forgive me. I've always wanted to do this;

to carry you across the threshold. Indulge me, if only a few seconds. It's just a juvenile dream of mine."

Indeed, juvenile dreams and heretical whims stood behind most of his actions. Those were the fruits of his Italian upbringing.

He put me down once inside and lit a lantern, affording me an opportunity to survey my new asylum. It was more than a hunting lodge. It was a trophy gallery with heads of wild beasts mounted to the walls, and pristine pelts covered the floor. It must have taken him years to accumulate all those trophies.

"Now you can get yourself situated," he said, pulling the cloak off my shoulders and hanging it on the deer head above the entrance. "You're safe here – at least for the immediate future. We're a good distance away from the city. Nobody knows about this place."

Ah, that secretive, intimate whisper. I bet he used it for absolving sins in the confessional. I wondered how many of his female sinners were tempted to stay behind for a bit longer.

"You killed all these animals yourself?" I asked, kicking off my shoes and burying my toes in the softness of the bearskin.

"Why would I display another man's catch? Everything within these walls is mine."

He made a decisive step towards me and squeezed my face, just like he did on Rue des Bernardins the night we danced *La Rotta*. His thumbs traced my cheekbones and tugged at the corners of my eyes. Surprisingly, Desmoulins was not rushing into the next kiss. His fingers lingered on my face for a bit longer and then slipped away, leaving me perplexed.

I realized the reason for his hesitation a few seconds later. We were not alone. There was another living being in the lodge – a woman lying on the bed against the wall. Having noticed chains coming out from under the blanket, I had to laugh. Desmoulins and his penchant for shackling his women!

I took a moment to examine the captive. Her eyes were closed, but I could tell from the shape of her eyelids that they were quite large. Her hair was the color of dirty snow. She was not born white-haired like Elinor, but she was not born a regular blonde either. No, she was a brunette who had greyed prematurely and was rinsing her hair with various herbal concoctions to give it that wheat-colored hue. I had seen elderly Spaniard women use that trick. But this one was not old. She must have been in her mid-thirties. Apart from a few superficial wrinkles around her eyes and in the corners of her lips, her skin appeared smooth and supple.

"Does this woman look familiar to you?" Desmoulins asked with a tentative nod in her direction, as if he was afraid to look at her for an extended period of time.

"No, I've never seen her before. Where would I have known her from?"

"Never mind. I was just wondering if you by any chance recognized her."

"Don't tell me she is the reason you became a priest."

"On the contrary, it was my decision to join the church that made her what she is now. I wrecked her life – *both* our lives."

"I believe you," I said with a sigh of fatigue. "You have that effect on women."

"Especially the ones I love." He produced a stiff shrug. "It's my curse. I always knew that about myself. Perhaps, that is why I confined myself to celibacy – or at least tried to. At any rate, I trust you to take care of her in my absence."

"You're leaving us?" I asked, not quite sure whether I was relieved or distressed.

"Reluctantly. I must return to Paris and try to free Mathias and the rest of your family. Remember my promise? I do not know when I'll be back. If she wakes up, give her food and water. The chain is long enough to allow her to walk around the room. Now, don't try anything foolish. I count on your good sense. I've gone through a lot of trouble to get you out of the city. I don't want to come here and find one or both of you gone. If something happens to you …"

"You won't survive it," I finished his sentence. "Is that what you were going to say?"

"Not quite. I'll survive something like that. I always find my way back. But Dufort is another story. He's impressionable and susceptible. If you die an unnatural death, God knows what that boy will do. Notre-Dame will lose its musical genius, and the bishop will lose a major source of income. Now you see why you must follow my direction. I am not joking. It's all very serious, my pretty child."

"I rarely do as I'm told," I confessed, "but for Dufort's sake I shall try. Just show me where the provisions are. I assume you don't expect me to go out and hunt."

The prospect of being stuck in a remote cottage in the company of a mad silver-haired woman excited and disturbed me. I felt like a heroine from one of those Wallachian fairy tales Mathias had told us around the campfire.

"I hope not to keep you here for too long," Desmoulins said. "How I wish I could promise you a happy resolution. Oh, and if this woman utters something outrageous, do not take offense to it. She is a splintered soul, my wretched Gisele. I could've given her the world, but she wouldn't accept my terms. Look at her now. So much for marrying an astronomer. Her endless quest for respectability … what a waste!"

I stepped closer to him and lifted my chin, assuming that a parting kiss was inevitable. I welcomed it. The first time it happened, I was too frazzled to appreciate his skill, and there were soldiers in the hall. I was hoping that the second kiss would paint a broader, more colorful picture of his amorous abilities. You can imagine my surprise when he did not take that opportunity to lock lips with me. He simply made a sign of the cross over my head and rubbed my cheek with his knuckles in a disturbingly chaste, almost paternal token. His gaze turned to the sleeping woman. With ineffable sadness and tenderness he knelt before the bed, squeezed her knees through the blanket and covered her hands, neck and shoulders with a dusting of superficial but fervent kisses.

The scene was beyond absurd. As I watched it, I felt another bubble of laughter rising in my chest. It was so comical to see Desmoulins lavish his ministrations on that old hag! I know I said she was not old just a minute ago, but clergymen over thirty-five are not supposed to lust after women their own age. This is why Satan puts in their way adolescent hussies like me. I had no trouble envisioning Lucius with his tavern wenches. There was nothing unnatural and distasteful about that. I could even imagine Dufort timidly rubbing the same wenches, looking for signs of exalted souls in them. But Desmoulins was my inquisitor, my man in black. He sneaked me out of the city just to salivate over another woman right before my eyes? Indeed, he was full of surprises, not all of them pleasant. I started thinking that he did not love a particular woman, only an assembly of traits. Suddenly I understood why he asked me whether the captive looked familiar. The physical resemblance between me and her was undeniable. If I were to live another twenty years, I would look like her. The nostrils, the cheekbones, the eyebrows, the earlobes – I had seen them before in the mirror. Desmoulins was drawn to those features and willing to worship them, the same way some women are drawn to a military uniform.

"There are some books inside the trunk in the corner," he said as he peeled himself off of the sleeping captive. "Most of them are in Italian. You'll find a manuscript of *The Decameron* I had started translating into French. The best segments are already finished. I didn't want you to get bored in my absence. You … you have use for that sort of thing, don't you?"

"Yes," I replied, curbing my resentment, "I know how to read. I read all your letters and even responded to some."

"I forgot." He brushed back his greying forelock. The realization of having to row back to the city, alone, daunted him. "I cannot collect my thoughts. Of course, you're literate. What made me doubt that?"

"Your handwriting is horrid, Monseigneur," I added.

"I know. Brilliant men often have sloppy handwriting. That's what my calligraphy master at Lisieux said." Desmoulins reached for his black cloak. "Just out of curiosity … What have you done with my letters?"

"I have destroyed them for your own good, Monseigneur. The content is stored in my heart. It was simply unsafe to keep those impassioned messages in writing."

"You did the right thing."

Those were his parting words to me. He put on his cloak and stepped into the night.

I did not feel like sleeping. When the rustling sound outside the window abated, I opened the trunk with books. On top of the pile lay *Le Petit Jehan de Saintré,* a romance by Antoine de La Salle. I was familiar with that title. The novel depicted the adventures of a thirteen-year-old knight instructed in religion and chivalry by a certain Dame des Belles-Cuisines who in turn wound up falling victim to a vulgar intrigue – a repulsive conclusion to a case of courtly adoration. The author himself boasted a colorful biography. Born a bastard son of a famous Gascon mercenary and a peasant girl, La Salle entered the Anjou court as a page and went to participate in numerous military campaigns and visit many lands – from the Kingdom of Sicily in the south to the Duchy of Brabant in the north. At the age of fifty-three he married a fifteen-year-old girl named Lione. Mathias admired that man, an adventurer after his own heart.

Mathias … I had not thought of my adoptive father or the rest of my makeshift family all night. Elinor was safe, and that was all that mattered. Why could I not bring myself to care more about the fate of the people in whose company I had roamed the Pyrenees, who had fed and clothed me for as long as I could remember? I should have been wringing my disfigured hands, half-mad with alarm. A grateful daughter and sister would have done just that. I was a callous, selfish girl, sprawled on bearskin with a book, while the Eliades were locked up in a damp, cold dungeon.

Having returned *Le Petit Jehan* to the trunk, I pulled out the unfinished translation of *The Decameron.* My knowledge of Spanish sufficed for me to be able to read the original Italian text. I skimmed over the French translation just to see how Desmoulins interpreted it.

The setting in *The Decameron* reminded me of my own predicament: a handful of youngsters hiding in a remote rural estate to escape the Black Death ravaging Florence. Having surveyed the collection of books Desmoulins kept in his secret hiding place, I noticed the recurring theme of disenchantment and mockery of ideals. Fallen damsels, errant knights, lascivious priests, old friends playing cruel tricks on each other. Those books were not compiled at random. They said something about the man who read them, about his worldview. That old trunk served as a portal into his soul.

A sonorous exclamation broke my reverie. "Child of Satan!" The house prisoner was sitting on the bed, her shackled hands folded in her lap, pale hair streaming down her straight back. I assumed she was addressing me. There was nobody else in the lodge. Yet she was not looking in my direction. Her eyes were fixated on the boar's head nailed to the wall.

"Are you talking to me, Madame?"

"Yes, I am talking to you, daughter of Beelzebub."

I had been waiting for someone to call me that. Daughter of Beelzebub! I was surprised it had not happened sooner. God knows, I had given the honorable women of Paris plenty of reasons to mark me as a hell spawn. And yes, somehow I had always known the accusation would come from a woman.

"Bonsoir to you too, Madame." I closed the book and shifted my position on the bearskin. "Are you hungry? Our mutual friend left provisions for us. Some bread and dried fruit. And a bottle of excellent wine. He's very thoughtful and gallant. You're lucky to be in his clutches and not someone else's."

Her head was twitching indignantly. "Pray, who are you? And what gives you the right to open your trap? Are you his accomplice or his latest victim?"

"I am his mistress," I declared proudly. *Mother of God, did I really say that?* "He professed his eternal desire for me. What's the matter with that?"

"What's the matter, you ask me? It's a matter of *time* before you end up like me. Mark my word, little witch. He'll convince the world that you're a murderess and put you on a chain."

"This is where you are wrong, Madame. You are the one on a chain. He trusted me with the task of watching you. You see, Desmoulins loves me. We are going to run away to Catalonia. He's just settling a few matters in the city. Then off we go."

She burst into soft, cackling laughter. "To look for the Philosopher's Stone? Is that what he told you? Amusingly enough, that is what he told me – eighteen years ago. I was exactly half the age I am now. As you can see, he's still looking.

He still hasn't found the infamous stone. Why? Because it doesn't exist. Although, I surmise he's gone through several female companions."

"I may not be the first, but I'll be the last."

"Keep telling yourself that, my sweet. You cannot possibly satisfy that man's demonic appetites. He's perverted and insatiable."

"So am I, Madame."

Guess what? I was ready to believe that about myself, about Desmoulins, and the two of us. I had a feeling that sinister man in black could introduce me to some scary pleasures.

After three days in the hunting lodge, I noticed an improvement in my overall condition. The fog inside my chest and my head began dissipating. I could breathe more deeply and think more clearly, as I had not done since leaving Spain.

I gave her food and water at regular intervals. During the day she got up from the bed and walked around the room as far as the chain allowed her. I was not afraid of her assaulting me. One time she allowed me to braid her hair. Having no comb on hand, I smoothed her pale tresses with my fingers and wove them into a loose plait. Denise had never allowed me to touch her hair.

Even though I knew her name was Gisele, I continued calling her Madame, and she continued calling me Child of Satan. Not that I minded that form of address. There was some truth in it.

She described in great detail the intimate things she had done with her subsequent lovers, bemoaning their lack of consideration and self-restraint and how unfavorably they compared to Desmoulins. She even murmured something about her dead baby who had been sired by one of those careless soldier boys. I did not ask her the baby's sex or how it died. I could tell she was beginning to regret her candor. At the same time, she needed to talk, and I was the only audience. I was thankful for the education she provided. Technical bluntness marked her descriptions. There was no vulgarity, pure science. After listening to her for a few hours I felt like I had already made love to Desmoulins. I knew all the sensitive spots on his body and the tricks to set fire to them. I pined for his return. That delinquent inquisitor with his wolfish grin inflamed my imagination. I pictured myself running my fried hands through the coarse, silvery tufts on his temples, kissing the veins on his neck.

The hag's voice startled me from my fantasies. "Don't get carried away, my sweet. The things I described don't apply to you."

"Look, Madame, you're just bitter over the simple fact that you're old, grey and chained up. I'm young and free. I'm going to Catalonia with the greatest scholar in Christendom. We are going to prove to the world that the earth is round, and there is at least one more continent."

"Then why do you keep those gloves on? Don't they hinder you?"

"Not at all. They are like second skin. They help me grip things."

"What are you hiding underneath anyway - vulture's claws?"

I pulled the gloves off using my teeth and wiggled my hands in front of her face. "There. Desmoulins has seen and touched them. Looks like strips of smoked ham. Nothing terribly frightening but can be a little distracting. So I keep them covered."

I had expected a squeamish wince and a spiteful remark, confident that in her thirty-six years of life the woman had seen far worse disfigurements. Her reaction caught me off guard. I was not prepared for that eruption of terror that followed. Pressing one shackled hand to her mouth and another to her belly, the captive trembled all over and let out a low-pitched, gut-wrenching groan.

"I know exactly who you are," she said, her voice calm and clear. "You were sent from hell to torment me, to remind me of my crime."

"Madame, I have no idea what crime you've committed. We are all guilty of something. I assure you, I am not from hell. I am from the Kingdom of Wallachia – which is close enough to hell. Do you know where it is? We are a staunch and proud Romanic people, surrounded by foes who do not speak our language: Saxons, Huns, Bohemians, Albanians.

Have you ever heard of Prince Dracul? We fled to escape his tyranny. For years we roamed Andalusia, Castile, Catalonia, Gascony, before coming to Paris. Now my family is imprisoned, and I don't even know on what charges. I'm the only one on the loose. But that is not the end of my tribulations. As fate would have it, I fell in love with three men. One of them was a pagan god forced to serve in the King's army. He's dead now. Another one is a fallen angel. And the third one is a demon working as a priest. That last one you know. You are so selfish in your grief. You think you are the only one suffering."

I do not know why I was telling her my story, only part of which was true anyway. Not that it mattered. Denise told me once that when you deal with a person in the throes of a fit, it helps to start talking about yourself and usurp the attention. The story does not need to be true, but it must be filled with tragedy and violence. I had a feeling the disheveled captive was deaf to my narration. Now her hands were folded as for a prayer. She shifted into a kneeling position on the bed.

"You spoke to her, didn't you?" she said, her eyes glistening. "My little girl. Well, she's not so little anymore. She sent you here, didn't she? She had a message for me. Talk to me, demoness. I don't know why I'm imploring you. After all, you are here to torment, not to comfort me. She'll never forgive me."

Ah, so the pieces of the puzzle were coming together. Now I knew that the dead baby was female and that the captive's crime was somehow tied to that death.

"Madame, I don't have to listen to this," I said. "I won't endeavor gagging you, out of respect for the owner of this lodge, who appears to still care about you for some odd reason, but I will plug my ears with chunks of bread. Now, if you don't mind, I'd like to finish reading *Il Filostrato*."

I put my gloves back on and turned my back to her. There was no more talk, only the clanging of the shackles.

Chapter 5

Soft and Deadly

(Blackfeather)

"A wilted cabbage leaf with a side serving of sonnets does not count as a meal." I keep repeating those words, even though they make no sense to me. If I had to eat at least once a day like most human beings, I would have died a long time ago. I would not have lasted into my mid-twenties.

To make a long story short, by age five I had lost all my relatives except for an English great-grandmother who lived in a tiny bucolic house on the outskirts of Gonesse with no contact with the outside world. For the next five years it was just me, the old lady and Chaucer.

Great-grandmother was a woman of letters. I knew *The Canterbury Tales* by heart. By age ten I had almost forgotten French. You can imagine my stupor when I had to return to Paris following the death of the old lady, who had raised me a perfect Englishman. I remember standing in the middle of the square, asking for directions in the language of our long-term enemies. I distinctly remember rocks and rotting carrots whistling past my ears. One rock grazed my forehead, knocking me down to the pavement.

The brief sonnet of my life could have ended right there, had it not been for the intervention from a young priest, who spoke a little bit of English. After chasing away the ruffians, he wiped the blood off my forehead and walked me to the University district, to the dining-hall of the college of Lisieux. The cooks needed someone to slice vegetables and wipe the tables after the rowdy scholars. I gained access to all the leftovers in the world, but somehow I was not hungry for food. I had my eyes on the tall tower where the University library was located.

Eventually, with some intervention from Desmoulins – that was the surname of the cleric who saved me – I was granted permission to enter the library for a few hours each Sunday. Desmoulins was one of the alumni, so he could open most doors with one snap of his long fingers. I was a neat, quiet, respectful boy, who could be trusted with books, which could not be said for the regular students. The head librarian realized that rather quickly and asked to have me moved from the kitchen into the scriptorium.

My new responsibilities included making sure that the ink bottles were filled and all writing supplies were in order. Needless to say, I rejoiced in the promotion, which afforded me more time with books. I spent all my free time reading and then ran to Desmoulins to report on my progress. Every Sunday he gave me a new list of titles to look up. Eventually, I was allowed to attend lectures. In the beginning I tried to sit at the very back of the room with my mouth shut, making sure that my pencil did not produce that unnerving scratching noise as it moved across the paper, but the masters, sensing my zeal, moved me to the front and called on me often. On several occasions I was asked to present whole segments of the lesson when one of the regular lecturers was out due to illness.

The next step for me was to become a licentiate – or a sub-monitor. Interest in all things English was on the rise, and my English roots lent themselves to the task of deconstructing the works of Geoffrey Chaucer and Sir Thomas Malory. I knew it was in my power to make Parisian scholars fall in love with the works of great authors on the other side of La Manche.

But then I ran into an obstacle. Apparently, in order to teach English literature, one needed to have a perfect command of Latin. To me that requirement made as much sense as putting chunks of beef into a honey cake. Latin was one subject I struggled with, only because I had started learning it so late. Once again, Desmoulins came to my rescue. After six months of intense tutoring, I passed the exam and received permission to teach. My class was tiny, my pay was meager, and my very presence at the University was often regarded as a joke. In those moments I reminded myself that I had gone from an orphaned kitchen boy to a lecturer.

So here I am – the black sheep of the Parisian academia! A benign distraction and a comic relief. But you know what? I do not need massive reverence. I am perfectly happy with my small, tightknit circle of Anglophiles. One day, when we have enough money in our hands, we will travel across the channel and visit all the places described in *The Canterbury Tales*. Alas, so far the only pilgrimage my students take is to the tavern. They like me well enough not to laugh to my face, but I know that behind my back they snicker at my exalted views on love, my lyrical poetry, my obsession with finding a muse and modeling my own destiny after that of the great lovers of the past. Sometimes I laugh at myself – incurable dreamer that I am – a euphoric fool with his head in the clouds.

The only man who would listen to me without interrupting or rolling his eyes was Desmoulins. Surprised? Despite his outward austerity, he possessed a deeply lyrical streak, just like me. He believed in the marriage of minds, the alliance of talents and intellects. The only difference was that I kept burying my muses, and he was still waiting for his. There are circumstances under which a man of God can open his heart to a woman without compromising the vow of celibacy.

To argue my point I used the incomparable Guillaume de Machaut, a composer and poet who had lived more than a hundred years ago, serving as a canon in Reims. Having survived several plague epidemics, he indulged in a late-in-life love affair with a spirited young maiden named Péronne d'Armentières, the muse as well as editor behind his lyric poem *Le voir dit*. Imagine close to ten thousand lines of verse, arranged in octosyllabic rhythmic couplets! Guillaume was in his mid-sixties, and she was nineteen. I could not recall anyone condemning him as a licentious old man. The consensus was that his affection, while not purely paternal or platonic in nature, had never been physically consummated. Perhaps, he was too old and ill to take full advantage of that opportunity.

To make a long story short, yes, a priest can love a woman, as long as that alliance produces artistic masterpieces and not a string of bastard children. An affair like de Machaut's fell into the same category as courtly love a knight would feel for his aloof lady. Every man of God should experience something of the sort at least once in his life. Periodic wars against the flesh exercise his will and refine his discipline. Inner conflict reasserts one's masculinity. Pent-up desire flushes out in the form of poignant artistic creations.

Yes, I babbled a lot, on subjects that were of tremendous interest to me but probably not to the rest of the population, not even my University colleagues. Desmoulins tolerated my babbling. He was also the only person with whom I could discuss my love life. He had taunted me good-naturedly about my romantic tribulations, especially after the deaths of my wives.

With each burial I was becoming more fragile and desperate to find a replacement. I needed to have a coltish, adolescent nymph prancing about me at all times. My tastes were very specific, through no fault of my own. Mature, matronly women held no appeal in my eyes. You have to admit, being tall and scrawny, I would look silly next to an ample-bodied woman. I would have trouble sweeping her up and lifting her to the skies. The lady of my heart needed to possess a very particular physique to enable me to do everything I wanted to do with her. I could not fall asleep without a pair of skinny legs wrapped around mine. Desmoulins understood my tastes, for they were very similar to his own. It was those acrimonious jokes that had kept my spirits from plummeting.

"Maître, you have that condemning look on your face," I said to him one day.

"Do I really?" His silvery eyebrow jerked. "Is it more condemning than usual?"

"You disapprove of my relationship with the Eliade sisters, don't you?"

"What makes you think I disapprove? On the contrary, I think it's marvelous that you fraternize with that family of devil-worshippers." He laughed his sinister laugh. "I'm only teasing you, as usual. I think that white-haired, red-eyed child sorceress is a perfect match for you."

"She wasn't my first choice," I confessed. "I would've loved to marry Agniese instead. She's a very droll girl with many talents. Her footwork when she dances, and her Catalan accent, even the way she scratches her head are infinitely endearing. But she is ill and will die soon. If I have a third wife die on me, it might send a message to the women of Paris. They'll think it's unsafe to marry me; that I have some peculiar Egyptian curse hovering over me or that I keep the skeletons of my dead wives stored in a closet."

"I think the women of Paris have already gotten the message – and they keep coming for more. They cannot resist your flamboyant, malnourished charm. You are very fortunate, Blackfeather, to attract so many naïve chits who do not mind your destitution or your sinister marital history."

"I'm also fortunate to have you for my benefactor," I added gravely and squeezed his cold hands. "Please, forgive me, *Maître*, if I do not tell you this often enough. I'm afraid to think where I'd be now without your intervention."

"Who knows? Maybe you'd be a commander in the king's army."

"With my physique? You must be joking."

"Physique is subject to cultivation, like everything else. Sometimes I think I did a horrible thing by introducing you to the University and encouraging all that poetic silliness that has nothing to do with the severe realities of the world. I exert such bad influence."

He laughed again, a tired, strained laugh. I noticed that his brow, always clouded, even on the brightest of days, appeared a little more furrowed than usual. I was fairly sure I knew the cause behind his anxiety. It had to do with some recent additions to the faculty.

"When Adrian Satigny arrives," I said, "I shall make a deliberate effort to snub him, give him the cold shoulder."

"Why would you do that?"

"Out of solidarity with you, naturally! I don't want that man, whatever his credentials may be, to think he can take your place. I'll do whatever in my power to keep him humble, even if it means turning my nose every time he passes in the hall."

I was only trying to demonstrate my loyalty to Desmoulins. I knew he was worried about the arrival of the new astronomy lecturer, so I wanted to assure him of my support. Alas, my ardent pledge was not well received.

"Blackfeather, what a stupid thing to say!" I saw his eyes flash with anger, genuine anger, not his usual humorous spitefulness. "Turning your nose at a fellow academician? You'll come across as bitter and vindictive and lose whatever fragile credibility you may have built over the years. I raised you better than that. You can put a few drops of poison into his glass when nobody is looking, but in public I expect you to be polite."

"All right, Maître," I muttered faintly, tucking away my good intentions, "I'll behave. I will not disgrace you with my rudeness. I will grovel before Satigny and kiss the tips of his boots."

"You'll do nothing of the sort. You will greet him with dignity, without any dramatic effects. This is not one of your amateurish morality plays."

Of course, all my plans to snub the newcomer went out the window. The moment Adrian Satigny crossed the threshold of the lecture hall, I found myself smitten – as only a man, a scholar, can be smitten by another. In many ways he reminded me of my first benefactor, from facial features to mannerisms. Although he was a lighter, warmer, more animated version of Desmoulins. Disheveled, radiant, self-deprecating and completely devoid of arrogance, approachable without plunging into familiarity, he instantly enchanted the students.

I was not present at the first encounter between Satigny and Desmoulins, but I imagine there was a fair amount of customary hand-pressing, head-tilting and exclamations along the lines of "I've heard so much about you!" on both sides. Maybe it was a blessing that I did not get to watch that scene. I was tremendously fond of both men and preferred for the three of us not to be in the same room at the same time, for then I would feel like I had to choose sides. I wanted the freedom to idolize each one of them. I knew they had much in common, but

I wasn't aware *how* much until later.

One early morning in July I was strolling through the University district, while most of it was still asleep. It was during those hours that I did my best writing. Emboldened by the recent success of *La guerre des bijoux* and my newly found love, I was working on a long prosaic piece with elements of courtly love and mystery.

Circling around the library tower, I saw a most enchanting vision. A slender woman was reading a book. And not just any book! *English Drama for French Audiences*. Can you guess the author? That's right. Yours truly. It was one of the few printed titles available in the University library. The head librarian was adamant about opposing Gutenberg's technology. I had to fight him to have the book put on the shelf. Begrudgingly, he agreed to compromise, but only because of all the good work I had done for him in the scriptorium in the past.

I paused in front of the bench and removed my cap. "Good day, Madame. May I ask what you are reading?"

She raised her enormous dark eyes. "Some drivel, to kill time."

I felt my empty stomach tighten painfully. "Drivel, you say? That's a harsh assessment."

"I've read many books in my life, hand-written and printed. I can tell the difference in content and execution. The new crop of humanists claims that anyone can read, and anyone can write. I imagine more mediocrity will become available in the years to come. Printed books are not as beautiful as those copied by hand. But then, not every book deserves to be executed beautifully. This one I'm reading now will probably end up in the back of my husband's bookcase after I'm done with it."

There was no malice in her voice, and her movements were laced with girlish immediacy. She was a good ten years older than me – the faint wrinkles around her eyes betrayed her age – yet her playfully upturned nose, gently rounded cheekbones and plump lips did not tie in with the image of a solemn matron espoused to an academician.

Unlike most married women, she was not wearing a veiled

headpiece. I took a moment to marvel at her long lustrous hair that was of a most unusual color: sandy, silver and chestnut threads mingled, evoking images of a fawn's coat. Judging from her eye color, she must have been a brunette in her youth. When she twitched her frail shoulders, she reminded me of a bird shaking rainwater off its wings.

"Your husband," I stammered, "is he as critical as you are?"

"Adrian? Oh, no. He doesn't have an opinion on drama or poetry. He's a wry mathematician and astronomer. He spends his days juggling numbers and reading star charts."

"So you must be ..."

"Gisele Satigny."

I bowed before her, still clutching my cap. "Madame! I'm most humbled."

She made a dainty, graceful movement with her hand, as if chasing away a pesky fly. "Straighten out. Don't strain your lower back on my behalf. I don't have any achievements to my name. I'm hardly Christine de Pizan."

"Your achievement is inspiring the finest scholar in France! Are you not the happiest woman on earth?"

"Well, Monsieur, if that is how you want to put it ... I have no right to complain. There's just one problem."

"What is it, Madame?"

"My daughter won't talk to me."

Daughter? I thought the Satigny were childless. "Children can be so ungrateful," I said. "If my parents were still alive, I'd probably aggravate them too. I hope your daughter's heart softens."

Madame Satigny rubbed her fingers together and pinched her lower lip. "There's a delicate nuance. You see, my daughter is dead. It makes our conversations difficult, as they take place inside my head. I call her name, and she usually answers. But lately she hasn't been responsive. She must be angry with me. Of course, she has a legitimate reason. I thought she had forgiven me."

Well, that was the most bizarre confession I had heard all week. Madame Satigny did not look me in the eye as she spoke. She was flipping the pages in the book, as if her daughter was hiding between them. Personally, I thought her mourning was a little excessive. I hope I have a right to speak on the subject, having lost several children myself. Now granted, they were all either infants or stillborn. Some claim that losing an older child who has reached the age of reason is more difficult. I had no idea how long ago it had been since Madame Satigny's bereavement or how old her daughter was at the time. God be my witness, I was not going to ask. My students were waiting for me.

"Well, it was a pleasure speaking with you," I said, putting my cap back on. "I hope your husband is enjoying his new post, and the young scholars are not driving him to insanity. I assume he's already met his new colleague, Monseigneur Desmoulins."

"Ah, that vile human being."

Those words were uttered with more fatigued disgust than raw anger.

If I could have a sou for every time someone called Desmoulins a vile human being, I would never have to teach again. I could spend the rest of my life writing poems and staging the kind of plays I personally found inspiring. I would never have to take another municipal commission.

"What he did to me," Madame Satigny continued. "It's the worst thing a man can do to a woman."

That statement could be interpreted in several ways. I chose not to venture there.

"Well, Madame," I said, adjusting my cap, "it was a pleasure meeting you. I suppose I'll be seeing you at the banquet."

"Which one? I've been going to banquets every night since our arrival."

"The one hosted by the assistant librarian. We can continue our discussion about printed books."

The assistant librarian, Julien Morel, occupied a modest but well-kept house in the vicinity of the University. His rank in the academic hierarchy was closer to the bottom, obliging him to humility and patience. He had to wait for his turn until his superiors had hosted the brilliant newcomer in their homes before inviting Satigny to his. I was looking forward to that occasion, actually.

The attendance was younger and more humble, making the dinner conversations more candid and stimulating. Down with pretense and formalities! Among the guests were: Daniel Dufort, the organist of Notre-Dame, and Johannes Métivier, who now had the same position I did seven years ago. Desmoulins introduced the blond youth as his estranged half-brother whom he was helping get established. I had toyed with the idea of bringing along Elinor as my companion but then decided against it at the last minute. Even someone as tolerant and welcoming as Julien Morel would feel uneasy having a twelve-year old showgirl under his roof. All right, maybe if we were the only guests, and if he did not have to impress someone of Satigny's bearing.

It was a small group of guests gathered around a small table, which made it difficult to carry on independent conversations.

As to be expected, the guest of honor took the lead and addressed Desmoulins, who was sitting to the left of him.

"Good to see you outside the University walls, Monseigneur. Gisele has recently shared a few heart-warming episodes from your past."

Desmoulins stuck his fork into a piece of stringy rabbit meat. "Oh, did she?"

"She told me you were friends in your youth. You taught her the foundation of Latin and helped her in a time of need. Why haven't you told me about your friendship?"

Desmoulins took a long sip from his wine chalice before responding to the question. "We are instructed to help discreetly and not herald charity cases," he said at last. "I had known and helped several women in my life. Gisele was just one of them. At any rate, I am glad she benefitted from those Latin lessons and continues to use the skill. So our friendship was not in vain. I wish I had been able to teach her more, but fate took us in different directions."

"Well, you made her the scholarly woman I am privileged to call my wife today. I am greatly indebted to you."

I took a moment to analyze what Satigny was implying. Did he mean that if Gisele did not speak Latin, he would not have married her? It was my first time seeing the spouses together, and I noted that there was not much gallantry or tenderness in Satigny's treatment of his wife. I had yet to hear him use a pet endearment or see him caress her fingers. He treated her as he would a fellow lecturer, with the same methodic amicability. Clearly, that man took the notion of equality of sexes rather seriously. I had no idea what he was like in private, but in public he was blunt and temperate.

Any time Gisele made an intrinsically feminine gesture, like curling a strand of hair around her finger, her husband frowned critically. I noticed she was not wearing earrings or any other jewelry. Her dress, although well-tailored, was devoid of embellishments. I wondered if Satigny was a secret supporter of the religious reform and embraced exaggerated simplicity of apparel. He seemed aware of his wife's external beauty and the effect it had on other men, but was unmoved by it himself. He wanted to showcase his wife's erudition instead.

Over the course of dinner he asked her questions pertaining to his work, obliging her to come up with highly technical responses. When she started quoting Nicholas von Kues, namely his hitherto unpublished writings on mathematics and astronomy, Desmoulins grew visibly disquieted.

"I feel so blessed," Satigny resumed with a kingly attitude, "to have lain my hands on the rare manuscript. I believe it's the missing key to the door that so many astronomers have been knocking on. I am very close to a breakthrough. And once I'm ready to demonstrate my creation, Monseigneur Desmoulins will be the first one to see it."

My Latin teacher excused himself under the pretext of having to visit an ailing widow. He thanked the host profusely, having barely touched the roasted rabbit. A few stringy morsels had been cut off but none eaten. Before walking out the door, he tapped the organist on the shoulder.

"You can stay if you want. I hear they're serving cherry cake for dessert."

Daniel Dufort did not say much all evening, yet all eyes were on him. That youngster could not make himself inconspicuous if he tried. Even while sitting, he towered over others, his fingers drumming against the edge of the table, composing or rehearsing. The light from the candle reflected off of his glistening red hair, creating the impression of a halo. I asked myself why he and I were not better friends. After all, were we not both Desmoulins' protégés? What could I do to remedy the situation?

"What are you working on now?" I asked him.

This seemingly innocuous question generated a defensive response. The organist immediately pulled his hands from the table, as if I had peeked at a music sheet, and recoiled from me. "Why do you want to know?" His hoarse voice lowered to a rattle, his pale blue eyes shooting frozen darts at me. "Do I ask you about your plays?"

"I'm sorry. I did not mean to invade your creative process."

"One does not ask to see a child who has not been born yet. As an artist you should know that. There are so many men in Paris who call themselves artists, yet they don't show basic courtesy to each other."

Ah, that reminded me precisely why Dufort and I were not friends. Being a genius, he could get away with rudeness, even violence. The bishop condoned his eccentric antics and his dabbling with Urban Gladiators as long as the boy kept bringing money into the precinct.

When the dessert was served, the Stone Prince picked out the cherries and ate them, smearing the sweet red juice over his mouth, but leaving the ravaged cake on the plate. What did one expect from a demi-angel raised by gargoyles?

I felt so sorry for Julien Morel. The poor assistant librarian had spent a hefty portion of his pay to host that dinner, and his guests were so unappreciative and self-absorbed. I tried to make him feel better by gobbling up the portion Desmoulins had left on his plate and the ravaged cake. My stomach was not accustomed to any meal larger than a walnut, so pain and nausea set in almost immediately. Still, it was a small price to pay for the smile of gratitude from the host.

There was no need for me to hurry home on that balmy July night. Hundreds of rose bushes lining the alley sprayed their fragrance into the air while the poet in me basked in the tepid, floral mystery. It was a night for clandestine trysts, confessions and revelations; a night for scheming and conspiring. Still nursing a belly ache, I wandered through the University grounds. I felt something monumental was about to happen; something crucial to the plot of the romance I was drafting. A writer must always be alert, and on the lookout for a potential plot twist.

My artistic intuition did not fail me. Passing by the dormitory complex, I heard voices. Those were not characters inside my head talking, no. They were real voices. Real people. A man and a woman engaged in an argument.

I hid behind the trunk of an orange tree, at once thankful for my slender constitution, and peeked at the scene before me. My Latin teacher was talking to Madame Satigny. Apparently he was back from visiting the ailing widow. That was quick! They stood facing each other, their profiles outlined against the dimming sky, their brows almost touching, their mimicry loaded with a sort of intimacy suggesting that the two were more than recent acquaintances. If I were seeing those two for the first time, I could have sworn they were former lovers.

"Congratulations on your nuptials," Desmoulins spoke, his neck arched and head inclined in his signature hovering pose. "At last, you've gained the long-desired respectability. Being a scholar's wife is more appealing than being a priest's mistress."

"Stop it."

"I've barely started. Don't ask me to stop so soon. Don't deny me the pleasure of taunting you. After fifteen years of silence, we can indulge ourselves a bit, just like we did in the old days.

"Jokes aside, I am thrilled for you, Gisele. Your husband was flashing his teeth at me across the dinner table. What else did you tell him about me? Adrian must think I'm hiding hooves and a tail under the cassock."

"He thinks nothing of the sort."

"You mercifully spared him the unsavory details? A wise decision, I'm sure. He must not be distracted from his work. So many eyes are fixed upon him – beady eyes, greedy eyes – searching for flaws. You two must have interesting pillow talk. I'd give my prized copy of Bernardo Gui's inquisition manual to overhear two minutes of it."

"Now, don't be vulgar."

I saw his cheek muscles twitching. "Don't be vulgar," he mocked her, as his voice dropped to a growl. "Listen to yourself. You're turning into a prude. Is this what happy marriage does to a woman? Did you tell him why you had to leave Paris? Did you tell him what you did to your daughter?"

"It was an accident."

"No, it wasn't."

"She tripped and fell into the fireplace."

"That's the version of the story you made up to comfort yourself. But we both know the truth, don't we? A one-year-old is not foolish enough to crawl into a blazing furnace, and yours was a cautious girl, not prone to accidents. I had observed her. She never put small objects into her mouth or bumped into sharp corners. Clearly, she was pushed into the fire, by the only adult who was in the house."

"No, you are the one making up stories to vilify me, just because I refused to be your peripheral plaything, refused to sit on a shelf between two glass jars in your alchemy lab. I bet you enjoyed the sound of my daughter's shrieks, the smell of her burned flesh. Deep inside you wanted her dead because she wasn't yours."

Desmoulins must have heard that accusation before, because he nodded wearily, his head bowing closer with each nod to Madame Satigny's.

"Yes, I had nothing better to do than wish death upon that premature mite. That is exactly why I brought you food and logs for the hearth after your lovers had turned away from you. The sight of your swelling belly must have spooked them. Who was wringing the blood out of the sheets when your daughter was born? Do you even remember? Don't think for a moment that I expect gratitude. What I did fell under minimal Christian duty. Our faith compels us to forget our own good works and not dwell on our own charity."

"Christian duty," she mocked bitterly. "Peddle that to someone who doesn't know your heart. The only reason you came was to *gloat*. It pleased you to see me starving and freezing. A loaf of bread and a few twigs of kindle wood were a small admission price. You always walked out with that smug look."

"You and your delusions ..." Desmoulins continued shaking his head. At some point his voice dropped to a whisper. I had to hold my breath to be able to hear him. "I always feared for you. Something like this was bound to happen. You were in a pitiable state during my last few visits. I should have kept a closer eye on you. It's too late now. Your daughter is dead."

"If she's dead, where's her grave? Show it to me."

"She's dead to you. Let's leave it at that. Would you rather hear that she was living somewhere in seclusion, disfigured?"

"Exactly how severe were her burns?"

"Severe enough, in my humble medical opinion. I did what I could for her."

"You wrapped her in a sack and whisked her away." There was no accusation in her voice now. She was merely reconstructing her memories. "You stormed into my lodging, pulled her out of the hearth and bolted out the door."

"I did what I had to. It was better that way. You were drunk, rolling on the floor and pulling out your hair. Would it give you comfort to see her distorted features with your own eyes? I don't know what pictures your rabid fancy paints in the night."

"Where is she now? What did you do to her?"

"Hypothetically speaking, even if she had survived the fall into the hearth, I never would've given her back to you. That much you can be sure of. You aren't fit to be anyone's mother. You're a menace to yourself, Gisele. Eventually you would've killed that wretched baby in some other way. I'm convinced of that. Your daughter was a burden. Admit it. You knew you were guilty, because you did not protest when I urged you to flee the city."

"I was in a state of stupor!"

"That seems to be your permanent state. You always have that vacant look in your eyes, even now. Put that sad incident behind you and be thankful that you didn't get caught. I could've turned you over to the authorities, but I didn't. I protected your secret then, and I intend on protecting it now. That makes us accomplices. The absurd things men do for love!"

She let out an eerie, chirpy laugh.

"Oh, you speak of *love*? I'm impressed. You have some nerve."

"Nerve is one thing I have in abundant supply. You won't like what I'm about to say, but my love hasn't gone anywhere. It's still here, lodged between my ribs. Every time I take a deep breath, it reminds me of its presence. Yes, I'm a little sick of it, to put it mildly. It's distracting as hell. It's kept me from enjoying an occasional affair."

"I'm sorry for wrecking your philandering prospects."

"No need to apologize. I'm stuck with my love, as are you. Since fate has brought you back to Paris, we need to find a way to go about our lives. I have no trouble keeping my mouth shut. Listening to confessions every day, I'm trained to protect the secrets of others. It's *your* mouth I'm worried about. For the love of God, stop dropping ambivalent hints about me in front of your husband and the rest of our colleagues. Now collect yourself and go back to Adrian. I'm sure he's wondering where you are at this hour."

By Jupiter ... Did I just hear all of this? I hope I remembered the best parts of the dialogue. What have I done to deserve such a meaty opportunity? The night sky opened up and dumped a most thrilling picaresque plot. That was my reward for not going home right after the banquet.

Looking back at my first encounter with Madame Satigny, I had thought she reminded me of someone. I had seen those features and mannerisms before on someone much younger. *Agniese* ... I remembered how one night after the rehearsal she pulled off her gloves and flexed her scarred hands in front of me. She must have decided that we were good enough friends, and since I was courting her sister, there was no harm in showing her burns to a future brother-in-law. I even remember the context of our conversation.

Agniese wanted me to understand why she could not twirl a tambourine on her finger. Her fingertips were numb and not as dexterous as Elinor's. For that reason she could not play violin or flute. I admit I was taken aback by the revelation but managed to keep a straight face. It helped that she had spoken of the disfigurement in a flippant, jocose tone, without any tension or anxiety.

It did not take me long to collect and string up the loose beads: Agniese's injury, her age, the astounding resemblance she bore to Gisele, and the dialogue I had just overheard. Of course, all those links could have been purely coincidental, but the writer in me insisted otherwise. *Agniese was Madame Satigny's long lost daughter and the object of her wrath.*

Desmoulins had pulled the girl out of the fire, treated her burns, handed her over to the Eliades for rearing and then told the stupefied mother that the child had died – if only to help her move on with her life. Or, perhaps, his intentions were not so benevolent, and he merely wanted to punish his old mistress for breaking off their affair. Was I missing anything? My analytical skills were rather sharp. I would have made a fine attorney or a procurator. Instead I was a writer.

While the details of the scene were still fresh in my head, I ran home and started scribbling the first chapter.

It happened at the height of the reign of King Louis XI.

In a small clay house on the outskirts of Paris, lived a dark-eyed maiden, whose interests were not entirely maidenly. She liked to count stars and calculate the distance between them. She took Latin lessons from a young theology student with a somber face and a wry wit.

I won't let another muse of mine die of starvation.

I kept repeating that vow, having resolved to see it fulfilled. No more burials due to malnourishment. My affair with the younger of the Eliade sisters was going to mark a new chapter in my love life. In only two hours after picking her up on Rue du Mouton,

I had asked her several times whether or not she was hungry, and every time the answer was an enthusiastic and unabashed "Yes."

The girl nodded her white-haired head and clapped her hands every time I pulled a treat from my pocket. I offered her an apple, and she ate it completely – including the seeds and stem. Then I offered her a bag of roasted hazelnuts, and she ate those before I could even say *"Bon appétit!"* When we stopped by a tavern for some bread, cheese and wine (at least, that was the modest menu *I* had in mind), my sweet Elinor ended up ordering roasted lamb in addition to the aperitifs. Of course, most of it ended up in her belly. I was not too hungry. I was more mystified than anything.

How could a creature so delicate be so ravenous? That imp was eating quickly through my meager salary. I took comfort in the thought that she was building up her strength for a night of frantic lovemaking, and that my generosity was going to come back to me tenfold.

After the feast at the tavern Elinor felt sleepy, as was to be expected. She was at that age when she took afternoon naps. We sat down in a shady spot by the river.

"Why do they call you Blackfeather?" she asked me, her head in my lap and eyes half-closed. "I don't think you ever told me."

"It is because my touch is both soft and deadly," I replied, running my fingers through her white curls. "That last bit is a joke, you understand?"

"I'm glad they died," she murmured, her rosy face rubbing against my thigh. "I'm talking about the women who came before me. Otherwise you wouldn't be with me right now."

She was right. I had never left a woman of my own accord, nor had I been discarded by any of them. One would have to die in order for me to move on to another. My muses tended to stick with me until the bitter end, which was an encouraging sign. I must have been doing something right to convince them to stay by my side despite the chronic hunger and frequent moves from one meager lodging to another. All of my wives and steady mistresses had died happy, without a word of complaint. I prayed that Elinor Eliade would be my last love, that God would allow me to keep her. We made such a splendid artistic duo. I had so many plans for us in terms of future productions. Perhaps, the other girls had been sent to me to season my soul in preparation for someone like Elinor. She was the youngest and the boldest of them all, definitely not shy about voicing her desires. That girl did not hesitate to ask for seconds at the table.

She was probably equally forthcoming in the bedchamber. I liked that about her, though I knew it would take me some time to grow accustomed to her candor.

When Elinor awoke, the sun was already setting, casting a rich cognac-hued glare on the water.

"I had the strangest dream," she said. "You and I were on a ship to England."

"Why, that sounds heavenly."

"Yes, except ... your face was very tense, almost morose. Then the wind blew, and your hair turned white, like mine."

I was close to telling her that it was not wise taking such long naps so late in the day, especially after such a large meal, but I held my tongue. After all, I had resolved to become more attentive to the physical needs of an adolescent female. We joined hands and proceeded to walk towards my lodging by the quay. Well-fed and well-rested, Elinor became awfully affectionate, rubbing her head against my arm like a cat in heat.

Suddenly, the short, rotund silhouette of Johannes Métivier materialized in front of us. I had not seen that boy since the banquet at Julien Morel's house.

"Can I speak with you in private?" he said. "Without the young lady. Can you give her something to play with while we talk? She doesn't need to hear any of this."

He pointed towards a looped rope hanging from a tree. The simple contraption like a makeshift swing – or a gibbet.

"Darling," I said to the girl, "I just need a few moments with Monsieur Métivier. We have some business to discuss regarding the new order of books for the library. It's boring, nothing that would interest you."

Elinor did not look in the least bit offended by the dismissal. She ran towards the tree, but not before rising on her tiptoes and giving me a kiss. A few seconds later she was swinging on the rope, her skirts billowing and skinny legs exposed.

"Make it brief," I said to Métivier.

"I shall try. Let's just say that you missed one hell of a skirmish at the University."

"It always happens when I'm off duty." I tried hard to

mimic disappointment. "Let me guess: the rector and the head librarian grappled?"

"Something even more exciting. Your new idol Satigny was taken into custody."

For a second my lungs became so constricted that I could not draw enough air to gasp. "On what charges?" I muttered at last.

"Possession and distribution of heretical literature. Tut-tut! And Satigny was just settling into his role so gracefully and comfortably. His teaching career was short-lived. Wild, isn't it?"

"I'll say ..."

"Where do I begin? Let's try from the start." Métivier rubbed the tip of his upturned nose. "That Morel fellow, at whose house we ate the worst rabbit stew, was looking for a misplaced book, something by St. Thomas Aquinas. I don't know what got into that man. Normally he's so calm and polite, but today he looked like a bundle of explosives."

"Maybe the head librarian subjected him to duress?"

"Maybe. At any rate, Morel and I embarked on a hunt for the missing tome. It was nowhere to be found. Eventually he started busting into individual classrooms and rummaging through the shelves. While going through Satigny's study, he stumbled across a very interesting title, the author of which was burned at the stake a few years back. La Fausse Révélation by Raoul Terrade. There must be no more than five surviving copies."

The title as well as the name of the author meant nothing to me. I was both relieved and ashamed to admit it. "You know more about forbidden books then I do."

"It comes with the territory," he said with a cryptic wink. "Don't forget who my brother is. At any rate, Morel felt compelled to report his findings to the ecclesiastic court. Think how poorly it would reflect on him if it came to light that he had been tolerating heresy within the walls of the University. The rest is history. Now your favorite astronomy lecturer is in the dungeon beneath the Palace of Justice."

I was still regaining my ability to breathe. "H-how do you know those things?"

With an air of infinite humility, Johannes inclined his curly head and laid his pink hand over his chest. "I have ears all over the city, my dear friend. We, little people, short of stature, rely on our wit and observation. This is how little white mice survive. But wait. I'm not done telling the story."

"There's more?"

"Of course, there's always more. I was just getting to the best part. When you are dealing with heresy allegations, it's never just one person. Over the course of the interrogation, a few interesting facts surfaced. Are you ready for this?"

"Yes!" I cried out in desperation. "Don't keep me in suspense."

"While Satigny was conversing with the torturer, another name came up – that of Josef Eliade. You know him, don't you? He's the grim, elusive one. Satigny confessed that the Bohemian urchin has been running errands for him, retrieving manuscripts from monastery archives. Of course, he claims that the book that landed him in trouble was not delivered by Josef. In fact, Satigny maintains he has no idea where it came from. So the next logical step was to arrest Josef Eliade. That part was easy, as he happened to be in Paris at the time. But you know who else is in town?"

"I don't know. The Pope?"

"Close enough. Anselm Viteri, the wolf of the Inquisition. He's visiting the bishop. Old Louis needed some moral support. So naturally, Viteri took a very active interest in Satigny's case. He decided that arresting Josef Eliade was not enough, but rather it would make sense to arrest the entire family. You have to give that man credit. I'm talking about Viteri. He's of the 'kill them all' mentality – breathtakingly efficient.

"In a matter of hours they captured Mathias, Denise and Sebastien. They are only missing the two Eliade sisters. The younger is with you, obviously. I don't think the Inquisition is interested in her.

"And Agniese … I saw her earlier this morning. She came by the University looking for Lucius. You know he's dead, right? A stab wound of all things! Nobody knows who inflicted it, and we're not likely to find out."

I laid my hand on Métivier's shoulder, begging him to

slow down. Too many arrests, too many deaths in one short conversation. "You need to give me time to digest what you just told me."

"I know, you were enjoying your idyllic rendezvous with your impish mistress, and I ruined it for you. I just thought it would be useful for you to know, in light of your, erm, affair, with one of the Eliade sisters. I know you were using their house for staging your shows, so now you have to find a new performance space. Such a nuisance, I'm sure."

Another chilling thought crossed my mind. "What will become of Satigny's wife?"

"Good question. I have no idea. She hasn't been seen since last night. I don't believe she's in custody, otherwise the guards would've told me; I'm friendly with them, and they keep me informed. Maybe she knew what was coming to her husband and she fled. Then again, maybe someone warned her – or forcefully took her out of the city. She is a ravishing woman, wouldn't you agree?"

"I suppose she is – if you like that type."

"Most red-blooded men like that type. In her short time here, Gisele gained her share of admirers. I mean, she has a good twenty years on me, but if she threw her supple arms around my neck, I wouldn't fight her off. I imagine there are several men closer to her age who would love to take Satigny's place in her bedchamber."

"You sound like you have some theories," I said.

"Do I ever! Not just naked speculations but facts that tie together. So far all arrows point at my dear brother. He is behind all this."

I felt obliged to stand up for Desmoulins, since he was not there to vindicate himself. "Now this is getting beyond absurd."

"You know it's not absurd. We both know my brother and Madame Satigny were lovers. Yes, I overheard the same conversation you did. In fact, I was standing a few paces away from you. I bet you had no idea you weren't alone because you were too busy plotting your new literary opus."

"This isn't about me."

"It's about *all* of us. We all have a role to play in this farce.

My brother could not reconcile with the fact that his old mistress had found happiness with another man, a man who also happened to be his academic rival. Not one but *two* reasons to hate Satigny! Knowing my brother's taste in literature, that book, in all likelihood, came from his personal collection. I'm willing to bet ten years in Purgatory that he is the one who planted the book on Satigny's shelf. Not with his own hands, of course. He would not risk his precious life taking a book like that out of his cell. He has that red-haired demon doing his dirty work."

"Dufort, you mean?"

"Do you know anyone else who fits that description? One night I saw Dufort sneaking into Satigny's study. He looked like a thief or an assassin and was hiding something under his doublet. He didn't notice me, but I surely noticed him. He is not a frequent guest at the University, which is why I thought it odd that he came, especially at such an unusual time of the day. Think about it. Dufort is protected by that mysterious order from the Vatican, making him the only person who can carry such books without endangering his life."

As much as I wanted to dismiss Métivier's theory as convoluted, I could not. To my chagrin, it made too much sense. I only knew one side of Desmoulins, the side from which I had benefitted immensely. It was no small struggle to accept that the same man who had advocated for me, who had helped me recover my French and advance my Latin, who had moved me from the street into a lecture hall, could also send another man to the stake for heresy. Just because I had never personally experienced Desmoulins' dark side did not mean that it did not exist. Of course, it was easy for him to continue feeling benevolent towards me, as long as I stayed in my place, kissed his hands in gratitude and did not pose any threat to him. And what if one day I did something to turn him against me?

"If it's any consolation," Métivier added, having guessed the cause of my silence, "I do not think that incriminating the Eliade family was a part of his plan. I firmly believe that the only person he wanted to eliminate was Adrian Satigny. The Eliades were just unfortunate collateral victims. I'm sure Viteri will find a reason to hang or burn them, just to make a point; just to make his presence in the city known. Their chief crime is being in Paris at the same time as Viteri. He does that sometimes."

I could not help but wonder what it meant for me, for my well-being. My name was tightly linked to that of the Eliades. Was I next? I threw a desperate glance in Elinor's direction. The girl was still holding onto the rope, swinging and twirling like an acrobat. She looked so sweetly absent-minded, and her laughter resembled a nightingale's warble.

"What am I to do now?" I asked the messenger. "Surely, you imparted all of this for a reason. You want me to take action."

"Look, my English friend, it's entirely up to you what you do or don't do. After all, you've known my brother much longer than I have. All my theories could be nothing more than residue from sibling resentment. If you think my brother is saintly and incapable of implicating another person, who am I to dissuade you? A man is entitled to his own delusions. However, if I were you, I wouldn't go home tonight. I'd find alternative lodging. And I wouldn't show up at the University tomorrow morning. I'd keep my head low and sleep with one eye open."

"But if I disappear without a warning, wouldn't it imply that I had something to hide?"

"And if you don't disappear, they might come for you, and then you'll feel silly that you didn't flee when you had the opportunity. I'm not saying your situation is easy or enviable. Forgive me for ruining your night of pleasure. I'm somewhat fond of you and I would hate to see your head roll into the same basket as everyone else's."

I do not know why, but I believed Johannes Métivier. To his credit, he did not stop at delivering the disturbing message and leave me to my own devices. He gave me a key to the room at the end of Pont Saint-Michel he had shared with the deceased Lucius Castelmaure. The rent was paid through the end of the month. Hopefully, I would not need to stay in hiding for that long. God willing, I would be able to come out in a few days and resume my work at the University.

I decided not to break the news to Elinor. I needed time to digest it myself prior to explaining to the girl that her adoptive parents and brothers were in a dungeon.

After three days of hiding inside the ugly hovel, even in the company of a lovely girl, I was ready to howl. To kill time and keep my thoughts from wandering into the darkest places, I continued composing my mystery piece. Of course, I did not have any writing supplies, so the creative process took place inside my head. Elinor was not always sympathetic, tugging at my sleeve and whining into my shoulder. Understandably, she was bored and puzzled. She did not understand why we had to stay inside and, most importantly, why we still had not consummated our love.

"Have you changed your mind, Blackfeather? Don't I please you anymore?"

"Of course, my angel," I growled, "you please me to the heavens and back."

"Then why haven't you done to me what you said you would? I'll have nothing to tell Agniese. And I promised to describe everything in great detail. My sister is a virgin, you know. She has three men after her, and she still hasn't done the deed."

Three men, bah! Elinor did not know there were only two left. The handsome archer was out of the picture.

"There is no need to rush, my sweet. Anticipation sharpens the ecstasy."

"I want to go home," she said suddenly. "I don't like this place. I thought your lodging was nicer than ours on Rue du Mouton."

"This isn't my lodging!" I shouted, jumping to my feet. There was no sense in keeping her sheltered from the truth any longer. "Poor as I am, even I can afford something better. I'm not here of my own choosing. We are prisoners here, while your parents and brothers are prisoners of the Inquisition. It's a stroke of luck that you weren't home when the guards came for your family. I didn't want you to find out like this."

The girl took the news very calmly. "So my dream *was* prophetic," she said. "You know what must be done. We must flee to England."

I looked at her in disbelief. "Do you know what you're saying? You think it's that easy?"

"Don't be afraid." She began patting my shoulder. "I'm

accustomed to living on the run. We've had to uproot and leave many times. It will be an adventure."

"Do you know how long it took me to rise up the ranks? Do you know how many pots I've had to scrub, ink bottles to fill before they allowed me to teach that one miserable course?"

"And you always complain about how poorly they treat you. If you go to England, at least you'll be among your own people who speak your language."

"They aren't my people. In France I'm too English, and in England I'll be too French. I don't belong anywhere, really."

"Then we can go to Spain. I speak most of their dialects."

"Grand, I'll depend on a twelve-year-old chit for survival! That won't be a blow to my masculinity."

Yes, I was beginning to realize that Elinor was going to be my last woman after all, because I was not long for this world. What possessed me to get involved with the Eliade family? I know the answer. That motley band of vagabonds tickled my poetic side. Like me, they had no country to call their own. Now I was paying the price for my sentimentality. Yes, I was painfully aware that my thoughts were cowardly and treacherous. Innocent little Elinor was ready to give her love to me, even though her own life was in danger, and I kept thinking of my own comfort and the things I would have to give up.

At quarter past ten Johannes came by. He made the decision-making easier for us.

His terse verdict: "You cannot stay here any longer," was delivered along with: "I don't have any news for you. I just don't like the lull. I think you should get out of the city, or better yet, the country. I don't recommend traveling by the river. Take the back roads. You can catch a boat once you reach Vernon. You'll also need disguises."

Mon Dieu, those were some stern marching orders! I had no idea where or when I would start following them.

I noticed that Johannes was carrying a sack over his shoulder. He dropped it to the floor, untied the strings and pulled out a nobleman's waistcoat and a brocade dress.

"Whose clothes are these?" I asked. I had never held such fine garments in my hands before.

"I got them from Aurore St. Laurent. She's going into a convent, so she won't need fancy dresses anymore. The waistcoat used to belong to her late father."

"Aurore knows?" I asked anxiously.

"No, she was just giving away old things, clearing out her house before embracing her new life as a nun. She knew I was friends with Lucius, so she trusted me with a few things to donate appropriately for her.

"Hurry and get dressed. The guards will be looking for a scrawny academician in black and a white-haired circus girl. I thought it would be amusing if you two could become nobles for one night. Just make sure not to behave like fugitives. Do not scurry, press against the walls or lower your heads. Walk slowly and proudly, like you have nothing to hide."

Elinor needed no further encouragement. She slipped the brocade dress right over her street apparel, which instantly created an illusion of ample forms, aging her a few years. She then wrapped her white hair in a bun and put the veiled headpiece over it.

"The banquet was such a bore," she said with a yawn, getting into character. "*Mon cherié*, can you believe we killed an entire evening among those dullards?"

In that moment I knew I would not perish. With a resourceful girl like her as my companion, I would survive.

Johannes discreetly slipped a bag of coins into my hand. "This also came from Aurore. She gave it to me ... just because. You'll need money to pay for the horses and the boat. You'll also need to eat. Well, maybe not you, but your mistress might get hungry."

Before pocketing the money, I squeezed the boy's hand. "Why are you being so nice to me?"

"Because you were always nice to me," he replied with a shrug. "I don't forget such things. Lucius let me stay in his ugly digs, and you showed me around the library. Besides, I'm annoyed at my brother. Many people are suffering because of him. I didn't want you to be among them, that's all."

I threw my arms around his short, soft body. "How can I repay you?"

"You can make me the hero of your next play. And make me tall and thin. I want long legs, damn it!"

Our trek through the slumbering city was uneventful. Not once did we need to employ our acting skills. I sensed Elinor's disappointment at being denied the opportunity to recite the phrase she had been rehearsing. I had no heart to tell her that in England it was not customary to use female actors. She would have to pretend to be a boy in order to play a female role. The farther we moved from the city's center, the bolder and freer I felt.

Alas, I let my guard down too soon. My Parisian ghosts were not ready to relinquish me just yet. I had one more unsettling encounter, just a few blocks away from the papal gate of all places. I saw two men wearing identical black cloaks. One was standing upright, his attitude haughty and dismissive, arms crossed on his chest. His interlocutor was slouching and wavering like a drunk, propped against the side of the building. A saddled horse was standing a few paces away. The men's voices sounded disturbingly familiar. I squeezed Elinor's hand, compelling her to stillness and silence.

A second later I learned that my anxiety was not unfounded. One of the men was my former Latin teacher. No amount of black cloth could obscure that posture. I had to rub my eyes a few times to make sure I was not seeing things. The man he was talking to was the late Lucius Castelmaure.

"Aren't you supposed to be dead, Captain?" Desmoulins asked.

"Well, I got tired of being dead. Now, if you don't mind, I'd like to return to the land of the living."

"I'm afraid that's impossible. You'll look very foolish, and so will I. You remember our agreement: you must leave the city. In order to start a new life – you must die first. I did my best to help you. Now it's your turn to fulfill your part."

"You weren't supposed to pierce the lung," Lucius said resentfully.

"You weren't supposed to squirm. I gave you that block of wood to bite into."

"That block of wood wasn't thick enough. My teeth went right through it."

"Well, excuse my lack of planning, Captain. I don't get approached with such requests every day, you know. You asked me to stab you in the back. Being a loyal, nonjudgmental friend I did just that. Now, if you don't mind me asking, what part about being dead don't you like?"

"I just … I just don't feel useful."

"If you want to be useful, go to Gonesse."

"To my dying wife, you mean? Not in a thousand years."

"The Archbishop of Reims has a summer residence there, one of many. It's called 'Le lit du lion.' There's a statue of a sleeping lion by the entrance. I believe he is staying there until August. Tell him the price of gold went up this year."

"What an odd message. What's that supposed to mean?"

"Trust me, he'll know what it means. He'll know what to do; what's required of him. Can you remember those simple words?"

The archer hesitated. "I think I can," he said at last. "I shall try."

Chapter 6

Just Words

(Lucius Castelmaure)

I always knew my death would be premature, stupid and devoid of any heroism. Do not ask me how I knew it. I am not endowed with what mystics would call foresight. I just did not see myself living past twenty-five. So at some point I stopped making long-term plans and immersed myself in momentary cravings. I was already on the path to destruction.

It all started with me winning an archery contest back in 1472, which was the last bearable year of my life. I took part in the contest on a whim. Even my father did not know about it until the very end. Had he known beforehand, he would have coached and lectured me into a stupor, and I never would have won. Papa had that effect on me. At any rate, my prize for taking the first place was being whisked off into a garrison, examined and interrogated by the recruiting committee and registered for training. That day marked the beginning of the end for me.

The next six months were a whirlwind of sweat, blood and confusion. I received frequent lashings for not following commands I did not understand. It was around the same time that I discovered women. Or rather, they discovered me.

One time I was heaving behind the barracks after yet another generous serving of lashes for God knows what offense, when I heard a whimsical voice say, "Such a handsome boy!" I felt kisses glazing over the fresh welts and the lacerations on my back, a tongue gliding up and down my neck and a pair of swift hands unbuttoning my trousers. My vision still blurred by the tears I had managed to keep from spilling, I leaned forward and collapsed with my chin between two ample breasts spilling out of a stiff velvet bodice. The woman started moving underneath me with admirable dexterity, without aggravating my injuries. She was a real master of her trade. All I had to do was lie on top, occasionally catching her lips with mine.

Handsome, handsome boy ... That's what they punished you for.

I felt compelled to correct her and explain that they punished me for being stupid and slow but then decided not to bother. As a woman, she saw things in her own light. She offered the right kind of consolation at the right time. Thus, my first experience of carnal delight was tightly linked to punishment. In my mind, I started expecting a sensual reward after every beating. Eventually, I started deliberately seeking punishment in order to give myself a reason to go whoring afterwards. Bitter medicine first – sweetmeats later. Eventually, my back became numb to the lash. I no longer needed to exert my willpower to suppress my cries. Sensing my indifference, my superiors suddenly backed away from me. Perhaps, they thought their goal had been accomplished. I had become hardened and resigned to pain.

The women continued plastering me from every angle. They greeted me on my way out of the barracks, and they followed me back to the doorstep. I was never unescorted – and yet always alone. What was that Latin word my tutor taught me? It evades me now. Pa-ra-dox? All that commotion, all that noise, and nobody to talk to. Clutter on the outside, and emptiness on the inside. My commanders shouting orders, Papa spouting criticism and women purring. *Handsome, handsome boy.* I know you will probably want to smack me after hearing my grievances. Here's a golden child bemoaning his fate!

What does it mean to be handsome? What privileges does it give you, really? It means that if you go into a tavern that also serves as an unofficial brothel, and you want to get both a drink and a whore, and you only have money for a drink, you can still have your drink and still get serviced below the waist pro bono. This is where the advantages of being good-looking end.

Still, even that trick is to be used sparingly. You do not want to become known as an opportunist who does not pay. Tavern keepers do not like it. That is a sure way to get banned from your favorite places.

Then there is the guilt factor. You remember that whores have to eat too. Some of them have children. And some of those children were fathered by patrons like me and the men under my command. It is your right to accuse me of being too soft-hearted. I'm certain my fellow officers have ridiculed me behind my back.

It was a promise I made to my mother while she was on her deathbed.

"Always be nice to women, my boy," she said in her serene, fading voice, "even the old and the ugly ones, even the mad and the ragged, even Moors and Egyptians. Just as the sun lavishes its warmth upon everyone indiscriminately, so shall you lavish your courtesy and kindness, my darling Lucius. You have no idea what one gentle glance from a handsome man can do for a down-trod woman."

In short, she was saying "Do not be like your father." She had to choose her words carefully, even in her final hours, and I had to make sure not to cry. Papa was in the next room, paying close attention.

I found that I slept better at night when I regarded that man solely as a soldier. It was easy to admire him when I thought of his military accomplishments. But when I thought of his qualities as a man, I found myself veering off into a dangerous territory: that of disloyalty and doubt. According to Papa, there were two kinds of people in the world: those who were "real people" and those who were "people, too".

Those in the first category—in which he placed himself, the King of France and, perhaps, a few of his comrades, did not need to justify their existence. Those in the second category had "a lot of apologizing to do." They were guilty by default, until proven otherwise. Guilty of breathing the same air and looking at the same sky as "real people".

Being nice to women was my subtle way of rebelling against Papa. When I could not pay for their services with money, I tried to pay with kind words and gentle—almost apologetic—touches. Keeping my cheeks smooth of stubble and my fingernails clean were just a few small tokens of consideration that set me apart from other men.

Maman, what would you think of your son now?

I spent my eighteenth birthday in the arms of another prostitute. Papa did not think I deserved a real celebration. My career was not advancing as fast as he would have liked. He blamed it on my sluggishness. He said I was slow on my feet and forgetful. At least he did not call me a coward. Thank you for that much, Papa. That skinny, weary grey-eyed woman was exactly what I needed. She was one of the older, less conspicuous ones in the brothel, probably in less demand than the others. She was grateful for my attention. When she found out that it was my birthday, she tossed in a few additional favors that would normally cost more. Moved by her generosity, I covered her hands with kisses. At some point we both said "to hell with agreements" and made love. Yes, I actually made love for the first time.

"How would you like me to keep you?" I asked her before crawling out of her bed. "As soon as I start making earnest money, I'll take you out of the brothel. You'll be all mine and no other man will lay his paws on you. Does that sound appealing?"

She looked genuinely moved. Apparently, she did not get many such offers. With a chaste, almost motherly pat on the cheek she pushed me out of the door into the damp night and wished me a happy birthday one last time.

Although prostitutes never give out their real names, she may have told one to me anyway, but that name escapes me. Whatever identity she may have had prior to settling in the brothel was of no consequence. The thought made me sad, and I knew I could not share my sadness with any of the "real people" because they would laugh at me. Prostitutes are not even "people, too".

Once again, I was alone with a pleasantly tingling groin, a foggy head and flaccid legs, trying to make my way to Pont Saint-Michel.

There were two cloaked figures walking in front of me: a man around thirty and an adolescent boy a few years younger than myself. A father and a son, I presumed. I could not see much. It was too dark, and I was too drunk. I only saw their silhouettes. My hearing, however, was sharper than my eyesight, and I caught a fair amount of their conversation. They were playing some sort of guessing game.

I overheard the man ask, "What do you think? Is she a witch or a cow?" He had a deep, languid, haughty voice that reminded me so much of my father's. Except that Papa would never play a game with me, not even on my birthday.

"Wait!" I heard myself shout. Dragging my feet, I darted towards the duo. "That game you were playing. Can I play it too?"

The boy turned around, and I saw his angular face framed by straight fiery hair down to his shoulders. The corner of his mouth twitched in contempt, as he turned to his older companion.

"Do you know this man, *Maître*?"

"You don't know me," I wedged in my reply, thus freeing the man from the need to reply in the negative. "You may have seen me on the street. I'm with the archers. We patrol the island. My name is Lucius Octavius Castelmaure, and today happens to be my eighteenth birthday."

"Congratulations," said the older man. "You have survived this long. Many soldiers are not so lucky."

"My name is Daniel Dufort," the boy introduced himself, tucking a flame-colored strand behind his ear. "Turning fifteen soon. I've been playing the organ at Notre-Dame for the past two months. I have a performance coming up in a fortnight. Ten original pieces. They say I'm the next Guillaume de Machaut. And this is Monseigneur Desmoulins, the holiest and most scholarly canon in the precinct." He turned to face his guardian and clenched his fists. "*Maître*, we cannot leave this drunkard on the streets. The night watch will collect him. How pitiful he looks! It won't be Christian of us. Can he spend the night in my cell? Please." He was not begging, he was demanding. "There's not another beating heart there except for the one-eyed cat."

"That ugly beast is still alive?" the man asked.

"Polyphemus is not ugly. He's just ... weathered. A champion mouser, too! Last night he brought two decapitated rats and laid them out next to my mattress. The only problem is that he doesn't talk."

Stupendous! Now I knew exactly where I ranked – up there with feral critters lifted off of the street. There was justice in that. Indeed, in my current state, I was no better than a one-eyed cat or a headless rat.

"Hungry for human speech, are you?" Desmoulins asked in a tone both reproachful and indulgent. "I suppose our conversations are not enough."

"More than enough. But they are always so ... profound and philosophical. Sometimes I want talk about something stupid and meaningless. This drunken soldier is just what I need. He's a godsend. Please, Maître. He'll be out of my cell first thing in the morning, I promise."

They were talking about me like I was not even there. But could I blame them? After all, I was the one who latched onto them on the street and interrupted their conversation. I was the one who begged them to include me in their absurd game without even knowing the rules. I was the one who could not shake off the gnawing feeling of loneliness, even after spending two hours in the arms of a seasoned prostitute. No amount of wine could dull the resentment from the knowledge that my own father despised me.

I never considered myself an envious man. Indeed, I was born with more advantages than one could wish for. I could look upon enamored couples without sorrow or bitterness, knowing that I could possess most women in Paris, with little effort. But when I saw fathers and sons engaged in an idle discourse that did not involve giving out orders, my jaw stiffened.

The two standing in front of me were not even a father and a son. Their relationship was that of a master and his dog, but the master was indulgent and oblivious, while the dog was pampered and ill-behaved. That overgrown pup could have any treat he wanted and was not expected to perform any tricks apart from the ones that pleased him.

"All right, you can have the drunkard stay in your cell," Desmoulins abdicated, "but only for one night. If the bishop finds out, he'll rant."

Ten minutes later we were inside the north tower of the cathedral. The walls in the cell were covered with images of creatures far more horrifying and repulsive than the gargoyles guarding the portal of the cathedral. Flame-breathing horses with wings, wolves with ten legs. They all came from the feverish imagination of the man inhabiting the cell. If I tried anything of the sort in my own room, my father would cut off my hands, one finger at a time.

"Do you like it?" Dufort asked boastfully, expecting a compliment. "I've thought about illustrating manuscripts. There's a book on demonology my master allows me to read. I hope to copy it one day and add my own drawings. When I meet the woman of my dreams, I shall give it to her as a present. A deserving woman would appreciate a hand-made gift, wouldn't she?"

"You're asking the wrong person," I said, still out of breath from the endless climb up the staircase. "I've never made anything in my life. Believe me, I have two left hands, and both grow out of my arse. They are only good for shooting arrows and breaking up brawls. Not everyone can be a genius like you."

Yes, I could get away with self-deprecation. It was one of the few benefits of being extraordinarily good-looking. Of course, Dufort immediately proposed a friendly bargain.

"I can teach you how to draw if you teach me how to shoot. What do you think of that?"

I did not know how to tell him I was not giving out archery lessons, so once again, I defaulted to self-deprecation. "I doubt anyone can teach me how to draw. My eyes, hands and brain do not talk to each other."

Dufort produced a sorrowful grimace. "It's a shame you have no faith in yourself. But can you still teach me how to shoot?"

I prayed to God to save me from this conversation. And sure enough, God answered. We heard an eerie sound reminiscent of that produced by a creaking door. A second later a mangy one-eyed cat slipped into the cell. The disquieting, vaguely diabolic sound was emitting from its blood-stained muzzle. The arrival of the beast elucidated Dufort's face.

"Meet Polyphemus," he said. "You know why we named him that, don't you?"

No, I had no idea. I inclined my head and opened my mouth, ready to confess to my ignorance, but Dufort rushed to my rescue. "Polyphemus was one of the Cyclopes in Homer's *Odyssey*. You've read *The Odyssey*, haven't you?"

Again, I had to respond with an indistinct groan. Truth be told, I had not read anything since my father cloistered me in the garrison. I had not touched or seen, let alone opened a book since winning that ill-fated archery contest back in 1472.

"Polyphemus is my best friend," Dufort continued animatedly. Why wasn't I surprised to hear that? "He only has one eye, as you can see, but that eye can perceive the invisible, things like spirits and shadows. He describes them to me. Thanks to him and his eye, I can peek into the netherworld. By day he makes his rounds around the precinct, keeping it free of mice. At night he returns to my cell to sleep by my side." He kissed the cat between the dirty ears and handed him over to me. "Would you like to pet him, Lucius? For luck. If you touch him, no harm shall befall you."

I had a feeling that politely declining the offer would not be acceptable, so I received Polyphemus into my arms. The flea-ridden creature, despite being scrawny, felt surprisingly heavy. He also did not appear to be any fonder of me than I was of him. With a belligerent growl, he swatted at my face. Thank God, by then I was sober enough to recoil. That night I myself came dangerously close to becoming one-eyed. A perfect closing gift on my eighteenth birthday!

Dufort laughed at the scene. He found it amusing. "Polyphemus always lashes out at those he likes," he said. "It's his way of showing approval."

The sound of his laughter made me cringe. It had an odd, feral quality. The boy sounded like someone who was accustomed to laughing and crying alone. No wonder! His primary audience consisted of a crippled cat and painted monsters. At the same time, he did not come across as shy or timid. His speech and demeanor resembled a cart without a braking pedal. He enjoyed the luxury of blurting things out.

As I was regaining my sobriety, a feeling of regret started setting in. The prospect of getting picked up by the night watch suddenly seemed more and more appealing. What possessed me to latch onto those two, of all men in Paris? I suspected it was going to be a long night with not much sleep in store for me. My juvenile host did not look in the least bit drowsy. He was going to keep me up with lame jokes, demonology anecdotes and references to Greek literature.

Now that my vision was not so blurry, I took a closer look at my new acquaintance. It is certainly good for a man to be tall, but at some point height stops adding benefit. Six foot is advantageous, but six and a half – superfluous. Those additional inches serve no purpose other than making you more visible and therefore more vulnerable. A human being does not need that many vertebrae. Same with facial features. Hollow cheeks look attractive, but Dufort's were too hollow. His excessive physical strength burdened him. He did not know what to make of it. I could tell it from the way he flexed his fists. It seemed as if Nature, in an angry, frantic attempt to create a perfect male specimen, came out with this … this thing. The Stone Prince. Yes, that was the nickname given to him by the new bishop.

Dufort sat on the floor next to me, pulling his long legs up and hugging his knobby knees. Judging from that awkward grin, I had a feeling he was going to ask me a question. And sure enough, he did.

"Tell me, what is it like, being with a woman?"

I felt my head tilt backwards involuntarily. *"Mon Dieu*, where do I begin?"

"I know the mechanical part," he said hastily, trying to make my job easier. "I want to know about the sensual part. Are they expected to feel what we feel? Pleasure, I mean."

"Women were made for our enjoyment," I said, taking the easy way out, "not the other way around."

The creature did not seem satisfied. "That's not what my master says."

"Well, if your master already answered your question, why are you asking me?"

"A second opinion, I suppose." Dufort shrugged his massive bony shoulders. "My master ... he hasn't had a woman in a long time. He is a priest, as you know. Understandably, it poses certain limitations. His vows oblige him to discretion and selectiveness. The woman has to be truly exceptional for him to take that risk. He won't endanger his soul or his reputation for just anyone. I don't even know if such a woman exists. Most of them are either cows or witches."

Cows and witches ... So that was the game he was playing with Desmoulins!

"Vows are just words," I said. "People make flippant promises all the time. The only vow I intend to keep is the one I made to the King of France."

There was no polite way to end that conversation. I removed my doublet, rolled it up and placed it under my head as a pillow. The mattress on the floor was wide enough for two, but I could not fathom sleeping shoulder to shoulder with that creature. In the past I had shared cots and bunk beds with fellow soldiers. It did not bother me to have someone tossing and snoring next to me. I just did not want the red-haired brat to get the wrong idea that we were equals, let alone friends, just because he sheltered me in his cell for one night and showed me his demonic artwork. I did not need him shouting my name on the street the next time I rode down Rue de Parvis with my commander and the rest of my company.

Dufort spent much of the night babbling, mostly to himself, drawing on the walls, scribbling in his notebook, humming polyphonies. I could tell he had a very vibrant internal life and a tightknit circle of imaginary friends. Towards daybreak he finally sprawled on the mattress, face down. Even with his eyes closed he looked arrogant as hell. I could tell that boy did not even aspire to be one of the "real people." He was the Stone Prince, an alpha-Parisian. Having made sure that he was fast asleep, I buttoned my doublet and slipped out of the cell.

Determined as I was to keep my word to the kindly prostitute who took such good care of me on my eighteenth birthday, I never saw her again. One evening I stopped by the tavern for a quick visit, just to assure her I had not forgotten about her, but she was not there. Later on, another wench told me in confidence that Jacqueline – that was the name of my one time lady friend – had died while trying to purge a baby from her womb. I came out of the tavern sober and bawling. This time I did not care if any of my fellow-soldiers saw me. What possessed Jacqueline to do such a rancid deed? I would have given her money, enough to take her out of the brothel, rent a cottage in the countryside and raise her child in peace. Perhaps, I had not been persuasive or prompt enough? Maybe I should have sent her money the morning after our tryst? Would that have made a difference? I suppose, I could not save every prostitute in Paris.

When I came home that night, Papa was still awake, sipping burgundy in his study.

"Lucius Octavius," he began. "I have some news for you. I wanted it to come from me."

I always got nervous when he used my middle name. "What is it? Did someone die?"

"Indeed, someone did die - the old Lucius. The lazy, slow, stupid Lucius. He is no more. I am pleased to meet the new Lucius, who has been promoted to a lieutenant." Papa filled another chalice with wine and pushed it towards me. "Congratulations, my son. Your commander will do the honors tomorrow morning."

I was not in a hurry to accept his token. My stomach was still in knots from what I had learned earlier. If I took a sip of that wine, I would only regurgitate it a second later. "So all those lashings were not in vain?"

Papa frowned and slapped his gloves against the edge of the tabletop. "Oh, stop. I didn't subject you to anything I hadn't been subjected to myself when I was your age. The good news is that now you have the authority to order lashings for others."

"Grand! Who'll be my first victim? Don't I feel like the King of France now!"

"And you should! You earned that promotion. I had nothing to do with it. In fact, you would have gotten it six months ago, but I deliberately asked your commander to hold off. I wanted you to spend a little extra time in the rank and file."

"Ah, so it's reverse nepotism?"

"Call it what you wish. I just wanted to make sure you were ready for this new responsibility. We both know that mentally you are a little behind your peers, so it made sense to wait. I do not expect you to move upward too fast. Otherwise you'll end up like Icarus, whose wings melted when he got too close to the sun. I am in favor of a slow and steady climb. We are on the right path. If you don't revert back to your idiotic ways, I think you'll do very well in your new position."

Papa did not anticipate any major military engagements. According to him, the country was still reeling from the last war. It would be a while before the king would muster the resources and the ambition for the next armed conflict. My promotion was perfectly timed. There would not be any opportunities for me to embarrass myself and the Castelmaure family name on a battlefield in the foreseeable future. Papa had more plans for me.

Now that I had a rank, it was time for me to secure a suitable match. That was one task I would gladly delegate to someone else. I wanted as little involvement as possible. Accustomed to the compliant, artless prostitutes who were happy with a coin and a kind word, I was a virgin in terms of elegant courtship. A few weeks before my nineteenth birthday I had my first encounter with the realm of respectable women—which also turned out to be my last.

Papa had a former comrade-at-arms named Jerome Poiron who had a summer home on the outskirts of Paris by the river where he held frequent banquets. Another passion of his was hunting. Once, Papa presented him with a pack of hounds. It was a most extravagant and obliging gift, the kind you would give to an enemy you wanted to keep closer than a friend.

Poiron had a plain and sickly unmarried daughter named Juliette, who was over the age of twenty. Remembering Maman's request to be nice to all women, even those I did not find appealing, I indulged Juliette with noninvasive attention.

Neither of us had much to say and her mother, who played the role of a chaperone, did most of the talking.

Madame Poiron's favorite subjects included family ailments. She used complex Latin terminology, butchering the pronunciation. Listening to her, I understood why her husband spent so much time in the saddle, hunting. I also understood why he was so anxious to get his daughter out of the house. The girl was shriveling up under her mother's influence like a small sun-loving yarrow bush in the shade of an ungainly old tree.

One day we managed to sneak away from the sickly matron. She fell asleep in the orchard, her withered bosom rising and falling beneath the embroidered chemisette. Juliette instantly revived, took my hand and pulled me inside the house.

"Come, Lucius. I must show you something."

It was the first time she called me by name, and she did it in a most intimate and animated tone. For a second I thought I had an entirely different girl in front of me. Anxious to see what sort of revelation she had in store for me, I followed her to the second floor. Still squeezing my hand, she led me into what looked like her bedroom. The place certainly did not look like her father's armory or a library. In the middle of it there was an enormous bed with four carved posts and a velvet awning.

What happened next was beyond absurd. Juliette recoiled from me, fell backwards on the bed and started pulling at her dress, undoing the bodice, panting and wheezing. Hooks and buttons torn from the fabric went flying to the floor. Her condition made me extremely alarmed. Thanks to her mother, I knew that lung disease ran in her family. Perhaps, she was having one of those dreadful attacks, when one's breathing passages become obstructed.

"What is wrong with you, Juliette?" I asked, rushing to her side and bending over her. "Are you suffocating? I'll bring you water."

"Get away!" she shrieked. "Don't touch me!"

The clarity of her voice reassured me somewhat. At least now I knew she was not choking. A second later I heard footsteps in the hall. Juliette's father and brother were standing in the doorway. The girl herself covered her face and burst into tears. *"Mon Dieu,* I'm ruined!"

Next thing I remember is standing outside in the orchard with Papa pacing back and forth in front of me.

"This is very serious," he spoke without looking at me, fingers interlaced under his chin. "Now you have to marry Juliette. There's no alternative."

I positioned myself in front of him, so he could not avoid looking me in the eye. "Papa, give me a chance to defend myself. I swear to you, this isn't what it looked like."

"You mean, Poiron's daughter threw herself on the bed, opened her dress and then forcefully pulled you on top of her?"

"Yes! That's exactly what happened. She looked like she was choking, and I was only trying to help her."

"Don't even start. Your poor mother would be disgusted. You have no respect for her dying wish."

"Papa, you know me!"

"Precisely. I know you too well." He shook his head and continued walking. "You've spent so much time with tavern whores that you have no idea how to behave with women of your own rank. It's a skill you'll have to learn, much like archery or fencing. This won't be a quiet or rushed wedding in some tiny provincial church. I don't want people to think we have something to hide. No, it will be lavish and public. It will take place at Notre-Dame."

Papa was no longer shaming me. He was strategizing. It was a done deal. There was no point in continuing to try to argue my innocence. The ailing matron, Madame Poiron, was already composing the menu.

The day before the wedding I had to go to confession, even though I had fewer sins than ever on my conscience. Still queasy from the incident at the Poiron estate, I had not done much drinking or whoring. I knew I should have used those final weeks of bachelorhood to indulge myself, but I honestly had no appetite for the things that once brought me comfort.

I saw treachery everywhere. Every woman seemed like a witch. Every cup of wine seemed poisoned. My comrades at the garrison clapped me on the shoulder, bombarding me with good wishes and rancid jokes, but I avoided their company too. The world around me smelled like the sewer. I am sure there was a dose of humor in my situation, but I failed to see it.

So when I found out that it was Monseigneur Desmoulins who was taking confessions that day, I chuckled. A perfect final stroke! I was already feeling like hell, and that arrogant priest could not possibly make me feel any worse. So I barfed up the story of my entrapment, expecting no sympathy. What sympathy can a handsome young officer from an aristocratic family expect? The Christian faith is not set up to treat the likes of me with kindness. Alas, I did not have any redeeming physical deformities or social disadvantages that would endear me to my confessor. I just had scars on my back from countless lashings. But who wanted to see those? There was no pardon for Lucius Castelmaure.

Desmoulins listened with great interest. Then he did something utterly unorthodox. Instead of absolving my sins and dismissing me, he told me a very similar story from his own youth. When he was around my age, a woman accused him of the same crime. That woman was his stepmother, no less. Apparently, the accusation caused a permanent rift between him and his father, who had up until that point idolized his son. I can only imagine what it felt like to fall from the pedestal in your own father's eyes. Papa had never spoiled me with praise. He had made it clear that he did not expect much of me. But even so, on the day he took Juliette Poiron's word over mine, something inside me rotted away and fell off, never to grow back. And Monseigneur Desmoulins had much more to lose than I did. To go from a beloved to a deviant overnight? Ugh ...

"Women can be very vindictive," he concluded. "There is a reason why the church warns us against them. It's not the lewd women of the streets we must fear. Even St. Augustine regarded prostitution as a necessary evil. No, it's those who come from reputable families that can bring about our downfall. I know it's not much consolation, but Mademoiselle Poiron must have been rather smitten by you to resort to such radical measures."

"It was totally unnecessary to drag my name through mud like that," I said sternly. "I would've married Juliette anyway.

One word from Papa would've sufficed. I never disobeyed him. It was his idea to make me a soldier, you know. It's not what I wanted, but I said yes. In my first year at the garrison, I'd taken many undeserved beatings. I realize it's all a part of the initiation process. But *this*? This is too much to bear."

"You are a very dutiful son, Lucius. God will reward you for your obedience."

"How?"

"By sending you great love, the sort of love they herald in sonnets."

"What use is it to me if I'll be married? It's like giving expensive riding boots to a man with no legs."

"Nobody says your wife will live forever, my dear boy. I hear her health is not robust. There's a good chance you'll become a widower very soon. You'll get your portion of the Poiron wealth and marry the woman of your choosing. Rest assured, your sufferings are not going unnoticed. You will get your reward from God."

"Well, Monseigneur," I said, straightening up, "have you gotten your reward?"

"I'm still waiting for mine. It's so hard to be patient and not lose faith when you see so many young people dying around you." He recoiled slightly and squinted. "I see you with a spirited foreign girl, a Spaniard, perhaps, with raven hair and a tiny waist. She'll sing and dance."

A foreign woman? Why, that sounded marvelous! I do not think I ever had a Spaniard. I had a strange feeling Desmoulins was describing his own fantasy mistress.

"That foreign woman, where do I find her?" I asked, growing genuinely excited.

"Don't worry, she'll find you – When the time comes. For now, go forth and try to be a good husband to your wife."

I came out of the confession booth partially comforted. Desmoulins no longer struck me as an aloof cleric. I saw him as a man, as a prospective friend. Even if that story with his stepmother was false, even if he told it just to make me feel better, I was still grateful for the intent. No, my heart was not singing. And it was not at peace. But at least it had stopped darting and jerking frantically like a rabbit caught in a snare.

On the way out of the cathedral I ran into the organist, whom I had not seen since my eighteenth birthday. The boy must have grown a few more inches. His hair looked longer, and his voice sounded deeper. He was turning into quite a contender. I wondered what kind of women he was drawn to. No doubt, Desmoulins must have planted the image of the dusky foreign enchantress in his mind. Most importantly, what kind of women were drawn to him?

Something told me he thought it beneath him to pay for intimate favors – since he was so preoccupied with the question of women feeling pleasure. He seemed far too interested in female physique, and probably the female psyche as well. My guess was that he wanted to be loved in the traditional and ever so ambivalent sense of the word. So he probably was aiming for a respectable woman, the very kind that Desmoulins warned about. Of course, respectable women would expect some material comforts. In his case fame did not translate into wealth. I knew that the bishop was hoarding Dufort's money. What did the child prodigy have to offer apart from his arresting looks and extensive musical repertoire? Was that enough to sustain a woman's interest? We had already established that daughters of Eve were capable of feeling the same sweet pulsations below the waist. But did they also appreciate finer things like music? Did they notice beauty that was not tied to things like garments or jewelry? That part I was not so sure about. The only female I had any coherent conversations with was my distant cousin Aurore, and it would be a stretch to call her a woman. A lieutenant in petticoats was more like it. She knew Latin and Greek and military history – all the things I was supposed to know. She could name the date and location of every battle back to the times of Charlemagne. I bet if she heard Dufort's compositions, she would approve. Alas, she preferred the company of her friend Diane, who was equally scholarly and unfriendly towards men.

To be fair, Dufort's place in life was a little unique – and unquestionably privileged. Staring into his dilated pupil, I became painfully aware of my desire to switch places with him, to become the Stone Prince for one day. A different kind of human. A different kind of good-looking. Trade my uniform for his liturgical sash. Trade my golden curls for copper strands. Trade Papa Castelmaure for Monseigneur Desmoulins. All my prior hostility towards him had been dictated by raw, juvenile envy.

"I've written a perfect hymn for your wedding," the boy said. "It sounds just like a funeral march. It's perfect for the occasion."

"I'm sure of that, but I didn't commission a hymn."

"I wrote one anyway. I don't expect you to pay me. Not with money. How about that archery lesson?"

"I don't trust you with arrows, Dufort. You'll blind someone, and I'll have another scandal attached to my name."

He bounced on his toes. "All right. How about a fencing lesson instead?"

"Deal."

I could not bring myself to deny him. He clasped my hand, nearly crushing my fingers. That boy had a grip! Perfect for squeezing the hilt of the sword. Pathetic as it sounded, this bourgeoning friendship distracted me from the travesty my personal life was about to become.

Being a perfect husband turned out to be easier than I had expected. My daily existence did not change much after the wedding. Juliette moved into one of her family's suburban homes in the vicinity of Gonesse, and I stayed in the city with my men. It did not take me long to forgive Juliette. I had a feeling the idea to incriminate me did not come from her. She was not fast or witty enough to devise such a trick. It must have come from her perpetually ailing Maman, whom I, thankfully, did not need to see. No doubt, the old witch was asking her daughter whether I was insulting or beating her.

Juliette did not expect tenderness or gallantry, but I gave it to her anyway, simply because it cost me nothing. I tried to make our obligatory couplings quick and painless, without any superfluous entourage. Night after night she lay on her back with her eyes closed, while I worked myself into a state of readiness, thinking of all the friendly whores waiting for me in the city. It usually took me between three and five thrusts to strike home, which translated into about ten seconds of discomfort for Juliette. As soon as she conceived, I left her alone altogether, tête à tête with her morning sickness, for which she was grateful. We were both relieved that we could stop copulation for the time being. With my procreative duty fulfilled, I could return to the things that truly mattered, things that required my attention in Paris, like the archers under my command and the new friends at Notre-Dame.

I am proud to say that I fulfilled my part of the bargain and gave Dufort that fencing lesson, which led to a standing tradition. Desmoulins, who had toyed with a sword in his adolescence as part of his traditional Italian upbringing, joined us. Most lessons were conducted in a secluded area behind the garrison. I had access to the fencing hall where my fellow soldiers practiced their skill, but I was not allowed to bring in outsiders. I did not want to compromise the lieutenant rank newly bestowed upon me. My authority was still fragile and subject to question. Papa watched me more closely than he did before my promotion.

Dufort got excited by the feeling of the weapon in his hand. As I had expected, the boy took to the sword. Licking his lips, his nostrils flaring, he would charge at his adversary. A few times I had to shout for him to slow down. After conducting a few of those lessons I started wondering if the relationship between the cleric and his ward was indeed as idyllic and cloudless as I had originally imagined. I had to pull Dufort aside a few times and have a stern talk with him.

"I don't like what I'm seeing, Daniel. You're getting too excited. That's not good."

"Are my movements not precise?"

"They are too precise – and deliberate. You are forgetting that this is only a mock duel."

"But it feels so real."

"See? That's what I'm talking about. If you stab your master on my watch, it will reflect poorly on me. I don't need his blood – or yours on my conscience."

"I'd never harm my master! Besides, his technique is as good as mine. For an old man over thirty, he's rather spry."

"Look, if you want to continue taking lessons from me, you must calm your ardor."

"All right," he resigned with a sigh that could freeze over the Seine. "I'll be good. You're taking the fun out of it."

"That's my job – to spoil your fun. You aren't five years old, and this isn't a wooden stick."

I admit I enjoyed every moment of it, playing a big brother to this clueless red-haired titan who had no idea how to control the immense physical strength bestowed upon him by nature, who was proud, petulant and intense. To my contentment, he listened to me. Up until then the only person whose opinion he respected was Desmoulins.

Whether I liked it or not, my fraternal attachment to Dufort grew with each lesson. Although my position as a soldier precluded me from engaging in a heartfelt dialogue with a civilian, especially one closely linked to the church, I often talked to him in my head, saying things I would never say out loud. The boys at the garrison were mere comrades, but this one I could call a friend.

I thought of the bizarre circumstances of our first encounter and my initial hostility towards him, his numerous acts of kindness I had interpreted as insults, from his offer to teach me how to draw demons to the depressing hymn he had written for my wedding. Looking back, I realized that those were the most sincere tokens of amicability anyone had offered me. I could not help but juxtapose the two of us. I was six foot tall and blond. He was six and a half and red. I had muscle, and he had wings. My origin was aristocratic, and his undisclosed. I was a Roman god, and he a Gothic angel. Both foreigners in this world, we were trying hard to make the best of our earthly experience.

After getting to know him better, I no longer wanted to trade places with him. You probably will not believe this, but I did pray for him to find his happiness – well, his version of it, which probably revolved around depressing music and monogamous love. It was too late for me. I hope those fencing lessons were not for naught. Perhaps, they would help him attract that nebulous woman he was waiting for, that enigmatic brunette who lurked in his dreams?

Four years went by. In that time I had risen to the rank of a captain and become a father to two girls, Marie and Amelie. Papa kept wrinkling his nose, stating it was unacceptable that I did not have a son. I must have been doing something wrong between the sheets to keep missing the mark.

"You need to work harder to produce that long-awaited Castelmaure boy," he would say to me. "It only took me one try to make you. You may not have turned out exactly as I had hoped, but at least I did not have a string of girls to drain my finances."

Personally, I did not care about the sex of my children – or their very existence. I did the polite thing and sent a fruit basket to Juliette. The first time I held my firstborn, she vomited all over my uniform. I took it as a bad omen and handed her back to the nurse. The young mother was in bed, with her face turned to the wall, pretending to be asleep or dead, which made my visit all the less awkward. There was really no need for us to talk. So when she gave birth to our second daughter, I did not show up at all. They were all doing just fine without me. What would I bring except for the stench of urban brothels? If I were to have a male heir, it would probably not be with Juliette anyway. According to the house lackey, she was not looking too healthy. The nasty lung disease plaguing the Poiron family had finally taken hold of her. It was not just her mother's imaginings. Juliette really was sweating through her bedsheets and coughing up blood. I had no desire to see that. I had my own problems.

It started with vague discomfort in the groin. Not pain or burning, per se, just disquieting tension that could not be relieved by emptying the bladder or copulating. Maybe I had been spending too much time sitting in the saddle? No, not more than usual. Then I noticed lumps on my inner thighs. They felt tender when I pressed on them, the pain echoing in my lower abdomen. It hurt to talk and swallow, even though I had no other symptoms of a cold. My throat itched and rattled. Similar lumps started forming around my neck, under my chin, behind the ears. The vice around my head grew tighter with each passing day. I caught myself removing my helmet during the day to give my wretched head a chance to breathe.

Like a wounded animal, I tried to hide my illness from the rest of the pack – and from myself, most importantly. When my solders and I went out to taverns after service, I drank a lot but did not grope any wenches. I had a perfect excuse: now that I was a father to two girls, I was obliged to behave in a more dignified manner. Somehow my comrades did not find that excuse convincing. I buried my gaze at the bottom of my wine cup to avoid seeing their crooked sneers and raised eyebrows. I desperately needed a new circle of friends who were not familiar with my past carousing habits.

Two people I could not bring myself to see were my friends at Notre-Dame. I avoided the parts of the island where I could run into them. One time Dufort's keen eyes spotted me as I was passing through Rue de Parvis. He ran out of the cathedral, jumped in front of me, grabbed my horse by the reins and asked me when our next fencing lesson would be. I replied, rather rudely, that I had already taught him everything I could, and there was no need to continue. He looked more puzzled than offended. And then he asked that dreadful question.

"Are you all right, Lucius? You don't look too good."

"Of course, I'm all right."

"My master says you haven't come to mass in several weeks."

"Notre-Dame is not the only place in Paris to receive communion. I'm busy, that's all. Now that I'm a captain, I have no time to play war with an old man and a boy. Now, if you'd excuse me." I spurred my mare and galloped away, my heart and stomach in knots.

Why did I utter those harsh words? Because I had to. Our friendship could not continue. What kind of sympathy could I expect from the Stone Prince, the sheltered virgin basking in delusions about eternal monogamous love? His blood was not polluted by disease and his memory by a multitude of awkward, sweaty, messy encounters with whores.

It was unexpected horror when I found my mare dead on the pavement in the wee hours of the morning. She had looked fine the night before when I had tied her up outside the tavern. It was as if someone had poisoned her. All I could do was lie down next to her, wrap my arms around her stiff neck and bawl. A few of my comrades came out, separated me from my dead mare, removed the saddle and the harness, then dragged away the carcass, leaving me on the steps of the tavern. A few more hours passed in pitiful, drooling delirium. At daybreak I heard an eerily benevolent, subtly accented voice above my head.

"Pray, Monsieur, what makes you weep on this glorious morning?"

I opened my inflamed eyes and beheld a man in his mid-forties, with curly black hair, a scarf around his neck and a small gold hoop in his right ear. Standing by his side was a youngster around eighteen, presumably his son, as he appeared to be a darker, more fidgety version of the man.

Why was I crying? Because my father despised me. Because I had never known true love. Because I felt nothing for my wife and children. Because I had just pushed away my only friend. Because curses, blessings, insults, compliments and oaths were just words, and words had no meaning. *Mon Dieu*, there were so many philosophical reasons.

"My horse died," I said out loud.

The man patted me on the shoulder and introduced himself as Mathias Eliade, a native of Wallachia, and presented me with a black Andalusian stallion. A part of me was reluctant to accept the gift. I feared the man was an agent of hell, offering me some sort of satanic barter. Did he want my pathetic sniffling soul? To my relief, Eliade's terms were perfectly reasonable. In exchange for the new horse I would take his son Sebastien under my wing and help fulfill his dream of becoming a soldier. The youngster looked good-natured and trainable. I had seen enough recruits in my life to be able to judge from the first impression.

When I mounted that stallion for the first time and galloped up and down the sleepy street a few times, I started thinking that, perhaps God had not turned away from me entirely and was ready to drizzle His benevolence on me again. The ride was so light and smooth that my long-suffering groin did not throb. For a moment it felt as if the clouds above my head started parting.

I knew what I had to do. I had to find Dufort and patch things up with him before too much time elapsed since our last conversation and his resentment set in. When I crossed the threshold of his cell in the north tower, the painted monsters on the walls greeted me with their gaping jaws like they would a prodigal old friend. The ugly one-eyed cat sniffed my boots and hissed.

"Is it too late to take my words back?" I said. "Let's pretend yesterday's encounter did not happen. It's … it's all piling up. The promotion, the birth of my second child. My body is a mess, and so is my brain. There are so many things you don't know."

"Save your secrets for my master," he replied. "I really don't need to know them. I have my own."

I took off my doublet, pulled up my shirt and showed him the scars on my back. In turn he rolled up his sleeve and showed me the fresh gashes on his forearms. Without a word to each other, we embraced. I did not care that I reeked of sweat and disease. Once again, my bones cracked in his grip.

"I was sincere about one thing," I said. "There isn't much more I can teach you. You've already mastered the key techniques. You'll need a new fencing instructor."

Dufort shrugged with a mixture of regret and relief. "I see no purpose in it. I cannot carry a sword at any rate. I'm not a nobleman or a soldier. It was just for fun. But you were right. We should stop those games. They border on mockery. Besides, my master is getting old and sluggish. It's not safe for us to play duel anymore."

I sensed that something had transpired between him and Desmoulins, a rift of some sort. Not that I found it shocking. One would have expected a conflict. Desmoulins came across as a very despotic man, and his ward was just coming into his own. Dufort was bound to rebel. I only wish I had the courage to rebel against Papa Castelmaure.

"Have you heard about Urban Gladiators?" I asked him.

"What about them?" He sneered spitefully. "Just a bunch of ruffians throwing rocks at each other. They don't use weapons – not real weapons at any rate."

"Yes, but the rules may change soon. The game is gaining

popularity. It's only a matter of time before nobles form their own league. They'll be lining up to fight the unconquerable Stone Prince."

Dufort's copper eyebrow arched. "What are you insinuating?"

"Nothing!" I punched him in the shoulder. "It was only a joke. Forget about it. I'm just glad we are talking again."

A few days after my reconciliation with Dufort I encountered a pudgy youth who introduced himself as Johannes Métivier, an estranged half-brother of Monseigneur Desmoulins of all people. We were sitting at a tavern on Rue des Bernardins. He looked me in the eye, as if we had been friends for years, and stated in a cool, matter-of-fact voice that he needed a place to stay. There was something sinister about his downbeat sangfroid that made me feel like refusing him shelter was not an option. So I invited him to stay in my room near the Pont Saint-Michel. I also ended up paying for the drinks that night. As soon as Johannes stepped inside my lodging, he nodded approvingly and made himself comfortable on the trunk, the only piece of furniture that could serve as a bed.

"You're very amicable," he observed. "I never forget that. Just as I never forget people who are not amicable. My adoptive mother was always sweet. Her husband? Not so much. Oh well, they are both dead now. That's why I'm here. Good night."

The next morning I woke up to the sound of munching and crunching. My guest had found a few apples and wheat cakes in the pantry as well as a jug of warm beer. I was a little peeved, because I kept those snacks for my female visitors, but I would not dare to show my annoyance.

"Rise and shine," he grunted, his mouth full of moist dough. "I've been thinking. Since you and I get on so well, we should partner in this venture."

"There's ... a venture?"

"Yes, the Gladiators. Don't tell me you haven't heard. I've been organizing the tournaments. The attendance has doubled since I took over. We need armed security. I thought that, perhaps, you and a couple of your fellow archers could keep those unruly ruffians anchored. Your presence alone will suffice. It will also give the movement an air of legitimacy. You want to attract wealthier spectators, don't you? They'll pay handsomely for attendance."

"I ... suppose I do."

"Then we need to have a few men in shining helmets flanking the arena. Of course, you'll get a cut of the profit. It's the least I can do for you after all the kindness you've shown me. I can be very, very generous, as you'll soon discover. I think it was fate, the way we met at that tavern."

Fate. There is nothing like a small man using big words.

In the end, I learned to appreciate the opportunity presented to me by Johannes. Supervising the street brawls helped me forget about my own illness. Watching the men split each other's lips and knocking each other's teeth out distracted me from the painful pressure in my lower abdomen.

But alas, the moment I left the tournament grounds, I was reminded of my predicament and the symptoms were not only physical, but mental as well. Imagine being drowsy and jumpy at the same time. One minute someone would call out my name, and the sound would slip right past my ears. Another minute I would shudder at the sound of a coin dropping. But I really knew I was in deep trouble when I started seeing things.

One night I was drinking on Rue du Mouton in the company of Sebastien, my latest recruit, whose father imported horses from Spain and sold them to my fellow officers. Mathias Eliade, true to his extravagant generosity, was supplying the drinks that night. The fog around my head was thickening, and at first I found the sensation comforting, feeling safe inside that humid grey cloud. Then I saw *her*, the fantasy girl whose image Desmoulins had planted into my head, the ambiguously Romanic nymph with black hair and heavy earrings. I do not remember whether her dress was red or blue, or if she was wearing much clothes at all. She stepped out of the fog with her arms outstretched, and enthroned herself on my knee.

"How do you like your horse, Captain?" she asked in the same faint, untraceable accent that the entire Eliade family had. "I hope Achilles is serving you well."

No, it was not a dream. The nymph was a real flesh and blood female with a name – Agniese. Her brown skin smelled of camphor and lavender. She writhed in my lap, running her fingers through my hair, and all I could do was drool over her clavicles. Only a few months ago I would be unlacing her bodice and pulling off her chemisette, but now all my amorous feats came down to drenching her apparel with my saliva and tears, for in my present state I could not do with her the very thing I had done with hundreds of women that came before.

At some point I asked her to touch my sword. It was the only remaining symbol of my manhood. I could not bring myself to kiss her properly; I knew if I touched her lips with mine, it would send a jolt of pain down my groin, so I limited my caresses to huffing and nuzzling. Of course, she took it as a sign of chivalry and gallantry. She probably got the idea that I regarded her as something exceptional and precious.

And indeed, I sensed that somehow she was different from my previous whores, a few notches above, perhaps. Her mother, Denise, told me later that Agniese was a virgin, and they, meaning the whole family, were saving her chastity for some high-ranking cleric. I wondered if the lucky rake was Monseigneur Desmoulins. I had seen him in the company of Mathias Eliade and knew his weakness for those feral, willowy darkies. But whom did the girl herself prefer? I had trouble imagining that she would willingly give herself to that. Never mind. I should not be slandering the man who had listened to so many of my confessions and who had taken so many fencing lessons from me. Desmoulins was fairly well preserved for his age. But would a girl of sixteen or seventeen want to spend her last moments as a virgin in the arms of that morose, silver-haired libertine? You tell me. What did I know about Agniese's tastes?

Still, I liked the idea of calling her mine, even though I was not able to do much about it. As long as nobody else possessed her, I could say that she belonged to me. All women in Paris were mine by default – unless they chose otherwise, which they seldom did. But how much longer would she remain a virgin?

I found out that she was also ill, and the progressive ailment of the lungs was called "white death" because it drained the patient's face of color. Agniese had a naturally dark skin tone, so her complexion turned olive. Still, the illness did not diminish her appeal. If anything, it added a touch of tragedy and elusiveness to her image. She still tried to dance, sing Catalan romances, tell Wallachian tales of horror and braid her sister's white hair.

I began catching myself having uncharacteristic urges. I wanted to do more than just throw her on the bench, pull up her skirt and do what I had done to so many other women. No, I wanted to put her into the saddle in front of me and ride with her slowly through the night, inhaling the camphor scent of her hair. What was happening to me? Was my own disease playing tricks on my instincts? Where were all of these chivalrous ideas coming from? Could I say that, for the first time, I was in love? Mother of God, Our Lady of Paris … if only you would cure me and restore my manly functions, I swear I would never touch another whore as long as I live. From that blessed point on I would only sleep with two women: my lawful wife and the Eliade girl. And once Juliette died, it would only be Agniese. For once, I would settle into that tender, courtly monogamy.

I felt like a fool pleading such a bargain with Heaven. I knew such a miracle would never be granted to a sullied man like me. The higher powers were fair in their austerity towards me. I felt the full sting of God's wrath when I finally saw Agniese in the arms of another man.

He had her pressed against the wall of a brick house on Rue du Mouton. To make matters worse, he was wearing my helmet! Still, the most humiliating surprise was yet to follow. When my men were done battering the bastard, I removed the helmet and beheld the face of my dearest friend, Daniel Dufort. I do not know what prevented me from killing him right there and then. I could have gotten away with it, too. I could have said that we caught him trying to molest a woman and had to resort to forceful measures. My men would have testified to that. I do not know what stopped me. Perhaps, it was the look in Agniese's eyes suggesting that she already made her choice. She did not mind being groped by that bony giant. The way she stroked his hair, the way she blotted the blood off his face hinted to a mutual attraction. So I did the agonizingly responsible thing and left the two virgins to work out the details of their first consummation. I suppose, that is what they call the highest, most transcendent form of Christian charity, when you put the happiness of others above your own. Believe it or not, I had never tried that before. My illness was forcing me to explore those other forms of love.

A week went by since the skirmish on Rue du Mouton, a week filled with contemplative prayer and self-righteous grins. I basked in my new role as the mercy-bestowing martyr. I felt my soul peeling off of my ailing body, seeping through the pores along with the sweat, soaring above the tiled roofs of the city. It was the most intoxicating feeling that even the strongest spirits in the tavern could not give me. With each excursion my soul wandered farther and farther from my body, but it came back every time. That return to earth was always abrupt, rude, suffocating and depressing. I still had a company of archers to supervise and a family to feed.

One night I was approached by Fabrice Bertrand, one of my comrades.

"It pains me to be the one to break the news to you, but … you'll be getting summoned soon. Our superiors are gearing up for a hearing. Your future is being determined."

"They've already demoted me," I slurred with a shrug. "I'm a lieutenant now, even though my men continue addressing me as Captain."

"It's only the beginning, I'm afraid. They are talking of harsher disciplinary actions."

"What the deuce have I done this time?" Honestly, I could not remember all my transgressions. I seized the boy by the breast of his doublet. "Tell me, Bertrand! I no longer trust myself to keep a record of all my crimes. Tell me, what do those inflated peacocks have against me?"

"For one, your part in that brawl epidemic," he replied, freeing himself from my grip. "They say you are contributing to the moral decay of the populace by rewarding violence with cheap spirits. Those are their words, not mine. I've been to a few gladiator tournaments as a spectator."

How could I explain to my commanders that the whole purpose of Urban Gladiators was to reduce street crime by providing men from all walks of life an outlet for rage? Had they not fantasized about impaling each other? Those street fights were a necessary evil, just like the brothels.

"Half of the company has been to the tournaments," I reasoned. "It cannot be the only reason why they are targeting me. There has to be more."

"You are also accused of instigating an assault on a holy man, the prodigy organist from the cathedral. They say you battered and injured him and threatened to have him pilloried. Do you remember anything of the sort?"

Did I remember that night on Rue du Mouton? Vaguely. I do not remember giving any orders to assault the organist. Not that my companions required explicit orders. I wondered who took the burden of reporting me. I could not for the life of me see Dufort tattling on me to his master and the bishop. He was capable of many things, as I had discovered that night, but not of downright betrayal. Was it one of the archers in my command?

"That holy man, as you say, was about to molest a woman," I countered, "one I happen to love. I suppose that part got omitted? He's one of the most brutal gladiators in the city. He had already fought everyone in Paris. He was expecting a team of fighters to arrive from Reims."

"Good luck explaining that during your court martial." Bertrand clapped me on the side of my neck, anxious to end the conversation. "Forgive me for ruining your merriment. At the same time, I did not want you to get caught unaware. I do not know when they will summon you. Hopefully you'll have enough time to prepare for self-defense."

Even in my intoxicated state, I sensed Bertrand's joy. He took great pleasure letting me in on the secret. Or was what he had told me all a lie,? Perhaps, his goal was only to aggravate me. As much as he pretended to be my friend, I knew that he had his sights set on my position. He was not one of the men who accompanied me on the night of the skirmish.

When I returned to my lodging that night, the old hag, my landlady, met me in the hall and handed me a folded note.

"A man from Gonesse came to see you," she said, shaking her grey head reproachfully. "He claimed to be your servant. Now, officer, if you can afford a servant and another home, why can't you pay rent on time?"

Remembering my pledge to my mother, I gave the ugly witch the most courteous smile I could produce in my state.

"Sophie, *ma belle*, allow me to explain a few things. That humble soul who came by has been serving my family for decades. He works for food. You shall have your rent money by the end of the week."

"I'll hold you to your word, officer."

Once inside my room, I lit a candle and opened the note, expecting it to be a reminder to send money home. In light of my recent demotion, I had been lax about feeding my nominal family in Gonesse. I comforted myself with the thought that the Poirons lived close enough and could step in if Juliette ran out of provision. They could not just let her starve.

The content of the note took me by surprise. I had to reread it several times. It conveyed the news of my youngest daughter's sudden demise. She fell asleep in her crib and never woke up. Well, that was quick. Who would have thought? My sweet Amelie … God, those words sounded so hypocritical. I was fairly sure she was mine, based on the physical description provided by the lackey. Juliette was not the straying kind. I had a hard time imagining her bedding another man, even if only to punish me for my absence. Yes, I could say with reasonable assurance "My Amelie." But, having never actually seen the girl with my own eyes, I had no idea whether or not she was sweet. Maybe she was a whirlwind of screams and vomit like her big sister. Now I would never find out. One thing I could do for her was light a candle for her soul. I did not even know yet if she was baptized. I imagine, Juliette had seen to that. At least, that was my hope.

I put on my night cloak and ran to the cathedral. Monseigneur Desmoulins was standing on the balcony. He already knew what had happened to my daughter. The lackey had taken great pains to make sure I got the news one way or another, so he had already requested a mass for Amelie.

"You should go to the funeral," he said, opening a box with candles. "I'm sure your commander will understand and give you a leave."

"No," I replied. "I'm not going back to my family. I don't want to see their faces, and I'm sure they don't want to see mine."

The fragile internal rod that has been keeping me up for the past few months suddenly crumpled. I collapsed in front of Desmoulins, clutching at his cassock. I remembered my own words, muddled sobs, though they sounded as if they were coming from someone else's mouth.

"I'm beyond redemption, Monseigneur. I've broken too many rules. Nothing can save me from court martial, only death. Sometimes I wish I would just get ambushed in a dark alley and stabbed. That would put an end to my vice, to my humiliation."

"Now that's a thought," Desmoulins replied as he placed his hand on my head. "To die – how convenient."

I stopped sobbing. "That was a figure of speech. I'm not ready to commit suicide. I haven't turned away from God entirely."

"Nobody says you have to die for real. But, perhaps, with a few theatrical tricks and optical illusions, we can convince your superiors that Lucius Castelmaure died. Of course, you won't be remembered as a hero. Your name will be forgotten. At least there won't be any scandals attached to it."

I confess I was intrigued. He made it sound so easy. "My superiors will want to see a body."

"They'll see it; no worries," he said, helping me up to my feet. "I can help you stage a convincing scene. I'll also help you get out of the city unnoticed. I'll even give you fake papers. You'll be able to start a new life anywhere you wish. One thing I cannot give you is common sense. My only condition – apart from you never murmuring a word about this pact of ours – is that you never speak to Agniese again. You will be as dead to her as you will to the rest of your family."

A few seconds elapsed before I could bring myself to agree to his terms. I had already relinquished Agniese to Dufort, but being forced to make that promise to Desmoulins added a new touch of finality to my ill-timed would-be love.

"I suppose, there are other girls like her," I reasoned reluctantly.

"That's the spirit, Captain. Now, it will only hurt a little bit. Just a pinch. A deep, hot pinch."

I recoiled from him. "Wait ... why will there be pinching?"

"You didn't expect to get out of this mess without a bit of bloodshed? We need a wound to show to your commanders. Now don't worry. I know a thing or two about medicine. I know the safe places on the human body. Come, Captain. Let the farce begin."

I let him stab me. Yes, you heard me correctly. I allowed my confessor, my fencing pupil to jab a knife into my back. I had a strong feeling before I agreed to allow him to that Desmoulins was not too preoccupied with my well-being. It was never about my reputation or my liberation, but about protecting his own shady interests. He wanted me out of the way so he could ravish the Eliade girl. But you know what? I no longer gave a damn.

I was becoming accustomed to having other people drag me into their schemes. First Juliette dragged me into marriage. Then Johannes dragged me into the Gladiator movement. It only made sense to let Desmoulins make me a pawn in his game as well. What else was I good for? So I bit into a block of wood, as he told me, turned my face to the wall and started counting to ten. *Un, deux, trois ...*

Then came that "deep, burning pinch" Desmoulins had described to me. Horns and thunder! As much I liked to think of myself as someone seasoned against pain, I was not prepared for the feeling of the knife slicing through my muscles. All those lashings at the garrison had not prepared me for this. I came close to losing consciousness. The wooden block fell out of my mouth, followed by a stream of vomit. My tormentor had to give me his shoulder to lean on and help me to my bed. All of this was happening at my lodging which we had entered through the back door to avoid an encounter with my landlady.

When I regained my consciousness, I was all alone in the dark, with a burning pain in my shoulder and a rancid aftertaste in my mouth. Vomit mixed with blood. Pray tell me, why the hell was I tasting blood? I thought my grim liberator said he was not going to touch any of the vital organs. Why did I have a bad feeling that the knife had grazed my lung? Well, I guess it was too late to protest. Now my job was to lie perfectly still and hope I did not die for real. Desmoulins promised to come back later in the day and bring some witnesses with him, so my staged demise could be documented. That man had thought of everything, including a few theatrical effects to make the scene more convincing. He created a puddle of blood behind the trunk. Much of it came from an old sickly pigeon that used to hide under the porch of the house. Desmoulins did not think twice about wringing the poor bird's neck. In his mind, it was a mercy killing. God knows how many rats he had sliced in the name of science.

So I lay there with my eyes closed as night turned to early morning. I felt the first rays of light tickling my eyelids. Was it the last sunrise of my life? If it was, I would spend it with my eyes closed.

I spent a few more hours, drifting in and out of sleep. Then I heard the door creak, followed by the pitter-patter of feet. The person who walked into the room was not Desmoulins. Then I heard the familiar melodic voice that made my heart jump.

"Lucius, thank God I found you."

It was the Eliade girl. Damnation! Her surprise visit was not a part of the plot, was it? Agniese tiptoed towards the trunk and took my hand. I guess she did not see the puddle of blood on the floor. Caressing my fingers she chirped and sighed and professed her love for me. Do not ask me what it took me to play dead, or near dead, when the only girl for whose sake I was willing to reform myself and give up whores, was calling me her hero and offering her virginity to me. You think getting stabbed was torture?

Blessedly, Desmoulins cut my torment short. He came in with his Bible and a flask of holy water, scolded Agniese for intruding on the last rites and treated her to a brutal kiss prior to handing her over to the soldiers and ordering them to remove her.

I heard my men scuffling around the room, whispering and grunting. I heard Desmoulins explain the situation to them.

"I found him bleeding in the middle of the night on the corner of the bridge. I did not know where else to bring him. He was bleeding profusely and I did what I could to patch up the wound, but it was so deep, as you can see from the puddle on the floor."

Fabrice Bertrand, my nemesis, was in the group.

"They can still try him, right?" he asked. "As long as he's still breathing, we can transport him into the barracks, right?"

"You'll do no such thing," Desmoulins interrupted him. "You'll let your unfortunate comrade die in peace. I don't expect him to last another thirty minutes. Gentlemen, Lieutenant Castelmaure has expressed a desire to be buried next to his infant daughter, who died a few days ago. He does not want anyone present at his bedside except for family. I hope I can count on you to respect his wishes and not make a spectacle of his death. This is your opportunity to say goodbye to him. I also trust you not to ruminate about his character."

One by one, my former comrades came by my deathbed and touched my hands that were convincingly cold and limp. Before long the room was empty. After making sure we were alone, Desmoulins snapped his fingers in front of my nose.

"You can open your eyes now. Sit up, stretch your limbs, empty your bladder if you need to. Then you'll be back to playing dead. The undertakers are coming in an hour. I want the world to see you taken out of this room in a casket. You'll ride out of the city feet first."

The situation was so ridiculous and bizarre that I came close to laughing. The scorching pain in my shoulder dampened my merriment.

"You surely are a man of your word, Monseigneur," I muttered hoarsely, my throat swollen and parched. "You did a thorough job hacking me up."

"Don't pretend like you're in agony. It's just a deep scratch. I didn't carve you up too badly."

He proceeded to wrap me in a sheet. By the time the undertakers showed up, I was completely covered. They did not see my face. It was hard not to wiggle with pain when they lifted me from the trunk, rather unceremoniously dumped me into the wooden box and loaded it onto a cart. The ride to the papal gates was long and bumpy. Every boulder on the pavement, and every pothole in the road sent a jolt of pain through my back. I winced and twitched inside the box, laughing internally at the absurdity of it. Desmoulins was riding next to me, singing a psalm to conceal any groans that might have been heard through the box.

Once we were outside the city walls, Desmoulins asked the driver to stop.

"We're here now. I've made arrangements with his relations to claim his body at this site. They'll take it from here."

The undertakers took the coffin off the cart and placed it on the ground. When the squeaking of the wheels abated, Desmoulins lifted the wooden lid and moved the folds of the sheet away.

"Congratulations, Captain. The mission was a success. You're a free man."

I opened my eyes and struggled into a sitting position. We were near what looked like an abandoned house with knocked-out windows and a crooked roof.

"You must be overwhelmed by all of this luxury," Desmoulins said, dragging me inside, "but to be fair, the ratty hovel you left behind in Paris was not much better. I wouldn't recommend staying here through the winter, but it's an acceptable place to convalesce. You'll find some food and water on the table. I also left you some money under the floorboards. Oh, and the documents! Your new name is Gerard Lemarchal. You are twenty-six years old, and you're a textile merchant."

"So this is it?" I asked, sprawling on my stomach and hugging a dirty pillow. "Is this where our paths separate?"

"Not yet, but soon, hopefully. I'll come by in a few days to check on you. If I find the house empty, it will fill my heart with joy. I'll assume that you're back on your feet and on your way someplace else."

Before leaving, he examined the wound once more,

insisting that it was not nearly as grave as I imagined it to be, and concluded it was a good thing that I was not continuing a soldier's career. I was too fragile, susceptible and skittish, and my frailties were bound to come out sooner or later. He walked out of the house before I could come back with any argument in self-defense. I knew he was right.

The basket with provisions left by my grim accomplice contained a loaf of bread, a slice of stringy smoked meat, some dry fruit and a small bottle of white wine. It was supposed to last me three days. Under normal circumstances I would have devoured it all in one sitting, but the aftertaste of blood in my mouth still triggered nausea. Left alone once again, listening to the whistling sound emerging from my chest, I could finally ponder what I had done.

Thankfully, Papa Castelmaure was away on business, training and reviewing a company in Amiens, which meant that the news of my alleged death would not reach him for a while. Would he go looking for my grave? Most importantly, would Juliette? I recalled Desmoulins saying that I wanted to be buried in Gonesse next to my daughter. It was logical to assume that Papa would head there. It would be a most awkward encounter between him and Juliette. They would realize very quickly that my death was a hoax. Would they give up on me and cross me out of their lives, or would they make it their mission to track me down and bring me to justice? Pondering all those possibilities was overwhelming. Desmoulins had kept his promise by getting me out of the city. It was up to me to figure out the rest.

For the first time in my life, I was the master of my fate. I strained my brain, trying to imagine my life without a routine, without orders, without obligations, and the new picture, to be perfectly candid, terrified me. Instead of the brilliant blue skies I saw a black hole.

What's wrong with you, Lucius? Is this not what you wanted? Oh, wait. You aren't even Lucius anymore. Your new name is Gerard. Get used to it.

There I was, a wounded beast, raised in captivity, suddenly

released into the wild. Despite having no appetite, I broke off a piece of the bread loaf and stuffed it behind my cheek. The sky was dimming. My comrades were probably heading into a tavern around this time. Dufort was preparing for the evening mass, rearranging his music sheets. Johannes was probably trying to clean up the puddle of pigeon's blood. And the Eliades? How would Sebastien react to the news? He must have heard it by now from his sister.

Most of all I missed my stallion Achilles. How perplexed and abandoned he must have felt without me. In whose hands would he fall now? Fabrice Bertrand must have snatched him up. Ah, such was the price of freedom!

After three days of idleness, stewing in my own doubts and regrets, I decided to venture outside of my shelter. Desmoulins had not come by having decided that I no longer needed him, or that I had already mapped out my itinerary and embarked on a journey south. Never mind that I had no means of transportation. So, having eaten the last walnut from the basket, I took the bag containing my fake documents and the coins and started walking back towards the papal gates. There was no place for me to go except back to the city. Perhaps, I could buy some shabby old horse with the money I had. At least I would be mobile.

I took the dark sheet that had served as my makeshift burial shroud and wrapped it around my shoulders to make it look like a cape. It covered my uniform, making me look and feel like a beggar. Nobody would recognize the former Captain Castelmaure.

At dusk I hobbled through the gate. After three days of absence, Paris felt foreign. It did not welcome back a prodigal son, but rather, was rejecting a traitor. I did not make it very far into the city because soon after passing through the gate I felt dizzy and had to lean against one of the buildings.

I heard the clopping of hooves, which made my heart leap. A sound so sonorous and so noble could only be produced by my trusty Achilles. And indeed, I saw the familiar silhouette of my stallion. The rider was wearing a Florentine hunting suit and I recognized Desmoulins at once. I rose to my feet and waved my arms to catch his attention.

"Alms for the poor!" I groaned, imitating a beggar.

He dismounted in haste and approached me, dragging Achilles by the reins. The stallion sensed my presence and let out a jubilant neigh.

"What the deuce are you doing?" Desmoulins asked me through his teeth. "Do you not realize the danger you're putting yourself in?"

"I got bored. You told me I was free to leave the old shack."

"Not to come back to the city, you idiot! If you don't stop this foolishness, I'll kill you for real."

"That won't take much effort."

"I was on my way to see you and reunite you with your horse. Didn't I tell you I'd stop by? Do you have any idea how much effort it took me to reclaim this bloody stallion? I had to make up a sentimental tale of how your surviving daughter wanted something to remember you by, so I arranged to have this horse taken to Gonesse. You realize I've told more lies in the past three days than I have in my sixteen years of priesthood?"

"You really butchered me, Monseigneur."

"Stop making up stories."

"Then why do I keep tasting blood?"

"I don't know. Maybe you bit your tongue. Maybe the ulcer in your stomach opened from all the cheap wine you've been drinking. Believe me, if I had pierced your lung, you wouldn't be standing here right now looking smug. I really don't have time to listen to your complaints. You have no idea what's happening in Paris; what a catastrophe I've been dealing with."

Now I was truly intrigued. "What catastrophe? Did I miss something?"

"Be thankful you aren't involved in it."

"Then who is involved? Someone I know? Please, talk to me."

"There is no point. You are dead. You have no part in this game. Here is your horse. Now get out."

"I cannot."

"What do you mean you cannot?"

"I feel like I'm leaving something unfinished. I want to make myself useful."

"Very well, then. I have a job for you. Go to Gonesse. The Archbishop of Reims has a summer home thereabout. The property is called 'Le lit du lion.' There's a statue of a sleeping lion by the entrance. Give the archbishop a message that the price of gold has gone up. He'll know what that means. Someone he cares about is in grave danger. That's all I shall disclose for now."

I confess it was a long message. I was not confident that I could memorize it, but nevertheless, I was flattered that Desmoulins trusted me with such an important task. It felt good to be riding Achilles again. He huffed and snorted resentfully after three days of being abandoned.

The estate of 'Le lit du lion' sat atop a green hill on the southwestern edge of Gonesse. I had passed it several times while making my obligatory conjugal visits and on several occasions had seen servants scurrying in and out of the house, but never the owner. I had always wondered who lived inside that villa half-hidden by cherry trees. This was my chance to find out.

Having reached the gate, I dismounted and rang the tiny brass bell. A woman in her late twenties wearing a silk chamber robe over her nightdress came to the entrance. "What do you want?" she asked rather curtly, seemingly unimpressed by the sight of my uniform.

"I'd like to see the man who lives here." Much to my embarrassment, the name escaped me. I realized that I looked like a drunken idiot, gripping the bars of the gate. "I have an important message for him from Paris. The price on silver has dropped."

The woman's plump lips puckered spitefully. "You disturb His Excellency at this hour with a ludicrous message like that?"

"It's not ludicrous, believe me. It concerns the well-being of his … of someone whose life he values. Please, Madame, I wouldn't be bothering you at this time if it wasn't important."

A few seconds later an imposingly handsome man around forty, whose features looked vaguely familiar, emerged from the villa. Ignoring my presence, he laid his hands on the woman's shoulders and pulled her away from the bars of the gate.

"Marguerite, my love, what are you doing out of bed?"

"I heard noise outside," she replied. "Some drunk wants to see you. He doesn't know your name, but maintains it's a matter of life and death."

"Well, it is!" I shouted hoarsely. Clearly, I had overestimated my strength. I was in no condition to travel, let alone on horseback. The ride from Paris had left me on the brink of fainting. Still holding onto the bars of the gate, I started slipping down to the ground. "Monseigneur Desmoulins says ... crown diamonds have been stolen. The price of silver dropped, and the price of gold ..."

"The price of gold went up?" the man finished my phrase, his voice trembling with alarm and impatience. "Is that what Desmoulins said?"

"Yes."

I released the bars and collapsed to the ground, my mission fulfilled. I could no longer see the couple, but I heard their voices above my head. I did not expect them to pay attention to the dying messenger.

"Forgive me, my love," the man spoke to his lady. "I must leave you for a while. I'm going to the city."

"At this time of the night?"

"Alas, I have no choice. My boy is in grave danger."

"Which one?"

"The one with red hair."

Marguerite repeated the question with an air of annoyance. "Again, which one? Forgive me for not keeping a record of all your progeny."

"It's my firstborn, the twenty-year old, who plays organ in Paris. I asked his guardian to give me a sign if there was any trouble."

"Your boys are always getting into trouble, so it seems. Every time one of them gets arrested, you run to the rescue. I feel like I'm being punished for not giving you sons. Your daughters have been perfect angels. When one of them elopes with some viscount, maybe then you'll twitch an eyebrow?"

"Don't start, my love. Not now. Go to bed. I promise to bring you something pretty from Paris to atone for my negligence."

"All right," she purred coquettishly. "And bring something for the girls too."

The last thing I heard before passing out was the sound of a long kiss.

The next morning the archbishop's mistress was in a much friendlier disposition. Having let me stay in the guest room overnight, she took the trouble of examining, cleaning and dressing my wound, while her nine-year-old twin daughters watched in quiet fascination.

"The wound isn't deadly," she concluded. "It won't kill you. I'm more concerned about the lumps in your neck."

Feeling suddenly exposed, I covered my neck with my hands. "Oh, those … They've been there for a while."

"You don't need to tell me." Having immobilized my face, she forced me to look her in the eye. "I know what causes them. I've seen them before on other men."

The pressure of her cold fingers felt oddly soothing.

"Where did you learn medicine?" I asked.

"At a convent," she replied casually. "I was a nun some years ago."

"I see …" I thought of my cousin Aurore who was on the same path. "What made you leave? You didn't like the food? I hear they serve the same tasteless mush day after day. Only the mother superior gets to eat delicacies like cheeses and smoked meats."

She patted me on the cheeks and released my face. "I see your sense of humor is intact. It's a good sign."

"Believe me, it's all I have left. Was it the master of this mansion who persuaded you to leave the stone walls?"

"Pierre didn't persuade me. Believe me it takes more than a boastful man to make me walk away from my vows. I did it on my own accord."

"What about his other lady friends? Are they also former nuns?"

"No, they are ordinary nitwits. True, I am not the only one, but I hold most power over Pierre. He always comes back to me.

Why? Because, unlike the rest of them – I wouldn't even call them rivals – I can actually carry a conversation and, God forbid, confront him when he's wrong. I have to set an example for my girls. His first big flame, Elisabeth Dufort, was fairly literate but completely devoid of wisdom and ability to compromise. She took it out on that miserable boy."

"Daniel *is* miserable," I agreed.

"You know him?"

"We were friends, I suppose."

"*Were*? Did you have a falling out?"

"In a way. Not exactly. It's a long story."

"Why do you speak of him in the past tense?"

"Because … because everything pertaining to me is in the past tense now. I'm not supposed to be alive. Everyone thinks I'm dead."

"Including Daniel?"

"Especially Daniel."

"And now he's in serious trouble. Does your wound somehow tie to it?"

"I honestly don't know anymore. There are too many bizarre things happening in Paris. I don't know if they are connected or not. There's some inquisitor in the city. What's his name? It's on everyone's lips now. Adolph … Adelme ... Anselm Viteri, that's right!"

The name must have been familiar to my hostess. She winced and bit her lip. "Pierre is walking into the heart of the storm. That should be an interesting encounter."

I could stay in bed and convalesce for a few more days. The hostess did not seem in a hurry to kick me out, even though she had every reason to resent me. I was the one who had disturbed her idyllic evening with my arrival and caused her lover to leave for Paris. But Marguerite turned out to be an assertive, sober-minded woman. I could see why the Archbishop of Reims was so attached to her. She was more than a fleeting comely diversion to him. We had a few stimulating conversations bordering on arguments, the kind I used to have with Aurore. Marguerite chided me for not seeking help for the cause behind the lumps in my neck and the persistent fever. There were remedies, apparently. I was not the first soldier in Christendom to contract the disease. She made me promise I would see a physician. She claimed many men had been cured by inhaling mercury vapors. Among the lucky patients was Pope Alexander VI himself.

"If you need to get home, I won't keep you here," Marguerite said to me.

"I probably should."

I suddenly realized that I had no home. I could not go back to my dingy hovel in Paris. I would never set my foot inside that city again. Now that I was a dead man and a free man, I could go to Gascony. I could open a tavern or plant a vineyard.

After leaving 'Le lit du lion' I stopped by the house where my estranged, soon–to-be-late wife lived. I could count the number of occasions I had spent a night there. I still did not know the layout of the home, so dragging my feet down the hall, I knocked on random doors.

I heard a gasp behind my back. "Look who's risen from the grave!" My trusty house servant, Giles, was standing in the hallway with a candle. With his free hand he made a sign of the cross. "Master Lucius …"

"I'm not a ghost, Giles. I know I look like one, but my soul is still attached to my flesh, miserly as it is. Please, escort me to my wife. I assume she's still alive?"

The servant nodded. "Yes, Madame Castelmaure is still with us, though she hasn't gotten out of bed since the death of the little mademoiselle."

"And how is my oldest, Marie?"

"She's in good health, thank God. Her maternal grandparents are coming to fetch her tomorrow morning. There's no need for the little one to stay in a house with so much death and sadness. If you'd like to see her, I could wake her for you."

I shook my head. Last time I tried to pick up Marie, she burst into tears. I was a stranger to her. The poor child did not need more aggravation. "Let her sleep. Only young ones can sleep so soundly. I won't stay long. I just want to see her mother for a few minutes."

"Of course …"

Before entering the bedchamber, I straightened out my doublet and smoothed my hair – as if it mattered. A gentleman never appears before his wife disheveled. I knew her condition was grave when I saw the pose she was sleeping in. Instead of lying on her side with her face to the wall, she was sleeping on her back with her hands folded over her chest, as if she had already died. Her cheeks looked hollow and her nose sharp. I walked in and sat down on the side of what was supposed to be our spousal bed.

"Bonsoir, Juliette ..."

Chapter 7

From the Mouth of the Wolf

(Anselm Viteri)

You always faint the first time around. There is no need to be embarrassed or reconsider your decision to join the institution that combats heresy. It is not a sign of weakness but a simple rite of passage. You can read every textbook on interrogation practices. You can even sit in on a trial or stand in the background against the wall in the interrogation chamber and still not feel fully prepared for your first independent proceeding. I certainly remember my first time. Would you like to hear about it? Maybe not before mealtime. I never tire of telling that story, especially when I have a young, wide-eyed novice inquisitor in front of me. When you see him biting his lip, clutching at his cross, hiding his eyes beneath the black hood, you feel that surge of paternal benevolence. You pat him on the shoulder, feeling the muscle tension through the fabric of the mantle, and tell him: "Listen, my son, it will be all right." And it will be. They will hear your voice, but they will not see your eyes.

Sometimes it is not a young man who needs your encouragement. Sometimes it is someone close to your own age. Sometimes it is someone as conspicuous and imposing as Louis de Beaumont de la Forêt, the bishop of Paris. Last time I saw Louis was back in 1475, a few years after he had assumed the position. He looked tired but optimistic. He knew he had quite a task before him, undoing decades of neglect by his predecessor, Guillaume Chartier. I saw that spark of determination in Louis' eyes and said to him, "Keep me informed of your endeavors. If you ever need to talk, do not hesitate to write to me. I don't want you to feel like you're all alone. It's a horrible feeling."

And he was just getting around to taking me up on my offer, after all those years of suffering in silence. Judging from the tone of his last letter I could tell he was overwhelmed with everything that was happening in the vicinity of the cathedral. He could not tighten all the bolts with bare hands. He needed a powerful tool to help him, and that tool was I. How could I refuse? Naturally, I was curious to see the extent of the damage and the neglect in the precinct.

When I finally saw Louis, my heart sank. What had happened to the ambitious, dynamic soldier of Christ I used to know? The abundance of grey in his hair, the wrinkles on his brow, the tremor in his hands. *Mon Dieu!* He did not look thirty-five. Worst of all, the hungry determined spark was gone from his eyes. He looked like a man with a huge chunk of meat lodged in his throat, perplexed as to what to do next, unable to swallow it or cough it up.

"I tried." Those were his first words to me. "Anselm, God be my witness, I tried."

"I know you did, Louis," I said, kissing his ring. "I'm honored that you summoned me."

I brought a bottle of excellent sweet wine. His face lit up when I pulled the cork out, and the sultry aroma of Basque vineyards filled the room.

"It's been so long since I smelled sunlight and freedom," he lamented. "I've been stuck in this wet, rancid city for too long."

"It's your cross to bear, Louis," I said. "You aren't some provincial priest."

"But sometimes I wish I were."

"No, Louis, don't start. I will not indulge your momentary weakness. That's not why I came here. God put you in this position for a reason. You weren't made for quiet provincial life. One day they will be reading about you at the University. You will enter history as the guardian of the ecclesiastic tradition, who managed to keep the infamous reformation at bay."

Two hours later, after the wine was gone, Beaumont was

reclining in his chair, fanning himself with the folio containing the latest canon court case, his sunken cheeks flushed.

"It's always the same two or three men in the precinct who make a bishop's life so difficult," he spoke. "In my case it's Desmoulins. That Flemish-Italian, or whatever he is, has been the thorn in my side since day one. He murmurs something about the right to carry a sword, and the young deacons start parroting him."

"Why does he need a sword?"

"So he can visit his mistress in the slums without endangering his life."

"A mistress? You mean Desmoulins has finally found a woman who corresponds to his lofty standards? I never thought that moment would come."

"I suppose. Maybe he just got desperate. The girl is half his age and dark-skinned. You probably think it's my fault, that I looked the other way and condoned that sort of behavior."

"I think nothing of the sort. You can only do so much."

"I tried to have a candid talk with Desmoulins. I advised him not to flaunt his affair. That darkie really had him bewitched. He took her on a tour of dungeons, including the one right beneath the Palace of Justice. He turned our judicious system into a joke to indulge that hussy."

Brisk, firm footsteps resonated from the hall. A hoarse, melancholic voice was humming a hymn. A few seconds later a red-haired youth stood in the doorway. I assumed it was the infamous organist, the Stone Prince, whose execution warrant, dating back to the 1460s, I still had in my possession. His gaunt face was covered in fading bruises and his left hand wrapped into some dirty rag.

"You called, Your Excellency?"

The bishop nodded and beckoned him with two fingers, as he would a skittish animal. Such delicacy was unnecessary, as the visitor did not look in the least bit disquieted. He stood in the door, six and a half feet of pure arrogance, propping the ceiling with the crown of his head.

"Monsieur Dufort, please come in," Louis said. "There is someone you should meet. I wanted this encounter to happen in closed quarters without additional onlookers. This is Anselm Viteri."

"I've heard about your savagery," the creature replied as he came in and plopped into the vacant chair, his long legs outstretched. "You did a marvelous job cleaning the Basque region of Egyptians and Moors. I think you'll be bored in Paris. There's nothing for you to do here. Not enough pagans or heretics. I assume, for you it's a pleasure trip."

Having paid his initial respects to me, Dufort started pulling loose threads out of his doublet. The fabric was an exquisite silver-blue color that emphasized the pallor of his skin and the red of his hair. Louis gave me his exasperated I-told-you-so look.

"What happened to you?" I asked, gesturing at his hand.

"It's a long story."

"I have time."

"But I do not." He pulled up his legs and assumed a more composed attitude. "I need to be somewhere."

"It's all right," I said, "I won't keep you. Give me the condensed version of the story. Rather, let me guess: it has something to do with the Urban Gladiators? The bishop has told me about your involvement with them."

"Actually, my injuries have nothing to do with the Gladiators. I got into a fight over a woman."

"Why, this is the most amusing yarn I've heard all week. And the bishop and I have traded quite a few."

The flippant smirk on Dufort's face turned into a feral grin. "Would I joke in front of someone like you?"

"Are you afraid of me?"

"I have no reason to be. The Inquisition cannot touch me. I feel perfectly at ease in your presence. That is why I tell the truth. I'm in love with a woman who happens to be in demand. Sometimes we must settle such disputes physically."

Judging from his twitching foot, he was anxious to go. Still, I was not ready to release him just yet.

"So who won the fight?" I asked. "Who has the lady's heart?"

Dufort had to think for a few moments before answering. Pensively, he ran his fingers over his mouth, as if trying to recreate the sensations from a kiss.

"It's hard to tell. I don't have much experience in these matters. Nevertheless, I am staying optimistic. She volunteered to wipe the blood off my face and bandage my wrist. Of course, this could have been an act of Christian kindness, nothing more."

"This mysterious damsel, is she pretty?"

"I am tempted to say 'yes,' but ultimately, it's a matter of taste. I have no idea what kind of women you like. If you are fond of frail brunettes, then yes, she is positively ravishing. If you prefer buxom blondes with poppy-red cheeks and cornflower eyes, then she is not your goddess. Does this answer your question?"

"More than adequately. I do hope this is not our last conversation, Monsieur Dufort."

Louis gave me another one of his plaintive see-what-I-must-endure looks and proceeded to massage his temples. "You're free to go," he muttered, shooing the organist away. "We expect your presence at supper tonight. Same goes for your master. I won't hear any more excuses of him visiting the sick."

"One more thing, Your Excellency. If you see Polyphemus, please let me know."

The bishop pulled his fingers away from his temples. "Polyphemus …"

"Yes, my cat. Well, he's not just mine. Polyphemus belongs to the precinct. He's been missing for days, and I have a bad feeling he is already purring in the lap of St. Thomas Aquinas. I'm trying to be philosophical about it. He was quite old, with foggy eyes and loosening teeth. If he is dead, we'll need to replace him. You don't want the cathedral and the cloister to become overrun by mice."

He clawed the air, imitating his pet, then leaped out of the chair and left the room, leaving behind the faint smell of frankincense.

"What do you think?" Louis asked me when the creature was out of earshot. "I asked him to stop by so you could observe him and give me your expert opinion. Is he truly a demon?"

"Absolutely." I knew Louis did not want to hear it, but I felt obliged to be candid. "That child should have been burned fifteen years ago."

Louis winced and pulled his head into his shoulders, waiting for my next blow to crash upon him. "So you think it's wrong that I tolerate his presence here? Even though he brings so much money to the treasury. His music is in such high demand."

"I have no doubt about it. Vice is always in demand."

Just because Louis and I were friends, I was not going to make it easy for him. As a friend, I had to be brutally honest with him. "Demons were also angels at some point. I must say, Dufort is quite striking in a way that challenges established standards of beauty. Everything in him is designed to mock what godly people consider to be righteous and good. Long flaming hair! If he had any modesty, he would crop it short and keep it covered beneath the hood. And his height! He doesn't seem ashamed of it one bit. He has no qualms about towering over bishops. He could have at least bowed his head. Obviously, nobody's taught him to lower his eyes or moderate his tone of voice before his superiors."

"It's Desmoulins' upbringing," Louis lamented. "He's the one who nurtured that creature, pampered his arrogance. There must be some diabolic pact between those two. They control the precinct. Desmoulins corrupts the young clerics by feeding them dangerous ideas, and Dufort entices the faithful with his infernal music.

"I also believe that they share a mistress; fornicate with the same witch, that dusky girl from the Dracul dynasty, who has raven claws instead of fingers. Her hair moves like a swarm of snakes. She's also a part of the pact. She inspires Dufort's music. Or, perhaps, I'm just exhausted and imagining things. This is why I needed your judgment, for I can no longer trust my own."

The bishop looked so helpless and bereft of pride that I felt a little embarrassed for him and for the entire church. Thank God there were no onlookers. I hoped that Louis did not display weakness before others. That would wreck whatever was left of his authority.

"I would like to hear Dufort play," I said. "Then I will give you my final verdict. And then you must decide what to do with him."

"What can I do? He's inviolable."

"In the ecclesiastic court, maybe, but not in the civil court. If sufficiently determined, I'm sure we can scrape up enough evidence against him to build a civil case. The boy is unruly and violent."

A few days after my arrival in Paris we received a piquant report from the University. One of the newest lecturers at the college of Lisieux, a certain astronomer named Adrian Satigny, had been accused of possessing a heretical book. La Fausse Révélation of all titles! It was the assistant librarian who denounced him, the humorless Julien Morel who broke out in hives at the very mention of the printed press or the notion that the earth was round. It was refreshing to see such a young man so fervently devoted to the old ideas. He was working against the tide sweeping his generation. For that alone he deserved a bottle of my sweet Basque wine. I had an entire case sitting in my guest room at the cloister. Poor Morel nearly fainted when I presented the gift to him. I had to assure him it was not a reward or a bribe but a mere token of appreciation. Although, I did like the fact that he felt so uneasy accepting gifts. It proved that his motives were pure. An inquisitor could use more men like him.

"Louis, this is your chance to shine," I said to the bishop, after Morel had left, "your chance to reassert your authority. Now, I want you to be in the frontline, not hiding behind my mantle. You'll work hand-in-hand with the ecclesiastic procurator."

I gave Louis a few moments to panic and hyperventilate. After all, he had not handled such a visible heresy case. He was about to confront his own fear of blood and scandal, to overcome his own squeamishness and skittishness.

"I shall put my foot down," he said, once his breathing normalized. "No more hand-wringing in the sacristy. I'll make you proud, Anselm."

Within a few hours of the report, Satigny was in custody. The arrest took place in broad daylight. The guards burst into the classroom in the middle of the lecture and seized the offender. The dramatic scene, no doubt, imbued the hearts of the scholars with terror, for they all were very fond of Satigny based on what I had heard; the man had managed to endear himself to everyone who came in contact with him. In addition to being erudite and eloquent, he was exceptionally handsome, one of the best looking heretics I have had the privilege of interrogating. I shuddered at the realization that very soon there would be nothing left of that beauty and eloquence. Before sunset this boastful and charismatic man, who thought himself above God's law, would be reduced to a mumbling, sniffling mass of broken bones and scorched skin.

Once Satigny was in my hands, I made sure to be stern yet courteous, never forgetting his academic accomplishments. All in all, I thought our dungeon conversation was productive. The condemned became very talkative before I needed to use any of the more intricate contraptions. A sheltered bookworm, he was not hardened against pain one bit. The very sight of the torturer's red hot iron was enough to make him talk. I asked him for names of his accomplices who helped him procure and distribute heretical books. Perhaps, some of his astronomy scholars had similar interests?

He begged me not to touch any of the Lisieux boys. They were all innocent. Most of them were regular rakes, spending every free moment in taverns. It was hard enough to convince them to read the assigned material, let alone the occult. No, the boys did not deserve to be prosecuted.

Then Satigny mentioned a free-spirited youngster whom he had hired to run errands for him, a certain Josef Eliade whose family lived on Rue du Mouton. They were a clan of wanderers from Wallachia, who had spent a few years in Spanish speaking lands. Perhaps, it was Josef who had slipped Raoul Terrade's book into the pile of perfectly innocuous material?

Now we were moving somewhere! In the end I got Satigny to confess that yes, he had indeed been collaborating with Josef Eliade in procuring anti-ecclesiastic literature. That official confession took just a little more effort on behalf of the torturer.

Having gotten what I needed from the hapless astronomy lecturer, I left him in the dungeon and went to see my friend Louis in hopes of gathering more information about that elusive Wallachian clan.

The bishop's eyes lit up when he heard the name of Satigny's accomplice. I could tell that surname was familiar to Louis. The puzzle was beginning to come together. Things were starting to make sense.

"I've always had my suspicions about Mathias," he said, nodding. "He is the patriarch of the Eliade clan, in case you are wondering. A man without a country is a man without allegiance and therefore without scruples or fear. He could be a spy or a mercenary. If his tales of serving Vlad the Impaler are true, then he is indeed to be feared."

Vlad the Impaler? Whoa! That was a name that did not come up frequently in conversations. Now I was intrigued.

"A man does not come out of serving a blood-drinking undead without losing his soul," Louis continued, his confidence building up. "Also, his rapid rise to prosperity and notoriety in Paris provides legitimate reasons for suspicion. Mathias was making too much money and too many friends. A vagabond does not achieve such success in such a short period of time without some help from dark forces."

"Go on, my friend, finish your thought," I encouraged him. "I think I know where you're heading with this, and I rather like it."

"To make a long story short, I do not think it would be excessive to arrest the entire Eliade family." Now the bishop was truly getting into the spirit of the Inquisition. For me it was nothing short of riveting to witness that transformation in him. "It is plain to see that Mathias' wife and children have all come under his influence. They've all been painted by the same brush. If there are any innocents in their midst, God will surely recognize them. Our duty is to make an example of them, isn't it?"

"Ah, that's my Louis!"

That day the torturer and his underlings had their calloused hands full! When the new batch of suspects arrived later that day, the furnace had to be lit again. When I went back into the dungeon, the Eliades were waiting for me: the patriarch, his Gascon consort and the two sons who looked nothing alike.

I assumed them to be born to different mothers, so different were their complexions, features and temperaments. One of the youngsters, Sebastien by name, was wearing a military uniform. He had just received news of promotion. I had to stifle a chuckle at the irony of it. Louis was not exaggerating when he said that the family had been on its way up.

One thing I learned is that when an entire family is accused of witchcraft or heresy, it is more practical to keep them together during the interrogation. It makes the process so much smoother and faster. Contrary to popular assumption, the presence of the loved ones actually weakens the fortitude of the one being interrogated. It is easier to be brave and obstinate when your parents and siblings do not listen to your shrieks of agony.

The Eliades proved me wrong. They turned my theory upside down. Perhaps, they were not a tightknit family after all. The boys did not seem moved by the sufferings of their stepmother. The woman claimed she knew nothing about the heretical book and she had very little to do with her husband's comings and goings. She said he was a lecherous goat that would mount any female between twelve and forty. That part was true. But an agent of heresy or sorcerer? No. Not to her knowledge, at least. Even if he made any unholy pacts, it was done without her involvement. She was a pious woman, who continued going to the mass and keeping faithful to her unfaithful husband. Not once had she taken advantage of his permission for her to bed other men.

And you know what? I believed Madame Eliade. I had seen many dishonest, insincere women in my practice. My hope was that her husband or one of the stepsons would speak up to save her. It was a pity that by the end of that conversation her fingers and toes were completely shattered. I had heard that she was quite a seamstress. Those rough but dexterous peasant hands had sewn many exquisite garments.

Then it was Josef's turn. He looked his usual sullen and unapologetic self. I could tell that Mathias Eliade was a lenient father who had never whipped his children. The boy did not believe until the very last moment that I would go through with the interrogation proceedings and subject him to the same manipulations I had used on his stepmother.

Even when the torturer's underlings chained him to the wall, he continued sneering spitefully. When the red hot iron grazed his downy chest, he let out a howl that sounded more indignant than anything else. For a few seconds he stood with his mouth open, glancing down at the red blisters. The second swipe of the iron brought him out of his stupor. Now he knew it was real. It was not just a bad dream brought on by one of Papa's tall tales about Vlad the Impaler.

After a few minutes of cringing, wailing and yanking at the chains, he calmed down and started talking like a respectful and reasonable human being. Just as I had expected, more interesting information came to light. Adrian Satigny was not the only scholar Josef had served. He had also run similar errands for Monseigneur Desmoulins. The two men were rivals, posing as colleagues. Both had been working on some mysterious optical contraption to magnify the celestial bodies. Both had been after the same obscure manuscript by Nicholas von Kues. Josef had known about their rivalry and played both sides. He confessed that it gave him tremendous pleasure to pit those two arrogant men against each other. Puppetry was a skill he had mastered as a child and used to entertain crowds at crossroads for small coins. Playing Satigny against Desmoulins elevated the game to a new level.

Eureka! My investigation had come full circle. The spears were pointing in the direction of Desmoulins. His patronage of the Eliade family made perfect sense now. Josef was running errands for him, and the sixteen-year old-Agniese was apparently warming his bed. In exchange for those favors, Desmoulins helped the whole family advance. Ah, this was too good to be true. All those flies caught in the same web! I had so much juicy material to present to Louis de Beaumont. Hopefully, he would know what to do with it. It was up to him to decide whether the Eliades would die on the gallows or at the stake, and whether their executions would take place on the same day or be spread out over the course of several weeks. The ecclesiastic procurator would pretty much endorse the bishop's decision. Once Louis communicated his preferences to the court, the procurator would see that they were carried out.

Before transporting Eliade into the holding cell where he would await execution, I allowed him to see his wife for a few minutes, so they could say goodbye. I was not so monstrous as to deny them a last conversation.

Her toes and feet broken, the proud Gascon woman was not able to stand.

"Damn you, Mathias!" she cried from her pile of straw. "Damn you for everything you've made me endure. For the years of truancy, all of your balmy lies, and most of all, for keeping Agniese in our midst. I always knew that little brown witch would kill us all. She's the reason why we're here. We're about to die, and she's free somewhere, cackling. She pledged our lives to Satan. This is her homage."

I felt there was not enough anger in her voice. Or, perhaps, she had exhausted her vocal cords while screaming in the hands of the torturer. Mathias was standing in silence, looking down at her.

"I should have killed her a long time ago," Denise continued. "I just couldn't muster the courage. I've never killed anyone before, you see. It's not a sin to send a hell spawn back from whence she came from. And that's just what she is. The lines on her palm have been erased for a reason. You've always kept her close to your bosom, Mathias, like some sort of diabolic amulet. Then I saw you look at her, the way you look at other harlots. I saw your lip curl and your teeth flash. Don't bother denying it."

Mathias sighed – as if awaking from a mid-afternoon nap – and nodded, his sweaty head bumping it against the bars of the partition.

"You know me too well, my love. Indeed, the wicked thought had crossed my mind. It is true that my feelings for Agniese were not fatherly. It was my plan to step in and scoop her up once Desmoulins got bored with her. I had hoped to sell her virginity at a high price and keep the leftovers for myself. Alas, plans do not always transpire."

"I knew it was time for me to act," Denise carried on, as if she had not heard her husband's affirmation of her fears. She was more concerned with finishing her own confession. "My vengeance had to be prompt and subtle. I knew the deadly power of herbs. So I prepared that brew and watched her take the first sip. You don't know how it delighted me to watch her decline as the first symptoms set in. It looked just like white plague. Hearing her wheeze and cough was music to my ears. I should have given her a stronger concoction. But I wanted to prolong her suffering. I was enjoying it too much. Now I'm paying for it."

It was one of those moments that made me regret that I had stopped taking painting lessons in my adolescence. What a picture that scene between the Eliade spouses would have made! A perfect illustration for a demonology textbook.

Louis de Beaumont was overwhelmed by the influx of new information that I presented with my usual eloquence and a little disappointed for not having chanced to see it with his own eyes. It was not customary for bishops to descend into dungeons, so he had to rely on my narrative to get the full picture.

"We need to bring this story to a logical finale," I said to Louis. "There are a few more people we need to talk to."

"At the interrogation chamber again?" Louis gasped.

"Hopefully, it will not come to that. The torturer needs a break. He was getting tired from standing so close to the furnace. We need to see our dear friend who likes to melt glass and mix powders."

To our surprise, Desmoulins arrived on time, looking more haggard than usual, his sunken eyes filled with feverish fire and surrounded by dark circles. Someone who did not know that man better would have concluded that he had spent the night in ceaseless prayer. He must have heard about the fate of the Eliades by now. No doubt, he must have been dismayed. They were his pets after all.

"It seems to me there's one family member missing," I said to him, skipping the introduction, "a green-eyed, brown-skinned maiden who appears to be the key instigator. According to her stepmother's confession, she has pledged the lives of the entire family to Satan."

"You have no proof."

The terse, lazy, unimaginative response disappointed me. Truly, was that the best he had for me?

"You are right about that, Desmoulins. It is hard to carry out a verdict in absentia. That is precisely why I would like to take a good look at her and maybe talk to her in the interrogation chamber. Would you be so kind as to take us to her?"

"I've no idea where she is. What makes you think I know her whereabouts?"

"She's your mistress, isn't she? You've made your affair with her public; taken her places where it's not customary to take women."

"I don't expect you to believe me, but Agniese Eliade is not my mistress. She made it abundantly clear to me that I am too old and too high-born for her, and it is not my habit to force my shriveled up aristocratic body on women. Moreover, I've permitted my protégé, Daniel Dufort, to pursue the girl for his own selfish pleasure. He is twenty years old now. A young man must start somewhere."

"Then we shall talk directly to Monsieur Dufort."

"He doesn't know her whereabouts either."

"Well, perhaps the torturer will help him remember." I deliberately kept my voice low and even. "I must say, that fellow is very efficient, as are his underlings. He does not need to verbalize his commands. He blinks, and they bring the right instrument."

Desmoulins let out a strange, jerky laugh that sounded like a cough.

"Good luck! You cannot extract information from a stone. And that is just what Monsieur Dufort is made of."

"But you aren't, and neither is his natural father – whoever he is. He won't be happy to hear that his darling boy had his thumbs crushed. He is still recovering from that squabble with the archers."

"You cannot do anything to the organist," Desmoulins said, his face assuming its usual austere mien. "In case you forgot, my protégé has immunity against prosecution in a canon court. I have a document to prove it."

I leaned forward in what was half-nod, half-bow. "So I've

heard. I'd like to see that paper. I hope you don't consider my request too intrusive."

"Fine. Give me ten minutes, and I'll bring it to you."

"If you don't mind, I'd like to follow you. I've been sitting in the bishop's room all day. My legs need stretching."

We left the bishop's palace and walked over to the cloister. Desmoulins dragged his feet purposely to aggravate me. Or maybe he truly was that exhausted. A few times he stopped, clutching his left side. His grimace of pain looked genuine enough. I did not begrudge him the delay. We both knew I was in command.

Walking down the cloister hall, we passed a young priest who let out a stifled gasp and recoiled at my sight. I do not believe he and I had ever met. Still, something inside him twitched when my clothes brushed against his. He sensed the menace, as a young buck senses the presence of a wolf.

We reached the cell at the end of the hall. Desmoulins took his time opening the door, pretending to struggle with the key. I loved every second of it, because every second he made me wait was loaded with dread. He could not keep up that charade infinitely.

"Aren't you going to invite me in?" I asked him once the door finally opened. "Then again, I really don't mind standing in the hall, spooking the young clergy."

"Please, come in," he muttered. "It might take me a while."

I watched him as he took off one of the icons on the wall concealing a built-in safe beneath. If he thought it was the most secure way to store confidential documents, I had bad news for him.

He was standing with his back turned to me, so I could only see his broad shoulders rising and falling. Apparently, his search was not going very well.

"I'm at a loss," he said finally as he turned around to face me. "The paper is not here. I've no idea where it could have gone."

"Naturally, it's not here," I replied. "It never existed in the first place. Our mutual friend Louis de Beaumont will be terribly embarrassed when he finds out that for all these years you've been playing him for a fool. Fortunately, I do have an execution order from fifteen years ago. It's not too late for me to send Monsieur Dufort to the pyre."

"I hope you won't conduct your process in the middle of a place of worship."

"Of course not. I have enough respect for ecclesiastic decorum. Didn't I just ask permission to enter your cell?" I sat down on his chair, which was uncomfortable as hell, picked up one of his writing quills and started practicing my signature on a piece of parchment. "But Monsieur Dufort must come out of the cathedral eventually. And when he does, my men will greet him outside and escort him to the Palace of Justice. You'll have the opportunity to stand right there and provide moral support as the underlings tear out his fingernails one by one. I predict, you'll tell me where the missing Eliade girl is before I'm done with Dufort's left hand."

"Go ahead," he said, "pluck out his eyes while you're at it. I don't really care about him much. I'm tired of his constant presence. If he were to disappear, it would be a relief to me – and to him as well. He's a miserable creature, a burden unto himself. If you don't believe me, just listen to his music. You'll know what I mean."

I took a moment to admire my calligraphy and then returned the quill to the inkbottle. My tutors had trained me not to leave dripping quills unattended. I did not feel motivated enough to tell Desmoulins what a rotten liar he was, and found it very interesting that he did not continue insisting that the document had been stolen.

"Let's make it quick and painless," I said. "I will offer you a generous bargain: You give me the missing Eliade girl, and in turn I promise not to touch that pet demon of yours. His luminescent red head in exchange for her greasy raven one. There's no need to drag Louis into this. You and I will go from here straight to your secret hideaway. Your protégé will remain unharmed in our custody. He won't be put to question without my instruction. His fate rests entirely in your hands. As you see, I can be quite reasonable."

Desmoulins did the right thing in the end, just like I thought he would. The fatherly feelings towards Dufort triumphed over his lust for the Wallachian wench. After all, he had spent fifteen years raising that beast, and he had known the Eliade girl for a few months at most.

When Desmoulins and I exited the cloister, I instructed half of my guards to accompany us, and the remaining half to wait for Dufort outside the cathedral. I gave them a detailed description of the young genius. They could not possibly seize the wrong man. I also thought it my duty to warn them that he was quite strong and equally obstreperous.

We travelled on horseback. Flanked by my men, I followed Desmoulins along the banks of the river. Having left the last row of waterside hovels behind, we took a dirt road into the woods. Our grim guide – an excellent horseman, by the way – kept the cowl of his cassock down. Perhaps to him it was a matter of pride, meeting a catastrophe with his face fully exposed.

Studying the lines of his forehead, nose and chin, I was reminded of his lofty origin. One could not ask for a more harmonious, aristocratic profile. He was one of those lucky devils who did not change much between twenty and fifty, whose skin dries and wrinkles with age without sagging, whose features retain their original shape, whose hair greys without thinning. Desmoulins had a right to be a little arrogant. I had trouble believing that any woman, regardless of heritage or statue in life, would reject him based on his age. It must have been the first excuse that came to his mind when he claimed that the Wallachian chit was not drawn to him as a lover.

I tried to imagine what was going on inside his head, what prayers he was reciting to keep that rigor over his visage. Would he wear the same mask walking to his own execution? In talking about Dufort's alleged death wish, perhaps he was referring to himself?

Once we reached the edge of a clearing, Desmoulins dismounted abruptly and headed towards what looked like a charmingly quaint and impeccably masculine hunting lodge. The shelter was inhabited, copiously illuminated and bursting with nervous energy. There was somebody inside, waiting and languishing.

Standing at the edge of the clearing, looking through the narrow window, I could see everything that was happening inside and hear their every word. I did notice that the infamous Transylvanian mongrel was exceptionally pretty. I understood why Desmoulins was so taken by her. The little witch was also happy to see him. She threw her arms around him, and for a few seconds he held her close – but then pushed her away.

"I'm sorry, I let her go," she said, nodding at the empty bed. "That lady friend of yours ... She's not entirely sane. She woke up right after you left. The first things that came out of her mouth were vile, but at least they made sense. She said you two were lovers, and that I'd never measure up to her. Then I showed her my hands, and she started babbling utter nonsense. Would you believe it? She thinks I am her daughter, the one she shoved into a furnace fifteen years ago. How is that possible? How can that sad, deranged woman be my mother? My God ... It's true, isn't it? You must've known all along. You deliberately arranged for us to meet. Don't tell me. I don't want to know. Then she ripped the ring out of the wall and ran off. I didn't stop her. I couldn't. Nor did I want to. She could be anywhere."

I confess I found her frantic monologue to be entertaining. I had no idea who this deranged woman was that she referred to, but her narrative had that dramatic, once-upon-a-time flare. Desmoulins was standing with his back turned to me, so to my chagrin, I could not see his facial expression.

"Get me out of here!" she pleaded, clinging to him and clutching at his cloak. "Let's go to Catalonia. I'm willing to go anywhere. My mind is made up. I should have taken you up on your offer when you first made it. Oh, Monseigneur! I want to spend the rest of my days with you."

I cannot imagine this was easy for Desmoulins. The girl's raven hair streamed over his shoulder. I took pity on him and helped end this heart-wrenching scene by giving the guards a sign to come in.

Still hugging Desmoulins, she lifted her head. "What's the meaning of this? What are these people doing here?"

"It's over, Agniese," he said. "Take my advice. Confess to everything. Don't make them take you back to the interrogation chamber. You've seen it with your own eyes. You know how those instruments work. Just say 'yes' and make it easier for everyone."

To my surprise, the witch behaved with dignity. Without any shrieks or protestations, she allowed the guards to walk her out of the lodge. I could not see her entire countenance. Her wild hair was drooping over her cheeks, with just the tip of the nose visible. Desmoulins was walking behind her, head lowered and arms crossed over his chest – an iconic monk pose I had seldom seen him assume.

It was around nine o'clock in the evening when we reconvened in the hearing room of the Palace of Justice. The Eliade girl had been escorted through a side door into the dungeon below. I asked the guards to make sure she was kept apart from the rest of her family.

Dufort was sitting in the defendant's seat guarded by two of my men. I quickly examined his face for any fresh scratches or bruises, but there were no signs that he had tried to resist arrest. With his legs outstretched, he continued pulling threads out of his mantle, holding them to the light and throwing them on the floor. He did not so much as look at his master, who took a seat in the judges' row, his cowl still down.

Louis was there too, drinking from his bejeweled flask. Judging from the flush on his cheeks, the flask did not contain plain water. Listening to the smacking of his lips, I was reminded that I had not eaten all day. One of the drawbacks of my profession is that occasionally, when I get pulled into an exciting case that keeps me engaged for weeks and days at a time, I put myself in danger of fainting due to malnourishment when I have to skip meals. My mentors have recommended keeping a bag of seeds, nuts and dried fruit on hand to keep my strength up.

"Now that everyone is accounted for," I began, "we can have an earnest discussion concerning the fate of the Eliade family. This is not a formal hearing by any means. The ecclesiastic procurator is not here with us tonight, but he has generously allowed us to use this space. I must say, this is one of the finest courthouses I've seen."

The door burst open and the Archbishop of Reims burst in, looking energetic and festive, with just a dusting of summer tan upon his handsome face. I noticed that his merriment had a nervous quality. His gaze kept wandering around the sitting room, appearing to be either seeking or avoiding someone in particular.

"I hope I haven't missed anything," he said, pulling off his gloves and stuffing them into his travel bag.

Louis de Beaumont grimaced in displeasure. "What brings you here, Pierre?"

"Boredom," the archbishop confessed unabashedly, "and a sense of vocational solidarity. I happened to be in the vicinity when a little bird told me there was a massive heresy case brewing in Paris. So naturally, I decided to come by and offer Louis my fraternal support. I want to see him bring that iron fist down." His eyes fell upon Dufort. "Bah, is this lanky devil on trial?"

"This is not a trial, Your Excellency," I repeated through my teeth. Who in the world did Pierre de Laval think he was, intruding like this? Oh, wait. He was the Archbishop of Reims, the man who would be crowning our next king in a few years. How could I forget? "It's just an informal, pretrial sitting. This young man on the defendant's bench is serving more as a witness. He had the misfortune of falling under some bad influence. But all that is to be remedied. After all, this is the purpose of the Inquisition: to instruct and redeem." I turned to address the organist directly. "Monsieur Dufort, allow me to point out that you have the most doting, selfless guardian in Christendom. For fifteen years he has been telling the world a lie about some immunity warrant that you allegedly possessed."

"It wasn't a lie," Dufort said, taking a break from his thread-pulling and lifting his head. "The warrant does exist. I can show it you, if you don't believe me."

He reached inside his waistcoat and pulled out a rolled up piece of parchment. At the sight of it Desmoulins exhaled and rubbed his forehead. "How did you get your hands on this?"

"With help from a good friend," the organist replied, "one who has no qualms entering a priest's cell and going through his possessions. Astounding ... A piece of twisted wire is a universal instrument for opening locks. And guess what? God did not smite him on the spot."

"Must be my brother Jonannes," Desmoulins muttered. "That conniving troll. After everything I've done for him. I knew I should have let him starve to death in his cradle."

I was a little surprised to hear that reference. I never knew Desmoulins had a brother.

"How I retrieved the document is of secondary importance now," Dufort resumed. "I've wanted to see it for years. There are a few rather interesting passages in it. Like this one, for instance ..." He unrolled the parchment and recited, "Upon reaching the age of twenty, the bearer of this document is free to forfeit his immunity privileges to another individual, male or female, French or foreign, Christian or otherwise. There it is, in Latin."

Yes, I could read Latin, thank you very much. I was just a little surprised by the sudden turn of events. So the document existed and looked authentic enough. The stamp in the corner and the cardinal's signature testified to that. Why did Dufort choose to quote the passage on forfeiting the privilege? That was my question.

"I am giving my inviolability to Agniese Eliade," he said. "See? There is even a line on the bottom to write in the name of the successor. I am twenty years old now. I can dispose of my fate as I see fit."

He sounded like he was talking as flippantly as if he were donating a garment he had outgrown.

"Monsieur Dufort," I said, stepping in front of him, "perhaps a little clarification is in order. I have a warrant for your execution. It is fifteen years old but still perfectly valid. There is nothing stopping me from carrying out the order. Without your immunity you become subject to prosecution like any other person in France. Do you understand that by saving that girl from the gallows you would be sending yourself to the pyre?"

"I do. We can settle this matter very quickly. Release her, and I'll take her place. I do not even need to see her."

Perhaps Desmoulins was right, and his protégé did have a death wish.

"And you realize that death by burning is not always fast and painless?"

"Maybe I'll get lucky and suffocate before the flames reach me. I've seen enough burnings in my life to know that such things are not uncommon. Do what you wish with me. I stand by my words. I'm willing to say this before the ecclesiastic procurator when he gets in tomorrow morning."

The room suddenly became very quiet, so quiet that one could hear the crackling of the candle wicks.

Pierre de Laval was the one to interrupt the silence with an exclamation. "My son!"

That was no usual appeal of a clergyman to one of his flock. The alarm and desperation in his voice betrayed a more earthly bond to the accused. I remembered vaguely that before Pierre de Laval had greyed, his hair had been a fiery red. Yes, it is not only sorrow that can deplete a man's hair of color prematurely. Excessive merriment and pleasure can have the same effect. At a closer look I noticed a resemblance between Laval and Dufort. The two also had a similar facial angle, with the forehead and the nose forming almost a straight line, as well as the somber brow ridge.

"My son," the Archbishop of Reims repeated, having regained control of his voice after the initial outburst, "think hard about what you are about to do. Are you sure you want to sacrifice your life for a girl who doesn't have much time? What a waste it would be. Even if she escapes the gibbet, she'll die of natural causes in a few months. And you, my son, are a recognized genius. You have decades of composing and performing."

Dufort inclined his head, as if trying to get rid of a cramp in his neck.

"Please excuse me from the need to explain myself, Your Excellency. I do not expect you or any other man of God to understand."

"All right then!" the Archbishop of Reims exclaimed, his voice echoing through the hearing room. "I wish to see that witch with my own eyes. I believe I'm the only one here who hasn't seen her. Show me that devious woman, for whose sake this impetuous youth is willing to give up his life. She must be endowed with some extraordinary gifts."

Louis shrugged and wiggled deeper into his armchair. "Indulge yourself. You didn't make this trip for nothing. She's in a holding cell right beneath us."

He made a sign for two guards to escort Laval, but the Archbishop raised his hand. "If you don't mind, I'd like to go alone. I've been to this place before. I know my way."

"Suit yourself but if you trip in the dark and break a leg, don't blame me."

Indeed, the archbishop appeared to be familiar with the layout of the Palace of Justice. He opened the side door that led underground while the rest of us sat and listened for the sound of his footsteps to abate.

Dufort resumed pulling threads out of his garments. His lips were moving and his feet twitching, as if he were rehearsing a liturgical hymn. I did not sense any apprehension. On the contrary, he looked perfectly relaxed and complacent, like a man who had finally achieved his life's mission. Through the crackling of the candles, I could make out the words of the chant.

Agnus Dei, qui tollis peccata mundi, miserere nobis.

It was no coincidence. Only minutes after giving up his inviolability, he was singing of the sacrificial lamb. How well-timed – and equally distasteful. No doubt, in his mind he had already exalted himself as a martyr. St. Daniel of Notre-Dame de Paris.

Fifteen minutes later Pierre de Laval re-emerged, wiping the sweat from his forehead.

"Well, the witch is dead," he announced with a mixture of triumph and disappointment. "I've traveled all of this way to see a dead witch. A little anticlimactic, if you ask me, but at the same time soothing. Now you can focus on executing the surviving Eliades."

Louis de Beaumont puffed indignantly. "How can she be dead? She hasn't even been interrogated."

"I didn't see any signs of torture on her body. It appears that she died of natural causes. She was ill, wasn't she? The anxiety from the arrest must have hastened her demise."

"Are you certain she's dead?"

Now it was Laval's turn to look indignant. "My dear friend, I've seen enough corpses in my life, those of heretics and witches as well as righteous people."

"What do you propose we do now?" Louis asked.

"You tell me. What do you normally do with the bodies of the defendants who die before being tried? Do you inter them in consecrated earth?"

Louis stood up from his seat and examined the wine stains on his robe. "We should burn her body just to be sure," he said. "It doesn't have to be done in public. We can dump it into the furnace of the interrogation chamber."

Pierre de Laval did not like that idea. "It's not fair to deprive the rats of the Montfaucon tomb of a well-deserved meal. They are God's creatures too. They depend on us for those occasional feasts. Though there isn't much meat on her bones, it's better than nothing."

"This is all strange," Louis de Beaumont said with escalating annoyance that stemmed from his inability to make sense of things. "If the girl had the gift of sorcery, why didn't she use it to heal herself? Perhaps, she was not a witch after all."

I remembered Denise Eliade's confession concerning the real causes behind the girl's illness. I decided it would be wiser to keep that piece of information to myself. Louis de Beaumont seemed eager to put the matter to rest.

"At this point, it is irrelevant whether she is guilty or innocent," I said. "She is dead now. Have the night men take her body to the Montfaucon tomb. She'll find herself in great company among traitors and miscreants."

While the two bishops and I were discussing how to dispose of the corpse, Desmoulins and his ward were sitting silently with their heads hung, mourning the death of their shared mistress. Once a satisfactory agreement was reached, Pierre de Laval walked over to the organist, sat down next to him on the bench, embraced him and whispered a few words in his ear that nobody else could hear.

"My son," he said out loud, "it appears that your sacrifice

will not be needed after all. Now that the young lady's death has been confirmed, you can keep your immunity. I cannot speak for everyone in this room, but I am outrageously impressed by your abnegation. This is the stuff of courtly romances. And I am grateful to God for our meeting – though I wish it happened under more pleasant circumstances. Life can be savage and hideous, my son."

Dufort twitched his shoulders, trying to shake off the archbishop's hands. "If you don't mind, I'd like to ..." He closed his eyes, while his mouth remained open. I kept waiting for him to request to see the girl's corpse. His reply surprised me. "I'd like to get out of here."

"I don't blame you one bit," Laval affirmed, patting him on the back. "It makes no sense for you to stay here in Paris. I don't imagine how you can continue living and working here after everything that's happened. Come with me to Reims, a place where you'll belong. We have a much better cathedral that has a much better organ with new pipes that will allow you to flaunt your talent."

Louis de Beaumont jerked like a cat roused from a nap by a drizzle of cold water. "Hold your horses, Pierre. As much as we've enjoyed your company, and as much as your surprise visit has brightened up this dreary evening, you cannot just steal my organist and take him with you."

Laval squeezed Dufort about the shoulders one last time and removed his hands.

"Let the young man decide for himself. He's not a prisoner here, is he? A talent of his caliber should not be sequestered. He's already given five solid years to your cathedral, Louis. I hear you've been keeping him in a drafty cell and hoarding his commission money. This is not how musicians are treated in most precincts."

Personally, I was impressed by Pierre de Laval's audacity. But then, he did not become an archbishop by being a wilting wallflower. I was curious to see how Louis would respond to such a bold lunge. Then I remembered that Louis was not very good at defending his interests or his territory. That was why he needed assistance from the likes of me. This time I decided not to come to his aid. I stood back and let Laval talk.

"The current king is old and sickly," the archbishop addressed the grief-stricken youth in his enticing voice. "He doesn't have many years left. You know what that means. There will be a coronation in the near future. Charles VIII will take the throne after his father's death. Wouldn't you like to play for the child monarch? I could introduce you to him."

Dufort lifted his head slightly. "Did you say there were new pipes?"

"Yes! New pipes, new keys, new pedals. But the current organist is old. His joints are swollen, and his fingers do not move as swiftly as they once did. He is a wise, benevolent soul, who has earned his rest. He would be glad to hand over his duties to a young successor. You will be loved and cherished, my son. You will have your own quarters with a massive bookcase made of red wood. You are welcome to have supper with me every night. And when the time comes, you will marry the worthiest, godliest woman and look at this juvenile infatuation as a passing fever."

If you asked me to voice my theory, I would say that Laval, in an act of fatherly concern, had killed the imprisoned Eliade girl with his own hands. That man was capable of anything. I had to admire him for that. He did what he thought he must, to save his impressionable, needlessly chivalrous son from what was essentially a suicide masked as an act of self-sacrifice. This is what I would have done for my Etienne, had he lived and not perished in that God-forsaken boarding school. Dufort's only fault was having survived the fever outbreak. He was alive, and my boy was dead. Had I sent Etienne to a different school, perhaps he would have lived also.

Case dismissed. My thirst for heretic blood had been satiated until the end of the month. I knew there would be more cases awaiting me when I returned to Bordeaux.

Sometimes the hunter chooses to release the wounded beast into the wild instead of finishing it off to take the carcass home to eat the meat and keep the pelt. Then, there is always the possibility of encountering that beast during the next hunting season.

Without a word of farewell to the rest of us, the triumphant Archbishop of Reims led the organist out of the hearing hall. Dufort did not so much as glance at his former master.

Chapter 8

On the Lion's Bed

(Pierre de Laval)

Please, don't faint. This revelation will probably strike you as shocking, but not every bishop dreams of becoming a cardinal, and not every cardinal dreams of becoming the Pope. Some of us are perfectly happy stagnating in our respective quarters, sleeping until eleven o'clock in the morning and allowing the faithful to kiss our rings on occasion.

My sister Jeanne and brother François kept telling me I would end up in the Vatican one day. "You'll be wearing red soon, Pierre. Wait and see." Those predictions made me chuckle, but I did not argue with my older siblings. They were entitled to their benevolent delusions.

François was made chevalier of the Order of the Crescent and became a favorite of King Louis XI. He went on to marry Catherine de Valois, daughter of the Duke of Alençon. And Jeanne was already married to René of Anjou, who had more titles than there were trees in the forest.

I was the baby of the family, and the underachiever. Notre-Dame de Reims was not just a stepping stone towards the Vatican, but my final destination. I did not need to climb any higher.

Having dumped most of my administrative duties to my vicars, I could dedicate my free time, which I had in abundance, to the pursuit of such philistine passions as winemaking, beekeeping and philandering. You should see my magnificent vineyards and orchards and taste my sweet honey. There is enough violence and impractical knowledge in this world already. We need more joy and pleasure. My three passions complemented each other. Women love wine and honey, and I love women – especially blondes. I always have a ripe apple in my pocket for a flaxen-haired minx.

Not that I ever needed treats – or titles – to entice the fair sex. In fact, I have pulled my finest conquests while empty-handed and dressed in layman's clothing. I do not need to impress women with my lineage, intimidate them with my power, or bribe them with my treats. All I have to do is smile. Sometimes even a smile is not necessary. A sliding, mindless glance will suffice. I find my wild popularity peculiar and amusing, because I do not consider myself exceptionally handsome. There are better looking clergymen out there, like my good friend Desmoulins, for instance.

If you put us side by side, you will see that he has a better posture, more balanced proportions, straighter teeth and more refined features. But you know what? All those advantages go out the window because he is so bloody intense and brooding, enveloped in some acrid cloud. Always grumpy, bitter, and disgusted with the world, spouting venom, pining for some unreachable feminine ideal that only exists in the sonnets of Florentine poets. Who wants to put up with all that angst for any prolonged period of time? See, this is why he is alone and has not fornicated in over a decade. If he loosened his cassock and lowered his standards a little, he would be flinging left and right! That winsome fusion of German and Italian would make him irresistible.

Thank God, we have different tastes in women. He likes mystical, ethereal brunettes, and I like earthy blondes. At least we will never get into a tiff over a woman. I would hate to lose a friend like him over a pair of breasts. Desmoulins is one of my absolute favorite people. And I cannot even say his given name out loud! He would kill me if I did. He hates his name. Personally, I think it is beautiful, so simple and yet melodic. It does not quite flow. Rather, it drops like a rock into the river, plunges like a dagger into the enemy's flesh. Of course, he thinks it is pathetic and lame, and there is no way I can persuade him otherwise.

And yet, when it was time for me to face the consequences of my philandering and find a substitute father for my firstborn, I immediately thought of Desmoulins. He was the only man cut out for the task.

I knew that Daniel was not an ordinary child, so he could not be placed with ordinary parents who would impose their ideas of propriety upon him by teaching him table manners and carpentry skills. He would rebel and possibly kill them, or they would drive him to suicide with their well-intentioned nagging. No, he needed another solitary soul, another proud hermit to show him how to exist and flourish apart from the vulgar pedestrian society.

Fifteen years later I had no regrets. Although, I confess, I did have some fears. When my estranged son had been handed back to me by Fate, I wondered how our relationship would pan out. How thick was the ice? Was I to try and break it with one blow or melt it first around the edges?

"Who are you, again?" he asked me after we left the Palace of Justice. I had just ripped him out of Viteri's claws. "Remind me."

"I am Pierre de Laval, the Archbishop of Reims."

"I see … And what brought you to Paris?"

"My desire to help you."

"Help me?" His voice was weak and low, like that of a man exsanguinated after a mortal wound. "Why would you of all people want to help me? My own father turned away from me. My mother killed herself. And my master …" He exhaled and shook his head. "I don't understand. You're a total stranger. What do you care?"

"I'm not a stranger, Daniel. And I care a great deal. Your interests are of utmost importance to me."

He took a gulp of air, remembering the proposition I made in the audience hall. "That's right, you need an organist. You thought they were going to burn me, didn't you?"

"Yes, there was an excellent possibility of you being sent to the pyre. Anselm Viteri likes to make an example on occasion. And yes, I do need a new organist. But that's not all. I'm not just offering you the position. I'm offering you so much more – a new life."

"So it can turn into a farce, just like the one I'm living now?" He tapped himself on the lips and cheeks a few times, as if trying to slap himself out of a dream. "What exactly did you whisper to me in the courtroom? First you told everyone that Agniese was dead, and then you whispered to me that she was alive. Which one is it?"

"She is not in pain."

"Stop talking in riddles."

"She … she is asleep."

"Well, is she going to wake up?"

"That is what I'm praying for. She should stay asleep for twelve more hours." I reached into the hidden pocket of my sleeve and pulled out a vial. Now that we were completely alone, I could share the details of my plot with him. "I purchased this potion from an apothecary in Verona. One does not trust a novice to mix such potent concoctions. It's not all herbs. There's a touch of snake's venom in it too, the kind that paralyzes the muscles and slows down the heartbeat. I went to see the Eliade girl in the dungeon. She was alive and awake when I arrived. And yes, she is divinely beautiful. I see why you are smitten by her. I explained my plot to her and gave her the potion. Within two minutes she was out cold. To an uninformed onlooker she's dead. The night men won't think to check for breathing or heartbeat. It's not their job to ensure that the person is truly dead. Their job is to take her to the Montfaucon tomb. That is what they were instructed to do."

"So she will wake up in complete darkness, on a pile of bones?"

"Not if we get there first. I told her it was a possibility that she might awaken too soon. As long as it doesn't happen in the presence of the night men. Dear Lord! That would frighten them more than it would her. Imagine a corpse coming to life before your eyes and leaping off the cart with a scream? I hesitated to give her a stronger dose. Her body was already weakened. It would be a shame if I killed her in the process of trying to rescue her."

I was peering into my son's face, hoping to see signs of bliss and gratitude, but instead only saw deepening perplexity.

"Does my master know about your plot?"

"Let us just say, he knows what I am capable of. He knows I'd never fail him. This is why he summoned me when he sensed danger. A young officer came by my estate and gave me the message."

Daniel frowned. "A young officer, you say?"

"Yes, an archer, I believe. Blond, handsome – and a little delirious. He could barely tie two words together. As it turned out, he had a wound in his back. It did not look deadly, but deep enough to cause him discomfort. At any rate, I left him in the care of my lady friend. He might still be there."

"Did he introduce himself?"

"I'm pretty sure he did. I forget his name. It sounds Roman. It's either Aurelius or Octavius."

"Lucius ..." Daniel whispered. "How odd. He came back from the dead to warn you."

"My son, people come back from the dead all the time. Death is only an illusion. In many cases, it's only the beginning."

"Now you're back to your riddles. So you didn't really come to cheer up our bishop?"

"No. In case you haven't sensed it, I don't have much respect for Louis de Beaumont. I came to help your master. He and I were best friends. Twenty some years ago we made a pact."

"How odd ... He never mentioned you. I didn't think he had any friends."

"We did not herald our friendship to the world. It was more of a stealthy alliance. I knew I could trust him with my most precious secret. There is no other man I would have chosen as a guardian for my child." There, I said it. My admission could not have been more explicit. I peered into his face, looking for signs of recognition. Even if Daniel comprehended my words, he did not show it. "Desmoulins was very fond of you."

"Like he's fond of his jars with powder?"

"He did not want any harm to befall you."

A shiver ran through Daniel's body. Instead of tightening his pale cloak, he ripped it off his shoulders and tossed it into the ditch. I did not ask him why he did it. The cloak symbolized his Parisian past.

"Desmoulins used me to incriminate his rival," he said. "He told me to deliver that heretical book by Raoul Terrade to the University and plant it on Satigny's shelf. He said it was a surprise gift for an esteemed colleague, and I believed him. It didn't occur to me to look at the title. It was never my custom to question my master. But he is the one responsible for that string of arrests. He knew Viteri was in the city. The wrath of the Inquisition did not end with Satigny. The Eliades' blood is now on my hands too."

Having parted with his cloak, Daniel ripped off his liturgical sash and reached for the cross around his neck, which I assumed, was also a gift from Desmoulins. The sleeves of his doublet rolled back, revealing thin, evenly spaced scars on his forearms. Perhaps, the past fifteen years had not been so idyllic for him. I had seen similar scars on the limbs of the young monks at Saint-Aubin d'Angers. I knew all too well what stood behind that calculated, ritualistic self-injury.

"I do not claim to understand the demons inside another man's head," I said, struggling to keep my voice steady and fighting the urge to embrace my distraught boy, "but I can assure you that your master did not intend for the Eliade family to suffer. It is not his fault that the arrow intended for Satigny pierced a few other people."

Daniel's mouth twisted, as if he had bitten into something bitter. "As usual, he did not think things through. He's not a very good strategist. His brain mostly stores Latin terms and mathematical formulas."

"There are older, darker powers at play. Your master was only an instrument. I assure you that right now he is completely devastated."

"Good. He should be."

"I pray that one day you can forgive him, remembering all the good he's done for you."

His tremors began subsiding.

"What will happen to him?" he asked after a brief moment of lull.

"He'll probably be dismissed from his clerical state, but between us, I think it will be a relief for him. He could never bring himself to walk away from his position of power on his own accord. Now he'll have no choice. He'll be better for it, you'll see."

At the end of the bridge, my servant was waiting for us with the horses ready. I told him to go back to "Le lit du lion" and tell Marguerite that I would be coming home soon. My son and I had a rescue mission to accomplish. I trusted my servant, but his involvement was not necessary. Also, in case things failed to go as planned, in case we did not succeed at extracting the girl alive, I did not want any witnesses. As the servant headed towards Gonesse, Daniel and I started moving in the direction of the Montfaucon.

We rode in silence, weighed down by the proximity of the macabre monument. In the past I had ridden by it several times but could never bring myself to approach it. This time I would have to overcome my squeamishness and enter the tomb. But listen, it was my plot, so I had to follow through with it. I had the key in my breast pocket. The night men were supposed to come by with the body. The plan was for us to remain in hiding until dawn and then go beneath the gallows. A few things were making me nervous. I was not worried about the night men. One could count on them to carry out the order. My greatest fear was that Viteri would change his mind about entombing the girl's body and burn it instead, as per Louis de Beaumont's original suggestion. I am sure Daniel was mauling the same thought.

"I'm very drowsy," he said abruptly as we saw the sinister skeleton of the gibbet outlined against the moonlit sky. "I know I shouldn't be. I haven't taken any potions. I just cannot keep my eyes open."

I helped him dismount from the horse and spread my own night cloak on the ground. "Rest a while, my son. I shall keep guard."

He was asleep before I could finish my sentence. At last, I could take a good look at him. He had the flashy, festive Laval coloring and the Dufort angularity. The rest of him was foreign, otherworldly. What if I were to introduce him to my siblings? What would Jeanne and François think of their nephew? One day, perhaps.

Elisabeth Dufort was not my first woman, although she was the first one with whom I broke my vow of celibacy. We met shortly after my ordination. At first she did not know about my religious career or my plans to become the abbot of Saint-Aubin d'Angers. I did not reveal all my cards at once. She was one of my incognito conquests.

If it makes you feel any better, I was not her first man either, though I was the first one who had gotten her with child. I remember her exclamations permeated with a mixture of giddiness and disgust, "I'm ruined, Pierre!" She knew my name, and that was about it. She laughed, pranced and covered her mouth to stifle nausea. An erratic girl, who must have bewildered her previous bedmates out of their wits. She slapped me when she said she loved me, and she kissed me when she said she hated me. Her physical appearance was unremarkable. Of all my mistresses, she was the plainest one, with wheat-colored tresses, a little darker than I normally liked, and bleak eyes, more grey than blue. No glaring flaws but no stunning assets either. Think of a common sparrow, a field chamomile in the human form. Still, it was with her that I experienced some of the most acute and exquisite sensations in my life. With one stroke she removed my skin, exposing every nerve. Whatever she did to me was nothing short of sorcery, leaving me both exalted and depleted. I wondered if she had used the same tricks on her previous lovers, or if she had saved up all in her repertoire for me.

Honestly, having lived through that delirium once, I was not sure I wanted to repeat the experience. A man cannot stay in a state of such arousal and agitation for too long. After a string of pleasant diversions, I had fallen into an obsession at the worst possible time. I had so many eyes fixated on me from every angle of the kingdom.

Elisabeth and I had never formally broken up, though I had gradually added on a few more women, just to diffuse the tension, as a perfumer would add alcohol to rose oil to soften the intensity of the fragrance. With each passing year I gave her more of my money and less of my time. After Daniel's birth, I tripled her allowance. I began gently withdrawing my presence, replacing it with material comforts. Is it not what tactful, considerate lovers do when the passion starts to wane? Elisabeth and I had the opposite problem. Our ardor for each other was not cooling. It was growing more burdensome and distracting, making it increasingly difficult to keep a secret.

Elisabeth was growing more demanding, always asking questions about my family, going through my things. One time I caught her rummaging in my travel bag. She was not checking for articles belonging to other women like handkerchiefs, earrings or hairpins. Items that belonged to my relatives seemed more interesting to her. Elisabeth knew I always carried miniature portraits of Jeanne and François. Perhaps, she needed them to perform a magic spell that would make my family accept her. God knows what was on her mind. All I knew was that she did not find her status of a pampered concubine satisfactory. Her discretion would not be bought with lavish gifts. She ended our affair with her death. Perhaps, there was some logic in it. Say what you wish about me, but I could not let myself fall to pieces over it. There were too many young monks at Saint-Aubin looking up to me for spiritual guidance and too many young blonde vixens seeking my affection. Let us not forget the little orphaned boy who needed a new home.

Now that boy was sleeping a few feet away from me. Sitting next to him on the spread open cloak, I could still smell the Parisian frankincense. Louis de Beaumont used the cheap stuff in his cathedral. He would never splurge on his flock. No wonder his clergymen were always coughing, sneezing and wiping their tearing eyes. Perhaps, he thought his faithful did not deserve better, or they did not know the difference. See, I ordered my incense straight from the Vatican. Nothing but the best for my precinct. That included the best organist in France. It would take forever to scrub the scent of Daniel's old home from his skin and hair.

Wallowing in the memories of my escapades, I came dangerously close to dozing off. The night had been equally exhausting for me as well. A few hours ago I had been forced to improvise the most daring and elaborate stunt in my life, and I had no way of knowing whether it would work.

The sound of wheels squeaking roused me from my reverie. I lifted my head and saw what looked like a giant beetle flanked by two dots of light crawling uphill towards the Montfaucon. I assumed it to be the cart used by the night men to transport the corpses of the executed criminals. The wooden box was supposed to contain the body of the Wallachian girl who had enchanted my son. I had only chanced to spend with her several minutes, but her composure impressed me. She did not crouch or whimper in the corner. She listened intently as I verbalized my scheme and then asked to be absolved of her sins in case that scheme did not work. I was honest and told her I was not entirely sure what I was doing. Before taking the potion, she kissed my ring through the iron bars. A brave, stoic girl, not the skittish urchin I had pictured. My boy had good taste.

From where Daniel and I took refuge, the night men could not see us. I glanced behind to make sure our horses were on the ground and made a few tentative steps forward. Now I could see the men with torches. They were speaking in subdued, weary voices. I could not make out the exact words. One of them burst out laughing, reminding me of a jackal's bark. His companion opened the door leading to the cellar, and a second later the crypt swallowed them along with the cart.

They did not emerge right away. Something was keeping them inside. What was taking them so long? Or, perhaps, my perception of time was skewed due to fatigue and anxiety. I could not spend another minute staring at the door of the crypt, so I shifted my gaze to my sleeping son. Having surveyed him from head to toe, I noticed a small knife attached to his belt. I pulled the knife out of the sheath and hid it inside my boot, assuming that was the tool he had used to slice his forearms; I believed it safer to remove all sharp objects from his immediate reach.

At last, I heard the door of the cellar creak. The men with torches came out and headed back towards the city wall, pushing the empty cart in front of them. After dumping their load, they moved swifter.

As soon as they vanished out of sight, and the squeaking of

the wheels faded, I shook Daniel by the shoulders. "Wake up."

He opened his eyes and propped himself on an elbow. "I had the strangest dream."

"You can tell me later, when we are on our way home."

He ran his fingers over the cloak on which he had slept for several hours, trying to remember how he got there. "Is it time?"

"I believe so." I nodded very slowly. "The night men came by."

He leaped to his feet and dashed towards the gibbet. I grabbed his arm and halted him.

"Wait. Before we go in, promise me something."

"Anything, Your Excellency. I shall be your most devoted servant. I'll perform any task, keep any secret."

That was not quite the response I was hoping to hear. The sky was just beginning to lighten. The first drowsy sigh of dawn stirred a chill inside my chest.

"Promise me," I said with paternal severity, "whatever the outcome, whatever we find beneath the gallows, you will accept it as fate. You will not do anything that would compromise your eternal salvation. Swear to me on the memory of your mother, for whose soul I pray each day, that you will not harm yourself."

This time he left me without an answer. He yanked his arm free and charged ahead. I walked behind him at a leisurely pace. A few minutes would make no difference. He could not get inside the cellar anyway. I had the key. And I had the knife that I had confiscated from him while he slept.

As he got closer to the grisly structure, he slowed his pace. Before reaching for the key, I took a moment to share one last bit of insight.

"It is a privilege to be able to bury the woman you loved, a privilege I turned down when your mother died. I never saw Elisabeth's corpse. It was buried on unconsecrated ground, because of the manner in which she had ended her life. I loved her above all others. She still has a hold on me. What am I trying to say?"

Daniel did not seem interested in what I was attempting to

convey. All servility was gone from his countenance. The same young man who was pledging eternal loyalty to me was now giving me that murderous look.

"Give me the key."

I fulfilled his request. It was endearing to see someone so obstinately, single-mindedly in love. "Do the honors."

The smell inside the cellar was not horrible, actually. More moldy than putrid. I had never been to a plague-stricken site – I had made it a point to stay away during the epidemic of the mid 1460s – but I had been told that those places smell the worst. I believed my sources. Those men were not squeamish or faint of heart. The rats and the maggots of Montfaucon did an excellent job removing the decomposing flesh. A deep bow of gratitude to Nature's sanitarians! The place seemed like fresh bodies had not been added in a while. I could actually breathe through my nose without feeling pangs of nausea.

Something crunched beneath my soles, pebbles or small bones. Of course, we had no source of light except for what was falling from the morning sky.

Daniel was stumbling in the dark a few paces ahead of me, shouting the girl's name. I yearned to tell him that there was no need for shouting. If she was dead, his cries were not going to bring her back to life. If she was asleep, they would make her awakening all the more terrifying. Still, I knew it was not the best time to appeal to his reason. That was why I kept my mouth shut and immersed myself into a silent prayer instead. Everything depended on the revelations of the following few minutes.

Having realized the futility of busting his vocal chords, Daniel fell silent and turned towards me, gulping the moldy air.

"Are you sure they came by?"

"Yes, I saw them with my own eyes. There are fresh indents in the dirt from the wheels, if you need proof. I'm positive she's here … dead or alive. I imagine the night men would dump her on top of the others. You have to keep looking. Do you remember what she was wearing? I hope to God they didn't strip her of her clothes. Sometimes they do that, if the fabric is valuable. Did she have any jewelry on her?"

I struggled not to laugh at the absurdity of the situation. There I was, Pierre de Laval, Archbishop of Reims, dispensing tomb-raiding instructions to my illegitimate son. Suddenly, from the depths of the tomb, came a high-pitched, hoarse voice singing a children's ditty.

J'ai vu le loup, le renard, le lièvre
J'ai vu le loup, le renard chanter
C'est moi-même qui les ai rechignés ...
I saw the wolf, the fox and the weasel, all three of them dancing.

You will have to excuse me for a minute. My narrative powers are inadequate to describe what happened next. A part of me is thankful that the darkness prevented me from seeing every detail:

My son, my beautiful, brave, talented son, plunged into the heap of skeletons towards that voice. Careful not to injure myself with a loose rib or femur bone scattered on the ground, I knelt.

Mother of God, Our Lady of Reims ... Thank you! I did it. I single-handedly rescued my son and his little sorceress friend. No assistance from human allies, only celestial powers. Did it mean that Heavens still regarded me with benevolence, even after all my liberties and transgressions? Perhaps, by rescuing this girl, I was atoning for my past sins. Seriously, this was the stuff of Florentine romances. Giovanni Boccaccio himself would be impressed!

I saw Daniel dragging the girl down the pile of bones. Just as I had feared, the night men had taken her clothes except for the white camisole that barely covered her hips. I noticed a few scratches and bite marks on her legs. The rats had already started nibbling at her. Their teeth must have brought her back to consciousness. How long had she been awake?

I ran out to fetch my cloak, which we had left on the ground at the bottom of the hill. I also roused the horses and took them with me. There was no need for us to spend another moment in that sinister place. Or was it sinister? Far from it. To me the

Montfaucon had become a place of triumph and salvation, a place where I had performed one of my early miracles.

When I returned to the foot of the gibbet, Daniel was sitting on the steps leading to the tomb, clasping Agniese in his arms, rocking from side to side. Her head tossed back, her tangled hair sweeping the steps. I threw my cloak over them. It was long and wide enough to cover them both.

"We should be on our way. I have a summer home nearby. We need to rinse those rat bites before they fester. You don't want her to get blood poisoning."

When the initial wave of rapture from the reunion subsided, Daniel stopped rocking and swept the girl's greasy raven curls away from her face.

"Do you know where you are?"

Agniese dug her scarred fingers into his shoulders, looked right through him and repeated the first line of the children's song. *J'ai vu le loup, le renard, le lièvre* …

"I see," he said. "You don't want to talk."

J'ai vu le loup, le renard chanter

C'est moi-même qui les ai rechignés …Her large swampy eyes communicated neither terror nor bliss. Her voice now inaudible, her lips continued moving, articulating the words of the ditty.

Daniel looked up at me quizzically. "Your Excellency, do you mind … taking a look at her? It appears that she's not fully awake. Should I keep talking to her or let her fall back to sleep?"

I wanted to tell him that girl was as awake as one could expect her to be from now on.

"Let her do what she wants. As long as her breathing is steady and her pulse is strong."

"Then I'll keep talking. Would it help her to hear a familiar voice?"

"I don't know how familiar it is to her, but it cannot hurt. She doesn't seem in distress. Look, she's not shrieking or trying to run away. Not sure how much sense she can make of your words, but keep talking. Maybe a few things inside her head will snap together, like two pieces of a buckle."

I could tell he did not like what I was saying.

"What do you mean?"

"I don't think she recognizes you." It made no sense to honey-coat the facts. "Perhaps I should have mentioned that one of the potential consequences is memory loss. Partial or complete, temporary or … permanent."

"When shall we know?"

"There's no way to predict. We have to wait and see. But you have to admit, it's a small price to pay for being alive. Come on, Daniel. Don't look at me like this. I am unable to perform three miracles in a row."

Marguerite Baudin would never admit to it, but I was the reason she left the convent. Do not believe her if she tells you that she had a sudden change of heart and decided to continue serving God in the world; that she had some unfinished business. That unfinished business was I – Pierre de Laval.

We met while on a pilgrimage. I do not remember the exact site – I have been on too many pilgrimages with so many women. I do remember being smitten by her playfully upturned freckled nose and the blond curl peeking out from beneath the veil. She must have been eighteen. We bonded over the early sonnets of Petrarch.

The conversation started in front of the statue of St. Sebastien and continued well into the night under the stars. It was a magnificent, magical night. I had not enjoyed the company of a virgin in a long time. After the pilgrimage we agreed to stay in contact through encrypted letters. Blessedly, Marguerite did no subject me to a hair-pulling, breast-beating farce of remorse. She was not opposed to the idea of continuing our acquaintance. We fitted so well together, both above and below the neck. I gave her a key to my Gonesse estate "Le lit du lion" and told her she was free to seek refuge there any time. None of my other lady friends had a key to that property, so the chances of an uncomfortable encounter were null. Something told me that even if faced with a rival, Marguerite would be able to hold her own. She struck me as a spunky girl, not easily intimidated. I knew she would make a fierce mother.

Four months into her pregnancy, when the habit started fitting a little too tightly around the waist, she packed up her books and informed the mother superior she was leaving. Of course, Marguerite could have told the old woman some weepy tale about being molested by a highwayman on her way to collect healing herbs in the woods. No, she would not stoop to evoking pity. The mother superior, a perceptive woman, respected that kind of candor. She even gave Marguerite a jar of honey and some bread for the road.

I confess I was delighted to have my little delinquent nun permanently situated at my Gonesse residence. Her feminine touch was not overpowering. Thankfully, she did not convert my austere predator's lair, my lion's bed, into a whimsical pleasure dome. Not that I would kick her out if she purchased new curtains made of turquoise brocade. Still, it meant a great deal to me that she respected my masculine esthetics and made very few changes.

She had waited out the rest of her pregnancy in my cozy library. Yes, "cozy" is a nice way of putting it. I did not have a huge room dedicated to storing books. To my great shame, I could not call myself an avid reader. I was not nearly as obsessed with the written word as my friend Desmoulins. He believed me to be far more scholarly than I really was, and I had no heart to disappoint him. I had access to obscure and forbidden books, and I gladly dispatched them to him, but I never read them myself.

My relationship with the universe was more tactile, more physical. I liked to work with my hands and other body parts. I liked planting apple trees, building bee hives, collecting honey, pressing grapes, squeezing women's breasts. I did not need to read to help me fall asleep. I always slept well after all those physical exertions. Even Marguerite read more than I did. All my collections of Aristotle and Petrarch were at her disposal. A few times I found her asleep with an open book propped against her swelling belly.

Imagine my pleasant surprise when Marguerite produced not one but two girls. To be honest, I was a little tired of having male offspring. Though being a father to daughters presented a new set of challenges.

When you have a girl, you have to worry about marrying her

off to someone reasonably respectable who will not mind her illegitimate birth, then all you can hope is that your daughter tolerates the husband you have chosen for her. When you have a boy, you have to wrack your brain about his status in society, then pray that your son likes the profession you have chosen for him. When you have several children out of wedlock, you have to get creative when molding their futures.

When I returned to "Le lit du lion" in the company of Daniel and his demented muse, I knew I could count on Marguerite's discretion and efficiency. Without needless questions, she ordered the servants to heat up some water for the bath. Our female guest reeked of the tomb, and we needed to scrub that smell out of her skin and hair. Daniel was reluctant to let go of her. The servants had to pry Agniese out of his arms.

"We're in a safe place now," I reassured him. "Nothing will happen to her. You too need a bath, though perhaps not as badly as she. What's left of her clothes will go into the furnace. Yours can be washed, but her camisole should be burned. It is better to leave the smells of Paris in the past."

He sat down on the bench in the hall and looked around for the first time. His gaze fell upon my two daughters, who were standing in the doorway, their hands joined.

"Who are these girls?" Daniel asked me.

"Your sisters."

"In Christ?"

"Yes, that too." I opened my arms, letting the girls know it was safe for them to behave as they would behind closed doors. "Jeanne, Clemence, come here! There's someone I want you to meet. This is Monsieur Daniel Dufort, a relation of yours."

They immediately ran up to me and clung to my sides, observing the newcomer with great curiosity. I bent down to kiss each one of them on the crown.

"Why is he sad, Papa?" Jeanne asked in a loud whisper. "Is he not happy to be here?"

"He's not sad, my sweet. He had a long and troublesome night, that's all. His lady friend was in danger, and we had to help her. But everything will be well in the end. Now show him some hospitality."

The girls detached from me and began circling around Daniel, stroking his hair and feeling the satin lining of his cloak. He shuddered every time their tiny hands touched him. Soon, very soon, I hoped, he would learn to accept and reciprocate sibling affection, which he had been denied for so many years. I had heard of his attachment to the one-eyed cat. If he could love an ugly beast, surely, he would grow to adore his younger sisters. Unless, of course, his heart was designed to love only the wretched and dejected.

"How handsome he is!" Jeanne droned wistfully. "Like an angel."

"Like a prince," her sister added with a sweet sigh. "I've never seen anyone so tall."

"You are right on both accounts," I said to the girls. "He is an angel, indeed, and his nickname is Stone Prince. He writes heavenly music. I commend you for being so perceptive."

Clemence, the more naïve and immediate of the two, pointed at Daniel's companion. "If he truly is a prince from a stone castle in the sky, then what's he doing with this witch?"

Jeanne yanked her hand. "Be nice!"

"I am being nice. I didn't say we should burn her. Papa, you'll exorcise her, won't you?" Clemence turned to me with a plaintive look. "The servants will clean her up, so she doesn't smell like death anymore, you'll purge her of evil, Maman will give her a pretty dress, and then there will be a wedding!"

Both girls started jumping and clapping their hands. They had never been to a real wedding before. Their seclusion was a painful subject for me. I did not know how I would bring myself to explain to them why they had never been to a banquet, a wedding or a christening party; why they spent their time with their mother, moving from one countryside residence to another; why their parents could not be seen in public together. It was only a matter of time before the word "bastard" would surface. I did not ask Marguerite how much she had shared with our daughters, but I trusted her to do it with her usual tact and precision, without needless drama. Perhaps, I underestimated my girls' ability to appreciate the unique benefits of their position.

You see, I did not worry about my sons as much. Somehow I knew they would find their way, and I was prepared to do whatever was necessary, even if it meant putting a safe distance between them and flushing out obscene amounts of money.

One of them, just a year younger than Daniel, had already decided to follow in my footsteps and enter the church. He was living in a Benedictine monastery near Piedmont, translating Greek manuscripts. Another one was pursuing a military career, stationed in the north near Lille. In fact, I had just visited him in April. He looked so imposing in his uniform, at the tender age of seventeen, that it brought tears to my eyes. My fourteen-year old, the only one with dark hair, showed great promise as a painter, so I arranged for him and his mother to move to Florence, where the boy could study under the auspice of great masters.

As you can see, I did my best to keep the fruits of my wanton passions as far from each other as possible. I can assure you, they wanted for nothing. I did not feel guilty about bringing them into the world. I was not spreading poverty or vice. No, I was giving Christendom a new crop of scholars, artists and generals, who would usher us into the sixteenth century. Still, I felt that my firstborn, Daniel, and the two girls were the most vulnerable ones and needed a little more affection and tenderness from me. For them I was willing to break my own rule of not introducing my children to one another. Naturally, it was a little disconcerting to see Daniel's tension escalate from the flighty affections of his half-sisters. Their hugs and squeals that would melt any other heart seemed to have the opposite effect on him. With every touch of their swift little hands the crease between his copper eyebrows deepened. I could tell it took him a great deal of self-restraint not to recoil.

"Girls," I said at last, coming to my son's rescue, "our guest is very tired."

I'm sure it was hard for them to understand how someone could be tired so early in the morning, but they obediently put on their protective beekeeper gloves and mantles and ran outside to check the hives. They had become experts at removing honeycombs without getting stung.

Their mother came into the room a few minutes later, a damp towel over her shoulder. "There's plenty of hot water left," she said to Daniel. "I have the most dutiful servants in the world. They always do more than what's asked of them. This time they boiled enough water to bathe a small company of soldiers." The color of his skin compelled her to feel his forehead. "You have a fever."

"But I'm not hot. I'm rather chilly."

"That's the first sign of an illness. I can hear your teeth clatter."

"I'm not ill, Madame."

"That's what my brother said before he died. Believe me I know what I'm talking about. Young men are so difficult. As a matter of fact, I just had a heated discussion with the wounded officer who came before you. What was his name? Captain Castelmaure."

"So he's alive after all? It's so confusing. First he's dead. Then he's back from the grave. I'll be damned if I understand."

Daniel kept staring at his hands, opening and closing them, as if he was seeing them for the first time. The swelling on his damaged hand was going down. He still had the dirty rag wrapped around it, holding onto it as if it were some relic.

Marguerite swatted him on the back of his head. "Go sit in the tub. It's not a suggestion but an order. I threw in some rosemary leaves. You'll come out clean and relaxed, just like your lady friend."

When Marguerite mentioned Agniese, he shuddered and jerked his head up.

"How is she?"

"Rather scuffed-up. We cleaned out the cuts and the rat bites and rubbed some cauterizing unguent into them. I hope we won't need to resort to mercury. Those rodents must've been hungry."

"Did she say anything?"

"Oh, she said plenty. None of it made sense. I am impressed by her worldliness, though. French isn't her native language, is it? She said a few things in Spanish. And then she lapsed into some bizarre dialect of Italian. We had several Italian girls at the convent, so I'm used to the melody of their language. Your friend's speech sounds coarser, more antiquated."

"Her adoptive father was Wallachian, I think," Daniel forced a reply and winced again, as if sand got caught in his teeth.

"Wallachians now call themselves Romans." I could tell that Marguerite welcomed the opportunity to flaunt her erudition as well as make conversation with my son. "Their language is distinct from that of Magyars or Saxons. What is the word they use to describe themselves? Romani or Rumeni? You surely do have a discerning taste in women."

Having discarded his mantle, Daniel was now pulling threads out of his shirt. Have you ever heard of a certain bird species that peck at their own breasts while in distress? That was the disheartening analogy that occurred to me as I was watching my son.

"Well, it doesn't matter where her family is from anymore," he said, throwing a detached button to the floor. "They are all dead, courtesy of my former master and the Inquisition. I think I'll take that bath after all."

He leapt to his feet, grabbed the towel off Marguerite's shoulder and walked through the door that the servant held open for him.

Left alone with the mother of my girls, I hugged her from the back and poked my nose into her scented neck.

"I have no words. You have been so incredibly patient and accommodating. I imagine it's a great disturbance to you, to have all of these strange characters arrive at your doorstep."

"Not at all. It adds excitement. I've been alone here for months."

"Sometimes I feel remorse. You probably don't believe that I'm capable of such emotions. What have I done? All my excesses … All those women and their children …"

Marguerite rotated in my arms to face me and dusted my collar with the back of her hand. The flippant and coquettish gesture warmed my blood as it always did. She was the closest thing I had to a wife. She did a myriad of casual, familiar little things that women do for their lawful husbands like fixing their clothes or smoothing their hair.

"I don't know what grievances your other concubines voice against you. I can only speak for myself. No grievances, no regrets. I knew what I was plunging into. I knew what an affair with a clergyman entailed."

"How could you know such things? You were so young."

"I had spent enough time in the convent to understand the ways of the world. I had heard enough conversations between the mother superior and the older nuns. They didn't mind seeing me go. They had already received the money I brought to the convent. The moment you spoke to me in front of St. Sebastien's statue and quoted Petrarch I knew that my life would never be dull again."

"Indeed," I admitted with a nod after a few seconds of deliberation, "quoting Petrarch always works like a charm. Ah, the curse of being literate! An unlearned girl, who had never opened a book in her life, wouldn't fall for such tricks."

We laughed and joined our smiling lips in a kiss. God, I needed that humorous respite after the tension of the past night. I came dangerously close to making some outlandish promise like dismissing my other mistresses and keeping her as my only one. If some higher power suddenly came down and forced me to choose only one woman of the ones I had in my scattered harem, I would choose Marguerite Baudin.

"What do you think of him?" I asked, reluctantly coming back to the precarious reality. "What is your overall impression? If you had to describe him in a few words ..."

"Sheltered and fragile," she replied, "despite his imposing physique. I surmise he was not raised to be an adjusted citizen. He was molded to perform a very specific task. You'll have to keep a close eye on him."

"I'm going to give him a dream life. I'll smother him in privilege. He'll never look back."

"It's not that simple, Pierre." She traced my mouth with her index finger. "People like him get very attached to places and select individuals. Don't expect him to make many friends at once, and don't take offense if he doesn't lap up your fatherly love. He'll bite your hand a few times before he starts eating out of it. At any rate, I hope I'm wrong. You asked my opinion, and I gave it to you."

And that was reason number seventy-eight why I loved Marguerite Baudin. She was not afraid to tell me that my firstborn was a social invalid, and my hopes of rehabilitating him overnight were naïve. Thank God I was going through this with Marguerite by my side and not someone like Nicolette de LaSalle or Constance Milet. Those two were afraid to part their hair on the wrong side to displease me. I found their servility to be exasperating. In the early days of our lovemaking they used to be deliciously cheeky and outspoken – before they found out who I really was. Looking back, I wish I had never told them about my position. There would have been more candor and spontaneity in our affairs. Nicolette and Constance were useless when it came to giving unflattering advice. Thankfully, I could always count on Marguerite to deliver the bitter truth between kisses.

In the end, her words proved to be prophetic. Daniel was not in a hurry to call me Papa. As his fever spiked, so did his resentment towards me. He decided I was to blame for Agniese's misfortunes. Convincing him to get out of the tub was harder than convincing him to get in. When I came in to check on him, he took a deep breath and submerged. Watching him sit underwater was unnerving, so I grabbed him by the hair and pulled him out.

"Look, I'm sorry I'm not an apothecary," I said. "Unlike your master, I know next to nothing about medicine and potions. I had to act quickly, so I grabbed whatever I had on hand. Given my lack of experience in such matters, I think my plan was an overall success."

"There was no need to drug Agniese," he replied, picking up a loose rosemary twig floating in the water. "I was perfectly willing to go to the pyre for her. She could've walked out of the dungeon with her memory intact. Everyone would've been happy, especially Viteri. That man couldn't wait to burn me. I liked my original plan."

"Well, *I* didn't like it. If God gives you children, you'll know what I mean. Right now you are making as much sense as Agniese. I think your fever started setting in back in the courtroom. You were delirious already when you offered your life for hers."

"I was perfectly lucid."

"Then you have a very unique understanding of pain and death. You think your moronic games with the knife have prepared you for being set on fire? I surmise you'd rethink your heroism and sing a different tune once the executioner tied you to the stake."

"Like I said earlier, I don't expect you or any other man of God to understand me. I gave up trying to make myself understood long ago."

"I leave you in Marguerite's care," I said. "You'll do everything she says."

He drew another deep breath and prepared to submerge again, letting me know the conversation was over. Mother of God, Our Lady of Reims, I had my work cut out for me! I kept my distance from Daniel for the rest of the day, playing with my daughters in the field, trying not to look in the direction of the house. The girls asked me a few times if there was going to be a wedding. After all, people always take a bath before they get married. Maman told them so. And why was the bride acting so strangely? And why was the groom so glum?

When it was time to make sleeping arrangements for the night, Marguerite instructed the servants to put both guests into the spare bedroom. It would be a little silly and hypocritical to talk about propriety at this point. I would be lying if I said I gave a damn about Agniese's maidenly honor. My love-struck boy had nearly walked to the pyre for her, so forgive me for not feeling too paternal or protective towards her. I felt no remorse leaving her alone with Daniel. Marguerite was in solidarity with me on that account. Deep inside I hoped that my son would not hesitate to take what he craved and deserved. Hopefully, Agniese's company would have a healing effect on him. Her body was not that badly damaged. Unlike the rest of her family, she had not gone through the hands of the same torturer. What were a few bruises and rat bites? They were no deeper than the ones Daniel had inflicted upon himself. Perhaps, licking her superficial cuts, he would feel some of his own pain retreating.

I knew the scene was not intended for my eyes, but I could not resist lingering by the door. The art of diplomatic, sensual seduction was clearly foreign to my son. His love, just like his music, had an aggressive, impetuous quality. He pulled the dusky strumpet onto the bed and resumed rocking her like he did on the steps of the Montfaucon tomb. Shrouded in Marguerite's nightdress, she draped over his arm, looking like a malnourished kitten in the clasp of an overly affectionate child who did not know how to moderate his own strength. I prayed that he would not inadvertently break any bones. He took her scarred hands and pressed them against his face, his neck and his chest. His skin, usually so pale, flushed from the mixture of fever and arousal.

Suddenly he loosened his grip, changed position abruptly, sprawled the girl on the mattress and proceeded to stroke the length of her body through the nightdress. I saw his hand slip under the fabric and expose the bruised calf. The veins on his forearms inflated. Oblivious to his ministrations and appeals, Agniese continued babbling in a mixture of French, Catalan and that feral Wallachian dialect. Daniel's frantic, clumsy caresses ignited her nerve endings, no doubt, but her mind was roaming some alternate dimension, probably the one where the souls of unbaptized infants go. The scene was disquieting. I decided I did not need to see more.

Walking away towards my own bedchamber where Marguerite was waiting for me, I heard a muffled gasp of confusion and protestation. It drowned in a stream of voluptuous whispers.

The next morning I woke up to three voices coming from the orchard. Marguerite was already up, standing by the window with a cup of cold mint brew. I joined her in contemplating the scene. The Eliade strumpet was dancing beneath the apple trees, singing a Spanish folk song, and my two daughters humming along. Agniese, her hair more wild and tangled than before, was still wearing her white nightdress. I noticed a small red stain at the level of her hip, which led me to believe that my long-suffering son had finally abandoned himself to the mercy of his instincts.

Three lovely Moorish girls,
went to pick olives,
and they found them already picked in Jaén,
Axa, Fátima, Marién.
Three vigorous Moorish girls,
went to pick apples,
and they found them already picked in Jaén,
Axa, Fátima, Marién.
Tell me: "Who are you, ladies,
who have robbed me of my life?"
"We are Christians who were once Moors in Jaén,
Axa, Fátima, Marién".

Of course, my daughters thought it was the most enchanting thing ever. They pranced around Agniese, clapping their hands and repeating the last line of the song: *Axa, Fátima, Marién.* When I put on my robe and came downstairs, Jeanne ran towards me.

"Clemence and I solved the mystery. We now know who Daniel's bride is. She's half-woman, half-bird. Her nose is like a sparrow's beak, and her hands are red and wrinkled like claws. See how she flops her arms as she sings? It's like she's trying to fly away. Maman has told us tales about such creatures. There are men who are part wolves, like that wicked Inquisitor named Viteri. And there are women who are part birds." I kissed her on the crown and urged her to rejoin her sister.

My son was sitting under the apple tree with his back against the trunk. The fever must have broken overnight, and his skin had resumed its natural pallor. His eyebrows were damp with sweat.

"I am glad to see you two reached an agreement last night." I sat down next to him. "Your friend appears to be in good spirits. Still out of her mind, but in good spirits. We're making progress."

"There won't be any more progress until she recovers her wits," he resolved. "It was unwise of me to stay in the same room as Agniese, especially in my feverish state. What happened last night won't be repeated. I mustn't touch her again until she knows who the bloody hell I am."

My blissful summer retreat, my fragile domestic idyll could not last forever. An archbishop must show his face in his precinct at least once in a while. So in early August I returned to Reims with my two newest family members. My vicars were happy to see me. I told them how much I appreciated their efficiency in running the show in my absence. To affirm my words, I gave each a pot of honey and a bottle of wine from "Le lit du lion." The two men were so thankful for the gifts, they kissed my ring with particular devotion and commented on how rested and refreshed I looked.

"My friends, I have a surprise for you," I told them. "I have spent all these weeks visiting cathedrals all over the country, looking for a new organist. And guess what? My search has been successful. Now Monsieur Buridan can retire in good conscience."

"What's his name?" my first vicar gasped.

"Patience, my friend. I told you, it's a surprise. I shall formally introduce him to you after the morning mass. This much I will tell you: his name is not entirely obscure. This gifted youth has become quite famous over the past few years."

As I had thought, my existing organist was relieved to see the replacement. The identity of his successor left old Jacques Buridan a little baffled.

"Your Excellency, you've lifted him out of Notre-Dame de Paris? How did you manage?"

"Why, I have my methods," I said mysteriously and smugly, adjusting the collar of my robe. It felt strange wearing ecclesiastic attire again.

Old Jacques was a perceptive man. He sensed that there was a story behind the story. Our closeness and mutual respect allowed for a little gossip. Well, maybe "gossip" is not the right word. I was confiding in someone who was of lower rank. Man to man, Christian to Christian, I considered Jacques Buridan my equal if not my better. I knew I could count on his discretion, so I did not shut him down when he asked me the question.

"Did something happen in Paris?"

"Of couse, there's always something happening in Paris. The culprit is Louis de Beaumont, who cannot control his men. His precinct is in utter chaos."

"Who is giving him trouble now?"

"Everyone. His deacons are sticking their tongues out at him. I think poor Louis reached his breaking point. I saw him briefly, and he looked like hell. I knew he shouldn't have accepted that promotion. Still, his greatest offense is not completing the repairs to the organ. A few years back he started replacing the pipes, and the task was never completed. As you can imagine, young Monsieur Dufort cannot wait another fifty years. He is bursting with ambition and creativity. He needs a decent organ. It's such a waste of life and talent, playing on a bad instrument. Wouldn't you agree?"

"Bring him to me," Jacques said. "I'll show him the registers and the pedals. The boy will taste of heaven."

Alas, the boy was not interested in tasting of heaven. He was determined to give me a taste of purgatory. Ever since I brought him to Reims, it had been one grievance after another. I gave him an entire wing adjacent to my quarters, with a fireplace and a balcony. After spending all those years inside a drafty cell with a one-eyed cat for a companion, you would think he would be grateful? Wrong. He said he had trouble falling asleep without seeing the familiar painted monsters on the wall. Are you ready for this? I told him he could decorate the walls to his liking, and he came back saying that he was not feeling any inspiration to paint. And the mattress was too soft. He was accustomed to sleeping on rougher bedding, with nothing under his head except for his own arm. Those downy pillows were giving him a neck ache.

But wait, I am getting to the best part. I married him and Agniese in secret. One night, when the cathedral was empty, I simply grabbed them and dragged them to the altar. I was treading a delicate line, taking certain liberties. I figured, if God had not struck me down for keeping several families in various parts of Europe, He would not strike me down for wedding my son to an imbecile. The girl's mental state had not improved one bit since we left my summer estate, and she was not able to say "I do", but since Daniel had already deflowered her, it was the lesser of two evils. He could now copulate with her every night with God's blessing, yet the stubborn boy held onto his resolution to abstain from intimacy until his wife showed some sign of recognition. Personally, I thought it was not good for his health, to deny himself marital privileges out of some nebulous principles. Carnal frustration was not contributing favorably to his mood.

Oh, and the precinct did not know about Agniese. Did I mention that? She stayed inside all the time under the auspice of a servant girl who was sworn to secrecy. I thought it would be prudent to keep Agniese out of public eye. I did not need any rumors of a dark-skinned, green-eyed maiden with burned hands parading on the streets of Reims. If the word got out and reached Louis de Beaumont or Anselm Viteri, they would surely recognize the Eliade girl whom they had thought to be dead. They would probably want to reopen the case, and that would also spell trouble for me as well. I seriously doubt that Anselm would want to take on the Archbishop of Reims, but he would probably find subtle roundabout ways to irk me by harassing select individuals I was fond of. I could think of a few physicians and merchants that he could latch onto and aggravate. So I explained to Daniel why Agniese had to stay inside at all times. I did not see it as the end of the world, because their quarters were very comfortable, spacious and well-lit. The girl lacked nothing.

Nothing except freedom and dignity, as Daniel pointed out. It was a complete disgrace what she had turned into, an insult to her proud Wallachian heritage. She was a truant soul, not meant for captivity. After having all her memories erased, she was placed in a box. What a horrible, demeaning fate for a girl who had trekked across Europe!

At some point, after hearing the same lament from him for the fiftieth time, I lost my patience and reminded him, a little brusquely, that he was here to perform a task, and that his emotional burden would be easier to bear if he focused on his work. He was not there to make a shrine out of his bleeding heart.

The choir swooned quietly over his celestial looks, aloof demeanor and sharp technique. They were a little disappointed by his refusal to share any of his original pieces. He played what was in the canon.

One night after the rehearsal he stormed into my study, fuming. "Why are they so nice to me?"

"They are fond of you. Get used to it."

"I'll never get used to it." He stood across from me, pushing his fists into the tabletop. "I find it most unnerving. Nobody in Paris was nice to me."

"This isn't Paris, in case you need a reminder. You are in the City of Kings."

"But I'm still me. People are the same everywhere. Come on, you can tell me the truth. You made them be nice to me, didn't you? You must've threatened them."

"I don't need to threaten anyone. I am not Louis de Beaumont. People respect me. Imagine that? I don't need to summon the Inquisition to keep order. This is a peaceful and civil precinct. Our altar boys do not get into brawls at the sacristy. And you know why? I'll tell you a little secret. Unlike Louis de Beaumont, I don't skimp on incense. I only burn the good stuff, the kind that does not give you a headache and a sore throat. After all, you are what you breathe."

Daniel continued burrowing into me with his dilated pupil. "Was this meant to be witty or amusing? Is this where I laugh?"

There was no point in continuing to maintain eye contact with him, so I proceeded to arrange the quills on my desk.

"My son, I would give up my bishop's ring just to hear you laugh once. Alas, nothing pleases you. You have the best musical instrument in France at your disposal. Does it mean nothing to you? You are with your natural father, who would do anything for you. The woman you love is alive and in good health. Whatever disease afflicted her in Paris seems to have retreated. I'd like to think the change of environment had something to do with her recovery. She spends her days singing and dancing. What more can you ask for?"

"It would be grand if she could remember who the deuce she was. So far she doesn't."

"Is it such a bad thing? Perhaps it's for the best to leave those sad events behind. It's time for some pleasure. Both of you deserve it. There's no crime in it. You're married."

"That thing you did ... that ritual you performed. Is it even lawful?"

"It is lawful enough. Why? Because I say so. Because I'm the Archbishop of Reims and your father. Men like me are not above the law. We *make* the law. The girl is ripe for lovemaking. I suspect that if you make your move, she won't fight."

"Precisely, she won't know to whom she's giving herself. She doesn't recognize me. I could be any other man."

"She may not remember your name, but her body will appreciate you – if you play your game right, that is. I know how daunting it can be when you are both inexperienced. If you are not confident in your skill, I can introduce you to a few women, discreet, patient, non-judgmental, who will teach you a few things. It pains me to see you so forlorn, my son."

His giant hands curled into fists. His knuckles sharpened. I would not be surprised to see the skin around them break and bladelike claws emerge.

"Do not call me that."

"Why not?"

"Because I cannot reciprocate. I cannot bring myself to call you father."

"Someday you might."

"No, I will not, Your Excellency."

"So you still resent me, don't you?"

"Not at all. I have no reason to resent you. To be truthful, I feel nothing for you."

I believed him. There was no venom in his voice, no desire to hurt me, which made his words all the more saddening.

"Nothing at all?" I asked, arching an eyebrow.

"Make no mistake, Your Excellency, I am impressed by the splendor of your quarters, and I am grateful for all of your efforts, as I know them to be sincere. But I cannot give you the sort of filial love that you want from me. I esteem you enough to be candid. I do not wish to deceive you or insult you with false endearments."

"Very well. If I do not have your filial love, then who does? That wolfish heretic Desmoulins, who pulled you into his dirty scheme?"

The boy did not respond at once. His silence was eloquent enough.

"I must go to Paris," he said at last. "There's some unfinished business waiting for me."

"Make sure to keep your papers on you at all times."

"Thank you for the reminder." He bowed before me and kissed my ring. A cold, formal token. "I shall return in five days."

"Travel safely. The choir will miss you, I'm sure."

"Not my choir. Not my cathedral. No my organ. None of this is mine."

"And I'm not your father," I murmured with a weary nod. "Yes, I've heard that before. And the sky of Reims isn't blue enough. May God protect you."

"Ungrateful, stubborn brat," I murmured when his footsteps faded. "Takes after his mother ... always conjuring undue drama. I offer him a fairy tale in Reims, and he'd rather go back to his Parisian nightmare."

So that was what raising children entailed. That was what regular fathers had to endure from day to day. I never thought I would say this, but after two months of putting up with Daniel's moods and grievances, I was actually relieved to put a little distance between us. The right side of my head was beginning to throb. Had he been like this to Desmoulins as well?

Then I heard divine singing coming from the adjacent room and my bubbling vexation cooled at once. The young Madame Dufort was standing in the doorway, laced up in velvet and brocade. How could I stay angry in the presence of that radiant creature? Helene, the servant girl assigned to our lovely guest had been doing a marvelous job taking care of her. She rinsed

Agniese's hair with rose water and braided it around the temples, accentuating the fine oval of her face. Having gone through many blondes in my life, I had never given a brunette serious consideration. There was a first time for everything. At age forty, I was still open to new explorations. In fact, I had never felt more adventurous and invigorated.

"Come here, my bronze cherub," I said, beckoning to her.

Agniese looked right through me. When I grabbed the bell sleeves of her dress and pulled her into my lap, she did not resist. Her back taut and straight, she graced me with another blank stare that was neither encouraging nor repelling of my advances.

Hope was condemned
By verdict of Fate
To be hanged for having me,
Hanging out with her.
Then comes Cupid with the sword
And cuts the noose short.
O Cupid, you were knavish.

"My son is a prudish, sentimental fool," I murmured, running my hands through the cool satin of her hair. "He likes to think of himself as principled. I can only hope that time and experience will heal him of his all-or-nothing attitude. In the meantime, your delectable gifts go untasted. It's a miracle that Desmoulins did not get to you first. He likes to plot his seduction slowly. This time he fell a little behind.

"But everything works out as it should, child. You are sitting on my knee, and we're all alone. Surely, it feels a little awkward, but it's not terribly wrong. When you think of it, father and son are of the same flesh."

Chapter 9

Bitter Herbs

(Aurore St. Laurent)

For the last time: healing is not a gift. It is a discipline, like carpentry or glassworks. If you manage to overcome your squeamishness and fear of blood, there is no reason why you cannot learn to clean, stitch and bandage wounds. So unless you can make a blind man see, and a lame man walk with one touch, do not call it a gift. Do not look at me like that. I do not possess that gift. I am among those mortal wretches who need to memorize the ingredients for a blood-stopping salve. I can lance and drain a blister from a severe scald, but do not ask me to pull a rotting tooth. I have a masculine grip – or so I've been told – and I just might break your jaw.

I am not exaggerating. It really did happen to me once. My aunt came to me with her ten-year-old daughter and said, "Aurore, I know you have a gift of healing. Please, help my little Mahiette." And she handed me what looked like a pair of pliers. The girl's face was covered in tears and drool. Her left cheek was red and distended, her eye swollen.

God only knows how long that abscess had been ripening and what home remedies they had tried. I knew my hand would not flinch, and I did not care enough for Mahiette to be disconcerted by her suffering. That little glutton had a habit of stuffing herself with honey cakes before bedtime. Her sheets were always covered with dried crumbs. She was also not diligent about scrubbing her teeth with a mixture of sage, mint, cloves, ground pepper and salt crystals. I had made a jar of that paste for the whole family, and most of my relatives laughed at me, including Mahiette's mother. Well, who was laughing now?

So we tied the sniffling chit to the chair. My aunt was holding a candle, and my mother was distracting the patient with stories from the Old Testament. I remember Maman's nasal cackling voice, the same voice that had been aggravating me for the past twenty-two years. I remember sticking the pliers into the red, throbbing cavern of Mahiette's mouth. I remember her squirming and kicking me in the stomach.

Normally sluggish and lethargic, she suddenly became rather spry. Still, I was stronger. I squeezed her knees between mine, practically sitting on her lap and flattening her against the back of the chair. Finally, I remember the triumphant hooting of the two women when the decayed molar emerged from Mahiette's mouth.

I allowed her to keep it as a trophy.

The wound itself did not bleed profusely. We sealed it with egg yolk and rinsed it with wine. But then a few hours later the patient started complaining about pain in her cheekbone and her ear. Apparently, while struggling to yank her tooth out of the socket, I inadvertently fractured the jaw. She spent the next few weeks with her chin in a sling, taking her meals in liquid form through a glass straw. My so-called "gift" was weaning her off the sweets.

My aunt was grateful for helping me restore Mahiette's fashionable slenderness. The girl's brocade gowns fit her again. My Maman, on the other hand, did not seem as pleased. It irked her to think that her marriageable daughter had mastered a barber's skill. If the word got out that Aurore St. Laurent was pulling teeth, a string of patients would line up.

My first male patient was my distant cousin Lucius, just a year and a half older than me, and decades younger in terms of mental development. Hurled into military at a tender age by his father, Lucius had become acquainted with the officer's whip and loose women much too soon, if you ask me. Too much corporal punishment paired with too much mindless fornication destroyed whatever rudimentary intelligence he possessed. I should probably mention that he was handsome and poor – both qualities equally irrelevant to me. The only trait that made him remotely interesting in my eyes was his skill with the longbow. Ironically, it was that very skill that had landed him in the garrison.

At any rate, he allowed me to touch the scars on his back. I also touched his other body parts the ones that were involved in helping him forget the pain inflicted by the whip. He demonstrated the biological process for me. He started it, and I finished it. Thanks to Lucius I learned how male anatomy looked and functioned, from the early stages of arousal to the explosive culmination. My mother was committed to the idea of keeping me in the dark for as long as possible – but I was even more committed to the idea of learning the truth. That truth proved to be neither appealing nor repellent. It did not make me want to try what Lucius had done with so many women.

Maman, who suspected nothing about our anatomy lessons in the bushes, had hinted on occasion that my kinship to Lucius was distant enough to make him an acceptable marital candidate for me. The fact that his side of the family had no money was the only unacceptable part. In the boy's defense, he showed promise. One day he would become a general and receive a handsome salary.

I cannot say I was wild about the idea of becoming Lucius Castelmaure's wife – or anyone else's wife for that matter. So when I found out that his father had arranged his marriage to Juliette Poiron, I felt relieved. An awkward alliance averted. I did not know the details of the engagement, but it sounded like there was some staged scandal attached to it. I could only guess what had transpired at Poiron's estate. I was fond of Lucius as a relative and a living anatomical specimen. God knows, I did not want to bear his children. Let another woman do that hard and dirty work!

I did not mind listening to his laments about his loveless marriage. The word "loveless" intrigued me. Did it mean that he considered love to be an essential component of marriage? Having bedded so many women of varying degrees of depravity, he still believed in love.

I believed in it too, for I had felt it. The object of my adoration was another woman, another amateur healer. Yes, such was the piquant nuance. I will not reveal her full family name, but her given name was Diane. She loved me too. Just like me, she had an overbearing mother nagging her, pushing her towards the altar. So Diane and I made a tentative pact to join a convent of our choosing and dedicate our lives to studying medicine and mixing unguents. We would live in the same cell, sleep in the same bed and then die on the same day, at the same time, of the same illness and be buried in the same grave. You have my permission to laugh. Diane and I were seventeen when we made that pact. We sealed it with blood behind the same bushes where my hapless archer cousin had shown me his arsenal.

Lucius was the only soul who knew about me and Diane. He had already told me so many of his secrets, so it was only fair that I should share mine with him. Eventually, Diane and I started including him in our games, if not as a participant then at least as a spectator. One of us girls would dress like a man – not from head to toe, but pick one piece from a man's wardrobe. We would take turns wearing my late father's old military doublet. A few times we acted out our scenes in front of Lucius. He always watched us with fascination. We knew he would not tell a soul, for in doing so, he would be forever depriving himself of such a delectable spectacle.

"May Neptune spear me," he said one time. "If you are so drawn to the doublet, why don't you get a real man? That way you won't have to play dress-up. There's a perfectly willing and capable man right beside you."

He did not understand. He was too obtuse and too blinded by his instincts. Not that I held his obtuseness against him, though – it did add a certain charm to our trio.

Once in my early twenties, I was basically waiting for a few family members to die, because with those vexatious people out of the equation, I could finally start living the life of carving wood and translating Greek and Latin texts that I've always yearned to live.

When my mother started showing signs of heart failure, I started making tentative plans for the future, touring

monasteries and cloisters, one of which would become my –
and Diane's – new home.

My friend Marguerite Baudin who was five or six years
older than me, raved about the Chelles Abbey located in the
Meuax area to the southeast of Paris. Almost all abbesses were
widows, daughters or sisters of kings and emperors, so they had
enough ties to the world and treated their sisters with leniency.
In vain had the bishops of Paris tried to reform the abbey and
elect the abbesses of their own choosing. Marguerite said it was
a great place for learning and forming alliances. Despite her
high recommendation of the Chelles Abbey, she herself had not
lasted there for too long. During one of the pilgrimages she met
a handsome, smooth-talking abbot who impregnated her with
twin girls. He later went on to become the Archbishop of Reims.

"I hope you are happy, Marguerite," I said to her. "You went
from being a woman of God to being a woman of pleasure."

"I am a woman of science first and foremost," she replied.
"And I intend to raise my girls accordingly. Pierre endorses my
pursuits."

Pierre was her leonine lover, the father of the pride. The
two girls he had with Marguerite were not his only children.
He also had a handful of sons tucked away in various parts of
Christendom. In fact, his firstborn was here in Paris, playing the
organ at Notre-Dame. A pseudo-celestial being, quite rightly
nicknamed Stone Prince. At any rate, the cathedral was not my
regular precinct. I went to the mass at St. Genevieve's. I had only
seen the famed prodigy from a distance, running up and down
the Gallery of Kings in his blue-grey cloak. Lucius taught him
fencing. At first I found that friendship odd, but then I thought
that my poor cousin probably got tired of being in the company
of his fellow belching soldiers and he pined for something lofty
and eccentric. Don't we all?

During one of his visits, Lucius confided in me that his
estranged wife was unwell and asked me to take a look at
her. After visiting Juliette in their Gonesse home I confirmed
that she had been stricken with that progressive corrosion of
the lungs known in the vernacular as the "white plague." The
treacherous disease does not discriminate, striking paupers

and nobles alike. If anything, nobles suffer longer, because they try to outsmart the affliction.

When the word got out that Madame Castelmaure was ill, my mother resurrected the possibility of me marrying Lucius. Now in possession of the Poiron fortune, he would make a more suitable groom. Of course, I would also have to inherit his two daughters, Marie and Amelie, but maybe if I got lucky their maternal grandparents would take them, and they would not be too much of a nuisance.

As you can see, Maman had thought everything through – but she had neglected to consider one minor detail: I wanted no part in her plan. As she lay on the sofa, panting and wheezing, her hand over her greedy, failing heart, thinking about merging the St. Laurent and the Poiron fortunes, I was making my own plans of retreating to the Chelles Abbey in the company of my beloved Diane.

Then the momentous day finally came when Maman expired – but not before she wheezed her final aria. I was going to give a portion of my inheritance to Lucius, as a don't-think-ill-of-me token, but he, conveniently, got himself killed in a street brawl. At least, that was my understanding. A few of his fellow archers had seen his body being carried out of his rental digs near Pont Saint-Michel. Between us, it was not the worst possible ending for Lucius. He had been battling some nasty groin infection contracted from one of his whores. He died a somewhat dignified death, worthy if not of a soldier, then at least of a street ruffian.

"There's nothing keeping us here," I said to Diane, stretching my hands forth, as we were standing on the steps of her house. "Pack your books, and we'll go to Meaux. We're free, my darling. Free at last."

I was always the one to outstretch my hands first whenever we met, and she would grab my fingers with the impetus of a child, but not this time. Instead, she locked her hands behind her back and lowered her head.

"How beautiful you look," she murmured apologetically and a little enviously. "How even this simple grey dress becomes you."

I did not like the sound of it. The fact that she started with a compliment was a bad sign.

"What's wrong?" I asked, taking her by the shoulders and walking her down the steps. "Talk to me. Has someone taken ill?"

She blinked and shook her head. "I cannot do this, Aurore. I cannot follow you to the abbey."

"Why not?"

"My parents have arranged a marriage for me. He's a widowed officer twice my age. He's crude and humorless, red-faced and bald, with jagged teeth."

I could tell Diane was making an effort to compile a list of her fiancé's flaws and detriments, as if it could soften my judgment of her cowardice.

"To hell with him." I gripped her shoulders and gave them a hardy, masculine shake. "You dislike men as much as I do."

"But I fear my parents even more. Please, Aurore, do not make it harder than it is. I'm not brave like you. In time you'd grow burdened by me. Your ship is sailing and I'm remaining on the shore. Surely, you'll find yourself a new friend. I hear there are some clever girls at the abbey. In time you'll see it's for the better."

This was no laughing matter, but I was not the crying type. I released my sniffling friend from my grip, adjusted the linen tucker around my bodice and headed back towards the gate, deaf to Diane's feeble pleas. Women were just as fickle as men! For all those months she had been nodding her pretty little head and agreeing with my every word, but when I finally showed up on her doorstep, ready to whisk her off, she suddenly turned retimid. Apparently, our plot that had hitherto remained but a nebulous fantasy became frightfully real. She was eager to dream out loud but not to take action.

One thing Diane was right about: I did not need an indecisive weakling by my side.

Did I tell you that the Chelles Abbey had a parallel male community? That's right! It was a full-fledged double monastery, the kind that had fallen out of favor after the Second Council of Nicaea but then revived some three centuries ago. It had initially started as an institution for the ladies, founded by Saint-Queen Balthild, wife of King Clovis II, but as it gained a reputation as an oasis of learning, a male contingent was established. The proximity of men did not deter me. Far from it. I welcomed contact with my brothers in Christ, as long as they were reserved and scholarly, not like Marguerite Baudin's rakish lover. I could sniff a lecher from a great distance.

The chief attraction at the Chelles Abbey was the marvelous scriptorium. Their nuns were world renowned as trained copyists and manuscript authors, assembling the memoirs of monarchs and saints as well as biblical commentary. One of the most prized titles was *The Royal Frankish Chronicles*, retelling the political and military history of the reign of Charlemagne. I was informed that some time would pass before I could gain access to that book. I needed to prove my trustworthiness first. Apparently, one of the girls who came before me committed the sin of turning the pages with greasy fingers after supper. The two nuns who received me at the gate and ushered me into the waiting room took a few moments to inspect the condition of the books I brought with me to ensure I treated them with sufficient care. They scrutinized the leather covers and the flaking edges. Then, with approving nods, they confiscated all of my literature except for the small prayer book and took it to the scriptorium. Now my personal library belonged to the abbey.

The name of the new abbess was Catherine de Lignières. Her predecessor, Elisabeth de Pollye, had held the position for forty-five years, her formidable spirit still palpable within the walls.

"What is your area of expertise?" Catherine asked me when I appeared before her. She was skimming over the letter of recommendation written by the priest at St. Genevieve's. "The Monseigneur does not specify your talents."

"Botany," I replied. "Medicinal botany."

"Excellent. We have an herb garden behind the dormitory. I'm afraid it's a little neglected. You are welcome to get some dirt under your fingernails."

I took the opportunity to present the small wooden chest

filled with gold coins. Three quarters of my inheritance. The abbess shot a glance at it and proceeded fussing with the recommendation letter. Monastery decorum dictated that monetary gifts were to be received nonchalantly.

"Just imagine: two newcomers in one week," Catherine said, folding the letter and sending it into the top drawer of her desk. "The other one came without any references, only extravagant declarations."

The familiarity of the abbess took me aback. Perhaps, she was testing me to see if I was inclined to gossip.

"Declarations of what kind?" I asked.

"She claims to be a mathematician and an astronomer. I don't know how long she'll last here – but then, I've been proven wrong before. She arrived disheveled and penniless, spouting Latin and tidbits of Greek. In her mind, that's her key to the scholarly community. She has that fugitive look about her. I'd be curious to hear your opinion of her."

"When do I meet her?"

"Very soon. The roof in the dormitory has been leaking after the three-day storm last week. The ceiling on the top floor has been destroyed. I hope you do not mind sharing a cell with her."

The abbess lifted her head and sealed our new alliance with a squint. Now I knew for certain that I was the one being tested and not the ranting astronomer.

I have no idea what Catherine de Lignières was talking about when she mentioned the dormitory room being damaged. I had expected to see muddy puddles on the floor, but apart from a few wet stains, the ceiling looked perfectly intact. The same two nuns who had greeted me earlier at the gate, showed me to my cell at the end of the hallway. I could swear I heard them giggle behind my back. It appeared that all novices were subjected to some sort of initiation prank.

I found myself standing in a tight square space with an arched window. My cellmate was a frail-boned woman in her mid-thirties with large dark eyes and sandy-grey tresses, her veil strewn on the floor. She was sitting on the mussed bed, her knees drawn up to her chin, rocking back and forth – a movement more characteristic of a long-term prisoner than a female scholar. I saw her tiny feet peeking from under the hem of her habit, restless pink toes curling and wiggling. She was biting into the rim of a tin cup. When I approached, she backed into the wall with the skittishness of a wayward child who had been caught committing mischief.

"You've come to throw me out, haven't you? The abbess wants to get rid of me."

Her girlish antics contrasted with the austerity of the setting.

"She wants nothing of the sort," I said, placing my travel bag on the table and keeping a comforting distance. "She said we are to share quarters until the leaky roof is repaired."

The sandy-haired woman responded with a jerk of the head. "This place is laden with anxiety. The abbess looks awfully nervous. She herself is afraid of being removed."

"By whom?"

"Our illustrious bishop, Louis de Beaumont. Haven't you heard? He is trying to stick his slippery fingers into the abbey. It is no secret that the men under his immediate auspice don't respect him, so he's trying to rebuild his pride by seizing control of the monasteries. A petty, backward tyrant – that's what he is."

She threw the empty tin cup across the room and proceeded to braid her hair, her fingers atremble.

"You don't seem to have much regard for that man," I noted, "and it seems you're not the only one."

"He burned my husband, you know."

"Did he now?"

"It was a magnificent bonfire. It really illuminated La Place de Grève. He burned so brightly, my Adrian, brighter than any other heretic. I was there. He didn't see me in the crowd, but he must have felt my presence, because I heard him shout out my name as the first sparks flew into the air."

I did not follow heretic trials, nor did I attend executions, but I could vaguely remember the scandal involving a certain astronomy lecturer from the college of Lisieux who was condemned for possession of heretical literature. It started coming back to me now. The trembling creature before me was Madame Satigny. It made sense that she chose the Chelles Abbey as her refuge, the place the bishop of Paris had not been able to touch. A heretic's widow on the run! And I had the pleasure of sharing a cell with her for the foreseeable future, listening to her confessions. At least I would not be bored. This was good. Diane had no idea what she was missing.

"Try not to despair," I said to Madame Satigny. "To quote the famed Arnaud Amalric, 'God will know His own.' If your husband indeed was innocent, you mustn't fear for his soul."

The woman wagged her hand. "I don't fear for his soul. I don't think much about him at all. He wasn't the love of my life, and he knew it. It didn't bother him. The sentiment – or the lack thereof – was mutual. He liked the idea of us being a learned couple. Two scholars traveling together, sharing a bed, that's all."

Honestly, what she described to me did not sound all that terrible. If I could, I would settle for such an arrangement – minus the shared bed. If I could find a free-roaming scholar who would be willing to keep me at his side and not burden me with sensual requests, I would jump at the chance.

"If Adrian was not your great love," I proceeded cautiously, "then who was?"

"The man who can rightfully take credit for most of my misery."

I fought hard to stifle a laugh. Men brought misery – what a novel idea! And of course, women always idolized those who made them suffer the most.

"You have me intrigued," I said. "Do share the rest."

Not that Madame Satigny needed any encouragement from me. She continued her narration on the same breath. "He was about a year younger than me, handsome, aloof and brilliant. He tutored me in Latin. I gave him my virginity."

"In that order? *Quid pro quo?*"

One's hymen is a small price to pay for knowledge, I suppose. Unfortunately, it is a price that can only be paid once.

"I don't remember the exact sequence of events. He and I toyed and tantalized for a while before we … consummated. He was very forceful and at the same time cautious. He could go from complete abandon to impeccable self-restraint. He knew when to push and when to stop. It's a very rare quality in men, as I later discovered."

Why did I have a feeling Madame Satigny had shared that story many times? Perhaps it was the fluid way in which it kept dripping off of her tongue, like a litany. She hugged her knees and resumed rocking back and forth.

"How did the other men enter the scene?"

"He discarded me. Or rather, I discarded myself to promiscuity. He made it impossible for me to continue the affair. His terms were far too demeaning. Perhaps he thought that becoming a priest would give him access to even more women. Still, even after our separation, he was not done tormenting me. He took away my daughter, the baby I had by another man. He slandered and exiled me then later he abducted me and kept me captive, all the while assuring me that he loved me."

All right, she could stop right there. I had heard enough. Her narrative was turning into one of those nauseating, weepy monologues that no self-respecting person would deliver while sober. And she was not even drunk. I had no idea what was in that tin cup, but I did not smell any wine. Although, I was curious to find out what she considered demeaning. What an odd choice of words for a woman who allegedly traded her chastity for a tome of Virgil's verse.

My cellmate never spoke on the subject of her former men again. She spent her days in the scriptorium reconstructing from memory the loose notes by Nicholas von Kues which her late husband had extracted from the monastery with help from Josef Eliade.

As I was finding out, she had not lied about her knowledge of mathematics and astronomy. Inside our cell we had a board nailed to the wall. She would spend hours in front of that board, scribbling formulas with a piece of chalk. So yes, she was a serious mathematician after all, not the delusional imposter I had taken her for on the first day. Forgive me, but the incident with Diane had left me a little dubious. Gisele was restoring my faith in the scholarly woman, who could love men and knowledge equally. Ah, if only I were a man ... It was comical and endearing the way her oversized habit flowed over her tiny adolescent frame. A few times she tripped over the hem and almost fell. I offered to hem the garments for her, to make them more comfortable, but she declined. Perhaps, she sensed that she would not be wearing them much longer.

After two months of tinkering with the herb garden at Chelles, trying to breathe some life into the depleted soil, I was ready to throw my hands up. Whoever had planted it clearly had no clue about the intricate diplomacy between various species. Rosemary, goldenrod and lavender were all fighting for water and sunlight, spouting their bitter aroma into the air. What barbarian had done this? It was like locking a tiger, a bear and a wolf together in one cage.

September was a perfect time to gather ferns and mushrooms that were vital to the blood-clotting unguents I have been mixing. There was a patch of particularly dense forest on the bank of the Seine outside Paris. The journey would take a few days. I invited Gisele to accompany me into the woods. She did not say much, only shook her head and turned away, her sandy-grey tresses drooping over her face. Apparently, my invitation awakened an unpleasant memory. Without pressing the issue, I took my travel bag and promised to bring her some wild raspberries.

One of my gifts to the abbey was an excellent bay mare named Artemis. I had bought her from Mathias Eliade, on my cousin's urging. Lucius was very pleased with his stallion Achilles, so he assured me that it would be a good investment. I took the mare with me to the abbey and told Catherine that she was free to use her for transport. After several weeks of idleness, Artemis snorted at me resentfully. She had forgotten my touch and my smell. It took me some time to win her forgiveness.

Before long, we were en route away from the abbey. Once I was securely out of Catherine de Lignières' sight, I pulled off my habit and promptly changed into the clothes I wore on the day of my arrival. My grey dress was a little wrinkled from lying in the drawer and fit me a little tighter than before – the bland and fatty cloister food had started thickening my waist.

It occurred to me that I was still the same Aurore St.

Laurent, minus the dowry. Two months of ceaseless prayer had
not softened me. I was still the same grumpy, acrimonious,
impatient girl, pining for something she could not grasp. I could
not say that my experience at the abbey had been transformative.
After my initial raid on the famed library, I realized that I had
already read many of the titles. One thing that kept me from
yawning with boredom was the companionship of Gisele
Satigny. The rest of the sisters – many of them coming from
families far nobler than mine – did not excite my intellect. I had
to laugh thinking how anxious I had been to leave my Parisian
life behind, and how restless I was already growing in my new
home. No longer a marriageable heiress, I did not feel like a true
nun either. Did the fifteenth century have a place for a woman
like me? It was all right if it did not. The prospect of being a
misfit did not terrify me. I could easily continue living like that;
huffing, sulking, growling and jotting down recipes for various
balms.

For the time being, I savored the solitude, the clopping of
my mare's hooves and the sleepy murmur of the river. Early
autumn was descending upon the Marne valley, brushing the
lushly foliaged banks with the first layer of gold. I followed the
curve of the tributary river westward towards Paris where it
flowed into the Seine. I had a general idea of where I was going,
but that idea grew vaguer with each passing hour. Of course,
there was nobody to ask for directions. The small boats floating
by were too far away. Even if I waved my arms and shouted, the
boatmen would not be able to hear me. By the time I resolved
to consult the map that lay folded in my travel bag, the sky was
too dark.

One good thing that came out of my brief stay at the Chelles
Abbey was that my intuition became refined. When you pray
so much, even without fervor, your inner ear opens up. I had
learned to heed the tacit messages sent to me from the heavens.
The realization of being lost was not accompanied by alarm or
embarrassment. I knew I was fated to get lost in the woods on
that night, just as I was fated to end up in the same cell as a
heretic's widow. Perhaps, the next morning I was going to find
the rare plants I needed. Perhaps, some playwright up above

was writing a tragicomedy, and I had a part in it.

I dismounted from Artemis and tied her to a young maple tree. Having sprawled on a bed of moss with my travel bag for a pillow, I fell into a deep, sound sleep – the kind I had not enjoyed in years.

My awakening was marked by a feeling of lucidity and determination. I had fallen asleep in an awkward position, yet my limbs were not bound by any cramps or stiffness. Amazing what one day apart from humanity can do! All the fog before my eyes, and the clutter inside my head had been cleared.

I untied Artemis, walked her to the river to drink and then continued my trek into the woods. This time I allowed the mare to lead the way. She in turn had some invisible guide. I do not know how much time elapsed since we left the bank of the Seine. I was not in a hurry to get anywhere, so I was not keeping track of time. In fact, time itself stopped when I saw where Artemis had led me.

We were standing at the edge of a clearing. The place was nothing short of enchanted. Every fern, every moss, every flower that came to mind was there – as if it had been sitting there, waiting for me as my reward. I had to blink a few times, rub my eyes and pinch myself. Having made sure I was not dreaming, I burst out laughing. For the first time, my laughter was not sardonic or bitter but completely raw and uninhibited. I had never laughed like that, with my lungs, heart, windpipe and throat in my life. Every organ responsible for breathing and vocalizing was involved. When the fit of merriment passed, I took out my gardening scissors and started clipping the herbs while I could. Such an array of healing plants had appeared magically out of the blue and would vanish just as suddenly. Now I would gather enough ingredients to last me through the winter. I probably should have brought a larger bag.

Then I heard Artemis snorting behind my back. Clearly, she was trying to draw my attention to something. She let out a neigh of alarm. I turned around to see what was agitating her and saw a black cloak caught on a log. The fabric had a few holes in it and felt moist to the touch. I examined my fingertips and saw dark red stains of drying blood. Some sort of grapple must have taken place here while I was asleep on the bank.

Instinctively, I picked up the cloak, as if it were a piece of evidence to be presented in court, and circled the clearing with my gaze. The salty smell of blood, all too familiar to me, reached my nostrils. I saw a trail of crimson on the yellowing grass. Holding the bundled up cloak with one hand, pulling my horse by the reins with the other, I followed the bloody trail into the dense sea of ferns.

Artemis bolted and jerked her head with another piercing neigh. I looked in the direction in which she was pulling me and experienced something akin to a revelation. Sprawled a few feet away from me was a *man*. Not just another male specimen, a mere compilation of anatomical traits and social privileges, but a man. A haughty patrician profile. A scholar's brow – high, clear and marked with superficial furrows. Coarse dark hair with swirls of grey. The breast of his blue doublet was stained in blood.

I knelt by his side and tried to prop his head up. He drew a spasmodic breath and opened his eyes. They were the same dark grey color as the water in the Seine. For a few seconds he stared at me, as if trying to remember where he was. Then his dry pale lips parted, and a drop of blood ran out of the corner of his mouth.

"Don't ... exert yourself in vain, mademoiselle."

I came close to taking offense to his words. *Don't exert yourself ... Don't dirty your pretty little hands.*

"You should let me take a look." I started undoing the top buttons of his doublet. "I possess some medical knowledge."

"I have no doubt you do." He stopped me with his glance. "Your hands smell of lavender. I can tell you've been gathering herbs. You don't strike me as some squeamish chit. But there's no need to intervene."

"Please, Monsieur, if you don't let me examine you, we won't know how deep the wound is."

"I know how deep. I'm a physician myself – among other things."

He locked his fingers around my wrist. I could tell that

his hands had once possessed impressive strength, and his voice, now so drowsy and faint, had once been melodic and authoritative.

"I assume there's another body lying nearby," I said, changing my tactic. "Should I be looking for another man in need of my care? If you are so averse to my help, perhaps your rival will be more appreciative."

"No, he won't. He's even more proud and defiant than me."

"You know him?"

"Yes, I raised him."

"So he's your son?"

"No, he's someone else's son. I just looked after him for fifteen years. Believe me, it wasn't my choice. I just couldn't say no. It's a long story."

"Fifteen years ... And it was his first attempt to take your life?"

"It was a long time coming. Like I said, he's a very proud, intense boy. Something like this was bound to happen."

"So it wasn't a random attack?"

"No, he actually gave me a chance to defend myself. He brought two swords and let me choose one. God knows where he got them. Well, I have my theories. It's not that hard to procure weapons. At any rate, it wasn't a duel in a true sense of the word either. More like a game that went too far. He came to visit me in this place. We had not seen each other since July. Odd as it sounds, I was pleased to see him. We split a bottle of wine and had a heart-to-heart discussion. He accused me of every fathomable sin, spouted a myriad of grievances, and I agreed with every word. He hated me, but he also hated his new life. He was wretched all around, past and present, from head to toe. I was wretched too. Before crossing swords we did not make any agreements to fight to death or until first blood. It just happened ... his blood flowed, then mine. We had taken fencing lessons from the same teacher, so we were equally equipped for the fight. I still don't know which one of us won."

I did not interrupt him. I was enjoying the sound of his voice too much. He closed his eyes again, as if it helped him save his strength as he narrated his story. When he paused, I suddenly realized I had been doing something utterly uncharacteristic – stroking the dying man's hair. Would you believe it? I had never done anything of the sort before. I had never caressed another human being except for Diane. Yet there I was, cradling his head, rubbing his temples, wiping the perspiration from his forehead, delving into the realm of hitherto unexplored sensations. And I had only known him for less than fifteen minutes.

"Do you have a name?" I asked when it dawned on me that we had not introduced ourselves.

"I believe so. If only I could remember ... It's Nicholas. Nicholas Van Der Molen."

"It sounds like a heretic's name."

"Indeed, that's what I am. Our merciful bishop released me. Good old Louis could've tied me to the stake next to another heretic, but then he decided that punishment wasn't sufficiently cruel. So he burned my books instead."

"Pleased to meet you all the same. My name is Aurore. I'm a delinquent nun, toying with the idea of becoming a hermit. Having forsaken domestic life, I'm not sure that monastic life is for me either."

He opened his eyes again and squeezed my wrist. "I have a perfect place for you. I own a hunting lodge not far from here. You can stay there for as long as you wish. I'm serious. If you don't like the animal heads on the walls, feel free to remove them. In the trunk you will find several books on medicine, as well as my own notes. Am I forgetting anything? No. Everything I have left is inside that lodge. I leave it in your hands. Good ... I can go in peace now."

"You think I will let you go easily?" I asked.

"No, I don't think anything is easy with you, Aurore."

His eyelids fused slowly never to open again. Having bequeathed his secret hideaway to me, he looked noticeably relieved. There was nothing more to say. I continued stroking his face, marveling at the perfection of the lines that seemed vaguely familiar. Even if our paths had crossed in another life, it did not matter. Now I knew why I had been summoned to that place.

When his cold fingers started shaking, I did something even

more out of character. I bent down and pressed my mouth to his. If he had any parting words, I did not want to hear them. Those words are rarely coherent. I held the kiss until his jaws relaxed.

I knew that the soil in the woods was dense, and it would take me hours to dig the grave. Before starting that task, I wanted to indulge my curiosity and examine the wound for depth and angle. Now that he could no longer protest, I unbuttoned his doublet and the shirt underneath. Beneath the bloodied fabric I saw something that made me gasp. It was not the stab wound but the word *Damnum* carved into his chest.

When I returned to the abbey two days later, I found my cell empty. Gisele was gone, leaving nothing except for the empty tin cup. Her bed had been stripped of linens, and the formulas on the board had been erased.

"What happened to my cellmate?" I asked the abbess, who was trimming the withering rose bushes in the garden. "Where is Madame Satigny?"

Catherine de Lignières' thin chestnut eyebrow crept up so highly that it nearly met the edge of her veil.

"Your friend determined it was not the best place for her. Not enough literature on the subject of astronomy. I told her she needed to travel to Venice for that."

Her explanation reminded me of the one my mother had given me some fifteen years earlier after my beloved dog Tybalt had vanished from the household. According to Maman, he had gotten bored of living in the city and run off to roam the fields. Three days later I had found his carcass in a ditch wrapped in a cloth and covered with flies. My parents had not even bothered to give Tybalt a dignified canine burial. I wondered where Gisele's body was lying.

"I don't believe that she left on her own accord," I said. "You made it impossible for her to stay. You kicked her out, didn't you? Or worse … You handed her over to Anselm Viteri."

I realized I was overstepping all boundaries of decorum, standing there before her, huffing through my twitching nostrils, fists clenched. Of all my vows that I have taken, it was the vow of obedience that I struggled with the most. I could not grunt, roll my eyes and mouth off around the abbess as I had done around my late mother. I fully expected to be reprimanded, and quite harshly too, for my insolence. To my surprise, Catherine Lignières responded to my outburst nonchalantly.

"I shan't begrudge you your ill manners, Aurore. After all, you've only been here for two months. You're still getting accustomed to the way of things. You are sufficiently shrewd, my girl. Once the voice of the world in you dies down a bit, you shall see things through my eyes."

"It might be a while," I warned her. "I haven't yet envisioned myself as the abbess of this place, not in my boldest fantasies."

Catherine flexed her back and tossed a stack of thorny rods into a heap.

"I rather like my position, you see. I worked very hard for this appointment, and I'd like to think that I'm doing a fine job running this abbey. Sometimes I have to make decisions that can be construed as uncharitable by someone as young and uncompromising as you. I applaud your passion and your keen sense of justice. Try not to lose those qualities."

"But you find them superfluous."

"No doubt, having principles complicates one's life, regardless of which side of the cloister wall you live in. It is no secret that Louis de Beaumont has been breathing down my neck for the past year. And once he learned that we've been sheltering a heretic's widow, his scrutiny doubled. I can feel him hovering over Chelles, licking his chops, looking for some loophole in the canon law that would allow him to slip in. I sympathize with your fondness for Gisele Satigny, but she was not the only nun here. I had to think of the other sisters and how my extravagant hospitality impacts them. Keeping Gisele here was unsafe – for her and for the others. Do you understand?"

"I do." Indeed, that was the sort of answer I expected from Catherine. "You gave up one of your own to appease Louis. Naturally, the hen submits to the cock!"

"Perhaps, a few centuries from now women will be equal to men. That day has not come yet. Until then we must resort to stealthy methods to protect our interests. That means forming advantageous alliances with other men, those who are willing to advocate for us. Take heart, my child. I did not leave your friend Gisele without succor. There is someone more powerful than our bishop."

"Kingly Louis XI?" I asked.

"Close enough. Pierre de Laval. I sent Gisele to him with a letter of endorsement and told her to ask for his protection. Pierre will never miss a chance to help someone persecuted by Louis, if only out of spite."

Of course! The Archbishop of Reims, Marguerite's lover. Why wasn't I surprised to hear that name?

"You do realize," I said, "that man never does anything for a woman out of the goodness of his heart. He will expect some sort of compensation for his kindness."

"And Gisele will give it to him gladly, I assure you. She doesn't strike me as someone who will yank at her hair and beat her breast after spending a night in the archbishop's bed. The man is not without charm."

Catherine inclined her head with a subtle air of nostalgia, which made me wonder if she was speaking from experience. Nothing astonished me at this point.

"So you are saying she's in good hands?" I asked her impatiently. At this point I only cared about Gisele's survival.

"Good hands indeed. Slimy but reliable. My dear, I've been alive for a few decades. I've learned to … interpret people. Simply put, Gisele Satigny is not nun material. She wasn't happy here at any rate."

"I'm not happy here either," I blurted out. "This place isn't quite how I envisioned it."

"I've sensed that for a while." The abbess wiped her brow and adjusted her veil. "This life isn't for everyone. I shall not keep *you* here."

Her stressing the word "you" meant there was no chance of me recovering any of the dowry I had brought to the abbey, which was perfectly fine.

So there I was aged twenty-two, orphaned, unmarried, friendless and penniless, with only a decrepit hunting lodge buried in the woods bequeathed to me by a dead heretic. I had no idea how well that lodge kept the heat in winter or if there was a place to start a fire. Oh, well, I had a few months to figure these things out. Thankfully, I was allowed to keep my horse and a few books. Catherine Lignières was not entirely unsympathetic. Without all those distracting shapes looming before my eyes, I could finally perceive the visage of the Almighty. Stripped of all the things that had burdened me in my old life, I could finally breathe.

Before retreating to my new home, I made one last visit to Paris. Having calculated the identity of the mysterious man in the woods, I stopped by the cathedral.

The new organist, Eustache Mazet, was a polite man of twenty-five who had received his training in Rouen. His appearance was completely unremarkable and his mode performance competent, if altogether unimaginative. He played a few classic pieces by Guillaume de Machaut and François Andrieu. I approached him after the service to welcome him to the precinct and to discuss a matter concerning my duty to the man who had died in my arms.

"I would like to request a mass for a dear friend who has passed," I said to the new organist. "I was hoping you would select a few suitable pieces."

His reply consisted of anxious, almost servile smiles. I noticed that his hands were trembling. He curled them into fists and pulled them into the sleeves of his tunic.

"I shan't impose my tastes on you, not knowing your friend. I think you should select the pieces." He looked away and coughed, which led me to believe that the incense was not agreeing with him. "Forgive me. I've only been here for two weeks. The size of the cathedral is a little overwhelming."

"How are you settling into your new role?"

"I don't know how long I shall last in this place."

"It takes a while to grow accustomed to a new instrument," I said.

"It's not just the instrument." My presence must have put him to ease. Or maybe he got tired of keeping up the façade of equanimity. His hands relaxed and rolled out from the sleeves.

"I don't believe the cathedral itself likes me very much. It's still grieving for my predecessor. The building is a living, breathing organism with a heart and a will of its own. You know this, don't you? The stones themselves reject me. I'm not the one they pine for. Please, do not think me a madman. I've spent enough time among the stones to know they are more alive than people."

I could understand Mazet to some extent. I spend most of my time among plants and have learned to interpret their wordless language.

"Late evenings are the only time I can stay and practice without interruptions," he continued. "And yet, that's the time of the day I fear the most. I'm never truly alone; I hear sighs in the staircase, a hoarse monotone voice mumbling. One time I came up to the Gallery of Kings for air and found splatters of blood on the balustrade. Where did it come from? I examined my hands for cuts over and over again. It's not the sort of thing I can report to the bishop so soon after arriving."

"You are right about that. Louis de Beaumont is fragile and easily startled."

Mazet snapped his fingers, remembering something. "One afternoon I came to rehearse and found this on the bench." He pulled out a folio and showed it to me. "He must have come by when the building was empty. Unless, some spirit delivered it on his behalf. He wants me to play it. I feel like I must perform his music, if I am to stay here."

I took the folio from his hands and flipped through the sheets. My vision instantly became blurry from the multitude of notes. Reading music was one skill I had not mastered. There was a brief letter attached.

To the people of Paris ... This is my parting gift, my final growl, a musical proof that stone can bleed.

"Then play it," I said curtly, returning the folio to him. "He has confidence in you. Maybe that will appease him and he'll stop haunting the cathedral."

Mazet cracked his knuckles and inhaled deeply, as if standing on the edge of a precipice. "I recognize it's a masterpiece, but

don't know how I'm supposed to play it. It must have been
written for two players. I simply don't have enough fingers."

He sat on the bench and laid his trembling hands on the
keys. The first measure of the hymn marked the last sob of the
fifteenth century.

About the Author

An only child of classical musicians, M.J. Neary is an award-winning, internationally acclaimed expert on military and social disasters, from the Charge of the Light Brigade, to the Irish Famine, to the Easter Rising in Dublin, to the nuclear explosion in Chernobyl. Notable achievements include a series revolving around the Anglo-Irish conflict, including *Never Be at Peace* and *Big Hero of a Small Country*. She continues to explore the topic of ethnic tension in her autobiographical satire *Saved by the Bang: a Nuclear Comedy*. Her cyber mystery *Trench Coat Pal*, set in Westport, CT at the dawn of the internet era features a cast of delusional and forlorn New Englanders who become pawns in an impromptu revenge scheme devised by a self-proclaimed Robin Hood. A revised edition of *Wynfield's Kingdom*, her debut neo-victorian thriller, was recently released through Crossroad Press. *Wynfield's War* is the sequel following the volatile protagonist to the Crimea. *Sirens Over the Hudson*, a social satire set in Tarrytown, NY during the Great Recession, is colored with the same dark misanthropic humor as the rest of her works. Her latest release *Blood of the Stone Prince* is a macabre tale of one beauty and three beasts set in late 15th century France.

Curious about other Crossroad Press books?
Stop by our site:
http://store.crossroadpress.com
We offer quality writing
in digital, audio, and print formats.

Enter the code FIRSTBOOK
to get 20% off your first order from our store!
Stop by today!

www.ingramcontent.com/pod-product-compliance
Lightning Source LLC
Chambersburg PA
CBHW070645180626
46817CB00006B/2251